THE FATED

AND THE

DAMNED

CHLOE HODGE

About the book:

Steamy, romantic, and dangerous, The Fated and the Damned is the deliciously dark conclusion to the Cursed Blood duology.

Please note: This series contains explicit content which may be triggering for some. This book will include explicit romance, mature language, violence, gore, reference to drug use, and emotional manipulation. This book is intended for readers 18+. This is book two, the final book in this duology.

The Fated and the Damned
Copyright © 2023 by Chloe Szentpeteri
First edition: February 2023

Paperback ISBN: 978-0-6453849-4-9
Hardcover ISBN: 978-0-6453849-6-3
E-book ISBN: 978-0-6453849-5-6

Special thanks and acknowledgement to:
Editor; Aidan Curtis,
Cover artist; Cover Dungeon Rabbit
Formatter; Rebecca Camm

Find me at: www.chloehodge.com
Instagram: @chloeschapters
TikTok: @chloehodgeauthor
Facebook: Chloe Hodge Author
Reading Group: www.facebook.com/groups/chloesreadingcoven

Also by Chloe Hodge

Cursed Blood
The Cursed and the Broken
The Fated and the Damned

Guardians of the Grove
Vengeance Blooms
Retribution Dies
Fury Burns

The Terrulian Trials
A Sky of Storms
A Forest of Fire
A Sea of Secrets
A City of Smoke
A Desert of Despair
A Kingdom of Conquerors

For all the spice loving, bad boy hunting, romantasy readers out there.
This is just the beginning you thirsty bitches.
˜It's corn˜

Did that dedication speak to your dark soul?
Do my stories bring you joy or mild amusement?
Want access to teasers, giveaways, memes, recs, and more?

Join my reading tribe!

Come and find us at Chloe Hodge's Reading Coven
www.facebook.com/groups/chloesreadingcoven

PROLOGUE
The Dark Queen

I'd forgotten the taste of blood. The metallic tang upon my lips, the surge of power slipping through my veins. A gentle buzz thrummed through my body, and I marvelled at every small sensation tingling beneath my skin. I was whole again. Beautiful and strong, soon to be unstoppable.

The underling fixed between my thighs picked up his pace as I arched my back, opening my legs in a simple command. His tongue swept up my centre, heightening my desire, my need for release filling me up in waves.

I fisted his hair in one hand, grinding my hips as I pulled him closer. A soft moan spilled from my lips and I paused, taking a breath before once more feasting on the neck of the witch hanging limply in my other hand. Her blood—the very essence of her power—misted past my lips, coating my tongue as I swallowed greedily.

This was what it meant to be alive. My enemies laid before my

 1

feet, my disciples responding to my every whim. I had forgotten what it was to have magic, and I had no qualms about restoring it.

The ritual circles my faithful flock had been casting to drain the girls of their vigour were no longer necessary now that my body was fully restored. The last few months I had been little more than a wraith as my power slowly returned, my body repairing a little more with each kill.

But now ... I was restored to my beautiful self. Better, in fact, no longer needing spells or ceremony to serve my dark magic.

I was no longer a witch, but something other. Neither living nor dead, but a new breed of chaos. My power was heightened, my thirst for blood and strength never sated. Gone was the hunger for feeble human food. My resurrected form could take power direct from the source—feed on witches like the vampires of old. Baba Yaga had even fashioned my teeth like them, enhancing the pleasure of each kill.

Witches were my sisters once, yet I felt nothing but joy when I drained them of blood. No sorrow or empathy, no regret or guilt. Not after witchkind had hunted me down, killed my followers and tied me up like a dog as they watched the flesh melt from my bones. No, I would offer them no mercy, no quarter, and I would take pleasure from ripping out the throats of every damned witch I destroyed.

Pleasure had been beyond my reach for too long. Any physical sensation at all, thanks to that wretched horseman. I'd expected pain for my treachery—torture by the hands of demons and

ancient creatures beyond even my comprehension—and indeed Death and his minions had granted me such for a time. When that didn't break me, he'd gifted me something so much worse.

An eternity of emptiness. I'd been but a speck of energy in a void of darkness. Incorporeal, unable to feel or speak or do anything at all except float alongside the other souls damned to a fate worse than death.

Trapped. What could be more horrible than the agony of physical pain? The absence of everything that made one alive. Just another ripple in a never-ending river.

It was worse than any hurt I might have felt by a blade. I'd have taken the stake over the desolation he'd wrought upon me any day, if only to feel something. Somehow, I'd clung to my sanity all these long years and, against all odds, my followers had defied the will of the gods—defied Death himself to bring me back. And, like any fool brought to their knees, I had learnt my lesson. Challenging a greater power was not without risk. My death had been the price of such stupidity, and I would not fall so easily again.

Not with an army of loyal worshippers at my back. Not with *her* in the picture now. The girl presented a problem, but one I planned to rectify soon. And now that my body was back to its former glory, my strength had returned. My ambition, with it.

"Faster," I whispered to the man on his knees, driving him harder against me as I reclined against my throne, sucking the last of the witch's power from her lips. Her body sagged, the light in

 3

her eyes flickering out as I took my last breath and shoved her away.

The witch thudded to the ground, her ribs caved in, her body deflated. Utterly drained of all her worth, which wasn't much—her power was weak, her magic little more than dregs in the bottom of a cup. And I was hungry, always *hungry*.

My minion gripped my thighs with two star-scarred palms, ravishing me with rapid strokes of his warm tongue. Pleasure surged, a breathy moan leaving my lips as I grinded against him. My black, varnished claws dug into the throne's arms as my core tightened and I came, high as a towering wave before it strikes.

When my thighs ceased their quivering, I looked down at the man between my legs, satisfaction roiling through me as he bowed his head in reverence. He had done his job adequately enough. I flicked my hand dismissively. "Go. Summon Yaga and bring the next prisoner."

He nodded, backing away a healthy distance before disappearing out through the crumbling doorway of the castle. My new stronghold was ancient. A crumbling, dilapidated sprawl of stone and creeping ivy. Once home to a forgotten king who'd no doubt fallen to a greater man, judging by the ruination of the keep. What it lacked in charm and sophistication, it made up for in location and security.

My followers assured me we'd be left alone. All because of a ghost story, no less. The entire household had been slaughtered once upon a time after an arranged marriage went awry. A result

 4

of treachery and greed between houses, supposedly when the other family reneged on their promises and ended that marriage early. The human wretches in the nearby towns said the spirits of the castle's previous inhabitants walked the halls and would kill any who dared enter its threshold. Nothing more than a folktale for superstitious humans.

I scoffed. Small-minded fools. Ones who I planned on wiping from the earth soon enough. They were beneath us, those gift-less creatures, and I would crush every colony and remind them of their place before I was done.

"My queen," a lilting voice uttered, breaking me from my thoughts.

My gaze snapped to its owner. She was a picture of grace—would have been disarmingly beautiful in her youth. Baba Yaga, my second, my most loyal servant among the flock. She bent her head as I gazed at her, a cruel smile carving her lips as she noted the limp body on the floor.

"Did the witch please you, Your Grace?"

I rose, padding over to the body and tilting her cheek with my toe. "She'd barely a drop of magic in her. Useless."

Yaga looked at the body with disdain. "A half breed, my brothers informed me after her capture. A mistake I will ensure does not happen again."

"The father was human, I presume?"

She dipped her head. "The blood of witches runs thinner by the year. They have grown lazy from idleness and peace, thanks to

 5

the wards erected around the village. The humans are none the wiser about their existence, and those that cavort with witches do so willingly or have their memories wiped soon after. The coven has been quiet."

"Not for much longer," I said with a small smile. "These wards you mention—they can be removed?"

Yaga grinned with pointed teeth, seeming to catch on to my thoughts. "It will be difficult. The councillors know now the banya was a ruse, and they will have strengthened their defences." She pursed her lips, pacing slowly. "I'll need to consult the tomes, but, yes ... I believe it's possible."

I padded towards Yaga on bare feet, my gown swishing through the bloodstained stones. "Your sensitivities put us in this mess." I clicked my tongue, my voice turning brittle. "Sentimentality has no place in this cult. You were sloppy, involving your son in my affairs."

My power trailed from my palms in misty red waves, snaking around Yaga's shoulders. I ran a nail down her arm, and she shivered at the touch, baring her throat to me in submission, her frame trembling with fear. Yet something like lust gleamed in her eyes, whether at me or in recognition of my power, I couldn't be sure.

Demons below, she was a stunning creature. One I might consider worthy of being my consort. But there was one other I had my eye on. One with great potential—power even he didn't know the limits of. And what a match we could make.

 6

I smiled and pressed a kiss to Yaga's mouth. She parted her lips as I swept my tongue in, a breathy sigh leaving her as I deepened the kiss until it was bruising. I sank my recently filed fangs into her lips, drawing blood which I consumed greedily. She moaned, arching into my touch, sweeping my long black hair over a shoulder.

She tasted like dark magic and black hell, the promise of power swelling in that blood. Powerful, but not nearly enough. I pulled away sharply, wiping my bloodied lips and sucking what remained off my finger, my hand tightening around her throat.

Her eyes widened, the flesh around her throat reddening until I let her go and she gasped, bending double. "See that the wards are destroyed. There's something I'd like to send to the witches. A gift from their true queen to her people."

Yaga bowed, her shock replaced with a dutiful nod. "It shall be done."

"And Yaga," I said dangerously low, "do not disappoint me again, or it will be your blood I feed on."

She bared her teeth and hissed but was wise enough not to challenge me. "My queen," she said simply before turning on her heel and storming away.

I smiled as I sauntered lazily to the arched window, gazing at the treetops and the city I knew lay beyond. With my power restored, the witches and their táltosok bodyguards wouldn't stand a chance.

Soon Mistvellen, the Kingdom, and the world beyond, would

 7

be mine.

PART ONE
THE CURSE OF
CONSEQUENCE

ONE
KITARNI

Red splattered in a crimson arc as my blade bit into pale flesh. One smooth slice and my opponent's lifeblood drained away, his throat torn open. The mess of battle never bothered me. I was a blood witch, after all.

A war song pounded in my blood, spurring my instincts as I moved quickly, purposefully.

These were my enemies, my prey, and I would spare them no quarter. I bumped into a solid wall and spun, a snarl on my lips as I came face to face with Dante. His eyes were dark murder, the gold ring flaring brightly in the dark.

He said nothing, did nothing but turn away and fillet his next victim. I ignored him—trying not to dwell on the absence of emotion on his face—joining András's side as three cultists closed ranks, trapping him against a thick, scarred tree trunk. Around us, the forest dripped with black, stinking of rot and ruin and the iron tang of fresh blood.

 11

A roar escaped my lips as I charged, sliding beneath a clumsy swipe by one man and gutting him in a flash of silver. I refused to acknowledge the glimpse of pink spilling from his stomach, moving on to square off with a man with sewed lips and eyes with pupils so dilated they were almost black. High on bloodmorphia, no doubt. The angry red line of his mouth looked infected, bubbling with yellow and pus-filled sores.

I grimaced, focusing instead on his movements, the amateur stance, and the white-knuckled grip on his axe. He moved, and I feigned to the left, changing direction at the last second to rotate and ram my blade into his chest.

Pained sounds answered, muffled and distorted from beneath his infected lips. What were they even trying to prove with such stupid ceremonies anyway? Was it some sort of sadistic punishment? I grunted as I pulled my blade out. Another fanatic felled. One less monster to defend against. I set my jaw, huffing a stray curl from my face.

András, having dispatched his attacker swiftly, studied me for a beat too long. "Someone's in a mood today."

I smiled sweetly, belying my frustration at a certain broody, towering wall of muscle looming nearby whom didn't deserve any space in my already muddled mind. "Just doing my duty."

András's eyes narrowed as he looked at the trail of bodies in my wake and mumbled, "If that's what you want to call it."

I looked at him coolly. "What's that supposed to mean?"

"A discussion for another time," he answered with a frown.

Planting a hand on my hip, I pinned him in my stare. "I—"

"Duck," András yelled. I didn't hesitate, sliding my leg out and crouching as he parried with a cultist. The ring of steel clanged in my ear, and I rolled to the side, narrowly avoiding a sword that glided beneath András's guard, dipping right where my head had been.

Adrenaline sluiced through my stomach, and I focused my attention elsewhere, shaking my head to clear it. A deep voice grunted with pain, and I snapped my eyes to the source. Dante. His arm was bleeding, and before my body could register it, I was moving. Running towards him with my sword raised and all my weight behind it as I shifted.

Damn it, even my body defied my determination to ignore the man, acting on pure instinct.

My blade connected with bone, and I grunted with effort, severing a clean cut through until a head thumped to the ground and rolled. When it finally came to a halt before a less than amused András, silence enveloped me—us.

I stared into Dante's eyes, searching for ... for only the gods knew what. My heart thudded erratically in my chest, and the hopeful girl in me longed, *ached*, to reach a hand out, to trail that stubbled jaw. To feel his arms around me, his lips upon my own.

Even after what he'd done, there was no denying how much I yearned for what was or what could have been. But the lies and deceit had opened a rift between us. Even if his reasons were valid, even if I'd have done whatever it took to save his brother,

 13

just like I'd have done anything if it was Eszter that Sylvie had been ransoming.

As if reading my mind, he lifted a hand and my heart galloped in my chest, anticipating his touch, needing to feel his flesh upon my own. Instead, he changed course, gripping his injured arm instead.

He cleared his throat. "It's only a flesh wound," he declared softly, daring a step towards me.

My walls built before my mind's eye, solid as stone, unbreakable as iron. And I hated that feeling, *hated myself*, for stepping away from that one small gesture. I swallowed the stupid lump in my throat. "Good. Get cleaned up, we need to move."

I turned away from him, feeling the distance widening that hole inside me even more. The hole that was growing to a chasm day by day by day. The wound I filled with anger and destruction and hate instead.

Two months had passed since Sylvie's resurrection. I'd almost died on that stone slab as Dante's mother—that vile, wretched creature—had fed from me, stolen my power and blood to bring the Dark Queen back from the dead. And Dante ... I hadn't been able to forgive him. Honestly, I'd been dealt some shitty cards and wasn't quite ready to face them yet.

Instead, I'd focused all my efforts on finding the crown Death had tasked me with hunting. A symbol of sovereignty in the Under World. The problem was, I had no clue where to find it, and hours spent researching with Margit in the castle library

had amounted to nothing.

When my brain grew too tired to take in information, I dedicated every spare moment to training. If we stood any chance of killing Sylvie, I needed to be strong. Body, mind, spirit. And hell, I could see the gruelling sessions paying off in the sleek new muscles of my body, though the latter was wanting. My heart was empty, just a blank slate wiped clean.

But these depressing thoughts were better spent with a drink in hand or a sword, and my blade had done enough damage for one day. There were witches needing help. My stomach churned as I gazed upon a line of four women bound by rope. They ranged from teens to a similar age to me, huddling together like sheep. I stalked up to them and swore at the sight of mottled bruises in purples and yellows lining their skin. Fucking cultists.

"It's okay," I said gently as I cut their bindings. "You're safe now."

Their eyes were wide, gleaming partly with relief and the haunted look of fear. To their credit, they raised their chins, seeming to find their bearings. I recognised a couple from the village. Hanna's friends.

A blonde witch—Elisabeth, I think her name was—walked forward and, to my surprise, knelt before me. "Thank you." Then again, quieter, tentatively, "Thank you." She looked up at me, one eye swollen but imploring all the same. A plea for forgiveness.

My heart panged with sorrow for what my kith had been through—what many would likely go through yet. I'd been joining

 15

the hunting parties for weeks now, scouring the woods for signs of the cult and cutting them down before they could advance to the village or Mistvellen.

Mama had informed us that more witches were disappearing, no doubt as sacrifices for whatever horrible rituals Sylvie required to return to her strength. We'd saved many girls, but there were always cracks in our defences, always loose threads the enemy had cut.

Most of our army remained in Mistvellen, training, scouting, protecting our greater city. All witches had been offered sanctuary should they want it, but many remained in the village. I suspected Caitlin had much to do with that, but there were some, like my mother, who refused to abandon any that would stay behind. "*We are all sisters,*" Mama had said fiercely the last time I saw her. "*I will fight for them until the end.*"

I glanced at the girl before me. I still recalled the feeling of wet mud clinging to my skin after she'd pushed me, laughing alongside Hanna and her other friends. I still remembered the vines that held me down and lashed at my skin time and again as they cackled over me. Each time I could have burned them to cinders, but I'd been too scared, not knowing how far I'd go.

But that was long ago now. Inconsequential.

Despite our differences, the horrible ways she'd treated me in the past, she was a witch. And we protected our own. I held out a hand in supplication, and she took it with a steady grip as I pulled her to her feet.

 16

"It's forgotten," I whispered for her ears alone. "All of it." We both knew what I meant. How far back that forgiveness went.

She nodded, relief easing the taut lines of her face. Her pretty features only hardened as she took in the slaughter around us. "The cultists have been attacking the village for weeks now, pressing in small waves and blocking our routes to the human towns. They take witches from their beds, somehow surpassing our defences. Without supplies and manpower, I fear we will not last the summer."

I sighed, sweeping a hand through my unruly hair. "We can send more soldiers, but Lord Sándor won't risk leaving Mistvellen unprotected against a greater force." I chewed my lip, my nerves writhing with anxiety. "Are the witches still in training?"

Elisabeth cringed. "Erika is doing her best with the time she has, and the táltosok are assisting when they can, but Caitlin has ..." She swallowed, looking away.

"She's done what?" I growled.

The witch's hands curled into fists. "She's agreed to meet with the Dark Queen to come to a mutual agreement."

I blinked. *What. The. Fuck.* "I'll burn in hell before I allow that to happen. Sylvie is murdering our people day by day, and Caitlin is considering a meet? *No.*"

"Trust me, I know how insane this is." Elisabeth met my gaze with her sky-blue eyes. "We need you, Kitarni. We need you now more than ever."

The witches surrounding Elisabeth nodded, their expressions

 17

fierce as they looked at me. For direction, I realised. For leadership.

My witch kith, who had once delighted in bullying me and belittling me, needed my guidance. Because they sensed my devotion to the cause? Or because of the power running through my veins?

An ugly, spiteful piece of me deep down wanted to let them suffer for their crimes, but ... no. I could never—*would never* turn my back on my own kind. My village.

I took a deep breath, letting the air sigh from my lips. "Okay. Okay, I'll deal with Caitlin. I'll come home."

Except it wasn't my home anymore. Never really had been, if not for my family and Erika. Elisabeth studied me as if she knew that too, and I didn't have the words or energy to broach that subject. Better to let sleeping dogs lie.

I turned, but three words halted my step.

"I'm sorry, Kitarni."

Elisabeth's voice was quiet, but to me it was loud as a bell tolling.

"What we did to you was wrong," she continued. "I'll always wish I could take it back."

My heart panged, but I didn't turn, didn't look at her as I said softly, "I'm sorry too." A sad smile curved my lips. "I just wish it didn't take the end of the world for you to realise that."

 18

TWO

DANTE

It was torture to be around her. Breathing the same air, inhabiting the same space, yet feeling like she was oceans away from my reach. I watched as Kitarni laughed, her smile lighting up the room, those hazel eyes gleaming with joy as she plotted with András and Margit at the edge of the training arena in the castle grounds.

After hunting down the cultists in the woods and freeing the witches, we'd ventured back to Mistvellen, but I knew Kitarni was itching to return to her village. So many stolen witches, so much death—it was wearing on her soul. We'd only been back one night, but it seemed my little hellcat hadn't had enough violence to sate her anger. Unfortunately for András, he was usually her sparring partner and, consequently, her training dummy.

András and Margit were the two people who could make her forget all the horror in our lives and bring some light back. It made my heart swell to see her so happy with them ... until I

 19

remembered she would never smile like that for me again.

I would never feel her hand upon my own, the press of her tender lips, the fiery embrace of passion—even the focus of that smart mouth and cutting tongue. Who'd have thought I'd miss being on the receiving end of her rage? A dagger to the heart would be better than the eternal ache, like an invisible hand crushing me beneath cruel fingers.

Now, I may as well cease to exist. She didn't acknowledge my existence if she could help it. Seeming too tired to make the effort, too defeated to try. I was beneath a heated glare or icy indifference, like I was no longer worth the effort of her feelings, good or bad. And that was the harshest pain I'd ever felt.

All because of my stupidity. I'd never meant to fall for her, but she'd branded herself on my heart like a scar that would forever mark my flesh. I should have been candid, should have told her that I was working for my mother. But, in my foolishness, I'd kept my secrets, too afraid to tell the truth in fear of the monster she'd make of me.

There are things I'd done to save my brother that would follow me to the grave. Witches had died because of me—because of the things Yaga had bid me do in the name of her queen.

But not *my* queen. There is nothing I would like more than to carve my blades into Sylvie's flesh, to watch her burn upon a pyre. It was the least that Kitarni deserved. As for my mother ... something hardened in my heart as I thought of that woman. She was the light of my family once, but she'd chosen dark magic and

even darker deeds over us.

She'd hurt my betrothed, blackmailed me with my brother. In my mind, my mother died long ago. I would see it destroyed, this thing that had replaced her, and I would happily be the one to do it.

My brother was beyond Yaga's reach now and, even if I'd gone about saving him the entirely wrong way, even if I had given up more than I could have ever imagined, I would have done it all again to protect him. Even if it cost me Kitarni.

It made me sick, that she was hurt because of me. Worse, it made me a coward. So many times had passed where I could have bridged the gap and tried to make amends, but I hadn't. It was easier to let her hate me.

I deserved it.

As if she could sense me looking at her, Kitarni's eyes locked with my own as she stepped back into the ring with András, spinning the pommel of her sword in her hand in warning.

My gut dropped from that gaze. A blank stare, empty of all emotion and impossible to decipher. For a moment it seemed like the world held its breath as we stared at each other. Then, like a thunderclap had broken the spell, someone walked in front of her, and she was gone.

Mine for but a moment ... and never again.

Or she would be, if I didn't stop drowning my sorrows in my cups and made a damn difference with my life. For Mistvellen, my people, and for her.

 21

What was it she was always calling me?

Insufferable.

An asshat.

Stubborn.

A small smile curled my lips. Yes, I could be stubborn when it came to the things I wanted, and there was nothing I wanted more than her. It's about time she remembered that.

I straightened my tunic, unsheathing my training sword and making to step into the ring.

"I wouldn't advise that," Margit said from behind me. Gods, she was like a wraith when she wanted to be, silent and deadly.

"And what, may I ask, are you referring to?" I asked, raising my brow as I looked over my shoulder.

She tossed her long black hair and smirked, those clear blue eyes glittering with amusement. "Do you really think she needs any more reason to run you through with a sword?"

I ran a finger down my blade, glancing at my cousin with a dark smile. "What makes you think she'll have the chance?"

Margit tilted her head. "Have you seen the bruises and scrapes András wears these days? And that's sparring with someone she actually likes."

"Ouch." I slapped a hand on her shoulder, making her wince. "Don't worry, cousin dearest. Violence is the least of my worries. In fact, I'm counting on it."

Margit scoffed. "This will only end badly," she sang, waltzing away with a dismissive wave. "Don't come running to me when

you're licking your wounds."

I turned my attention back to Kitarni, who was holding her own against András. She was good. Really fucking good, but she could be better. Stalking towards her, I blocked her blow with my sword, saving András from a harsh whack to his ribs.

"Allow me to cut in," I said smoothly.

András looked at me gratefully, then shifted subtly, giving me an 'are you sure you want to go there' look. When I didn't move, he sighed under his breath, taking up a perch in the shade of a nearby tree.

Kitarni's glare was murderous. "I was doing perfectly fine sparring with András."

"Ah, she speaks. A good sign." I grinned, pointing my sword at her. "Your footwork is sloppy and you're favouring your right leg. Sheer strength will only get you so far."

"I'm not sparring with you," she snapped. "Get out of my way."

I shifted my stance and raised a brow. "Too afraid to take me?"

She gritted her teeth and I knew I'd hit a nerve. "Nothing would give me more pleasure," she said, an angry rumble releasing from her chest as she rushed me. I batted her sword away easily, side-stepping at the last second and forcing her to stumble past me.

When she charged at me again, her eyes brimming with fury, I deflected each blow, then grunted as she punched me in the jaw,

 23

spitting out blood onto the compacted dirt. She followed that up with a sharp thwack to my ribs, then a stab to my stomach. I could only imagine how she wished the training blade was of true, sharp steel.

Damn, she was certainly not holding back, which is just what I'd counted on. My little hellcat wanted to play dirty? Fine by me. I rubbed my stubble with one hand, my smile growing wider.

It only infuriated her more.

The next flurry of movement had me on the back foot, but after recovering I advanced swiftly, anticipating every step and swing of her sword until she was panting heavily, her back pressed against a stone column. Her arms trembled as she held up her guard, her sword buckling as she struggled against my own.

"You are strong, Kitarni, but you're ruled by emotion. Every expression tells me a story, and every step taken in anger gives me an advantage. Let go of the pain and let your sword be your anchor."

She glanced away, her teeth gritting.

"Look at me." She struggled against me futilely, huffing. "Look at me, Freckles."

That name made her face crease, uncertainty flashing in her eyes just long enough to allow me to swipe her sword away so that it clattered to the ground. I leaned my hands either side of her head, caging her in so that our faces were mere inches apart.

Sweat dripped down her brow, her hair plastered to her skin as her chest heaved with effort. When she looked at me again, it

was with pure wrath. "Let me go, Dante." The words were slow and measured, every word coated in dark warning.

I had the sense she meant more than simply letting her walk away from this encounter. "Never," I replied in a deep voice, the muscles in my arms cording as I shifted even closer.

Our lips were a breath apart and I longed to close that gap, to steal her kiss and drown myself in her. The sharp inhalation of Kitarni's breath was enough to tell me her body wanted that too. For a moment, the world seemed to still—nothing but the heated air between us and the tingle from every whisper of our bodies pressing together.

"I will never give up on you," I said quietly. "We can't keep doing this, Kitarni. How long will you continue to ignore me? I need to explain, I need to tell you—"

"Don't," she snapped, her eyes searching my own, her torso shaking as it brushed against mine. Her hands crashed against my chest, sending me back a step. "I gave you so many chances. What is there to say? You betrayed me. Betrayed us. What can you say that will make me forget that?" She shook her head, her jaw hardening. "I will not yield, Dante. I won't."

She kneed me between the legs and I gasped, doubling over as pain wracked through my body, unable to do anything but watch the rigid line of her back as she stormed into the castle. Perhaps trying to talk to her through sparring wasn't the best idea, but damn it all, it was worth a shot.

I wasn't stupid, I knew it would take work and perseverance.

I'd have to try harder, but I wouldn't stop. Not until I had her once more.

Not until she was mine.

THREE

KITARNI

"It's so gods-damned good to see you." I crushed Eszter in my arms, smiling at the familiar floral-and-honey scent of her hair. She laughed, the sound muffled as she buried her head in my shoulder, nuzzling in.

I hadn't realised until now just how much I needed this. Needed my family. Mistvellen was my home now, but there was nothing so comforting as being reunited with my sister and mother. It helped to have some time away from *him*, too. After that heated little moment in the sparring ring a few days ago, I'd needed an escape. Returning to my village was the next best thing, even if it was mostly to oversee operations here.

"I missed you too," she whispered, pulling back with a wide smile. "The house has been so much quieter without you in it. Everything has just been ..." Her voice trembled, and I tugged her closer again, propping my head atop her own.

It had only been a few months since I'd seen her, but she

27

seemed different somehow. Grown. The softness to her face had hardened ever so slightly, the gentleness of her eyes now bearing the weight of a woman who'd known hardship.

"I know, little one," I said gently. "I know."

We stayed like that for a while, just soaking each other in, enjoying the embrace between two sisters. Two souls whose threads bound them together.

A soft rap at the door had us both swivelling to find a mop of glistening blond hair and green eyes. I grinned, beckoning our guest to enter. "Eszter, I'd like to introduce you to my friend, András."

Eszter untangled herself from my arms and dipped into a small curtsy. "It's a pleasure, Lord ...?"

I snorted. "Lord of Being A Pain In My Ass."

András ignored me, his lips widening with amusement. "See what I put up with? A rare treasure, your sister," he said to Eszter. He took her hand and pressed a kiss to her knuckles. "The pleasure is entirely mine."

He peered at her with intrigue, eyes glimmering with the kind of shine that promised mischief. My eyes darted between them. "Oh no. Absolutely not. Eszter is off-limits, so keep your filthy paws away."

"Kitarni, you wound me. I am nothing if not a gentleman." He placed a hand over his heart, shooting me an affronted look.

I laughed, Eszter chuckling her amusement too as her eyes swept over András from head to toe. If I wasn't mistaken, there

 28

was interest in her gaze, though from her letters I knew she was head over heels for Lukasz. I might have warned her about *Sándor* men, but she seemed so happy, and hell if I was going to be the jealous, overbearing sister.

"I'm a big girl now, Kit, I can handle myself."

I blinked. "Please tell me you didn't grow up *too* much while I was away."

Eszter's cheeks turned bright pink. "Gods, Kitarni," she grumbled, knowing exactly what I meant by that. "Not one minute through the door and you're prying already."

My smile turned devilish. "Just doing my duty. I don't think Lukasz would be too happy to hear you're flirting with another táltos."

András stiffened. "Lukasz is courting you? No one tells me anything," he groused.

I smiled victoriously. "Did I fail to mention it? Well, now you know." I padded to the table, taking a seat and plopping my boots on the back of another chair. I cast a sideways glance at my sister. "So, have you kissed him yet?"

"Kitarni!" she chided, her cheeks turning a shade of beetroot as she ducked her head sheepishly.

"Oh, don't mind András," I said, waving a hand. "He loves the gossip."

He grinned, sliding into the seat beside mine. "It's true, I feed on court gossip like the village drunk on that swill you call ale here. I already know we're going to be good friends, Eszter."

29

I rolled my eyes. *Pompous ass.*

She cocked her head, her lips quirking shyly. "What makes you say that?"

"If I can put up with this one's bad tempers, swearing, and general haughtiness, then you will be a breath of fresh air, I'm sure."

My mouth fell open to argue, but I couldn't even deny it. True. All true. András only smirked knowingly. I flipped him off with a chuckle and turned to find Eszter looking at me oddly.

"What?"

She laughed, shaking her head. "It's just, I've never seen you like this. You seem different."

I shifted in my seat, feeling slightly uncomfortable with that assessment. "How so?"

Eszter walked gracefully to the cooking fire and looked over her shoulder with a jerk of her head. I grinned, sparking a fire with a click of my fingers. She set about arranging cups, boiling some tea, and placing some palacsinta on the table. An excited squeak left me as I reached for the sweet, rolled pancakes. An even more undignified noise followed as I took a bite and the chocolatey fruits exploded in my mouth.

Gods, it was all so familiar it made my heart ache with longing. Homesickness—not for the creature comforts or familiarity of a place, but the warmth of the people in it. Okay, fine, a little bit for the creature comforts.

Amused, András raised a brow at me, then watched Eszter

 30

quietly, thoughtfully, an expression I couldn't glean on his face.

My sister set the cups on the table and took a seat across from us. When she saw my inquiring glare, she laughed again. "Gods, stop looking at me like that. I meant it as a compliment, Kitarni. I've missed you like hell, but moving to Mistvellen has been good for you. This village holds bad memories—bad blood—but now?" She assessed me with a keen eye. "The way you hold yourself, the conviction in your eyes ... you're stronger. Happier. I always knew the potential you had. I think perhaps you've finally realised that too."

My heart swelled. My sister, ever the observer, wise beyond her years. It had been difficult to compartmentalise everything that had happened since leaving this village. So much blood had been spilled since then. And tears ... many tears. But for the first time since the incident in the cultists' clearing, I realised how right Eszter was.

Sorrow still stalked my footsteps, and anger filled my cup, but I had come so far, had taken all the shit from my past and forged myself into something stronger. Even if I'd lost the potential for something else before I'd ever fully grasped it ...

I didn't have the words to respond, so I reached my hand out to clasp hers. A gesture she immediately understood. She knew me so damn well.

"How have you been?" I rasped. "The village—"

"Is in shambles," she said with a wince.

My lips pursed. After spending the last few months picking

31

off witch hunters and intercepting messengers, I hadn't expected good news, but if what Eszter said was true, it was worse than I'd thought.

András sipped from his tea. "Is Caitlin Vargo still the High Witch of your coven?"

Eszter's face darkened, her lips turning to a scowl. "Unfortunately. The coven is a mess. Witches are disappearing in droves and our resources are fast depleting. Caitlin's leadership is crumbling by the day. Each of her decrees are more foolish than the last."

"Are the laws in this town not governed as a democracy?" András asked.

She shook her head slowly. "Not exactly. The councillors have a say in signing off on small matters, and each councillor is responsible for certain assignments and units, but the High Witch's word is law. It's always been that way."

"Well maybe it shouldn't." I coiled a curl around my finger, chewing on my lip. "Caitlin's dictatorship has never been formally contested before, but now is the time for change. Under her leadership the witches are suffering, women are being dragged away right under her nose and she does nothing. I only have one question. Why?"

Eszter looked at me with sorrow in her eyes. And in a voice barely audible, she whispered, "I don't know."

A frustrated sound escaped my lips. "What is the point of fighting against Sylvie and those fanatics if we can't protect our

own? Who does that make us in the end if we can't protect the ones we love?" I glanced at András, noting the concern in his eyes, the set of his jaw.

"There are always casualties in war, but the innocent should not suffer the wicked," András said. He sighed, raking a hand through his shiny blond locks. "Lord Sándor has provided soldiers to defend the witches and guard these borders. These are highly trained men. They would not shirk their duties or abandon their posts."

My frown deepened. "Erika would never allow our people to be taken without a fight. Something is wrong. It just doesn't add up."

Eszter said, "There's a reason for that. Caitlin has been sending Erika on scouting missions—Lukasz too. With the cultists blocking all trade routes and water outlets, we're running out of food. We can survive on what our earth magic can harness for now, but it's not enough to last. Especially when the weather cools. Erika isn't here half the time, and without her there's no one to lead our forces, small as they are."

I steepled my fingers together, propping my chin on their tips. "So you're telling me she's sending our best warriors out on meaningless quests while our village remains vulnerable against attack? No one to command the táltosok, no one to train the witches?"

Eszter nodded. "Exactly. Mama has been doing her best to ration our food and water and to keep the soldiers in line, but

 33

there's only so many places she can be at once. If Sylvie sent an army to attack, we'd fall, Kitarni. All of us."

András swore under his breath, all evidence of his cheery temperament gone. He glanced at me—asking for permission, I realised. It was still odd to me, to have anyone deferring to me, much less my betrothed's best friend. I wondered if Dante begrudged me András's company, then thought better of it. The asshat had probably asked András to watch over me in his stead. Shoving that thought aside, I nodded my acceptance and András left our house without a word, stopping only to nod politely to Eszter.

He was headed to find the táltosok, no doubt. To find answers and to take charge if no one else would. I wondered how many remained in the village at any given time. A mere handful, if witches were being taken from the town. From my experience fighting alongside the táltosok, they were not a people who took their duties lightly. How had no one ever seen the cultists come? Were women stolen from their beds by thieves in the night?

I shook my head. What a mess. If Dante were here ...

I swallowed. My betrothed would have ripped someone's head off for allowing the village to fall into chaos. I imagined a small part of him might delight in it if that head were Caitlin's. He'd demanded to come, of course. Even though we weren't speaking, he still managed to frustrate me to no ends. But Mistvellen needed him more than I did right now.

Maybe always. My anger towards him was still too raw to

analyse and I had needed space, time, and a physical target to unleash upon. Unfortunately for András, that had been him in the sparring ring.

My friendship with him and Margit was all that was keeping me from falling apart—and Imre's baked goods. Specifically his bejgli. The poppyseed or walnut sweet rolls melted in the mouth, gooey with just the right amount of sugar. I must have eaten cartloads of his pastries by now, and he never failed to give me a bear hug and a grin when I visited him. Margit had threatened me with about a thousand curses if I were to get any stains on the books in the library.

"Books," I muttered to myself, the glimmer of an idea forming. "Are the histories and lore on our coven still kept in the temple? I know we have records dating back hundreds of years." Eszter pursed her lips, and I sighed. "Don't tell me, they're under lock and key by Caitlin?"

She smiled apologetically, confirming my suspicions. "Caitlin has remained holed up in the temple, admitting the councillors only when calling a meeting. Its halls are no longer accessible by the witches."

"What!?" My blood heated, my fingers curling into fists. "She doesn't allow the townsfolk to worship the gods? In wartime we need their blessings the most."

Eszter said nothing, but I sensed the anger seeping from her, thick and oily. To deny the witches their right to worship was a low blow. Even the High Witch had no right.

 35

My stomach curdled like aged milk. Caitlin fucking Vargo. She would be our coven's end if she didn't pull her finger out of her ass and act. Our people were dying, being stolen out from under her nose. Soon they'd be starving. The gods would not watch over them without prayer.

"Fuck this," I snapped. "Caitlin's reign is *done*. The council is not a dictatorship, it's a democracy. It's time the witches remembered their power."

Eszter stared at me with a small smile curving her face, those honey-brown eyes lighting up. A soldier's smile. "You're planning something already, aren't you?"

I smirked. "What would you say if I was?"

My sister tossed her long hair over a shoulder and raised her chin. "I'd say what are we waiting for?"

It was a cloudy night, which suited my needs perfectly. Shadows masked the white glow of the moon as Eszter, András and I stalked through the temple grounds. I'd dressed all in black to avoid detection, and it was a good thing, too.

Caitlin had guards patrolling the temple grounds, because of course she thought herself more important than the entire fucking town. I gritted my teeth so hard they hurt. She was an utter fool, and a fool in power was more dangerous than most.

Eszter skirted the flowers and bushes with practiced ease.

 36

We'd had our many mischievous quests in our youth, but the way she moved like smoke was impressive. As if she glided rather than walked.

Our boots made no sound as we ran across the grass, halting behind pillars and plants. If I wasn't so worried about getting caught, it might have been fun. I'd studied the soldier's movements from afar as they circled the area, performing sweeps once every few minutes, though they switched it up on occasion.

Smart. Annoyingly smart. It made it harder for enemies to sneak behind their patrols and today, that enemy was me. If the táltosok saw me and András they'd ask no questions—their allegiance certainly didn't lie with Caitlin—but I didn't want to cause confusion or risk alerting Caitlin to our presence.

I glanced at my sister. "You know what to do."

She nodded devilishly, streaking towards the outer garden to intercept the guards before they made their next sweep. Eszter made a striking distraction, one I knew they'd have trouble keeping their eyes from.

Seeing András and I would only rouse suspicion, and the thought of Caitlin's withered fingers grasping a tighter foothold on this village was unacceptable.

"Kitarni," András whispered, motioning me towards the rear of the building. I had a good view of his ass as he moved. There were worse things I could look at. I smirked. Much, much worse.

We dashed into a rose bush, a thorn scraping against my exposed cheek. The sting reminded me of the last time Eszter and

 37

I had been in this position, spying on the councillors. Caitlin had been hesitant to act then, too. *Nothing* had changed.

András threw me a grin that was all white teeth and victory. "An entrance fit for a queen, my lady," he purred, jerking his chin at the window above.

I rolled my eyes and huffed. "I don't remember it being so gods-damned high."

"I'll give you a boost," he said quietly, lacing his fingers together.

Frowning, I judged the distance, then shrugged. "Your funeral."

"All right, on three. One, two—"

Ignoring his little pep rally, I stepped into his hands, opting to climb him like a ladder rather than be tossed up the wall. He grumbled as I put one boot, then the other, on his shoulders, but the window was still too high. "I'd say sorry, but we both know I'd be lying," I said.

"What ... for," he panted, shifting under my weight.

I grinned as I stepped onto his head and was answered with a string of colourful curses. Much better. Now I could get a solid grip on the ledge without flapping my arms and legs about.

If anyone looked, we were done for, but as I heard Eszter's lilting laugh float across the gardens, I relaxed. She had them wrapped around her finger.

"See you on the other side," I said to András, and slipped inside the witch's lair.

FOUR

KITARNI

I vaulted through the window, landing lightly on my feet in the temple's rear chamber. The room was dark and silent, which meant Caitlin had likely retired home for the night. I breathed a sigh of relief. Lady Luck had finally graced me with her presence.

Just in case, I strained my ears, narrowing my eyes for a hint of any candlelight. Only dust stirred as I made my way through the room, careful to avoid bumping into any furniture. There was little light to see by, so I risked conjuring a small flame into my palm.

The room was threadbare, littered with a few books and scrolls, but otherwise occupied only by an alter at the far end of the room. I studied a small statue of Istenanya upon the stone slab, surrounded by unlit candles and paraphernalia.

The mother goddess. *The blessed one.* It was she we prayed to most to nurture and keep us safe, though I had a feeling Hadúr,

the god of war, would be worshipped in bountiful tides soon. Witches needed protection from the cultists, but we needed our blades to be sharp and our minds even sharper.

I looked around the room, casting an eye over the few books present. Titles on simple spells and potions, herbal uses, and earth magic castings. Nothing out of the ordinary or worth locking up. No, those books would be somewhere secure.

After hunting through the entire temple, my findings had come up short. I raked a hand through my hair in frustration. András would be growing impatient, and Eszter would be long gone by now.

Where could they be? Surely Caitlin wouldn't hide such valuable items in her home? The books I sought contained our history, dating back to the first witches of our coven. Such things were timeless treasures, and given the increased guard presence around the temple, I was inclined to follow my initial instincts.

I returned to the rear chamber, glancing at the statue of Istenanya. The firelight almost made it seem like she was watching me, scrutinising my every movement.

Please, blessed mother, I prayed. *Show me the way. Give me a sign.*

She merely stared at me with outstretched arms, a look of love and affection adorning her beautiful face. I followed the angle of her palms, my eyes dropping to the ground. A rug lay settled over the stone. The corner of it was flipped, as if someone had scuffed it in a hurry and hadn't bothered to right it.

Dust plumed as I pulled the rug back, stifling a cough as

the cloud climbed my nostrils. "Hello," I said quietly, grinning to myself. "What do we have here?"

A trapdoor leading underground. To a cellar? Or something else? My skin prickled with awareness, the beast within stirring as if sensing danger. I glanced at the window, pursing my lips. András would be pissed at me for not bringing him, but we needed the spells in those books. Something—anything—to overthrow the High Witch without inciting a coup. If the coven stood any chance against Sylvie, strength in numbers—in unity—was our best bet.

Fuck it. I hefted the trapdoor open and stared into the pitch black below, climbing onto a ladder that had seen better days. Honestly, I was surprised Caitlin even had the strength to get down there.

The ladder groaned as I descended, the wood creaking with each boot I placed on the rail. Without a free hand, I'd been forced to snuff out my fire, which left me in total darkness in the tight space. My chest constricted, breaths coming shorter as the ladder seemed to go down, down, down into the gods only knew where.

Coldness greeted me the further down I went, the air musty and stale and ... metallic? A dampness settled in my bones, my instincts warning me to turn back, to find light again. I'd never been one to back down from a challenge, and I wasn't about to now. My gut was always right.

Unfortunately, my gut could be a real bitch sometimes.

 41

A scuttling sounded in the dark and I stiffened, holding my breath, hoping against hell it was just a rat. The hairs on the nape of my neck raised, and I shivered once more. Not from the cold this time, but from something that didn't belong here.

There it was again. A skittering—the steps too uneven to be a witch. The sound grew louder as it approached. My heart thudded beneath my ribcage, threatening to give me away. Sweat beaded on my forehead, my palms clammy with fear. What the fuck was down here?

With shaking fingers, I raised a hand near my face, conjuring a small flame to life.

And screamed.

A twisted face appeared before me, so distorted by shadow and smoke it was impossible to make out what was what. Fear rooted me to the spot as this being hurtled towards me with a horrifying gait. Paralysis crawled through my veins, pinpricking over my skin as I could do nothing but stand there and wait for the blow to fall.

Move, Kitarni. *Fucking move!* The beast inside me roared in defiance, writhing and raging deep down in my stomach, and somehow, my limbs jerked back in response.

I sucked in a breath and exploded. Red surged from my body, crashing upon the beast with a thunderous clap. It yowled, the sound so unearthly that my bones trembled, threatening to buckle beneath me.

I'd left my sword at home, and my throwing knives and the

tiny daggers in my boots wouldn't be much use against the creature before me. A nightmare, a parasite which had no place in the Middle World. I knew what it was the moment I saw it: *Guta*. A spirit from the Under World known for inflicting paralysis, then violently thrashing its victims, leaving bloodied, broken corpses in its wake.

The demon screeched, still writhing from the magnitude of my power. But what could kill a creature not of this earth? I rolled, narrowly missing a swipe of a clawed hand as I sprinted down the tunnel, shoving it against the wall as I passed.

It crashed into the stone, howling once more as it gave chase. I stumbled down the tunnel, my light flickering treacherously as I ran. It was a maze, this underground labyrinth, never-ending, always turning.

My breath came in gasps, panic constricting my chest, my lungs not filling with the air I needed. A sob tore from my throat as I heard the scuttling increase. It was right behind me, one wrong turn, one stumble ...

I racked my brain for a solution, a way out of this mess, but I couldn't go back without facing the demon. I also couldn't run forever. A flash of red scrawl appeared on the wall beside me—an arrow—and I didn't hesitate to heed its guidance.

I threw fireballs blindly over my back, hoping to slow the spirit. It hissed and screeched so loudly I felt my ears would bleed, but it never slowed, never stopped.

The dirt floor crunched beneath my boots, my legs screaming

as the muscles burned from exertion. I'd never run so fast in my life. When at last it felt like my body would betray me, I crashed into an open chamber.

"Hello, Kitarni," a low voice said, right before something slammed into my head.

My head barked with pain, a throbbing so violent my skull threatened to crack in two. Something wet and sticky ran down my temple, congealing in clumps over my brow. Groggily, I sat up and tried to blink back the fuzziness to no avail. I jerked, finding myself bound by ropes to a chair, the material chafing against my wrists and around my ankles.

"No." The word was soft, almost pleading as I writhed, my breaths growing shorter, heavier as panic swelled my chest. The ropes stung as I clenched my fists and pulled, and the scar on my sternum burned as memories flashed through my mind—of a blade sinking into my chest, my blood being drained, cultists chanting and a world full of so much red.

A small whimper escaped my throat and my heart thundered hard enough to tear from my chest as I sucked in small, desperate gasps. At this rate, I was going to black out again. Sweat dripped down my back, beading over my temple as I bent over.

Breathe, Kitarni, just breathe.

I squeezed my eyes shut, taking one deep breath through my

 **44**

nose, expelling the air through my lips. Another, then another, until I could form some rational thoughts ... until the sounds of footsteps shuffled along the damp, cold floor.

I whipped my head around, trying to see past the curtain of hair falling in front of my face. Someone had removed my boots, stealing away the hidden blades stowed in each. I tried to summon my magic, but my power was sluggish. Besides, if I tried to roast Caitlin or use my blood magic, I'd have a demon to answer to.

Shit.

The world was still blurry, but I saw a shadow—no, two shadows—standing over me. And a voice. Grating, pretentious, ugly in every note. One I knew too well.

My vision slowly cleared, and there she was. The High Witch and chief councillor herself. Caitlin. Fucking. Vargo.

Shiiiit.

She sneered down her nose at me, her wrinkled lips pursed in disgust, like *I* was the monstrosity in the room. The demon, however, remained blurred. Most likely hidden by a spell, blocking it from my sight. Or perhaps it had no true face and was just a constant mask of shadows and filtered light.

It seemed calmed by her presence, almost as though tethered to her command by an invisible leash. And I supposed it was. The Guta would not be in the Middle World without a summoning. Only dark magic could beckon demons from the Under World and bend them to one's will. It was an abomination, brought forth only by the darkest and most forbidden magic.

 45

Its presence loomed over me, ominous in the dim light of flickering candles. My heart galloped in my chest, sweat sliding down my face as I forced myself to breathe. To form a plan and buy myself some time.

A flash of movement drew my eye, and I peered over Caitlin's shoulder, spotting a glimpse of grey skirts. I followed the fabric higher. A female figure wriggled against iron chains built into a stone wall, her mouth gagged by a rag. Wide, brown eyes stared back at me in terror.

And all around her ... blood. Dark brown blotches splashed violently over the walls and the dirt.

The thundering in my chest retreated deep into my stomach as fear, slick and oily, oozed through my veins. My pulse throbbed in my neck, thump, thump, thumping to every shaky breath.

"Caitlin." I gasped, slowly turning towards my captor. "What have you done?"

I recognised the witch tied up. She looked barely old enough to have had her first bleed—a timid, mousey girl whom I'd never really had the chance to know. In fact, I wondered if anyone had ever really bothered with her at all. The kind of person used to blending into shadows, not immediately missed. I knew the feeling well. I'd learned to embrace the darkness on purpose.

My throat constricted as her muffled protests sounded through the gag.

Summoning a demon and holding a witch prisoner like this was the highest transgression, especially from the High Witch

 46

herself. If the coven found out, she would die by fire. I narrowed my eyes. *Painfully,* and hopefully slowly.

The bound girl sobbed, drawing my attention once more. Tears tracking down her dirty cheeks, she stared at us—at me— imploringly. I swallowed, my heart panging for a sister witch. I knew that look in her eyes too well. A lamb led to slaughter, an innocent who learned from heavy fists and sharp tongues just what the world was capable of.

Caitlin smoothed her skirts, lifting her chin. "I did what I had to. You gave me no choice, Kitarni. Our coven is crumbling. The return of the Dark Queen threatens all we hold dear."

"All *you* hold dear. Your position teeters on a cliff. All it would take is one small push." I smirked, cocking my head. "You're threatened."

Her eyes flashed with warning, those wrinkled lips curling with disdain. "You have always been a thorn in my side. Defiant, crass, disrespectful. I knew you were trouble from the moment you came clawing out of that abomination's womb. We should have let you die."

My stomach twisted at those hateful words. Caitlin was rotten to her very poisonous core.

"I suppose you blame me for Sylvie's return." A bitter laugh escaped my lips. "You know her resurrection was inevitable. Neither the gods nor Fate herself could change that card. Not when they had help from an inside source."

Caitlin stiffened momentarily before smoothing her skirts

down. "I don't know what you're talking about."

"Don't play dumb, Caitlin," I snapped. "The only way the cultists could bring Sylvie back is with spells wrought from dark magic—knowledge contained within a certain book kept in your care. Did you think I wouldn't work it out? The banya and I had quite the enlightening chat before she sank her blade into my chest."

Her face tightened, the lines around her lips crinkling further as those slate grey eyes narrowed. "How dare you imply that I would consort with those fanatics. A dangerous accusation against your better."

"My better?" I scoffed. "There is nothing better about you. High Witch or no, the truth will come out, and the witches will have your head."

Caitlin lifted her chin as she sneered, her gaze raking over my bonds. "Even if what you say is true, you won't live long enough to tell the coven."

The demon at her side shifted closer, the utter wrongness of its presence on this plane sending invisible bugs skittering down my arms. Oh, I had no doubts she would make good on her promise. I wriggled my wrists ever so slightly. There would be no escaping the ropes by force alone, but magic on the other hand ...

I lifted my chin. "I'm curious, Caitlin. Why did you give the banya the book? Wait, forgive me, I meant to say Baba Yaga."

Caitlin's face twisted impossibly further. "Do not say her name in my presence. That woman is a disgrace to witchkind."

She took a calming breath, seeming to contemplate whether to answer for a moment before she sighed. "I knew there was no stopping Sylvie's return. Long before she was resurrected, I kept a close watch on the cult's movements. I knew they would come one day. They never stopped searching for one with the Dark Queen's blood."

Intrigued, I eyed her cautiously. "If you knew I was Sylvie's descendant, why not give me to them sooner? Why not make a deal with the cultists?"

She scoffed. "If it were up to me, I'd have bartered your life for our village's protection long ago, but I couldn't be sure if Sylvie's magic ran through your veins. I kept my eyes on you, but during all these years you never let it loose, that dark power. It was only when the Sándor pup arrived and Nora announced your betrothal that I knew. It takes a rare treasure indeed to catch Lord Sándor's eye. Why else would he match his son to a peasant daughter? To a *Bárány?*"

"My father was one of Lord Sándor's closest friends, you ignorant twit." I smiled coyly, unable to help myself. "I suppose it could easily have been my beauty or sharp wit. Or perhaps my exceptional performance in bed?"

She slapped my cheek hard, the skin stinging from the imprint of her withered hand. She was surprisingly strong for her age, but I wouldn't let her see me wince. "You never knew when to keep your mouth shut. Such a disappointment. Your father would be turning in his grave if he knew what a whore he'd sired."

"Don't talk about my father," I hissed, my blood heating as I stared at her defiantly and lifted my chin. "If he were alive, he'd be by my side, fighting to dethrone you."

"But he isn't alive, is he? Your precious daddy isn't here to fight your battles and you'll be joining him soon enough as food for the worms beneath my feet. I'll even sing a song in your honour as we hold vigil. The girl who would defy death for the witches who scorned her, with only her mother and sister to weep when she is gone."

"You would do all this to secure your position as High Witch? And when I'm gone, then what? Join the cult? Offer them more sacrifices?" I shook my head sadly. "You betray your own kind. Sending witches as sacrificial offerings to keep Sylvie preoccupied will only keep you safe for so long. When the Dark Queen is ready, she will come, and she will slaughter everyone. What will you do when the witches are burning and the village is black with the rot of her curse? What will you do when she comes for your heart?"

Caitlin turned to me slowly, her eyes dead and flat. "There is no price too high to pay for power, child, and I shall have plenty of it before that comes to pass. This coven is lost, but there are many more to rule."

I raised a brow. "It might have escaped your notice, Caitlin, but you're well past your prime. No coven will bow to a High Witch as old as you—not when they have their own elders in place."

50

She smiled, a cold and cruel thing that didn't reach her eyes. "For now. But I won't be challenging them as I am, girl. I'll have the blood of maidens running through my veins."

My eyes followed Caitlin's line of sight as she looked at the other witch like a piece of meat. And I supposed she was, in a way. "Dear gods. You're going to drain her? Steal her vitality?"

Her lips pressed into a thin line. "I'm not a monster, Kitarni. It gives me no pleasure to do this to a fellow witch."

"No," I spat. "You're worse than a monster, hiding behind propriety and excuses. This is sick, Caitlin. You're deranged and no better than the cultists you despise so much."

She slid a curved blade from a leather throng at her hip, fingering the arc of its steel as she took one step closer. Then another. "As I said, Kitarni, I'm only doing what I have to."

I swallowed thickly as she approached, cold murder in her eyes. "Wait," I snapped. "Just tell me one thing: why not fight for our freedom? Why not take a chance?"

She laughed. "Only gamblers bet on those odds, Kitarni, and I haven't the resources to play with. I am not a queen, nor am I her fool. I refuse to be played like one."

Anger roiled inside me, the beast roaring to be freed. "You're right, Caitlin, you're nothing but a coward. If you had any honour, you would be standing with the coven, fighting until your last breath for every witch with a drop of magic in her veins. We have the táltosok, we have our power, and when Sylvie's army comes, we will show no quarter. And you? Your memory will die with you. The world will never know your name."

"Pretty words, but they fall on deaf ears. *I* will be alive. That's more than I can say for you." She advanced until she leaned over me, the shadows flickering over her face making her appear like a demon. But I knew better. Demons were creatures bred for carnage and chaos. Caitlin was so much uglier.

The girl tied to the wall sobbed, fresh tears tracking down her cheeks as she writhed uselessly against her bonds. I looked at her and smiled. "It'll be okay," I whispered. "It's going to be okay."

I didn't know if I was convincing myself or her.

"You know," Caitlin said conversationally as she ran a finger along the blade, "contrary to what I said before, I think I will enjoy it this time, and I—" She paused, sniffing the air. "What's that smell?"

I looked around innocently, then sniffed alongside her. "Smells like a hag about to get her come-uppance to me."

Caitlin glared at me, the smell forgotten. "You have plagued me for so long, girl."

"We have been lifelong nemeses," I agreed cheerfully.

She paused, uncertainty flickering in her eyes as she looked between my own. *Oh yes, you should be afraid, Caitlin.* Every minute she'd spent blabbering on, I'd been singeing the ropes with the slightest flare of magic. Demon be damned. It was either that or being carved up.

"Do you want to know what I think?" I said with a wide grin, revealing too many teeth. "You talk too fucking much."

 52

A fireball erupted in my palms, instantly feeding on the ropes around my wrists, and I jumped up instantaneously, jamming my fist into Caitlin's stomach. She wheezed, bending double as I slammed my other hand into her face so hard something *cracked*.

She crumpled to the ground and I turned my attention to the demon. It circled me slowly, menacingly, every second that ticked by feeling like an eternity as it watched me with soulless, pitch-black eyes.

It lunged, and I had all of two seconds to dive out of the way, rolling over my side to land in a crouch, fire blazing once more. I tossed a fireball in its direction, staring in dismay as the flames simply sputtered out with a wave of its clawed hand.

That hand raised higher before it, a slow ascent of a long, furred arm shrouded in smoke and shadow reaching for me. My fingers and toes started feeling numb, that odd sensation tingling in my extremities as slowly, paralysis began overtaking my body.

I was sinking into an abyss, too dizzy and still too disorientated from having my head bashed to focus the dark magic in my blood. My stomach dropped as I stumbled, the fire in my palm winking out as I fell.

That hand reached closer, closer, and all I could think of was him. My dark knight. The man who had taken all I'd had to give. I pictured his handsome face, tousled hair and dark eyes lined with gold. Lips I yearned to kiss, if only one last time.

My eyes began to flutter closed. I didn't want to see my death. Didn't want to look at that thing while it tore me apart. But I was

already breaking. Nothing could hurt more than the pain that had already cleaved me in two.

A bloodcurdling roar sounded, and my eyes snapped open, watching a dark shape hurtle across the room, twin blades unsheathed and eyes flashing in the dark.

"Dante," I managed to breathe.

He moved like a demon himself, swords glinting in the candlelight, his chest bare and tattoos gleaming like smoke as he moved. He slashed, landing a blow to the demon's waist, causing it to shriek so loud I thought my eardrums would burst.

Black blood sprayed the ground, bubbling and hissing as it sank into the dirt. Dante moved as though in a trance, slashing, rending, lunging forwards and then nimbly retreating. Like one of the black wolves of his clan he attacked savagely—a man with nothing to lose. *Or perhaps, everything,* a small voice inside my head dared to hope.

The demon hissed, swiping its claws across Dante's back as he turned. Dante gritted his teeth against the pain, but still he persisted. It wasn't until he'd backed the demon into a corner that it opened some sort of portal in the ground, jumping through it and disappearing at last.

As soon as the demon left, warmth seemed to spread through my body. Slowly, I could wiggle my toes, then twitch my legs and roll my hips.

Dante's breath came in ragged pants as he crashed to his knees and cradled my head in his lap, checking me over for

wounds. When he seemed satisfied, he held me for a moment, running a knuckle down my hair and cheek with a featherlight touch before he withdrew sharply, as though burned.

"Are you hurt?" he rasped.

I couldn't answer yet, my tongue still firmly lodged against the roof of my mouth. All I could do was stare into the bottomless depths of those dark eyes. Eventually, I blinked repeatedly, darting my own towards the girl chained in the adjacent room. He nodded, searching me hesitantly, but at my insistence he huffed and stalked away.

A string of curses reached me moments later, followed by the rattling of chains and his deep voice speaking in low, soothing tones. The sobbing of the girl came next, and a minute must have passed where he comforted her, letting her cry it out.

When my limbs became fully responsive and I could move my jaw, I stood up slowly, making my way into the other chamber. The girl saw me enter, and she flung herself on me, squeezing as tight as she could.

I hugged her as fiercely as my weak limbs could manage as she wept into my shoulder, threatening my own eyes to tear up. Dante just stood back and waited, his arms folded, lips twisting as his gaze fell upon Caitlin.

She was still unconscious, and I wanted it to stay that way for as long as possible. When I broke apart from the witch, I held her face gently in my hands. "What's your name?" I said softly.

She sniffed, sagging a little beneath my hands. "Léna."

 55

I smiled, tucking a strand of her mousey brown hair behind her ear. "You're safe now, Léna. No one will harm you."

Her brown eyes darted to Caitlin, and I hushed her, turning her head back to my own. "She won't hurt anyone ever again, I promise. I need you to be brave now, okay? Do you know the way out of here?"

Her lips wobbled, eyes brimming once again, but she lifted her chin and nodded.

"Good. I need you to tell the táltosok patrolling nearby to meet us outside the temple. Then go and fetch my mother, Erika, and Lukasz. Can you do that?"

"Yes," she answered meekly. Then stronger, "Yes."

"Go," I whispered, and she grabbed one of the candles and flew out the door, leaving me alone with Dante.

We stared at each other in silence, the tension between us so tangible a knife could cut it. He stood just an arm's length away, his eyes unreadable as he gazed at me.

"Thank you," I breathed, laying a hand on his chest. He stiffened ever so slightly beneath my touch. It felt like a thousand words went unsaid as the silence stretched. He placed his hand on my own, warm and calloused, and we just stood there. Seconds passed, but it could have been an eternity.

"Kitarni, I ..."

I held my breath as I waited for something—anything—to mend this rift between us. But my heart fractured even further as he closed his mouth and shook his head. Anger rippled through

me. How could I be so stupid? I'd shut him down in the sparring ring back in Mistvellen, still too angry to let him in, but now we were alone together at last and he couldn't muster a few words? I'd get more substance from a damn rock. At least they didn't break or betray. How could I ever trust him again? He had taken my heart and crushed it beneath his boot. I knew better than to pick up those pieces only to give it to him again.

Tears glimmered in my eyes, but I refused to let them fall. I had spent too many on Dante already, shed over countless nights and idle moments when alone.

We had so much to say, but as I pulled away, the window closed, my heart breaking further apart, crumbling into ash. I looked into his eyes, drowning in pain and sorrow and regret, but it was too late for us now. He had his chance, and I couldn't wait for words that would never come. A future that would never pass.

"Don't," he said quietly. "Don't shut me out again."

I gaped at him, opening my mouth to spew vitriol when Caitlin stirred on the ground, groaning softly as she came to. Dante moved immediately, placing one of his swords—still black with the demon's blood—against Caitlin's neck. "Say the word and I will end this wretched creature."

A part of me wanted to see her blood drench the ground, to see justice brought to Léna, to the coven and to myself. I was so angry. It would have been too easy to let her bear the brunt of it, but it would be a kindness to end her life so quickly. Caitlin needed to pay for her crimes, and there was only one punishment befitting her treachery.

"No." I shook my head, my lips curling as I glanced at the miserable creature. "She will be tried the witch way. By burning at the stake." My gaze slowly shifted to Dante, and I knew he could see the conviction there. "Bring her to the square. This ends tomorrow."

I turned on my heel, feeling as though I was turning my back on everything that was. Just before I stormed out the door, I heard Dante speak.

"You were born to lead, Kitarni. I know you will rule well."

Those words sank like a stone in my stomach. I wanted to scream at him, to shake some sense into him, but I paused, anger roiling within me, hands balling into fists.

"You're right, Dante. I will rule," I said quietly. "By your side. A thousand worlds away, and none."

FIVE

DANTE

"You idiot!" András said, glaring at me as we stood guard at the outskirts of the village. "You stupid, hard-headed fool. You—"

"I get it," I growled, pacing back and forth like a caged animal, only my cage was of my own making. "I made a mistake."

András scoffed, throwing his hands up in the air dramatically, his face dark under the gloomy sky. "Made a mistake?! You had the perfect opportunity to make amends and you pissed all over it. The wolf lord of Mistvellen, cowering before a woman scorned. Please. Dante, if you lose her, you'll regret it for the rest of your life."

"Don't you think I know that?" I said, storming over until I was inches away from his face. "Not a day goes by where I don't think about what I did. How I didn't try hard enough to keep her safe or why I didn't just tell her the truth. Every hour, every minute spent apart from her is *agony*. She will never trust me

 59

again. And even if she did, I wouldn't deserve it anyway."

András looked at me for a long minute as we faced off, until suddenly he swung, his fist connecting with my jaw with a loud crack. "Pull yourself together man. You've had plenty of time to mope about your actions and, quite frankly, I am over your moods. You're like a bear woken mid-hibernation." He huffed. "The Dante I know would make things right and forge a way forward. *Stop* worrying about the past and *start* thinking about how you can make up for everything you've done. By the gods, man, she's going to be your bloody wife."

I rubbed my jaw, staring at him in surprise. It took a lot to rile András, but I couldn't blame him. I'd been poor company for the last few months, and the only way I'd managed to work through my misery had been by focusing all my attention—and perhaps aggression—on hunting cultists and securing my city's safety. A bear awoken indeed, and the cult kept on poking it. *Me.*

Every time we freed a kidnapped witch, a little piece of my soul seemed to stick back together, though nothing would ever clear the mark my mother had left on me. I'd never hurt a witch, but I hadn't stopped the atrocities against them either. My mother's little blood rituals were proof of that. It wasn't until my father had confessed his plan to have me married to Kitarni that I knew she was the one they'd been looking for.

I hadn't meant to care for her, but before I knew it a few insults, shared fights and a shared bed had me realising I was in over my head. From the moment I'd met that wild flame, I'd been

burned, and I wanted to walk right back into her fire. I'd never wanted to cage her, but I should have tried harder to keep her safe, to keep her far from my mother's reach. I may as well have sunk that blade into Kitarni's chest myself. The thought made me sick to my stomach.

"Kitarni has made it very clear she doesn't want to repair things. She will go through with the wedding, but it won't be for me."

"You're still not getting it." András sighed, slapping a hand on my shoulder, forcing me to look at him. "It's not about you. It's not even about her. Together, you're unstoppable, a force to be reckoned with. I believe your fates are wound together and, regardless of your feelings, the gods have bigger plans for the two of you. The choice you must make is whether you want to follow that fate or deny it. For both of your sakes and the rest of our damned souls, I hope you choose the former, because something tells me you're both the key to our kingdom's survival."

His words rang with the clarity of truth. I wasn't foolish or self-indulgent enough to think I could save anyone. I wasn't the hero of our story, clad in golden armour to rescue the fair lady. Kitarni was more than capable of rescuing herself. She could bring the world to its knees if she dared.

She would fight blood against blood. There was nothing Kitarni wouldn't do to save our people. She was a warrior, and I, her dark knight, to command as only a queen could.

Mistvellen was in danger, and I would throw every ounce of

my strength into fighting for it—for the witches I had wronged and for my people. With the witches' magic, the táltosok and our wolves, we stood a chance. A slim one perhaps, but any sliver of hope was worth dying for.

I raked a hand through my hair and faced my second. "You've been a good friend, András," I said, clamping my hand on his shoulder so we mirrored each other. "I'm sorry for letting you down. You're like a brother to me. You deserve better."

He smiled solemnly. "Everything you did was for the right reasons, even if you're a damn fool sometimes. For you, Lukasz or Margit, I would have done the same. Maybe with a bit more finesse but ..." He crossed his arms, giving me an appraising look, his green eyes shining. "Loosen your coin purse and we'll call it even."

I grinned. "If we get through this, I'll get you a damn castle of your own to lord over."

"And get rid of me that easily?" he asked, looking affronted. "I think not."

"My lord," a guard approached, nodding his head respectfully. "You've been summoned to a council meeting in the temple. The elders wish for both of you to be present."

I grimaced, sharing a loaded glance with András. "I guess we're to weigh in on Caitlin's fate."

"There's nothing to decide," András hissed. "The witch can burn for what she's done."

I thought of Kitarni's determination—how she'd already

62

decided how to punish that old hag. Caitlin's treachery was the highest sin among witches. She'd taken the blood of her own, twisting it into dark magic to use for her own selfish gain. There was no way she wouldn't pay with her life for what she had done.

"I think we're going to see just that when the sun comes up tomorrow," I replied. "But I don't think that's the only reason we've been summoned."

András groaned. "It never stops, does it?"

"The wheel of fate keeps turning, my friend. We're just along for the ride."

The atmosphere in the temple was gloomy, everyone's mood as thunderous as the storm building outside. The gods stared down on us from high, their morose faces flashing ominously with each lightning strike.

Kitarni sat beside her mother, her back ramrod straight and her face emotionless as I entered. The flickering flames on the nearby sconces made her look like a vengeful goddess, wicked and unforgiving, and fuck if I didn't want to worship every inch of that woman. She was power personified. She was perfect.

András took the empty seat beside her, the pair thick as thieves these days. I was glad for it. Truly glad she had found family in Mistvellen. If not in me, then in better men and women.

I smoothed out my tunic and smiled at each of the councillors—

 63

noting Iren's absence—as well as Eszter and Lukasz. My gaze passed over Kitarni, but she was pointedly looking anywhere else. The dismissal was blatantly obvious, but everyone seemed accustomed to our rituals now. All were aware that my efforts to court Kitarni had all but been cut off at the balls.

Once we were seated, Nora looked us over, one by one. "You all know why we're here. Caitlin betrayed us in every way imaginable, and she must pay for her sins. Tradition dictates she die by the stake. Are there any objections?"

No one answered. The only one who might've tried to protect Caitlin was Iren, and the spider was missing. Erika's dark eyes flashed, a vein in her neck pulsing so hard it seemed ready to jump ship. "I think we're all of the same mind. The gods will pass judgement before she leaves this world," she spat. "May Death find her in the next."

"Then it's agreed," Nora said, her lips pressing together. "A pyre is being built as we speak, and Caitlin will be tried in the morning." She sighed, shaking her head, her brows downturned. "This is the first time in our history that a High Witch has ever faced prosecution. There will be an uproar among the other covens."

Kitarni stood up slowly. "Then let it serve as a reminder to those who would turn their backs on their own. Times are changing, but one thing will always be certain. We do not betray our blood, and we do not cower. Anyone considering walking the path towards cultism and Sylvie's tyranny will think twice after

hearing about Caitlin's death, and any witch foolish enough to ignore that warning will soon find themselves bound to a pyre thereafter. I'm sick and tired of the in-house fighting and the squabbles of power. It's time for all our sisters to come together and face the evil at our doors."

"Istenanya knows we need all the help we can get," Erika grumbled, smoothing out her long braid.

"I've sent word to the covens in Transylvania. Two of the five have answered our call," Kitarni replied, her eyes burning with determination.

I didn't let my surprise show, but my fingers curled ever so slightly in my lap. By the look on András's face, he hadn't been privy to this information either. It seemed Kitarni had been busy indeed in the last few months. Just what else had my hellcat been planning?

Except she wasn't my anything yet, even if I still thought of her as such, still claimed her as my own, even if she wanted nothing to do with me. But no one, not Sylvie, nor any other would-be pursuant would have her. *Mine.*

"How many witches does a coven make?" I asked, turning my head lazily towards her.

Her hazel eyes pinned me beneath their weight, and I couldn't help but let my gaze travel down her face, to the full lips I'd once claimed so fervently. She bristled—or perhaps shivered?—ever so slightly, but did not falter as she replied, "There's around one hundred women to a coven, give or take."

One hundred. Fuck. "It isn't enough." Not nearly.

Kitarni grimaced. "I am working on the others, as well as our network in Budapest. But as it stands, my influence is … limited."

"Which brings me to the next item on our agenda," Nora said. "The matter of succession. With Caitlin out of the picture, a new High Witch will need to take her place. There has only ever been one way of doing so."

"A trial of magic," Eszter whispered, her eyes drifting to her sister.

Nora nodded. "As is customary. But I have a different proposal in mind. Our coven is breaking and with war coming, we don't have the time for ancient rites of passage. I suggest a vote on the next High Witch. To make it fair, it must be unanimous, and all present will partake, as this decision will affect both the witches and the táltosok. Are we in agreement?"

A slow smile spread across my face as I studied Nora. A strategist knows when to make their move, and this plan was carefully conceptualised. I had to wonder how long she'd had this in her arsenal. With Caitlin out of the way and Iren absent, Nora had shifted the battlefield and opened the way for a new leader to come calling in one fell swoop. A woman who would lead us all to safety through fire and blood.

I stood slowly, my movements smooth, my face set as the warrior, the lord of Mistvellen. "I cast my vote for Kitarni Bárány to become High Witch."

It was a pin drop in the silence, and it sent a wave surging

around the room.

András didn't even bother to hide his shit-eating grin. "Aye, the blood witch has my vote."

Kitarni shot him a glare, but her eyes glimmered as one by one, each one of her family and friends bent the proverbial knee. My girl would be lady of Mistvellen and High Witch of her coven, and *no one* would reasonably be able to ignore her summons then. She would gain her armies and the aid required, and maybe, just maybe we'd stand a chance at surviving Sylvie's wrath.

Nora nodded, smiling warmly as she extended her arms towards the group. "Then it's settled. The decision is unanimous. Kitarni will be ordained as the new—"

Her words were swallowed by the temple doors slamming open, vines creeping around the edges, latched on from Iren's outstretched hand. She smiled coldly as she approached, her cape fluttering behind her, those grey eyes calculating.

"I vote Iren Gábor for High Witch."

Well, fuck.

Things were about to get a lot more complicated.

SIX
KITARNI

ren sucked the joy out of a room like a vampyr from Transylvania sucks blood from its victims. *So close.* I'd been so close to securing the power I needed to convince the other covens to come to our aid. As lady in waiting of Mistvellen and the new High Witch, they would have been forced to grant me an audience at the very least. Iren stood in the way of that, and she knew it.

No matter, I would do things the hard way, because when had it ever been any different?

"We've already cast the vote, Iren," Mama said sharply. "You're too late."

"Come now, Nora, we both know all councillors need to be present for decisions like this," Iren said sweetly, slipping elegantly into the chair closest to Dante. "Not to mention, our High Witch is still very much alive."

"Caitlin gave up her rights the minute she sold out our sisters,"

Erika said darkly. "The witches need a leader now. Performing the trial of magic only slows us down."

Iren's blonde hair swayed as she tilted her head. "Now more than ever we need a strong leader. A smart one." Her eyes cut like daggers as she looked me up and down dismissively. "Kitarni is young and brash, and she's also no longer part of this coven. Not in the way that we need."

My fingers curled into fists, but it was Dante who answered, "And who better to offer resources and men to fight for your cause? Who better to offer refuge for witches when the time comes? Your people are being taken by the day. They are dying, Iren, or have you so easily forgotten whilst you've been away?"

Shit. This was quickly spiralling. We didn't have time to play 'who's the better wordsmith'. Morning was approaching and, come the dawn, we'd be burning a witch at the stake. Everything was going to change, and if we didn't present a united front, the witches would break. *Our coven.* It would be chaos.

Iren placed a hand on his arm, her long nails clutching him almost possessively. She looked at Dante, batting her lashes, leaning too close towards him. Her gaze flicked to mine ever so quickly, and I saw red. My power thrummed in my veins, sensing my anger and the white-hot surge of possessiveness roaring through my blood at the sight of her sharp fingers touching him. My husband to be.

"Away strengthening our ties to the other covens. You're forgetting I have connections of my own, wolf lord," she purred.

"I am no blood witch, but I am powerful, and I have no plans to let this coven fall. Perhaps you'd be better off with a woman with more ... standing. A marriage to the future High Witch would better serve you and your people. A marriage with me."

Over my dead body. The chair squealed as I stood up and planted my hands on the table, red misting around my fingers as I stared Iren down, my words slow and measured. "Get. Your. Fucking. Hands. Off. Him. Before I burn them off."

Silence. Then tinkling laughter, melodic and utterly out of place as Iren chuckled and removed her hand, her finger sliding down his own before she rested her palm on his cheek and tilted his gaze towards her. For a heart-stopping moment I thought she might kiss him, and that image alone nearly made me explode.

Iren knew it, too. A volatile leader, brash and violent, was hardly a fit one to lead. I would not fall prey to whatever new games she'd concocted so easily, but I'd be lying if I didn't picture her dying a hundred gruesome deaths just then.

Everyone gaped, looking between Iren and me as though we might start a war of our own, and oh, was I tempted. Unfortunately, disintegrating Iren probably wasn't the best way to gain the coven's support. I huffed, taking a deep breath and forcing myself to stay calm.

Dante grabbed Iren's wrist where she still touched him, squeezing it tight enough that she winced. When he smiled coldly, I shivered, feeling myself unreasonably turned on by the sheer savagery in that look.

"Touch me like that again," he said quietly, "and I'll break each of your fingers." He let her go, his lips curling with disgust. "Belittle my betrothed again, and I'll rip out your throat."

Goddess save me. My heart thumped in my chest, my body flaring with heat at the icy rage flashing in the gold rings of his eyes. The dominance masked by the calm and collected way he held himself. It was terrifying. And it was everything I wanted.

Iren swallowed audibly as she snatched her hand back and moved away. Even if I'd wanted to, it was impossible to hide my smirk. I didn't need Dante fighting my battles for me, but this was more than that. Iren wasn't trustworthy, being one of Caitlin's spies and, let's face it, a spider's web is never finished. If Dante wanted to put her in her place, I'd happily watch her squirm any day.

András breathed in deeply, then smiled cheerfully as though nothing had happened. "You mentioned a trial of magic?"

He was good at easing the tension like that and right now this room was about as chilly as a graveyard in full frost.

"It's one of our most revered customs," Eszter explained, ever the peace maker, though the slight curve to her lips told me she'd enjoyed seeing Iren knocked down a peg too. "Candidates undergo several tests of strength, endurance, and the mind. The winner is decided by the coven, and she is then proclaimed the new High Witch."

I needed no encouragement. "I'll do it. I'll go against Iren in the trials."

Iren's smile was wicked. "I was hoping you'd say that. We'll see who's more fitting to lead, fire girl, but might I suggest one stipulation?"

"What do you want?" I snarled, sick of her games and feeling exhausted. My body felt stretched, my bones wrung out like wet rags. Dawn was a few short hours away and I desperately needed to sleep. Even if I hated Caitlin and everything she'd stood for, watching a witch burn would be no small feat. Mama had told me what it was like to witness a burning, and that story had stayed with me long after.

"I wish to make a deal with you," Iren continued. "The loser in this contest will walk away from the coven. Forever. No looking back no matter what."

Mama sucked in a breath. "How can you propose such a thing? We're at war Iren. Personality clashes aside, we all have a part to play."

"Our being at war is precisely why I ask. We can't afford Kitarni to lose control of her powers because of an emotional response. The last time that happened, she set fire to the village. What happens when one of her friends get hurt? Or his lordship?" Iren circled the table slowly, her blonde hair glimmering in the firelight. "You saw how protective she was of Dante just now. What happens when he is threatened? She could destroy us all. She might be powerful, but the beast inside her, the product of Sylvie herself—it's unhinged. She's not just a blood witch. She's a monster."

A *monster*. A lump formed in my throat, and my veins ran cold at that word, everything inside me shutting down. She had a point. My power was destruction, and I'd managed to rein it in until now, but the possibility of losing control was awfully real. Too horrifying to consider. Iren had knowingly exploited that by using my jealousy for her own means. A spider with the worst kind of bite.

I closed my eyes, letting my fingers clench before gently unfurling. Maybe she was right. Maybe I was a monster, but the more I thought about it, the more I realised maybe that wasn't such a bad thing.

"*Magic can make monsters out of all of us,*" Dante had once said to me.

And maybe that's exactly what the coven needed right now. My eyes snapped open, and I walked purposefully to Iren, extending my hand.

"Kitarni," Dante warned, his body tense as he surveyed us. But he wouldn't stop me from doing what I needed to. He never had. It's one of the things I'd respected most about him.

Ignoring him, I looked Iren in her grey eyes, letting the dark red power in me flash within my own. "You want to seal your fate so badly? Fine. I accept your proposal, and when I win, nothing will make me happier than to see your back as you walk away from this coven."

She grinned, cocking her head dangerously as her palm slid into mine. "You have yourself a deal, little blood witch. See you

at the burning."

Iren walked away, disappearing like smoke through the temple doors. The breath shuddered out of me as I looked at the wide eyes of my friends. My family.

Eszter shook her head, her brown eyes wide. "I hope you know what you're doing Kitarni. Because there's no going back."

SEVEN

KITARNI

The rain shrouded the square in mist, foggy tendrils blanketing the stones beneath our feet. An unseasonably cold morning, but the chill in my bones cut deeper with the dread of what awaited me.

I took no pleasure in death—it's a miserable and filthy affair. I was used to the piss and shit and blood by now—had killed enough cultists to know what the body does when it shuts down and smelled enough corpses to recall the sharp sting of decay in my nose.

But we weren't burying bodies today or leaving them to rot. Today, Caitlin would be cleansed, body and soul, and she would burn for what she has done. My stomach roiled, anxiety swimming deep inside me.

I did not want to hear her scream.

I did not wish to see the fire claim her.

Such wants were ill afforded. I felt Dante move beside me,

his shoulder brushing softly against my own, the barest touch. It was enough to send awareness skittering down my arm, and though he did not speak, I knew it was his way of being there for me. He was always a rock to lean on. A pillar of strength against all obstacles.

The breath shuddered from my lungs as I finally looked upon Caitlin. Her withered face crinkled into a sneer, and in her old eyes I saw her condemning me to a fate worse than death. But no matter. She'll be the first to know about that. Death himself will greet her with open arms and whatever might pass for a wicked grin in that void-face of his. I didn't want to think of what torment he'll have planned.

Mama, flanked by Erika and Iren, approached her. The pyre itself was simple. A wooden pole raised on a landing in the centre of carefully stacked and bound kindling. There were no ladder or steps to climb. Why create more work for the táltosok when a living torch was already in their midst?

The councillors might say the words, but I would be the one to light the fire.

I was the match, the executioner.

Mama raised her arms, and the chorus of voices dipped to a hum before falling silent. My sisters stood at my back; their eyes raised at the woman who betrayed them. The woman who sold them off like chattel, who trafficked their blood in return for the promise of power and fed from their innocence.

No one stirred as the wind clawed at our shawls and our

hair whipped in the stillness. Even Caitlin herself was silent, the air ripe with the stench of her fear. A coldness in my stomach that belied the temperature told me Death was somewhere close, waiting to collect, to lead her home.

"Caitlin Vargo, High Witch of the Green Coven, you are sentenced to burn at the stake for your crimes," Nora said, her voice amplified so it boomed across the square. "Do you have any last words before Death takes you?"

My blood pounded in my ears, so loud I wondered if Dante could hear it. My heart-rate quickened, my breathing sharp and rushed. He stiffened by my side, leaning just a little closer to me. His warmth seeped through my tunic and into my skin, cleansing, clarifying my thoughts.

The crone lifted herself up, jutting her chin into the air with the authority of a woman used to looking down her nose at others. For so long, she had looked at me that way. As something beneath her. Ugly. Wrong. But I had never pretended to be anything except me. It was the lies and secrets of others that had masked my true skin. And now that I knew who I was, I would cower no longer.

Caitlin couldn't strip me of my dignity when I was a girl. She wouldn't do so now that I was a woman. A witch worthy of being in this coven and someone who would always defend her own.

"Everything I did," Caitlin rasped, her words throaty with emotion, "I did for the good of the coven. Before your blood soaks the earth, you will remember the protection I afforded you. One lamb does not a wolf satisfy. But a flock will feed a thousand."

I stared at her piteous form as murmurs broke out among the coven. Surely no one was foolish enough to believe her? One soul or many, she had traded lives for her own selfish gains. It didn't matter if her arrangement with Sylvie had bought the coven time, she had murdered witches and, in the end, her own greed and fear had turned her wicked with lust for more power.

Before I could point out as much, my mother strode towards the people, disgust etched into the creases around her downturned lips. "A lie however beautifully crafted is still poison from a serpent's tongue. This woman is a traitor, a murderer, and a thief. She has broken our creeds and abused dark magic. Opened the veins of our sisters in an attempt to steal their magic and corrupt another coven as High Witch. In this, there is no forgiveness. Under the eyes of the Mother and all that is sacred, I sanctify that Caitlin Vargo shall burn with the rising of the sun. What say you, my sisters?"

I stepped forward, my eyes never straying from Caitlin's face. "Aye."

A collective of voices sounded behind me, all acknowledging the order, all agreeing as one.

Caitlin shrieked with rage as everyone turned on her, then her splutters of protest turned to whimpers and pleas, begging, utterly diminished in her final hour. Mama looked at me firmly, nodding once, and I took a deep breath.

Dante stepped beside me, and I allowed myself to look at him before the world changed course once again.

His olive skin gleamed, the set of his chiselled jaw and full lips stern as he looked at me. Those eyes burned into my own, deep and perilous and filled with my darkest desires. But his lips curled up ever so slightly to the side, a single dimple winking into existence, and he nodded. Just once, enough to convey his encouragement, and his strength. Enough to say I could do this.

His hand brushed against my own, his knuckles scraping against mine with the most fleeting of touches. A tiny gasp escaped my lips, and I didn't dare let myself dwell on that contact, not as I focused my gaze on the witch before me and raised my arm.

"No," Caitlin screamed. "Please, don't do this, don't—"

Her words fizzled out as I focused on my task, the whole world blurring as I pointed my finger and let my power come rushing to the fore. I was the executioner, and I would not shy from my duty.

"*Burn.*"

The kindling burst into flames, crackling and groaning as the fire licked the wood and caught until it encircled Caitlin entirely. She thrashed at her restraints, her chest heaving, her neck taut from where she stretched her face as far away from the flames as possible.

Warmth blazed in my direction, searing and harsh against my cheeks as the flames climbed higher and higher, the smoke making my eyes water and my throat dry out.

Then the screaming started. Soon after, the smell of burning flesh permeated the air.

I didn't want to watch this. Didn't want to see or smell or face the destruction from *my hand*, but I didn't look away. Not for a second while the rain misted down and the clouds rumbled with the voices of the gods.

Dante wrapped his arms around me. I let him, too frozen to push him away, too horrified to do anything but stand there as the flames crept towards the sky and the screams were soon silenced.

I, too, wanted to scream and vomit and curl myself into a ball anywhere but here.

But I didn't look away.

Long after Caitlin's body was unrecognisable, I was still staring.

EIGHT

DANTE

She trembled by my side, small and silent beneath the weight of my arm around her waist, but not once did her eyes stray from the atrocity before us. Kitarni had never shirked her duty, nor would she allow herself to appear weak in front of the others.

The fact she was allowing me to hold her at all spoke volumes to her discomfort. Her body was warm, her curves nestled against me. I'd craved her touch, her smell, for so long, but the moment the shock wore off and she came back into herself, the anger would return, as would the rage she harboured deep inside.

I wanted to hold her forever, but I knew it wouldn't last. The best I could do was distract her from her thoughts and the horror before us.

"Are you ready for the trial?" I whispered in her ear, tightening my hold on her before she could storm away or shrug me off.

For a moment I thought she wouldn't answer, but she shivered where my breath kissed her cheek, her lips parted and shaking. "How can I be ready for something I know nothing about? Iren already has the advantage because she knows what's coming."

"If it's power they seek, then yours is beyond Iren's capabilities. She is a green witch, where you have fire and blood magic in your veins." I scoffed. "It's hardly a contest."

"Power alone does not make a leader, Dante," she replied stiffly. "You above all people should know a good leader must earn respect and *trust*, not demand it."

Well, shit. A kick in the balls would've been better. "I do know that. Gods, Kitarni—"

"No," she hissed, stepping away from me and turning, at last, away from the charred husk upon the pyre. "You don't get to do this. You don't get to act like everything is fine—that we're fine—just because the world is burning around us."

I steeled myself for her rage, ready to take everything she'd throw at me, because I deserved it—and she needed a distraction. Her mind was elsewhere, but I knew what was going through her head. Iren had hit a nerve calling her a monster, playing on her worst fears and every insecurity she'd carried for all those years in her youth. And now to be the one to end Caitlin ... it wasn't just an execution, it was gods damned torture. It shouldn't have been her, but even I could admit it gave her power. A sign that she would do anything for her people. Nora knew it, and Iren did too.

So, I would take the brunt of Kitarni's pain and frustration and let her channel her anger into me. If she couldn't love me,

 82

then I would take all the worst parts of her and still want her anyway. Maybe it was selfish of me, maybe I needed to let her go, but I would bear it, because nothing would kill me quicker than not having any part of her at all. If Kitarni thought I would tire and give up, she clearly didn't realise how deep my stubbornness ran.

"I can't forget what you did," she continued quietly. Her eyes brimmed with tears, the restraints she'd so carefully built around herself beginning to snap. "You never even apologised. You never even—" She swallowed, her voice thick with all the words she wouldn't say.

"Kitarni," I tried again, reaching out a hand, but she took another step away. "I know it's too late for forgiveness, but I swear, not a day has gone by where I haven't kicked myself for my wrongs. There will never be enough words to say how much I'm sorry. I'm so fucking sorry."

A single tear slid down her cheek, her eyes swimming with hope and desperation, but she looked around at the whispers and sidelong looks from the witches, and I knew she was lost to me. Kitarni would rather suffer in silence than appear weak to her sisters. A leader needed to be strong, and a High Witch needed to put her people before herself.

Her shoulders squared and her hands curled into fists as she hardened her heart and turned away. A better man might have known then to let her go, but I was not a good man. Neither a hero nor a saint, but a damned demon put on this earth to end

anything that got in her way. I'd seen the hope in her eyes, and it had restored some of my own.

András's words echoed in my thick skull, and I knew now.

There was nothing I wouldn't do to get her back. I would raise the dead, walk through hell and back for that woman.

If she was a monster, I was too.

And so long as she was by my side, I was perfectly ok with that.

Laszlo whimpered beside me, pawing at my leg for attention as I stared across the clearing at the two witches. I scratched behind his ears absentmindedly, my eyes fixed on the brown-haired beauty as she squared off against Iren.

The two couldn't be more opposite. Iren was waifish, with blonde hair cut in a sharp bob and piercing grey-blue eyes, her mouth curved with a cocky smile. Pretty, but all sharp angles and bones. Her eyes lacked warmth, hard as stone, like she'd forgotten how to laugh. I wouldn't be surprised. As a spy, perhaps even an assassin, there are things she would have seen and done that can't be taken back. Sometimes life has a way of setting people on the right path, and sometimes the decisions we make set us down the wrong one.

Gods, did I know that better than anyone.

I looked to Kitarni, Iren's opposite in all ways. Glowing olive skin, long curly brown hair that had a mind of its own, full lips and eyes that sparkled when she laughed. And those pants ... those fucking leather pants that made me want to squeeze her ass and bend her over.

My girl. My beautiful little hellcat.

I wondered how different things might have been if she'd let her power consume her. If she'd picked the wrong side to fight for, or placed her trust in someone who'd only ever have used her. Caitlin deserved her fate, and I knew Kitarni would give everything she had to win the fight today. The coven needed someone who wasn't afraid to break the mould and reshape the world if that's what it took.

Iren wanted power and, the funny thing was, I had no doubt she held qualities that could make a good leader. But she served only for her own gains. The question was whether she would fall into line and take orders if she failed this test. And she would fail, Kitarni would make damn sure of it.

The women circled each other slowly, assessing for weaknesses, judging each other's every movement. Iren was fast, prancing around like a skittish horse, but Kitarni was methodical.

The rule was simple: disable your opponent without causing severe bodily harm. I guessed destroying Iren was out of the question then. Folding my arms, I watched impassively. Iren was at an advantage with her earth magic, but Kitarni's fire magic would be a more difficult beast to wield. I tensed as the women stopped moving and a horn sounded, signalling the beginning of

 85

the fight.

Iren lashed out, a surge of roots splitting through the soil aimed right for Kitarni's legs. She darted back, burning them easily with a swish of her fingers. Iren didn't stop, shooting vines so fast they were a blur, one of them slicing Kitarni's cheek open as she narrowly avoided being fully bound.

My eyes narrowed as blood dribbled down her cheek, my fingers itching to wreak havoc of my own. Lukasz put a hand on my shoulder beside me, his brown eyes stern as he shook his head. Right. To intervene in a sacred ritual—especially as an outsider—would only earn severe punishment, possibly even banishment.

Kitarni grunted, her hands moving with precision as she fought off barrage after barrage of greenery, the arena lighting up with pops of colour from her fire. Sweat beaded on her temple; her brows pulled together. I could almost see the cogs in her mind turning, wondering how to fight a foe she could not touch.

Fire and blood magic were both too dangerous for her to equip with the odds stacked against her.

Iren laughed as her vines slipped past Kitarni's defences time and again, the cords slicing Kitarni's flesh like a knife through butter. As she focused on the vines flying at her face, she didn't notice the root curling quietly towards her boot until it was too late.

With a sharp tug, the root wound itself around her ankle and pulled taut. Kitarni crashed to the ground, seething as the line pulled her along like a hooked fish. Red wreathed her hands,

glimmering in her eyes, but just as quickly it disappeared. This wasn't a battle she could win by blood magic. With a frustrated snarl she slammed the ground with one palm, fire catching on the vine until it burned all the way to Iren's fingers.

Iren shrieked, clutching her hand to her chest, her eyes filled with bloody murder. She closed her eyes, her spine locked and her hands outstretched as she summoned the very earth ahead of her—soil, rocks, and roots quaking and ripping from the ground as it floated up. Her eyes snapped open, and my stomach twisted with fear as she hurled it with a grunt.

Kitarni wasn't quick enough. The earthly matter collided with her torso, sending her flying backwards and skidding along the ground.

"Kitarni," I yelled, just as Eszter did. Our eyes met—a mutual need to protect her, to defend her against all odds. But Nora, white-faced and grim, whispered words in her ear. Whatever she said was enough to get the girl to back down, her eyes shimmering with fear.

Lukasz grabbed my arm before I could do anything stupid. "Go to her and you'll forfeit her chance at High Witch," he hissed. "Kitarni will be banished from the coven."

I looked into my brother's eyes, seeing them soften at the pain in my own. To see Kitarni suffer was unacceptable, but to cause her to fail would be even worse. I swore, shaking him off, tearing my gaze back to her crumpled form, then to Iren.

The latter was grinning victoriously, already assuming she'd

won the match.

"Get up Kitarni," I whispered. "Get up."

She groaned, her fingers twitching as she pulled herself together, dragging her nails through the dirt slowly as she rose. Iren's smile faltered, and a part of me wanted to howl like a wolf at the fury on her face.

Kitarni limped to a stand, favouring one foot and clutching her stomach with a grimace. Her face was a mask of dirt and blood caked her cheeks and teeth, but she was smiling. *Smiling* as she raised her hands and unleashed her true power.

That's my girl.

Fire erupted from her hands, rising higher and higher into the sky like a tidal wave that could crush towns and wipe out everything in its path. Heat seared into my skin, making my leathers almost unbearably hot. Sweat dripped slowly down my chest and, for a moment, it felt like the world had stopped as we all stared in awe at her might. Slowly, the fire came crashing down, curling like a snake around Iren's form, enclosing her behind a wall of flames, red hot and then flickering sapphire blue.

Iren gasped, sweat pouring down her face in waves. She conjured vines, the earth, roots, but everything curled inwards and fizzled to ash from where she stood. In mere moments, Iren's flesh would begin to melt, and the best part was Kitarni hadn't laid a lick of magic on her.

The spider shrank back, her limbs twitching.

And Kitarni ... her eyes blazed like the sun, scorching and

unstoppable.

"Yield," she commanded, lifting her chin, her hair billowing from the power still pulsing from her hands.

Iren uttered a strangled cry of frustration, but she lifted her hands palm upwards, and with a submissive bow of her head she choked out, "I yield."

One test down, one to go.

NINE
KITARNI

I devoured my chicken paprikash like it was my last meal on this earth, groaning as I savoured every drop of the juices. Mama had made it—a special treat for winning the contest, she'd said. With the explosion of flavour in my mouth, the warmth of the hearth and the comfort of my mother and sister beside me, I could almost forget the looming threat of Sylvie and Death. *Almost.* He would have my head if I didn't deliver on my promise of finding the crown.

But that was a problem for another day. For now, I was happy to celebrate some small wins.

Iren hadn't just yielded to me with the combat trial. She'd bowed out entirely, too proud to endure a second beating of her ego. I had no doubt she was licking her wounds somewhere, cursing me for my victory.

"I'm proud of you," Mama said, beaming at me over her bowl. We were having dinner in the family home, András, Lukasz, Erika

 90

and *him*, joining us. "I never expected to see a Bárány heading our coven, but there's a peace in me now, knowing you will lead us to safety."

"You earned your place," Erika agreed, her dark eyes sparkling. "Iren will be nursing her wounds for a long time to come. You should've sent her on her way, turned her own foolish bargain against her."

A foolish bargain indeed. It was stupid, agreeing to leave the coven if I'd lost, but I'd had no choice. Iren had backed me into a corner, and who else could I bet on if not myself? Desperate times called for hard choices. It was just a godsend that I'd won, or else I'd really be in the shit. Kind of hard to protect people if you're not allowed anywhere near them.

My skin prickled, and I glanced at Dante, finding him watching me, weighing my merit. Our relationship had shifted ever so slightly, though I didn't dare unpack what that meant just yet. I couldn't ignore him any longer, not with so much at stake. We needed to work together if we were to stand any chance against Sylvie. More than that, I needed this marriage for the power it would grant me. He'd made it clear he wanted me to rule, but just how much leverage did that give me? Would Farkas allow me to make decisions on behalf of Mistvellen and my coven?

I didn't want to marry Dante like this—with so much unresolved between us—but I would. I'd told Mama as much not long after Sylvie's resurrection, but those words had been fuelled by hot tempers and the sharp stab of betrayal. A few months of brooding had helped stoke those flames. Even so, I would bind myself to him right now if it gave me the means to lead as I needed to. To protect my family.

András slurped his meal noisily from beside me, and I frowned at him sidelong before turning my gaze back to Mama and Erika. "I might not like Iren, but she is useful. There is no better spy, and as much as I hate to admit it, she has connections we need. Banishing her now would be short-sighted."

"You trust her? Despite how close she was with Caitlin?" Lukasz asked, raising a brow.

I studied the táltos sitting across the table, noting the way his hand rested on my sister's and trying not to smile. He noted the direction of my gaze, the corner of his lips tipping up. I hadn't had the chance to get to know him yet, but he had already done more for me than I could ever repay. In the time I'd been away at Mistvellen, he'd been overseeing my family's protection personally. Mama had even allowed him to stay in the house and ... oh gods. I blinked, slowly looking at Eszter's face. She looked radiant, as always, her cheeks rosy and her golden-brown hair shiny, but there was something different about the way she held herself. No longer as timid and childlike, but with a woman's countenance and a seriousness to the eyes.

Well, fuck. I looked back at Lukasz with a hard glare, his dark brown skin turning several shades paler, but to his credit he clasped Eszter's hand harder, anchoring himself for dear life.

Good. I smirked, cocking my head as I answered him. "I'll

be keeping her on a short leash if that's what you're asking. She'll be accompanied by a set of guards whenever she leaves the village. Preferably with someone we trust when carrying any correspondence. In fact, she'll be leaving first thing in the morning."

Mama blinked. "And just where is our little spider heading?"

I smiled, lounging back in my chair. "Now that I'm High Witch, the leaders of our neighbouring covens might be a little more amenable to the idea of answering our call."

"And if they're not?" Dante asked, his voice a deep rumble.

For the first time since Sylvie's resurrection, I didn't shy away from his gaze. I was done feeling sorry for myself and letting my anger rule me. If I didn't get past what he'd done, if I couldn't even be in the same room as him without those feelings overcoming me, he would be my ruin. This man was mine. For better or worse, whether I wanted him or not.

I stared deep into those brown eyes ringed with gold. His face was lined with stubble, the reddish glint to his dark brown locks gleaming in the candlelight. His hair had grown longer over the last few months, and he'd tied it back with a leather thong. It made his cheekbones stand out, the sharp cut of his jaw deadly and—I hated to admit—even more delicious.

"They will," I replied with a secretive smile. "Let's just say I offered them a little incentive."

"Gods," András groaned, rolling his eyes. "That's never a good sign."

"Stop whinging, András, or I'll demote you from the ranks."

He scoffed. "My orders come from Dante, so until you two are married, you don't have the power to do any such thing."

Everyone's eyes immediately swivelled to Dante, and I felt my cheeks heat as awkward silence followed. Damn it András. The táltos looked at me sheepishly and I kicked him under the table, only for Lukasz to immediately straighten and grimace instead.

Oh my gods. I wanted to die right then and there. Clearing my throat, I looked to my betrothed and took a deep breath, then smiled sweetly at my family. "Actually, seeing as we're on the subject, I have an announcement. Dante and I are moving up the wedding."

He stiffened slightly, his eyes flashing, the only sign of his surprise—and maybe his anger.

"Kitarni, that's ..." My mother faltered, her smile strained, her brown eyes lacking the usual warmth that accompanied the smiles I so adored from her. She was the only one who knew my real intentions. That the wedding was just a means of gaining power in the world beyond our coven. A world currently ruled predominantly by men with resources and soldiers I desperately needed. "That's—"

"Wonderful," Eszter gushed, rushing around the table to envelop me in her slender arms. "How soon? It'll be at Mistvellen I suppose? Oh let me take care of the dress, please, it'll be my gift to you. I can get new fabrics, use my earth magic to make flowers ..."

Her voice became background noise as she droned on about things I'd never dreamed of for myself. What any girl would dream of for their wedding. But I found I couldn't focus as I risked a peek at Dante, who was smiling as everyone congratulated us, not a chink in his armour as he let this information roll off his back like a duck out of water.

When he turned to me at last, it was with a predator's smile and eyes glittering with the promise of danger.

"Nothing would make me happier," he said smoothly, rising from his seat and stalking towards me, "than making Kitarni my wife." He placed his hands on my shoulders, squeezing a smidge too hard for comfort.

"So are we going to talk about what happened tonight or do I have to force it out of you?" Eszter asked, popping a chocolate in her mouth as we lay side by side on my bed.

I grimaced, stuffing my mouth with one, two, three chocolates to avoid the conversation. She twisted her head, glaring sternly, and I rolled my eyes in response, savouring the creaminess in my mouth as I chewed slowly.

"I might have forgotten to inform him, but what does it matter? A wedding was coming either way, I just … gave it a nudge."

"You know, at some point you'll need to refer to *him* by his name again." Eszter sighed. "Kitarni, are you sure about this? I

know you'll do anything for the coven, but this is forever. Do you really want to marry Dante while things are so strained between you two?"

I shrugged. "My feelings have nothing to do with it. As far as I'm concerned, nothing has changed since the betrothal was announced. This marriage was always about power. Farkas wants the blood of my ancestors to flow through his grandchildren, Mama wants the coven and clan to reunite, and I want the influence that comes with an elevated position. At the end of the day, if we don't stop Sylvie and stop the spread of corruption, what we want doesn't matter."

Eszter shuffled to face me, and I rolled over so we were nearly nose to nose, like we'd lain so many times before as children, whispering secrets and telling stories when Mama thought us asleep.

"It matters to me," she said quietly, her soft doe-eyes glimmering. "I know you still feel something for him. I know you're hurting and you want to believe in him again. You might not believe it, but I think you can repair what was broken. What he did to you was wrong, I'm not denying that, but is it possible the things he did were for all the right reasons?"

I shut my eyes, not wanting to open those wounds again. I didn't want to feel the pain of his betrayal, nor let those aches come to the surface. It still hurt too much. I rubbed my hand absently over my chest, right over the scar from where his mother had stabbed me.

"I'm not sure we'll ever get back to that place again, Eszti," I murmured. "I'm not sure he even wants to."

"Bullshit."

My lids snapped open as I blinked at a sharpness in her voice I'd never heard before.

"You think I don't see the way he pines for you like a lost puppy? He's broken, Kitarni—more than you realise. Beneath that perfect smile and the cool, calm exterior is a man who's *hurting*. His mother is a sadist. A gods damned nightmare. And his actions led her to hurt the one woman he was meant to protect."

My heart panged with sorrow. I knew his mother had done some damage. Hell, anyone would carry some trauma if they learned their long-lost mother had turned out to be very much alive and, subsequently, a murderous bitch. But how could I truly understand if he wouldn't talk to me? He'd never really tried ...

Or had I just not wanted to hear?

I pawed at my eyes, grunting as I shifted onto my back. My body ached from today's trials, and there were bruises all over my body to prove it. Iren had done a number with her little trick today. Gods, if I was human, she might have killed me.

Sighing, I glanced sidelong at Eszter, who was waiting patiently for me to work through my emotions, and oh, wasn't that just the wellspring that kept on giving? I thought of the last few months spent in misery, avoiding Dante at all costs despite wanting the very opposite, because it was hard to admit but ... I missed him. His warmth, his voice, those damned dimples.

Everything. Which only made it even harder.

I said calmly, "So I should forgive him because he has mummy issues? We all carry heavy burdens, it can't all fall on me to lighten his load to make him feel better."

"You're right. The pair of you are holding the weight of the world on your shoulders. Wouldn't it be easier if you shared that? Did you ever wonder what it would have been like in his boots? She'd ransomed his brother, Kit. His family."

Guilt speared through me, my stomach knotting with the thought of Eszter being in Lukasz's position. If Baba Yaga had threatened to kill my sister, I'd have done anything—everything—to save her. Including what Dante did to me.

"I know you'd pull apart the world to save me. Love is your greatest strength ... and your biggest weakness." Eszter's face softened and she took my hand gently. "I can't tell you what to do or how to feel, Kitarni. That's for you and you alone to work through, but I will say that being human—as much as a táltos can be—isn't something you can fault him for. In our world, full of magic and power and mystical things, we can't afford to forget the parts that set us aside from darker beings. He made mistakes, but he did it with love in his heart."

Tears pricked my eyes, the pain in my chest blooming. "Who made you so wise?" I asked with wobbling lips. "Because you sure as shit didn't learn it from me."

She chuckled, wiping away the salt tracking down my cheeks. "You taught me more than you know. I've always looked up to

you. My big sister and my fierce protector. I love you more than anything and I always will, but there's a space in your heart that Mama and I can't fill. You've been hurt so many times by the ugliness in this world, don't you think it's time you allowed yourself to be loved?"

My heart squeezed to hear those words and I burst into fresh tears, chest heaving and nose sniffing as Eszter pulled me into her arms and we just lay there bundled together, two halves of the same soul.

She was right. I'd always looked out for her, always tried to solve my own problems and go it alone, but I couldn't do it anymore. It would take a village—a damned congregation of covens—to face what was coming. I had to lead, but I didn't have to do it alone. I had my family and friends and, despite everything, I knew I'd always have him.

I just had to figure out how.

TEN

DANTE

We need to talk.

That's all the parchment said on the front page, slipped under my door just moments ago. I frowned as I turned it over, the script on the other side piquing my curiosity. The letter instructed me to meet at the temple in due haste, and it was signed *K*.

My heart did a panicked flip as I paced the small room I was staying in at the village inn, my stomping wearing out the threadbare rug and no doubt the owner's patience, too. Fuck. I'd fought numerous monsters, cultists and men, yet a simple sentence had me losing my shit like a man caught mid-romp by their mistress's husband.

Not that I had ever been in that situation, but a certain blond-haired rake had. Where was that asshole when I needed him? I swept a hand through my hair, plucking my shirt from the cot and taking a breath as I glanced out the slitted arch that passed for a window.

The hour was late and a harvest moon glimmered from the midnight skies beyond, yellow and seemingly close enough to cast a rope around tonight. I'd take it as a sign of good luck because I'd damned well need it for the storm brewing. Kitarni didn't do things by halves, so the meeting could go one of two ways.

I'd be on the receiving end of her wrath before we'd eventually lay everything on the table, talk it out and come to a mutual agreement to set aside our differences and work together for the good of our people.

Or—and a very big or at that—she'd forgive me. Give me another chance. Gods, what I wouldn't do to hold her again. To see her smile on our wedding day with some small slither of joy. Anything would be better than a marriage born of hate and disappointment.

I hadn't had a chance to speak to Kitarni about her *announcement* last night. I'd gone along with her charade with gritted teeth and charming smiles, but if she thought being my wife meant she'd be able to make decisions for both coven and clan without the courtesy of informing me, she had another thing coming.

Hadur's blade, I needed a stiff drink.

I sighed, donning a light shirt and loose pants, not bothering with my leathers. After the rain during Caitlin's execution, the air was thick with humidity and hot as hell. With Kitarni's temper, the heat would surely worsen.

Something I craved and feared in equal measure.

The door groaned in protest as I left my quarters and swept through the inn. It was mostly empty, just a few witches deep in their cups laughing together in the corner of the room. They whispered together as I passed, and I flashed them my dimples before I left, an explosion of giggles following my footsteps.

Let them talk. I couldn't care less what gossip circled me, but if a bad word was said about Kitarni, they'd soon think twice if I caught wind of it. I liked to think I was a fair ruler, but my leniency only went so far. Mercy was a foreign virtue when it came to hurting my family. Ironic really, given that protecting Lukasz was what had put me in this mess in the first place. He couldn't be blamed for my actions though. They were all on me.

The temple stood tall and proud in the distance as I walked through the square, breathing in the heady floral scent of wisteria and rose wafting from the gardens. The pyre was still sitting in the town centre, giving the usually peaceful village an ominous feel. The hairs on the back of my neck prickled with awareness, and I found my pace quickening as I hurried to move past it. The dead didn't scare me. I could control them, after all, but this business with Caitlin and my mother felt decidedly unfinished, and that foreboding haunted my every step.

I didn't like surprises and a nagging tug in my chest told me our luck would give out soon. Something bad was coming and we were woefully unprepared. I just had to hope we'd covered our bases because, when Sylvie came for us, it would be with

102

vengeance in her black heart and an army at her back.

My skin prickled at the thought and, before I knew it, I was standing at the temple doors, frozen with both hands pressed against the ingrained wood. Gods above, is this what I've been reduced to? I shook my head and pushed, heaving the doors open, a gust of wind slamming them shut behind me.

The thud echoed through the room, but all I saw, all I heard, was her. She was dressed in a thin shift, a simple shawl covering her shoulders, her curls mussed as though she'd had trouble sleeping. But then, if she was dressed for bed, why had she called me here so urgently? I walked down the aisle into the small chamber at the rear of the temple.

"Dante?" She looked me up and down with wide eyes, noting the thin shirt and pants. She rushed towards me, then slowed her steps, pausing a healthy distance away. "When I got your note, I thought the worst. What happened?"

My brows scrunched together. "I was going to ask you the same thing. I received a letter too. You didn't send for me?"

Confusion clouded her features. "No, I—" Her wide eyes shuttered before they snapped open and she swore colourfully, her hands meeting her hips. "Oh, that sneaky little ... I'm going to kill him."

Of course, I should have known. The conniving little shit couldn't help interfering in things he absolutely shouldn't. "András," I grumbled. "The handwriting matched your own, so I just assumed ..."

"This stinks of Eszter's handiwork just as much." She shook her head. "I can't believe they'd do this! When I'm through with them, the pair will wish they'd never ..." Her voice trailed off as she leaned around me, shock registering on her face. "Dante! The doors!"

She lunged behind me and I turned just as the doors shut with a resounding bang, a ruckus following as something clanged, sliding against the wooden grain. I pushed, swearing as the doors rattled. They didn't budge.

"I'm ever so sorry, but the doors appear to be jammed. I'm afraid you're stuck in there for the night," András called innocently from the other side, sounding remorseful.

Liar.

"András," I warned, "open these bloody doors or I'll wring your neck."

"Not an option," he said cheerfully. "You and Kitarni need to work your problems out and seeing as you're both equally stubborn, we thought you needed a little push in the right direction."

"So you're locking us in here?" Kitarni fumed, her mouth gaping.

"All you need to do is talk to each other. And until I am satisfied with the outcome, you'll remain in there as long as it takes."

"I'm sorry Kitarni," another, softer voice came muffled through the door, "but this has been a long time coming. For

both of you."

Kitarni ran her hands through her hair. "This is so childish. Let us out. Dante and I can have a rational conversation without being shoved in a cell."

András yawned. "If you're both so mature, you'll be out of there in no time. Then you can punish the children when you're ready. Until then, we must bid you farewell. Our beds await."

"Sorry," Eszter squeaked quietly. The sounds of shoes scuffing echoed until the temple doors thudded shut, leaving Kitarni and me in awkward silence. I didn't miss her quick glance at the open window, but even with the desk to assist her, it was a stretch and one I didn't think she'd dare bother to look so undignified to reach.

She looked at me warily as she paced the room and I watched her quietly, arms folded against my chest. Gods, we really were stubborn. An age went by and still no one spoke. The tension was taut enough to slice with a knife and my stomach knotted; András might have moved onto the top of my shit list, but he had a point. This had gone on long enough.

As if coming to the same conclusion, Kitarni finally deigned to look at me. A glare, admittedly, but I'd take it. "Why are you staring at me?" she snapped.

Despite myself, I couldn't help the small smile gracing my lips. "This is the first time we've been alone for a while. Being cornered like this reminded me of our first meeting in the woods, after being attacked by those wolves. You were so angry, you threw

105

a dagger at my head."

She paused her relentless stalking and folded her arms. "You deserved it. You were being a dick."

"And you were being a haughty brat," I replied with a smirk.

Her eyes flared and I'd be lying if I said I didn't enjoy the spark of defiance, the retaliation that would surely come if I pushed her. Her eyes tracked my lips and I smiled wider, goading her further.

"You know what your problem is? You're still the same arrogant asshat as always. Some things never change," she hissed, her voice wavering. "Even if ... even if everything else has." She looked up at me, a thousand questions in those hazel eyes, and pain that made my heart ache with a need to protect her, wrap my arms around her.

"Not everything," I whispered, daring a step, then another.

Her palms found my chest, halting me, as though she was fighting an internal battle. "Then why?" she asked quietly, looking up through her lashes. "If what you say is true, why didn't you trust me? Why didn't you tell me what Baba Yaga had planned to do with Lukasz, or what she'd been doing to the witches?"

I sighed. "When my mother ..." *No, not that. Not for a long time.* I tried again. "When Baba Yaga ordered me to find the blood witch, I never expected that same witch would be my future bride. When I met you in the woods, I knew you were the one they'd been looking for. Everything was so complicated after that."

"So, what, I got off lightly because of our betrothal, yet the

other witches were murdered?" She shoved me away with surprising strength, her words cold and biting. "Was it complicated enough for you when she mutilated their bodies and drained them of blood?

I growled in frustration. "I didn't know what she was doing with the witches. Until Hanna, I had no idea about those rituals."

"A poor excuse," she scoffed. "You were a fool, Dante. She played you like one of those chess pieces you love so much, and you didn't stop to think about the consequences. People are dead because of you."

My blood heated, and I felt the darker powers in me swimming to the surface, my shaman magic begging to be released. But there was no bringing the dead back here. Only a harsh and bitter taste of the truth. Because everything she said was all true.

"Don't you think I know that?" I snapped, running a hand through my hair. "I am a murderer. My soul is dirty. No matter how much I wash my hands, they will always be stained. Call it sheer stupidity for not seeing what was right in front of me, but it's the truth." I sighed, sliding against the wall and resting my elbows on my knees. "I thought she was dead. For years, I thought she was lost, and when she came back into my life ... I was blinded by a child's love for a mother he thought dead long ago. I did as she asked without question *because* she was my mother. And I ... I know I should have done better. Been better. Once I realised what she was doing to the witches, I defied her requests and she blackmailed me with Lukasz's life. You came into my life not long

 107

after."

I tipped my head back against the wall, closing my eyes. Flashes of Hanna's mutilated body swept through my mind, the guilt inside me overflowing. Just another burden to bear, another soul ripped from this world because of the cultists and their dark magic. Because of *me*.

Kitarni stood there, watching me in silence for a few beats, and I waited in the stretching silence for a rejection that would cut me to ribbons. Instead, her voice was gentle. Contemplative.

"Your mother manipulated you. She twisted your love for her and poisoned your morality for her own gains. You might have made mistakes, but in the end, at least, you did what you had to for the right reasons. It doesn't make it right, but I can understand now." She sighed, walking to the desk and perching on the edge. "What I can't figure out is why you wouldn't trust me to help you protect him. We were meant to fight this fight together."

I studied the calm exterior of the fiery queen before me as she tried to tame some of her locks. Beneath the slow, methodical movements of her fingers lay a deep anger, and I feared we'd only just scratched the surface.

"I thought I was protecting you by keeping it to myself, that you'd be safe in Mistvellen. I knew you'd never abide being left behind, which is why I drugged you. Aside from locking you away, it was all I could think of at the time. I never wanted to cage you, Freckles, nor did I want to lie."

She swallowed hard, her fingers gripping the edge of the desk

so hard her knuckles went white. When she looked up, her eyes were molten rage. "Your secrets almost cost me my life, and those of many others."

I rose from my position, reaching out a hand, letting it drop awkwardly. "I know. And I'm sorry, Kitarni. So very sorry."

She bit her lip, contemplating everything I'd told her, studying me as if searching for any hint of a lie. When the silence stretched so long it became deafening, she finally spoke once more.

"Was any of it real?" she asked quietly. "Did you ever really want me?"

I stepped towards her, shaking my head. "I never wanted you, Freckles. I—"

"And there it is," she interrupted. Her lips twisted with hurt for a split second before she smoothed her face out. She'd gotten too good at hiding her emotions, pretending she was okay. And it was all because of me. I couldn't have that, so I took another step forward, turning her chin towards me.

"Want is a base desire, and what I feel for you goes far beyond that. I need you like I need air to breathe, and sustenance to keep me nourished. You are both my biggest failure, and the biggest victory I might ever achieve. I can't do this without you. I won't."

The breath sighed from her lips. "How do I know I can trust you again?"

There was no simple answer to that question, but the hope that sparked in my heart was like embers catching, spreading hot and heavy in my being. So, I spilled every truth inside me, and I

didn't hold back for a damn second.

"You don't. But I will spend every waking minute proving my worth to you. I will fight for my people, and I will die for yours. Nothing can change what I did, but maybe everything I do now can help those who need it most. I will fight for you Kitarni. If you'll have me."

She nodded slowly, biting her lip. "I'm still so gods damned angry at you, but I'm glad you told me and ... I understand. I would have done anything to keep my family safe." Her eyes raked over me, seeing down to my very soul, and she pushed against my chest with her hand, the tiniest of smiles twitching her lips. That little gesture, it was enough. More than enough. "I still think you're insufferable though."

I chuckled, capturing her hand in my own. "And you're still a stubborn witch."

Her eyes narrowed as she thrust her chin up, and I couldn't help but grin at her haughty attitude. "Your place in my good graces is still tentative at best, so be warned: your honeyed words are sweet, but your actions speak louder. Pushing me is not in your best interests right now."

She was right on all accounts, which is *exactly* why she needed pushing. She'd bottled up her pain, shoved it deep down and put all her energy into fighting, training, being the person the world needed. But this anger inside? It needed an outlet. It needed *release*.

"You're right. Which is why I would've thought you'd jump

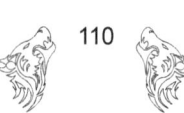

110

at the opportunity to shed blood. I lied to you Kitarni. I drugged you, hurt you through my actions."

A warning sound rumbled in her chest, and the sound was so sinful that excitement coursed through my veins. She pushed me away. "Stop. I know what you're doing. I don't need to hurt you to feel better about this, Dante."

"You didn't seem to have a problem with it when we were training," I purred, circling her. "I know you've thought about it. Driving a knife through my heart, carving out pain as I did to yours. Don't you deserve some relief?"

Her hands clenched into fists, blood-red misting up her arms as her shawl dropped, forgotten. "Hurting you will solve nothing. It won't ease the pain."

"No," I agreed, breathing in her ear. "But it will give you the release you've been so aching for. Let it go, Freckles. Let it out."

Her teeth gritted together as I came to a stop before her. "You think you're doing this for me, but I know you, Dante. This is as much for me as it is for yourself. You want to hurt for what you've done. To feel the pain bestowed on so many before you."

I stiffened at the truth in her words, glaring down at her as she stepped so close her chest brushed against my own. "Is that so? And just what are you going to do about that?"

She stared at my lips, her hands moving up my chest slowly, stirring something deep inside me. Our breaths mingled, sharp and slick with keen awareness of each other's bodies. "I will be your judge. And I am going to punish you."

111

She shoved me so hard I slammed into the wall with a grunt, my spine tingling and something besides me toppling over. Her hand slipped into my hair, her nails scraping along the roots until she pulled it back roughly, baring my throat. A groan escaped me, my cock hardening, aching for her touch.

Her smile was feral as she looked up at me, her kisses gentle until she bit down on my neck, licking over the hurt as she pulled my head back even further. She was a goddess, her curls framing her face, her eyes still swirling with anger and a touch of lust.

Those full lips captured my own in a brutal kiss, rough and painful and everything I'd dreamed about for the last few months. Her tongue melted against my own and I gave myself to it fully, closing my eyes as her hands slipped under my shirt, exploring, sliding over every ridge.

I hissed as a sharp pain flared on my back, immediately cooled by a golden, healing glow. My eyes snapped open, finding the room filled with smoky tendrils of black, my magic responding to the pain. Only, it didn't seem angry, merely curious. She'd burned me—burned my shirt to cinders—and somehow, I had no marks on me to prove it. The stark contrast between hot and cold had my dick throbbing, and she hadn't even touched it yet. Fuck, this witch would be the end of me. Her magic flared against me again and again, and I sucked in a sharp breath as her nails clawed down my back. I braced myself as her hands trailed down my stomach, but instead of inflicting pain she shucked off my boots, then unbuttoned my pants and roughly removed them.

 112

I sprang free and she licked her lips hungrily, smiling slyly, rising and grinding against me, daring me to explode all over her. "Fuck, Kitarni, keep doing that and I'll come before I'm even inside you."

"Maybe it's my way of punishing you," she purred. "Or maybe I want to be punished too."

Gods have mercy. I grabbed her nightdress, ripping it in two, exposing the generous swell of her breasts and claiming one nipple in my mouth, nipping it and sucking before taking the other.

She moaned, and I smiled wickedly. "You're so wet, beautiful," I whispered in her ear. "I can feel how much you want this. Do you want my cock inside you?"

"Yes," she replied breathily, arching her back as I slipped my finger inside her, circling with my thumb. I pulled my finger out, sliding her taste across her lips and inside her mouth.

"I'm going to fuck your mouth so hard you'll be seeing stars. And then I'm going to claim every inch between those beautiful thighs."

Another moan answered me. "Do it," she said at last, fucking my hand and making those sweet, sinful noises that made me want to explode. "Do it, Dante. I want it. I want all of it."

"As my queen commands."

ELEVEN

KITARNI

"I need you on your knees," Dante said huskily, his tone sending shivers down my spine.

I dropped instantly, barely noticing the scratchy fabric of the rug as my eyes came level with the sheer length of his cock.

It might have frightened me once, the thought of taking him like this, both of us simmering with old hurts and anger. But now, I'd never wanted it more. Every brutal, punishing moment made pleasurable through the pain. Because he might have begged to be punished, but he was right. I needed release and, right now, I ached to have him inside me, hard and without restraint.

I took him in my mouth, tentatively at first, sucking and sweeping my tongue over the sensitive tip, then harder, deeper, until he was hitting the back of my throat. He groaned, tilting his head back, and I felt myself become impossibly wet at seeing his pleasure, at every thrust as he grabbed the back of my head and

 114

pushed in even further. I thought I'd break, but I managed to relax my throat, hungry to take what I wanted.

My back arched and I grabbed his ass, raking my nails down him so hard I drew blood. He grunted, thrusting harder in punishment, manipulating my head so he was so deep I was nearly choking. I wanted more, the kind of filthy, unrestrained sex that would send Christian women to hell under the eyes of their god. But I was far from holy and I would burn in brutal rapture for this moment.

"Fuck, Kitarni. I love the way you look with your lips wrapped around me." Dante's thrusts came faster as he neared climax, groaning, his hand fisting my hair so hard it hurt. Tears blurred my eyes from the pressure, but I refused to stop, waiting for the moment he shuddered, spilling into my mouth. I licked up every drop as he watched me with shuttered eyes, but we weren't done. Not by a long shot.

He lifted me up like I weighed nothing at all, planting me on the edge of the desk, swiping the contents off so they went crashing around the room. "Spread your legs, Freckles," he commanded, pinching my nipples, then licking over each.

I did as he asked, feeling utterly exposed as he grabbed each leg and tossed them over his shoulders, proceeding to do something I'd never dreamed of. His tongue slid up my centre, and I yelped, grabbing onto the edge of the desk to steady myself, melting into him.

Fuck. What was this magical bliss? This heady torture? I felt

myself coming apart, panting as I writhed against his mouth, moaning as his tongue flicked over the most sensitive spot. Pain shot up my ass and back from the desk jutting into me, and I grunted.

Dante stopped, eyeing me from between my thighs, and I whimpered, shoving myself into his face. He smiled, his mouth slick from me. "My good girl. You taste so fucking good. I want to taste your release."

I shivered, trying to squeeze my legs together to ease the mounting ache, but he lowered my legs and spread them even wider, kneeling before me. His finger pushed inside me quickly and then withdrew, his hands flying up to cup my cheeks, squeezing momentarily before he began licking again.

A groan escaped me, loud and desperate, and that wet finger of his slid between my ass, circling. I cried out, bucking into him, feeling so much pleasure riding that wave that my legs began quivering, the pleasure so deep I burned the table where I gripped it.

Dante laughed and, before I could take a minute to recover, he grabbed me, spinning me around and shoving me over the desk. He lined himself up behind me, thrusting in so hard, so deep, I cried out, panting. He kicked my legs apart so I was spread eagled and bared, unable to move as he pounded.

His cock filled me up, every sensitive nerve set on fire as he took me savagely, desperately, as though the world might end tomorrow and he needed every inch of me. I moaned, pressing

back into him, my eyes nearly rolling back into my head. That finger of his found my ass once more, and I writhed so much he fisted my hair at the back of my scalp. He pulled me so taut my back arched, allowing him to hit a new angle in my body that had me screaming.

"You are mine, Kitarni Bárány," he growled from above me. "Say that you're mine."

I licked my lips, feeling the wave of pleasure readying to crash out of me. "Yes. I'm yours. I've always been yours."

A deep rumble escaped his lips, and he sucked in a breath. "Finish with me, Freckles."

Gods, yes. He didn't have to tell me twice. I moaned as he quickened, thrusting harder, faster, so brutal that my release flooded my body as I clenched around him. We came together until I dropped, panting over the table, Dante resting his temple against my back.

We stayed that way for a minute until our breathing harmonised and my heart stopped racing like a beating drum. He scooped up my tattered nightdress from the ground and knelt before me, using it to clean me up with the gentlest of touches.

Honestly, I was still finding it hard to fathom what had just happened and where this sex demon had sprung from. We'd been intimate before but this? If this was the real Dante unleashed, then I was all fucking for it. I knew the charming lord before me was without mercy on the battlefield, and I more than liked the dark side of him in the bedroom too.

Or the temple antechamber, so it happened.

When Dante finished tidying me up, I finally looked around the room, wincing at the mess we'd made. It looked like a storm had roared through the chamber, breaking numerous items and overturning just about everything we'd touched.

I raised a brow. "Next time we decide to have angry sex, let's try not to destroy everything we touch, okay?"

"And ruin all the fun?" He snorted, tugging me to the ground and into his arms. Beads of sweat ran down his neck and chest and I stared at them, mesmerised with the paths they tracked over every plane and ridge of muscle.

A small smile crept over my lips as I admitted, "I suppose there's something exciting about being so reckless."

"Naughty little hellcat," he reprimanded, shifting me so we could lie down beside each other.

He traced idle circles over my hips, then up my stomach, landing over the scar on my chest. My skin tingled as he pressed his lips to it, then took me by the back of my neck and kissed me deeply. Slow, sensuous, and without the urgency of before.

When he pulled back, he stared into my eyes seriously. "I know it will take time to restore what we had, but I meant what I said, Freckles. From today until my last, I will earn back your trust. I will earn my place by your side and, together, we will stop Sylvie."

I sighed. He was right, of course. Our history wouldn't just go away, but it felt so good being with him again and finding

this small peace. I wanted to stay in the moment forever. Forget our problems, forget the war and the rest of the world. But such dreams were not to be. "It won't be long until she attacks. There's so much to do here, so much to prepare. I fear for my people."

"Our people," he corrected, tucking my hair back from my face. "Your problems are my own, as are those of the witches here. We'll get through this Kitarni. I have connections too. The táltosok are few and far between, but there are more clans across the Kingdom. I have already asked for aid."

I nodded. "We'll need all the help we can get, but at least with Caitlin gone, we can restore order to the village. Any willing witch will resume training tomorrow, under Erika and Lukasz's guidance, and with Mama and Eszter's assistance in leading, I'll be able to focus on the next task."

"The crown. Your bargain with Death." He frowned, pinning me under his scrutinising gaze. "Tell me you aren't planning something that's going to set a demon on our asses?"

I bit my lip. "I might have decided to use the crown's power before giving it back to him."

He straightened. "Kitarni, it isn't wise to anger the horseman, nor any other being from the Under World for that matter. When Death finds out you kept it from him, he'll have your neck."

"I'm not afraid of him," I scoffed. "We have a mutual respect. Besides, he's busy playing house with Fate. Now that his prized pony is back in the stable, I'm sure he'll be otherwise occupied for a while."

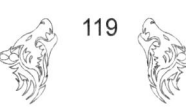

"I wouldn't count on it," Dante grumbled. "Just what do you mean to do with the crown anyway?"

I frowned. "I'm not certain yet. Death said his ring gives him the power to rule, but I'm betting the crown is even stronger, given its significance. I suspect he'd intended it for Fate, to rule by his side."

"And Sylvie stole it before she was executed, knowing whoever held it would have magic strong enough to conquer a kingdom—to conquer the world."

"Yes. The fact she hasn't made a move yet tells me she hasn't been able to retrieve it, which means it must be somewhere heavily guarded. Or perhaps ..." I trailed off, eyes widening. "Oh fuck."

"What is it?"

I looked him dead in the eye. "I know where to find the crown. There's only one place Sylvie could hide it where no mortal could enter. Only one place she could access through her dark magic and have power enough to conceal it from immortal eyes."

Dante's eyes widened in understanding. "You think Sylvie was plotting with Fate even before her execution?"

"It makes sense. After Sylvie failed to overthrow Death the first time, she must have persuaded Fate to her cause. The crown would have assured both got what they wanted. Fate would have dominion over the Under World and, in return, Sylvie would have the mortal realm to wreak her havoc. Together, they would have been unstoppable."

Dante shook his head. "But before Sylvie could use the crown, the witches saw her burned at the stake."

I nodded, excitement filling me. "Sylvie was clever enough to cover her bases, which means wherever the crown is, it's undetectable by Fate and Death. And I know just the place it is hiding.

Dante blew out a breath. "The crown is in the Under World."

I smiled grimly. "Looks like I'm going to hell."

TWELVE

DANTE

I heard the scuffing of András's boots just in time to cover Kitarni's gloriously naked body, which was a true shame. She was a drug I'd never have enough of and, even after spending much of the night continuing our antics, the less logical part of me was standing to attention.

The golden rays of dawn filtered through the high window in the chamber, but I'd been awake long after Kitarni and I had ceased our lovemaking, plagued by thoughts of the crown and the Under World.

She wanted to travel to hell, right into the belly of the beast. Before Kitarni's theory about Sylvie's hiding the crown there, I hadn't thought it possible for mortals to visit the realm. Even if the crown was in the Under World, venturing there would be a fool's mission.

What manner of monsters roamed that ethereal plane? Worse still, what if Death sensed her presence the moment she arrived?

These questions and more had raced through my mind all night, chasing the sweet mercy of sleep from my reach.

"What's happening?" Kitarni mumbled, rousing and blinking sleepily like an owl.

Before I could answer, a clang sounded and András opened the door, a bundle of clothing in his arms and a shit-eating grin on his face. To his credit, he didn't even blink at my state of undress. "Well, aren't you two a sight for sore eyes?"

Kitarni squeaked in protest, holding the rug tighter to her chest and I scowled at him as I grabbed my pants and slipped them on. "Finally letting the prisoners out, are we?"

He ignored me, looking around the state of the room, his eyes roving over the scratches and bruises covering my body. That smile grew impossibly wider. "I figured you'd need some time to figure things out. How right I was. Glad to see you're both mostly in one piece."

"Stop gloating and hand me the damn clothes, András," Kitarni said irritably, though her usual bite was half-hearted at best.

The pair continued arguing like an old married couple and I glanced between them with a small smile. Their exchange was made even more amusing by the tattered rug wrapped around her frame and the bird's nest that passed for her curls, compared to the glowing blond hair and pristine clothes András wore.

As frustrating as it was, his interference had certainly helped mend the rift between Kitarni and me. She still needed time to

123

heal, to trust in me again, but talking alone had done wonders. And the anger she'd held for me, well ... I was feeling it today. In all the right ways.

Her training was paying off. She had been toned before, but the lingering softness to her belly and the roundness of her thighs had hardened to muscle, and she was *strong*. Now to continue testing her swordsmanship against a real opponent. I had promised, after all, to teach her in the ring.

"Enough crowing," I said at last, at my wit's end with the duo. Honestly, one András was bad enough, but the two of them together just spelled trouble.

András huffed, tossing the bundle at her before turning around. "Just remember who brought you little lovebirds back together."

I dragged a hand over my face, keen to change the subject. With so much to do, coupled with the gnawing dread about Kitarni's safety, I felt restless with the need to act, to keep busy. "What news do you bring?"

András's back stiffened, his preening and gloating forgotten. "That's why I'm here so early. We've received word from the scouts. Cultists have been spotted drawing closer to the village."

"How many?" Kitarni asked as she pulled a tunic over her head. "You can turn around now."

His eyes were steely as he did. "Around twenty-odd. One of the witches accompanying us said they appeared to be lingering around the border's edge."

"Near the wards?" Kitarni gasped. "Gods. Sylvie means to expose us to the humans."

My eyes snapped to hers. "Surely she wouldn't risk drawing their attention? If the wards fall, the humans will rally. That's problematic for everyone."

"She wants the witches persecuted. For us to be hunted just as her followers were after her death. It won't matter if the humans discover her cult, she will destroy them without hesitation."

"There's also the matter of the other things residing in the woods," András added. "The corruption has spread nearly as far as the outer reaches. If left unchecked, those monsters will have free reign."

"I don't understand," I said, looking between them. "The creatures are unable to travel beyond the forest's edge."

"Yes, but only while the wards are in place," Kitarni replied. "The power in the spells hiding us from human sight ensures no one can get in without the magical signature required. But in the same way, the wards are responsible for keeping things from getting *out*. Right now, they are all that stand between those monsters escaping and wreaking havoc on the world."

The weight of what she was saying crashed down on me. "You're telling me Sylvie alone has the power to destroy them?"

Kitarni nodded, her face grim. "A few months ago, I would have said no, but now that the banya has been proved false and Sylvie is alive ..." She sighed. "Mama used to tell stories about our ancestors and the creation of the first wards. Once upon a time,

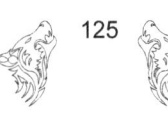

after Sylvie's demise and when the first banya was honourable and good, the coven worked beside her to construct the initial charms to protect us from the eyes of humankind. It took a village to harness strength enough to manage such a taxing task. Since then, every banya over the generations has been charged with maintaining them—monitoring their strength and injecting magic when required. Even your mother must have kept up with the ritual ... until she became a cultist and began practicing dark magic."

"Yaga was responsible for them?" I asked, blinking. "That makes sense. She could lead Sylvie right to them."

"Sylvie was powerful before her death, but since her return ..." Kitarni scrubbed her face tiredly. "She's not a witch anymore. Not mortal. To be honest, I don't know the limits of her magic."

"Which is why you're so determined to go to the Under World." I sighed, reaching out to stroke her arm.

"Pardon?" András said, baffled. "Did I miss something integral here? You want to go to hell?"

Kitarni winced. "Well I'm not thrilled by the idea, but I suspect the crown is hidden there, so ... yes?"

He blinked, staring at her in shock. Ah shit. I braced myself for the fallout. Three. Two. One.

"Are you out of your fucking mind?"

"András," I said quietly, raising a hand. "If Kitarni is correct, it might be the only way to defeat Sylvie."

His glare turned on me. "You're siding with her on this? Did

you get hit too hard in the head while you had your little angry sex war?"

"I know it's not ideal," Kitarni said calmly, "but if she can dispel the magic of those wards, we won't just have to worry about Sylvie's army, but a host of cross-bearing men armed with pitchforks and torches. The creatures will escape and kill anything in their path. Thousands will die, András."

Silence filled the chamber. András hung his head, picking at some invisible lint on his clothes, and Kitarni blew out a breath, pacing with her hands on her head.

"How many scouts are on patrol?" I asked my friend.

He looked up at me, his face souring. "Not enough."

"Then we take a unit now, kill any cultists lurking near the borders, and set up a guard around the perimeter. It won't hold long, but we might be able to buy some time at the very least."

Kitarni nodded. "I'll have Erika send some witches to assist. Your soldiers could use some magical aid."

"And you?" I asked gently. She'd normally be the first to dive headlong into battle, but she seemed preoccupied with her thoughts, a permanent frown creasing her brow. "The coven must prepare. This new information demands care and I must convey it delicately, so we don't cause a panic. I need to get our affairs in order."

Pride washed through me as I looked over my betrothed. She was a born leader. If anyone could put this village to rights, it was her. "What are you going to tell them?"

She cocked her head, a small smile gracing her lips. One that meant mischief. "Everything. It's time for a coven meeting, and I'm going to lay all the cards on the table. Sylvie thinks she can outsmart us, but she's not the only one with a few tricks up her sleeve. I have a plan."

I grinned, striding over and kissing her deeply. "Of course you do. Give em' hell, Freckles."

"You too. Be safe."

I'd barely left the room before I heard the crinkling of paper and the thud of items being rifled through. Oh yes, she was up to something, and I hoped by all the gods that it would be enough, because we'd need nothing short of a miracle to save us.

The smell of spoiled eggs and rotting carcass permeated the air as I stalked through the Sötét Erdő with Lukasz and a small group of soldiers. Everywhere we looked, a black, viscous substance oozed from branches and pooled beneath our boots. Any remaining plant matter had either shrivelled up and died or the tendrils had curled into themselves, trying to hide from the corruption.

It worsened every day, leaking closer and closer to civilisation. Soon, it would be upon the village and, not long after that, consuming the golden glow and vibrant purples of the fields surrounding Mistvellen.

The mark of the damned. I'd never imagined the fate of the world would tip because of a cult of dark worshippers and bloodmorphia addicts. Men waged wars for land and glory, for women or treasures. Perhaps some even revelled in watching the world burn, but this ... this was the destruction of all things. All peoples.

It had to end. The cultists *all* needed ending, none more than Sylvie and my mother.

Did it make me a monster that I didn't care about destroying so many lives? I squared my jaw. Maybe, but I didn't care. They'd made their choice; they'd threatened the ones I loved.

Lukasz held up his hand and we stopped, crouching low as something traipsed through the undergrowth. No, not just one thing. A group of tündérek walked through the treeline up ahead, their faces impassive, their steps near silent. Earth faeries, by the looks of their dark skin, and the odd fae who had antlers or green whorls trailing down their arms and legs. One thing remained the same between all though, and that was the black staining their cheeks and necks, oozing out of their ears.

Lost to corruption and deadly as hell.

I held my breath as we all stayed preternaturally still, a gift of the táltosok blood running through our veins. They hadn't noticed us, and as the seconds passed into agonisingly long minutes, we finally relaxed at Lukasz turning to face the group, his hand half-raised to signal the move.

His eyes widened, and I turned instantly, finding myself face

to face with a faerie, her teeth bared and her eyes pitch black. She shrieked, swiping with claws that would have opened my throat, and I jumped back, her dagger-like nails narrowly missing me and scraping the front of my armour.

She hissed and I drew my twin blades, using the motion to curve them instantly and sever the head from her body. It thudded to the ground, rolling to a stop, her expression frozen in one of fury.

Answering howls sounded in the distance and I grimaced at Lukasz as the ground rumbled beneath our feet—what could only be a stampede of hooves seemingly galloping towards us. Lidércek and the faeries that had passed earlier.

Fuck.

"Group together," I barked at the men, raising my swords and readying my stance. "Don't give them an opening." We formed a huddle, spines pressed back-to-back. My power sizzled under the surface of my skin, whispering sweet nothings in my ear, begging for release.

But not yet. One faerie wasn't worth the strength of conjuring my necromancy. Not when my blades yearned for the taste of more dark blood.

The faeries arrived first, their beautiful faces twisted with eerie grins. I moved, my swords like flowing rivers, carving a path through flesh and bone. The male fae ahead fell before he could raise a hand.

Lukasz cursed behind me, battling two lithe females armed

with swords. Apparently, Sylvie had seen fit to equip some of her mindless soldiers. The realisation didn't sit well. Not because we'd have any trouble dispatching small numbers like this, but because it boded ill for the coming war. Cultists, creatures, humans ... what else did Sylvie have up her sleeve?

I planted my feet beside my brother as the others broke off against their opponents. He glanced at me and nodded and I flashed him a grin; it all reminded me of the old days when we'd spar side by side, always formidable, always unstoppable as a team. We ran together, charging the faeries and disarming both with practiced twists of our wrists.

The faeries shrieked and we dispatched their heads in one swift strike, black blood splattering our cheeks as we turned, facing each other with mirrored movements.

Behind us, the lidércek approached, their hooves sliding as they came to a stop, causing leaf litter to dance as it fluttered in the air.

"Dammit Dante," Lukasz said, his brows pulled together. "I had them."

"Oh?" I raised a brow, rolling my neck as we stepped into line besides each other, slowly advancing. "Could've fooled me. You've grown slow, fattened by Nora's cooking."

Lies. Even with a little extra weight, he was still cut with hard muscle, but the look of outrage on his face was certainly worth it.

Lukasz grunted, lunging against a tündérek, countering her blow and answering with a riposte. "My swordsmanship is still as

sharp as my tongue."

"You were always quick-witted," I agreed, not even bothering to look as I thrust my sword into a tündérek's stomach before running, sliding on my knees through the dirt and slicing through his opponent's stomach. "Not quick enough to beat me, though."

Lukasz shook his head, grinning at me slyly as he grabbed my arm and heaved me to my feet. "Glad to see you're as arrogant as ever. Kitarni hasn't tamed the beast inside you yet."

I scoffed. "Tame me? She's wilder than I am, and that's just how I like it."

"I don't want to know," Lukasz said, grimacing. He assessed the damage around us. Thankfully, only a few soldiers had superficial wounds.

With a flick of my wrists, the excess blood on my blades flew off and I wiped them on my leathers before sheathing them. "You and Eszter seem to be getting quite cosy," I said, folding my arms as I watched the unit take a breather.

Lukasz smiled slightly, shaking his head. "I'm a gentleman, remember? You're not getting anything out of me."

I grinned. "You know, if you so much as cause her sister to shed a tear, Kitarni will rip your head off."

My brother frowned. "Why do I get the sense you're oddly delighted about that fact?"

I shrugged, my smile revealing all my secrets, but I cocked my head, growing serious. "Everything will change soon. Sylvie's army is weeks away at best, perhaps even days. Tell Eszter how you

feel. She's a kind, good-natured girl. Don't let the war destroy that."

Lukasz looked at me, seeing right through me as he had a knack for. "She is not her sister, Dante," he said softly. "And I am not you. I know you're just looking out for me, but I have my own mistakes to make, my own lessons to learn. Letting anything happen to Eszter will not be one of those mistakes. I've made arrangements. She will head to Mistvellen on the morrow."

"Does Eszter know about said arrangements?" He looked at his feet, which was answer enough. "She won't go," I said gently. "The Bárány women are stubborn as mules. She won't leave her sister."

"Then I will strap her to a horse myself," Lukasz snapped, his brow furrowed.

I knew his frustration wasn't grounded in me. My brother was a good man. Loyal to a fault, gentle and kind, and capable of thinking on his feet. Despite my teasing, he was a good soldier, too. Life had always been a competition between us—to be the better warrior, to be a smarter strategist or a wordsmith when in talks with other allies. We'd grown up a bit since then, maturing the way a seed does through its cycles through life. Only, we didn't get to come back if we perished. There was no renewal period, no second chance.

The world was a funny place. Regardless of our parentage and bloodline, my brother was my brother, and that was that. But I knew there were challenges he'd had to overcome, nonetheless.

133

Racial differences as well as being born a bastard. Mistvellen was a diverse city and one my family was proud to call home, but there's not a place in the world where shadows can't mask the malevolent. There would always be those who feared what they could not understand or did not bother to know.

Still, Lukasz had always put Mistvellen before his own needs. Father had never treated him differently despite Lukasz's mother, and that simple act alone had been the difference between a hard life and a cherished one. A life where Lukasz had been educated, trained, respected and, more importantly, loved.

Only now, Lukasz might have found *the* love of his life. An altogether different kind that threatened to turn level-headed men into mindless sheep and steadfast soldiers into distracted partners. I knew because a piece of me was always with Kitarni. Wondering if she was okay, if she was in danger, if I could do anything to stop her from being a gods damned hero and just let someone else save the day.

But no one would.

No one *could*.

"Just be careful," I said finally. "The last time I got in the way of a Bárány, it ended badly. I wouldn't recommend it." I studied the táltosok, seeing that the wounded had been patched up and everyone was ready. "Let's keep moving."

Lukasz nodded, taking point, and this time I slid into position beside him, stealthily moving through the undergrowth. Gods, it stank so fucking bad, and with blood splattered all over

me, I felt like gagging.

The woods were eerily quiet as we moved, nothing but the fire of a couple torches to guide our way. The flickering light played tricks on my eyes, making it seem like the shadows were alive and creatures big and small were hunting us. I scrubbed a hand over my eyes, blinking back the fogginess settling over me.

My spine tingled with awareness and the hairs on my arms stood on end, warning me that something wasn't right, not that anything was in this forest anymore. By the sidelong glance he gave me, Lukasz felt it too. Either cultists were close, or we were approaching the wards. I hoped to hell it was the latter and not a combination of the two.

Ahead, a shimmering light caught my gaze, and I pointed it out to Lukasz, knowing he'd likely already seen it in what looked to be a clearing. *The wards.* We'd made it. Cautiously, we eyed the ground and nearby trees for traps before pushing the last sticky black leaves aside and wading through.

The sight made me freeze in my tracks.

Five pikes stood before us, lined in a neat row before a translucent wall that shimmered silver, then black, then blood red. The fractured light seemed frantic, as if tampered with and corrupted like the woods around it.

Spiked at the top of those pikes were five heads, their faces twisted, clotted blood dribbled down the wood and pooling in a small lake where the stakes embedded into the ground.

The táltosok scouts who'd sent word to the village.

My stomach turned violently, but it wasn't even the gruesome display which had my bones feeling brittle and my heart racing. Written in their blood upon the ground were three words that had my blood turning to ice.

I am coming.

"These men were tasked with patrolling the border and protecting the wards," Lukasz said, his face grim. He shook his head. "Those sick bastards."

"The Dark Queen knows we're onto her." I blew out a breath, looking back to the heads on those pikes, unable to tear my gaze from the faces of those men. They'd been interrogated, no doubt. Tortured for information and forced to watch each other's suffering. There was no way to know what they'd given up—the number of our forces, our weak points, anything—but what little they knew was still too much, especially given the message. "We've been compromised," I said, turning to Lukasz and the others. I pinned a táltos by the name of Bela under my stare. He was the quickest runner and could convey my message the fastest, gods be willing. "What little time we had has just been shortened considerably. Get back to the village, tell Kitarni and the other councillors what you've seen. Convey Sylvie's message and make ready. The hourglass has run out."

Bela nodded, removing his heavy armour and sword before taking off through the woods. The gear would only have hindered him. I just had to hope no other surprises were lying in wait to catch him off guard.

 136

"Move out," I commanded the others, but as Lukasz turned, I put my hand on his shoulder. "Wait."

He glanced at me quizzically, and I shook my head. We didn't have time for sentiments, but I felt compelled to confide in him, now more than ever. Life was too fucking short. Sylvie's actions only proved that.

"If the end of days is upon us, it's important you know that I'm happy for you. I haven't been here—really here—the last few months, and I've been too damned caught up in my own shit to pay much attention to anyone else's, but if anything good has come of this mess i'ts meeting your match." I cleared my throat, hoping my rambling was making sense. "You and Eszter? You're a good fit. Just don't fuck it up."

Lukasz shook his head, a wry grin on his face. "Don't go getting soft on me now, Dante. We need you at your most merciless if we're going to win this fight."

The humour fell flat on both of us, but I set my jaw, let my soul harden as I faced the men once more. "You can count on it. Believe me, Brother, you haven't seen the worst that I can do."

THIRTEEN

KITARNI

By the time I'd rifled through grimoires and old tomes until I'd finally found the spell I was after, I was a sweaty mess. After one look at my clothes and the state of my hair, Eszter had clucked her tongue and shoved me into the tub, a pleased grin on her face.

The rest of the day had passed in a blink, my nerves shot and my anticipation making my stomach curdle. My plan wouldn't be easy to carry out but, if it worked, it might be our only saving grace.

I just hadn't counted on needing to implement it so soon.

I had just finished up the town meeting when a táltos sprinted out of the woods like he was running for dear life. The minute I saw his face, I'd known something was wrong. My heart had just about leapt out of my chest, because my first fear had been for Dante's life, but a few hushed words later, and it had felt like the world had tilted ass up.

 138

I am coming, her message had read.

There were those three words again, the same ones Sylvie had screamed as Dante had carried my half-dead ass in his arms when we'd fled the cultists' encampment months ago. My stomach threatened to revolt. It's not that I had ever doubted her conviction, but I had hoped for more time or more of a game plan. Just ... more.

Naturally, the announcement that we'd have to move my plan up to, well, today, had not been received quite so calmly. But everyone had their orders, and whether they liked it or not, this was our best option.

I huffed. And it had all been going so well.

The village was a blur as witches spread throughout the town square like wildfire, herding children and gathering precious possessions as they went.

I sprinted up the path, efficiently dodging witches as I went, my boots pounding over the dirt and past the stone statues of the turul guarding the doors. A group of witches were already inside gathering supplies, and I nodded to a few I recognised. Elisabeth— the witch we'd rescued in the woods—and a few other faces I'd never forget.

Hanna's faithful friends. Less than a year ago I would have flinched to see them, or more likely still, blended into shadow before they could see me.

Everything had changed. Now I saw only fierce determination in their eyes and a willingness to help. Girls who'd grown into

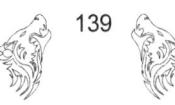

women, united by a common enemy and stronger together, as women always were.

I nodded to each witch, and they bowed their heads—actually bowed—as I walked past. They had never done so for Caitlin, and that kernel of knowledge made me smile. Still, it would take some getting used to. Mama and Erika were stockpiling crates gathered from the antechamber, and I skidded to a halt as I approached.

"Is there enough for the spell?" I asked, peering into their boxes.

The crates were filled with white candles, crystals, chalk, and various other trinkets, as well as grimoires and valuable artefacts that had been with our coven for generations. Our history lay in those crates ... and our future.

Mama nodded, her brown hair frazzled, the odd curly tendril escaping her bun. "It will suffice. These items are necessary, but whether the spell works or not will depend on the people's magic, not so much the tools used to create it. Ingredients are necessary, but they mean nothing if not used correctly."

"Do you really think it will work, Kitarni?" Erika asked, her brown eyes solemn. "With this many witches?"

"It has to," I replied instantly. "It will work *because* of our numbers. Power combined is magic amplified. Trust in Istenanya. The mother will see us through."

Erika shifted the weight of her crate and put a hand on my shoulder. "Never mind the gods. I have faith in you. That is enough for me."

I smiled, shoving all my fear aside and putting on a brave face. The truth was, I had no idea if this would work because I'd never tried it before. Spells weren't my strong suit—one mispronounced word, one misstep, and they would all pay the price.

A cost I couldn't afford.

But thinking that way would only reflect badly to the other witches. The spell would work and my only regret would be missing the look on Sylvie's face when she realised, she'd been played. I smiled again, and this time it was genuine; if that bitch thought she'd destroy us in one fell swoop, she was in for a surprise.

"Let's go," I said, hefting the last crate into my arms. "Laura should have readied the herbs by now."

We filed out the temple and I looked back on it one last time, bowing to the gods in their stained-glass windows. Every blade of grass, every blossom tree, had all been a sanctuary once upon a time. A place of worship and a garden of escape.

It might be the last time I see them.

As expected, Laura was waiting in the square, the dried herbs required for the spell bundled in neat rows by her feet. The curvy witch bowed her head as we approached, her long black hair swaying in its braid.

"Rosemary for protection, mugwort for cleansing, and stinging nettle for strength."

"You've done well, Laura. Have the witches draw a circle, placing the items just inside the ring. When it's complete and everyone is gathered, we can begin."

She turned, barking her orders at anyone within range who didn't have a child or animal in tow. Impressively, most of the witches appeared to be accounted for, packed and ready nearby. In less than an hour, they'd managed to cram their lives into a few meagre sacks or onto carts.

Sadness panged in my stomach as I looked around me at the place I'd once called home. But, as I watched mothers and sisters scurry about, I realised the endearment didn't quite ring true. Home had never been the roof over my head, the town, or even the woods I loved so much. Home was my family.

I lifted my gaze over the thatched roofs, the stone giving way to ivy and the flowers in bloom, catching sight of golden locks in sunlight belonging to a girl with goodness in her heart and hope in her soul. To my sister. And to my mother, who was grace and wisdom and a reminder of a person to aspire to.

Beyond them, past the village proper and to the border of trees where sickness threatened to rupture, Dante appeared. Blood streaked across his face, his dark hair glinting red in the sun. Yes. Home was not 'where'. It was 'who'.

And Dante, for all the crap he'd done and all the shit he'd pulled, a part of me would always see that in him—for the family he'd gifted me and for finding a place where I belonged. There were other things too, things I was still tentative to explore.

He collided with me, wrapping his large arms around my waist and squeezing me tight before he held me at arm's length. "I hope you know what you're doing, Kitarni, because Sylvie isn't

far behind us. I expect she'll be here by nightfall at the earliest, tomorrow morning at the very latest."

"That's all the time we need," I said, leading him towards the square. "Thanks to your messenger, we've had enough time needed to prepare."

He glanced at me sidelong. "What's your plan?"

I grinned, winking at him. "You'll find out soon enough."

"My little hellcat," he said with a chuckle. "Causing trouble as always."

"You wouldn't have it any other way. Let's get to work. Gather the táltosok and make ready to leave."

He bowed, extending his arms with a rakish grin. "Your wish is my command." I watched him go, staring a little too long at his ass covered in blood-slicked clothes. There was something about a man dressed for battle that just did things to a girl. Images of last night sprang to mind, of being slammed against the wall, then slammed by something else. Dirty words that had made me wetter than a wellspring.

Down girl. I turned towards the square, focusing on the task at hand. Mama dipped her head at me just once from the centre, Erika and Eszter by her sides. One by one, the witches gathered around the circle, and those that couldn't fit stood behind them, hands placed on each other's shoulders until forming a seemingly endless spiral of bodies.

They all parted for me as I strode towards the middle, nodding their heads respectfully, murmuring encouragement

or well wishes. Fear shone in the eyes of many, but there was determination and fury, too. Not at me, but at what was to become of their town and who threatened it.

I fisted my hands as I came to my place in the centre, letting the nails bite into my skin painfully. I needed the sharpness to ground me and keep my mind focused. Mama handed me the book containing the spell and I took a deep breath as my family left me, Eszter smiling softly before she became one with the coven.

I cast my eyes over the circle one last time, studying the many candles with their flickering flames, the bones and herbs and crystals that scattered over rock and soil and the roots of the earth. Then I began reciting.

The spell was simple enough, but the words were ancient and complex. An old, forgotten language unknown to humankind and feared by the supernatural world. Feared ... and prized.

The words spilled from me, slowly at first, quietly, but the longer I spoke, the atmosphere shifted. The air rippled with magic, the world beyond our circle darkening until it shuttered, replaced by a sphere of smoke and shadow, writhing like a creature of the night.

My words deepened, my voice becoming louder, mine and somehow not. All around me, witches chanted, repeating my words, swaying faster, more violently with each passing second. I was drowning in power and the beast inside me revelled, drinking in every drop flooding my body, roaring victoriously as it slithered

 **144**

through my veins and passed beyond my fingers.

Soon there was no light and it was near maddening to be blinded by nothingness, but the magic was working, the sphere growing larger, larger, encompassing the entire square and then beyond, stretching clawed fingers towards the edge of the town and up the very trunks of the woods surrounding us.

That ethereal voice rumbling from my throat deepened and then, suddenly, the last line of the spell was finished. I came back to myself, slamming into my body with a sudden awareness that had me gasping for breath and reeling from a shockwave.

My vision cleared and I was falling to my knees when strong arms caught me, lifting me up. I saw Dante's face, his dark brown eyes, the chiselled jaw so delectable I couldn't help but run my finger along it. His chest rumbled against me, then his mouth was on mine, claiming, devouring, as if the magic I'd just expelled called to something deep inside him, too.

His tongue curled around me, sinfully sweet and dangerously tempting. I could have lost myself in the scent of leather and musk and earthen things. The faint smell of blood and sweat overlapped it and, maybe it made me fucking crazy, but that combined with his possessive touch made the junction of my thighs so slick and my mind conjure things I wasn't even ashamed to think of.

At last I pulled away, suddenly aware of all the eyes on us. "Dante," I breathed. "Everyone is watching."

"Let them watch," he whispered, his lips pressing against the shell of my ear. "I want them all to know who claimed you. I want

them to know you're mine."

The breath whooshed out of me as he set me down and, to my surprise, the entire coven dropped to one knee, their heads bowed in submission.

"What are they doing?" I hissed, looking around frantically.

Dante's smile was predatory. "I don't know what you did," he said slowly, "but the power you just showed ... it was incredible. The whole village was shrouded in shadows."

I shook my head. "It wasn't just mine. It was the power of the coven. Our power combined."

"Maybe you're right." He lifted my chin with his finger. "But you were the one to harness it. To take on the magic of so many is no easy feat, Kitarni. Be careful if you do it again. The magic you used was old and combining power like that is addictive. Don't let it consume you."

I swallowed. He didn't need to tell me twice. I still remembered vividly how it felt to have Dante's magic in my veins. It had been intoxicating and I'd almost lost myself to the ecstasy of that feeling—almost let him bleed out while I had been oblivious.

Never again. I couldn't afford to lose someone I loved—or myself, for that matter. I'd be no good to my coven if I turned into a power-lusting strumpet. I smoothed my pants down and faced the villagers, who were still watching us curiously, waiting for their orders. Despite not being able to see any visible changes, I knew the spell had worked. I could feel it all around us, a strange awareness of the ancient magic, as if it settled over my shoulders

like an unseen cloak.

"The spell worked," I said to the witches. "Once we leave this place, Sylvie will be none the wiser. It should buy us enough time to get away safely to Mistvellen, but we need to leave right now. I want all children and elderly near the front of the convoy. Those of you willing to fight can take your orders from Erika or Lukasz. The rest of you, move out."

Dante looked at me in surprise as the crowd dispersed, taking my hand gently. "That's the plan? You're leaving the village?"

I hung my head. "If there was any other way, I'd take it. I know this is their home, but villages can be rebuilt. If leaving means they get to keep their lives, then I'm willing to make that sacrifice. They might hate me for it, but if we can get them to Mistvellen, at least they'll be safe."

He pulled my head back gently, staring deep into my eyes. "No one hates you Kitarni. The witches respect your judgement. You're their High Witch now, and you're doing what you must. It's a wise decision and my father will happily accommodate the witches. It's likely many have family in Mistvellen. Daughters whose fathers or brothers remain there, and witches who can be reunited with old flames.

"The old ways are done, Kitarni. This is the future we wanted. A chance for families to remain together, for witches to have the right to choose how and where they want to live their lives."

My heart leapt at his words, hope rekindling deep in my stomach. Everything he said was true. It was exactly what I'd

dreamed being the lady of Mistvellen might accomplish one day. Under other circumstances, it would be a joyous occasion indeed. But for now, our task was to get them there safely.

One step at a time, Kitarni.

I lifted my hand, curling my fingers around the back of Dante's neck and into his hair. "I'd like to see that future. But first we need to get these people to safety. And then?" I smiled devilishly. "I recall a certain lord telling me about his fondness for jewels on the fairer sex."

The ring in Dante's eyes flashed. "Not the fairer sex. *You.* I want to see them on you, and you might also recall that I mentioned I want you naked while you wore them. But I have a feeling you're talking about a different kind of jewellery."

I elbowed him gently. "Why not have both?"

FOURTEEN

DANTE

The Dark Queen's followers approached, seeming to glide along the ground with their dark robes like a wall of smoke gathering from a wildfire. Their mutilated faces were twisted into grimaces or stitched lips, their mark of faith to Sylvie. To us, they were simply the masks of the damned. Fools hellbent on destroying all in their path, all because of their belief.

Christians, pagans, dark worshippers; our beliefs were so different, and it was that fact that made faith so dangerous. That fact that had humans burning witches at the stake and cultists cutting out hearts and draining bodies of blood.

Were they so different in the end? I had to think so. Humankind had many flaws, but despite their ruthlessness towards witches—or those unfortunate human girls who were labelled as such—their savagery was born from fear, not a need for power.

Yet power was always what it came down to, and Sylvie had it

 **149**

in droves. I cocked my head as I studied the approaching cultists, waiting for the moment the Dark Queen arrived.

I wanted to see her face the moment she realised what Kitarni had done. Wanted to see how she'd retaliate, knowing she'd been duped. It didn't hurt that Baba Yaga would likely be with her, ever the loyal servant to kiss and cower at her feet.

My anticipation piqued as the woman who'd once been my mother did indeed arrive, her lips painted red, her eyes lined with dark kohl. She was so thin she looked like a wraith, buried beneath a black tunic and a fur shawl too hot for the warmer weather.

Hatred boiled inside me ever hotter, but it was the woman beside her who stole my attention. Sylvie was breathtaking. The kind of beauty that men wove ballads about or sung sonnets for. Her tawny skin was golden, flushed with health and a youth belying her true age. Long brown hair hung braided down her back, and the leathers clad to her curves left little to the imagination.

Gone was the woman risen from the ashes, half-dead and bearing the pallor of death. The Dark Queen was restored and, though at first glance she was pleasant to look at, I knew the ugliness inside her. The hollow where her heart should be and the emptiness in her soul. It shone through to the outside if one only looked beyond the veil of beauty.

I wondered how much blood it had taken to renew this form. How many witches had died to get her here. My stomach twisted. Too many. The answer would always be too many.

150

Sylvie's lips curled with triumph as she spotted the witches, and she lifted a single finger into the air, pointing it towards the coven she hated so. "No mercy."

This morning, those words would have made even my stomach twist, but instead I smiled as I heard the soft whispers of Kitarni's own lips moving from where she stood beside me, her hands clasped with those of Eszter and her mother. The Bárány women, standing together as they chanted a spell, strengthening their existing enchantment. United like they always would be in all things. Kitarni trembled beside me and I placed my hand on her shoulder, lending her my strength should she need it.

Sylvie's forces rushed forwards, their eyes glimmering with the madness of bloodmorphia, their weapons raised. An eerie cry sounded from the dark wave as they crashed down upon the witches and táltosok alike, and I braced myself for the moment we'd all been waiting for.

The witches stood fast, their faces determined and weapons of their own raised high, but as the enemy attacked, their blows went straight through them. Again, they struck, met with thin air as they attacked. Confused, the cultists looked at each other, then back at Sylvie, whose red lips twisted in a slash of anger, her brown eyes flashing.

"What is the meaning of this?" she hissed as she approached, waving her arm through a nearby witch. Her arm passed straight through her, and the witch in question smiled wickedly before her body disappeared before my very eyes.

Sylvie's brows creased, and then her face morphed into something ugly and sinister as she bared her teeth, her eyes turning pitch black as she screamed. The sound was so chilling it skittered down my spine, settling into the crooks of my bones and the pit of my stomach.

The Bárány women ceased their chanting and the illusion fell away. Like a shockwave, all the witches and táltosok in the village disappeared, leaving the town quiet as a graveyard. There was nothing but the odd tinkle of metal or shuffling feet from the cultists as they looked on with gaping mouths—mostly. Many had sewn them shut.

I glanced at Kitarni, who grinned at me like a child on Szent-este morning. "An illusion spell," I said, smiling as the witches continued to wink out of existence through the water's reflection we peered into. "Kitarni, you never cease to surprise me."

"It was the only way I could think of to get everyone out safely," she said simply. "I managed to harness the spell to make the copies act as realistically as you or I. There's a magical signature to every spell, but I took a gamble that Sylvie would be too distracted by her need for revenge to notice it."

"Well, your bet paid off," I replied, sitting down on a log once the bespelled water returned to normal. "We'll reach Mistvellen tomorrow. I've sent a messenger bird to the castle asking my father to send troops to escort the caravan to safety. We might have delayed Sylvie, but who knows what other monsters roam

the woods."

Kitarni frowned, her gaze darting to the trees surrounding us. "I don't like how exposed we are right now. The Sötét Erdő is no place for children, and that's when it's not dripping with corruption."

Nora settled onto the log beside me with a weary sigh. "The children will be protected. The witches would give their lives before allowing a single hair on one of their heads to be harmed."

"The táltosok too," I said. "They will be safe, Kitarni. I swear it."

Her face softened as she looked at me, but I could tell the worry ate at her insides by the way she kept glancing into the darkness surrounding us. Somewhere along the encampment, a baby wailed, its mother hushing it softly.

I shifted uneasily. I'd heard of creatures in the Under World that stole away children in the night, whisking them away to feed on later. None of these creatures existed in our realm, but after seeing the demon Caitlin had conjured back in the village, I'd begun to wonder what other monstrosities we might see.

There were spells to harness dark magic, of course, but a summoning was an altogether different feat. To allow darkness to enter our realm, however briefly, was to allow carnage, and as Caitlin had never dismissed the demon ... was it possible it was still roaming the Kingdom?

If one entered our realm, it was a very real possibility that others could too, and I'd begun to wonder if the doorway between

realms had been opened.

Opened and perhaps ... left ajar.

The concern niggled at me, burrowing deeper beneath my skin, but it was a theory I wasn't yet ready to discuss with Kitarni. She already had her hands full with her new position as High Witch, and I didn't want to worry her any more than she already was.

No, we'd discuss it upon our return to Mistvellen, and hopefully Margit would have some insight into the matter. Better yet, she'd have *seen* something that would help us in the days to come.

I worried about my cousin. Fierce as she was, she was alone in ways no one else would ever understand, assailed by her visions in waking moments and whatever nightmares ailed her in rest. Despite the respect and courtesy afforded her by her station, she was still seen as strange by those at court. A beautiful, odd creature. In my opinion, her uniqueness made her even more precious, but I knew she didn't feel the same way, much as she pretended otherwise.

It's why she spent so much time in that damned dungeon beneath the library, keeping company with spiders as they weaved their webs in that dusty chamber and she weaved visions with her mind. The books, at least, I could understand. Sometimes I wanted to hide away myself, forget about my responsibilities and just lose myself in a fictional world. But such luxuries weren't meant for lords and ladies with the end of the world just a stone's

throw away.

Kitarni climbed into my lap, wrapping her arms around my neck as she stared deep into my eyes. "What's on your mind?"

So much for not worrying her, though the gods knew honesty and communication was exactly what we needed right now. After everything we'd been through—everything I'd put her through in the last few months—it was the best fresh start I could offer us. I smiled, pressing a kiss to each of her wrists.

"I haven't been able to shake the feeling that Sylvie's actions have consequences that extend beyond our realm. When Caitlin summoned that demon back in your village, she would have had to open a doorway to allow it through. But she never sent the demon back, and by failing to do so ..."

"She left the door open," Kitarni said, frowning. "You think more demons can pass through?"

"It's just a theory, but if I'm right, then it means we have more problems to worry about than just Sylvie. I'm not sure how the witches' magic will stand up against dark magic, not to mention demons."

"It won't," Nora said, her mouth set in a grim line. "Earth magic is bound by nature's rules. We can harness it, borrow it, but what is life in the eyes of creatures who crave ending it? Demons don't abide by the laws of man, and they certainly don't balk in the face of nature's gifts. The proof of that lies in the dying forest around us. Dark magic is, and always will be, unsatiable."

That declaration didn't sit well with me, but every word spoke

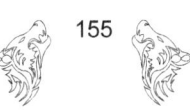

the truth. The witches of this coven would not be able to stop the creatures from the beyond, and neither would the táltosok. Our powers of animation were useless against monsters neither dead nor truly living.

"What about my powers?" Kitarni asked, settling back in a way that rubbed against my cock. Not that she noticed, too deep in thought.

I cleared my throat, shifting her ass to perch on my thigh instead. "Can you defeat them with the blood magic running through your veins?"

Her brow creased and she cocked her head, silent while she considered it. "No, not defeat them, but perhaps control them. I couldn't say for sure until I learn more about it. Maybe Margit will have some answers."

I nodded, coiling a strand of Kitarni's curls around my finger. She moved back into my lap, wriggling her ass back and forth like a cat readying for a nap. I was all too aware of her mother sitting right beside me, even as my dick wanted to spring to attention.

"Keep grinding on me, and I will be forced to fuck you in front of the whole camp," I whispered into her ear.

My little hellcat only chuckled under her breath.

Good gods, this girl was going to be the death of me. Since we'd fucked ourselves stupid in the temple the other night, I'd been craving her touch like an addict. I couldn't get enough of this woman.

My finger traced down her outer leg, settling on her thigh

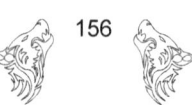

protectively. As soon as we got back to Mistvellen, I'd be showing her just how much I approved of her victory over Sylvie.

Nora stood up, smiling fondly down at us. "I'm going to check on the children and Eszter. She'll be so excited to see Mistvellen."

"She's going to love it," Kitarni said. "You both are."

Nora stroked her daughter's cheek, the simple gesture full of love and adoration, and then she disappeared among the throng of witches.

I reclined on the log, happy just to have my girl in my arms and a quiet moment together. There hadn't been much time for stillness since Sylvie's resurrection, and we hadn't been alone at all apart from the night in the temple ... and the chamber below it where I'd found Kitarni, Caitlin and the girl.

Kitarni was almost too silent, which was never a good sign. She always had a million thoughts running through her brain, which meant she was plotting or worrying. If I had to take a wild guess, I'd pick the latter.

My hand trailed up and down her leg, shifting closer to the junction of her thighs, then scraping along the sensitive skin above her pants. She gasped, arching into me.

"Dante, everyone will see," she said breathily, giggling girlishly as she glanced at the witches camped several metres away.

"Mm, maybe the idea of that turns me on." I slipped a finger down her pants and inside her, finding her already so wet for me. "Maybe it turns you on too."

She batted my hand away with a warning glare, then turned

to face me, her eyes glimmering with excitement. "That's off limits tonight. We've got something else to do."

"Does it involve ravaging you against a nearby tree?" I said quietly.

Her lips curved into a devious smile, one that I instantly recognised as scheming. "Not quite." She was silent for a beat, and when she spoke, her words sent an ominous chill down my spine. "I think I know how to test our theories, but you're not going to like it."

I pressed a kiss to her lips, moving my hands up to feel the delicate column of her neck. "Tell me."

She took a deep breath. "You and I are going to have a chat with a certain horseman. It's time we met with Death."

FIFTEEN

KITARNI

My boots were silent on the forest floor as Dante, András and I wound our way over sleeping bodies and past the personal belongings of the witches. There wasn't much. What little they could grab was tied up in rucksacks, their entire life packed away in one bag. The sight of the few precious children tucked tightly into their mamas' arms sent a sharp pang through my chest.

Letting the town burn to ensure their safety was a small price to pay, but it didn't make the decision any easier. The knowledge that they'll have a roof over their head and food in their bellies from a life lived in Mistvellen helped, but there would be some who begrudged me for uprooting their lives and bringing about change.

Some who would cling to old traditions and past principles that I no longer wished to uphold. Not when it broke up families, and certainly not when it prevented women from reaching their full potential. What's the point of being part of a female only coven when the very rules and regulations strip us of our greatness?

András nudged my arm, pointing to a gap in the trees surrounding us, and I changed my direction, aiming for the veil of darkness not splintered by the light of crackling torches dotted around the camp.

It was hard not to wrinkle my nose at the stench that climbed my nostrils the deeper we tread. A decay that clung, gripping on for dear life and never letting go. András frowned as he evaded dripping branches and mouldy logs.

"Remind me again why we're travelling deeper into this godsforsaken place?"

I elbowed him, teasing, "Afraid of getting your fancy pants dirty?"

He looked at me blankly, his brow rising. "They're expensive and they make my ass look impeccable. Why would I? Some of us take care of our clothing, instead of shredding it like beasts."

My cheeks heated at his insinuation, because yes, back in the temple when Dante and I had been together, clothes were the furthest thing on my mind. Dante smirked at me, clearly enjoying my embarrassment, and I huffed as I focused on avoiding a particularly gruesome rock pulsing with black veins.

Beyond the rock the woods opened to a small clearing, nestled in between trees bunched closer together which would grant us privacy—or protection from any creatures looking for a snack. It would put us in overly familiar proximity to Death, but

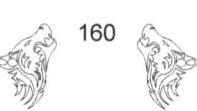

it was a risk I was willing to take. He still needed me, after all.

As if he read my mind, András asked, looking around warily, "Just how do you propose we summon him if we don't have the spell?"

"When I was younger, on the *Elátkozottak Napja*, Death visited our home, seeking the blood of witches."

András cocked his head, a few blond curls falling into his eyes. "Like he does every year on the Day of the Cursed, right? I've heard the stories. But I thought he couldn't harm you if you had the proper spells in place."

"True, but Eszter, innocent as she was, ran out to protect the livestock. When I ran after her, I found Death in the barn. He warned me about the lies—about the banya." I shook my head, thinking back to that night long ago. "He'd practically handed me the truth about Baba Yaga, and I'd been too clueless to understand what he'd meant. He knew all along who the banya really was."

"Gods great and small do so love their riddles," Dante grumbled. I noted his hands flexing, as though he was itching for the pommels of his blades, the soldier in him responsive and ready should danger approach.

That would all depend on Death's mood. And to think I could have been using a cleaner, more comfortable clearing for something far more enjoyable. The thought only soured my mood and made me clench my legs together.

"So he let Eszter go and then what?" András asked, his curiosity piqued. "You're still alive, which means he mustn't have

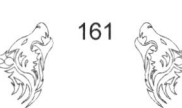

been too peckish that night."

I rolled my eyes at him. "He didn't want my blood, András, he wanted me. And this"—I turned around and lifted my shirt, letting him see the three blackened scars imprinted on my back, writhing faintly as they always have—"is the mark he made for it."

"Fuck me," András breathed, stepping closer and reaching out to touch them.

Dante grabbed his wrist before he could, looking at me sharply. *Possessive lordling.* "How do we know this will even work?"

"We don't." I smiled at him wickedly. "Call it a hunch. And boys? Be on your best behaviour please. He doesn't appreciate bad manners."

Dante and András shared a look, the former dropping his hand and nodding at his friend. Hesitantly, András's palm pressed against my scars. I was surprised Dante hadn't demanded to do it himself, but he'd never been the overbearing type. Possessive perhaps, but never stifling. At least ... not with his friends.

I closed my eyes and breathed deeply. I didn't know where to start or what to do, but I pictured Death in my mind and pulled at the otherworldly magic slithering on my back like one would a tether. When I had the image vividly in my head, I said his name, just once.

"Death."

For a moment nothing happened, nothing but the sounds of Dante and András's breaths and the frantic beating of my heart breaking the silence. Just as I'd thought it hadn't worked, I

felt a chill lift my hair, ruffling the thin fabric of my shirt, and a collective intake of air from the males beside me.

When I opened my eyes, it was to shadow and smoke and the familiar hooded guise of Death and his faceless mask. Once fully formed, I found him leaning against a tree, picking at his bony fingers as if there was dirt beneath his nails—not that he had any.

"Summoned with the chime of a bell like a common house cat," he remarked, turning his head towards me and pushing off the tree. "You're lucky I'm feeling curious. What does the fated one wish of me now?"

I quirked a brow. "Fated one? A little on the nose for you, isn't it?"

The shadows curling around his feet crept up my arms, caressing my neck. "Blood witch, seeker of justice, breaker of bones, does it matter what name you bear? Your fate remains the same, as does those of the warriors you walk with."

"And what do you know of our fate, Horseman?" Dante remarked.

Death's faceless gaze swivelled to him. "The forgotten son, come to restore a legacy. Tell me, how was your mother when last you saw her?"

Dante bristled. "Very much alive, unfortunately."

Death laughed, the sound chilling me to my bones. "For now. Her thread is entwined with yours, but that may change. The cards are never set, and even my darling wife cannot prevent that."

"So you tied the knot," I said with no small amount of amusement. "Congratulations, I guess?"

His gaze made my skin tingle like little bugs biting me all over. "Her murderous tendencies are little more than a distraction, especially when it comes to the Middle Realm. She's where she belongs. By my side, as my queen."

"And she's not pissed at you for whisking her away from her games here?" I crossed my arms. "I find that hard to believe. She wanted her prize and I am willing to bet she'd do anything to get it."

"You're young and mortal," Death said, his voice melodic and old as the ages. "I could try to explain the depths of our relationship, but I'm afraid you haven't the time nor the capacity."

I shrugged. He was probably right. They had millennia—eternity—after all. One little love spat was probably just a bump in the road for them. Even if she was scary as all hell and had never learned to share. "As long as you keep her in check, you can play happy families as much as you like. We have enough to deal with earthside. Which brings me to why you're here."

"You want to know about the demons," he stated. Death circled the three of us unnervingly, András looking like he wanted to be anywhere in the world but here.

"I don't hear you denying their presence in the Middle Realm. So it's true then, a door has been opened to the Under World?"

"In a sense. The spell your prior High Witch used to create a temporary portal allowed the guta demon into the Middle Realm.

164

However, she never severed the spell."

"Meaning the portal remains open and demons can come and go as they please," I said, scowling. Caitlin fucking Vargo. Even when dead she was a pain in my ass.

Death waved his hands. "Unfortunately for you, dark magic always comes with a price. Your elder never paid, upsetting the balance of this world and the next."

"She paid with her life," András said, cocking his head. "I'd call that the ultimate price."

Death turned, laying his bone fingers on András's shoulders. To my friend's credit, he didn't cringe, but his lips pursed with distaste. "Dead by witches' hands. No blood was spilled when she conjured the demon, and no payment was made before she died. Payment owed to *me*."

Of course it was. Istenanya's tits, things kept getting worse. I cocked a hip, resting a hand on it in annoyance. "Let me guess. You won't close the door until you receive said payment?"

Death chuckled. "You assume much. Even if I wanted to, I cannot close the portal. This is a mortal affair and demi-gods cannot intervene. I'd have thought you of all people would know that well enough by now, Kitarni."

"You can't be serious," I scoffed, gaping at him. "You're the king of the Under World, are you not? Can't you command the demons to stay put?"

He floated towards me, his robes billowing out, the stench of decay climbing my nose until I felt so sick my eyes were watering.

"And what makes you think I want to?"

I bristled as the coldness of his breath scraped along my cheekbones, but my insides heated with anger. What use was having power of his proportions if he refused to use it? Dante watched us carefully as Death got a little too close for comfort, his hands blatantly moving to the hilts of his swords, not that they would be of any use against the harbinger himself.

András's sidelong look begged me to keep calm, to not react to Death's baiting.

He should have known better.

"Your precious wife planned to overthrow you, conquer the Middle World, and claim ownership to all kingdoms. She may not have succeeded, but her interference and agreement with Sylvie created a ripple that affects us all. You owe *me*."

Faster than I could blink, Death grabbed my throat, his bone fingers wrapping tightly around my neck before he lifted me off the ground like I weighed nothing. My legs flailed as I hung like a limp doll, at the mercy of the supernatural being before me.

"Unhand her," Dante snarled, his blades out in an instant as he charged. András joined him, his own sword angled, grim determination on his face, because they both knew their attacks would be futile. But they did it because we were family, and goddess bless their soft and squishy hearts for trying.

Death didn't even bother looking at them as he stretched one finger out, flinging them away so hard they each careened into a tree trunk and were bound by smoky tendrils of black.

 166

I wanted to scream, to cry out in anguish, but I could only choke as my vision shuttered, my pulse fluttering feebly in my neck.

"Let me make one thing clear," Death hissed quietly. "I owe you *nothing*. I am death. I am despair. Mortals don't know the meaning of fear until they step into my world. Once, witches revelled in my power, and humans likened me to a devil. What I am is so much worse."

"Maybe so," I rasped as his fingers eased ever so slightly. "But with all that power, you cannot touch me. Not yet."

Those curled fingers of his released me, and I thudded to the ground unceremoniously. I gulped in precious air, looking to Dante where he thrashed against his binds, a murderous gleam in his eyes, the muscles in his neck corded as he strained. I nodded my head just once, to let him know I was ok. He didn't look any less menacing, but it was worth a try.

Death leaned back, smoothing his robes and conjuring a throne made of smoke and shadows to sit upon as he regarded me. His voice was tinged with mirth as he spoke, and I imagined him to be smiling.

"In all my years, I've never met a witch so bold as to bite back. None except Sylvie, at least. You manage to surprise me, little one. I enjoy your tenacity and our little visits. I wonder if I'll enjoy torturing you even more when your time here is up."

I blinked at him. "Lucky me for having such a gentleman caller. Is that how you treat all your friends?"

167

Death chuckled, the sound grating down my bones. "Be grateful it wasn't worse. Now, ask of me what you seek. I have been away from my land for too long."

I shook my head, not even bothering to go there. Time hardly mattered when you're eternal, so why the rush? The fact he was impatient at all suggested all wasn't sunshine and roses downstairs—or whatever passed for the Under World. I really had no idea what to expect of it. But if he was eager to return, perhaps his reign was still in danger after all. From Fate? Or from the demons? I tucked that little kernel of information away, focusing on my current task.

"I wish to make a bargain with you."

He cocked his head. "You are yet to fulfil the last promise you made. Don't think I have forgotten about the crown, girl. I am waiting, and my patience grows thin."

I smiled sweetly. "You will have the crown. Retrieving it, however, will be easier if you assist me with our little demon problem. Surely it's in your best interests to have them locked back in your own realm? Not to mention a certain wife of yours who, not so long ago, was aching for the power of the crown. If you're not careful, other precious creatures might find their way out that door. Creatures who, this very minute, might already be planning their escape."

Death was preternaturally still as he looked at me—through me, it felt like. When the tension had stretched so taut I feared he might snap, he purred, "A blood spell will close the door. One

already in your possession. You need only consult the tomes kept in the care of the all-seeing one."

My fingers itched with the urge to burn his robe to cinders. Why must every answer always be in riddles with these damnable demi-gods? I sighed, pawing at my eyes as I considered his words. There was really only one woman who fit that description. A woman with a penchant for bloodmorphia and a sass that made mine look like child's play.

"Margit." I smiled coolly. "So once the door is closed, will that send any demons on this plane back to hell?"

Death steepled his fingers. "Their connection will sever, and they will return to the Under World."

Good. That was one problem solved. There was no way we'd be able to defeat demons on top of Sylvie's army. It was a long shot, but I quirked my brow, pacing the clearing. "Any chance you have any knowledge rattling in that skull of yours that will help us win this war?"

Death laughed, cold and merciless. It was answer enough.

"Mortal affairs," I said irritably, blowing out a long breath. "Right, got it."

He rose, floating towards me eerily and stroking a knuckle to my cheek, then running his hand down my bruised neck, seeming to delight in whatever he saw there. Or maybe he was savouring the memory of hurting me. Who knew with him? He was hot and cold, helpful and then decidedly not.

"Always a pleasure, my dear," he rasped.

"I wish I could say the same," I muttered, but I raised my chin. "Thank you for your ... assistance."

"Use this knowledge wisely. But remember, Kitarni: all magic has a price, and the cost of that spell is a high one. Be sure you're willing to pay it."

He dissipated into nothingness, transporting back wherever the hell he came from. Dante and András were freed once he'd left and the former rushed towards me, taking me in his arms. I nestled my face into his chest, unable to shake the oily, slick feeling of dread in my stomach.

SIXTEEN
DANTE

Portals to the Under World, cultists razing villages, humans going on witch hunts ... it was shaping up to be an eventful summer. I swiped my hands through my hair, tying half of it in a knot as we approached the castle gates. The day was sweltering, my shirt sticking to my back and my leathers slick against my thighs.

The scent of lavender was thick in the air and the fields either side of the long dirt path leading to the city hummed with bees as they spread their pollen. The fields had always brought me joy, reminding me of simple times. Reminding me of Yana. A mother turned monster. I had no issue raising my sword against her now.

I rolled my neck, watching Laszlo as he bounded along, tongue lolling out, those honey brown eyes ever watchful as he surveyed the landscape. The loyal mutt had grown on me over the last few months, showering me in kisses whenever I saw him. He hadn't left Kitarni's side, sleeping in her chambers, guarding her whenever she roamed the castle or beyond.

I wondered if she'd remain in her quarters, or if she'd return to mine. The bed had never felt emptier over the last months, the room never hollower. She rode beside me, quieter than usual, contemplative. After Death—the fucking prick—dropped his ominous warning last night, she'd been lost to her thoughts.

Her hair was tied into a messy bun by a leather thong and I could see the beads of sweat dripping down the column of her neck, disappearing beneath the light white shirt she was wearing. I wanted to lick that neck later, then continue licking down that collar bone, her breasts, the most sensitive part of her.

When we got inside, the first thing I wanted to do was make her scream as I buried myself inside her.

But before I could do that, my father would be waiting and he'd grown impatient with us both. Our impending nuptials had been delayed, swept aside under the excuse that war was afoot. He knew better, of course, but my good standing and his respect for Kitarni only strayed so far. Duty above all things—that was his expectation.

It was just as well that Kitarni was on the same page, needing this marriage more than ever to secure goodwill and position with the other covens. As Lady of Mistvellen and co-ruler of this keep, they wouldn't refuse her. How could they? Human villages bowed to men and men alone, but we weren't human, and we certainly weren't foolish enough to think so little of our women.

The lord and lady ruled equally in Mistvellen. A táltos and

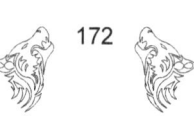

witch side-by-side, powerful, unbreakable. So long as Kitarni and I were together, we would stop at nothing to keep our people safe. Once we killed Sylvie, we would bring in the dawn of a new era. One where covens and clans could co-exist, families could remain together, and all kinds of magical beings could live in peace without the fear of cultists or humans.

The realisation of that goal would all depend on our next moves.

A horn blared and the portcullis opened at last, soldiers streaming out to assist the witches and lead them to their new homes. Boys ran out behind the soldiers, their eyes wide and toothy grins even wider as they spotted mothers and sisters. The latter shouted with joy, many dropping their things and charging towards their kin.

"Have you ever seen a more beautiful sight?" Kitarni asked softly, her eyes shining as she watched them all.

I laid my hand on her thigh, enraptured with the smile transforming her face into one of hope. Utterly devasting in its beauty. "This is what change looks like. These families never should have been separated in the first place."

"And they never will be again," she replied fiercely.

We dismounted, passing our horses' reins to the stableboys and heading for the castle. "Come, Father will want to be debriefed and see to it that our guests are settled in."

She slipped her hand into mine. "Not guests. Citizens. This is home now. All our homes."

I squeezed her hand, grinning as we walked up the streets. Home. I liked that word coming from her lips.

My father strolled down the streets, the scar puckering on his cheek as he grinned, those brown eyes alight. Lukasz found me, bumping my shoulder as we approached the lord of Mistvellen.

"My sons," Farkas's voice boomed, his hands reaching around and clapping us both on the back. He wasn't a very sentimental man, so this public display of affection was a little surprising. To Kitarni, his gruff face softened further as he placed a hand against her cheek. "My daughter. It does me well to see you."

Kitarni's cheeks flushed and I smirked to see her blush—a rare sight on her pretty face. She hugged him fiercely, not caring about the watchful eyes and he melted in her embrace. "It's good to see you, Farkas," she said quietly.

When they broke apart, the lord of the keep watched the procession of witches filing in, his expression turning grave. "What happened?"

Lukasz ran a hand through his short hair. "There is much to discuss. Sylvie attacked the village"—he raised a hand to stall Father's impending outburst—"*after* Kitarni ensured everyone was out. All witches and táltosok are accounted for."

The lord's scowl deepened, turning his scar a violent shade of red. "And Caitlin?"

"Dead," I remarked, my lips curling at the reminder of that woman. "Burned at the stake for colluding with the enemy and drawing blood from her own."

Father spat on the ground, then stroked the stubble on his chin. "That woman deserved her punishment and worse." His eyes shifted to Kitarni. "I take it the coven is under new advisement?"

I smiled victoriously, wrapping an arm around my betrothed's shoulders. "You're looking at the new High Witch."

His keen eyes raked over Kitarni and he nodded with approval. "Good. We're in this for the long haul now. Sylvie will come for us again. That attack was only the beginning."

"Witch's tits that man can talk an ear off," András huffed, sliding his back against the wall.

I grunted my agreement.

We'd been at it for the better half of the day, discussing war tactics and the next steps in protecting our city against Sylvie and her cult. Naturally, Father was furious about the coven abandoning the village—it was an extra point of defence and a place we could keep an eye on the humans' movement—but wasn't too proud to admit Kitarni's decision had been the right course.

Every witch, from the longest living elder to the youngest babes, were all alive ... for now. I grimaced, not liking where those dark thoughts could lead. I owed it to the coven, to all the fallen witches, to see that it remained that way.

"I noticed you haven't told him about our encounter with Death," András added disapprovingly. Such a mother hen. "He's

going to find out eventually."

I shrugged. "There's no use in worrying the man until we find out more. Which is precisely what we're going to do."

András straightened, spotting his 'friend' at the end of the hall. "What you're going to do. I have more important things to do."

"Like getting your cock wet?" Kitarni asked with a wicked grin, her eyes sliding to mine hungrily.

My hand was on her instantly, curling over her back with featherlight touches, lingering near her ass in sweet promise.

"Oh, you're one to speak, defiling the temples of our gods," András scoffed. "At least my trysts are behind closed doors in appropriate spaces."

"People go to temples to bend the knee in prayer. You can hardly blame me for worshipping something else while on my knees," she bit back playfully.

"Lords have mercy," I muttered. They were insufferable, but I was all for it. We needed some normality in our lives right now and their senseless bickering was just fine with me. Besides, I had plans of my own—and I was growing impatient to see them through.

Apparently, I wasn't the only one, because as soon as András had clapped me on the back, swept his blond, already perfect locks into place and strode purposefully towards his lover, Kitarni was pulling on my arm and dragging me into a dark space.

A storage cupboard, by the looks, filled with rusted armour

and forgotten things. I didn't have time to investigate as her mouth pressed against mine, bruising, demanding. She bit my lip and pulled back, grinning wickedly, an excited glint in her hazel eyes.

Fuck. Yes.

SEVENTEEN

KITARNI

'd been waiting all day to be alone with Dante. War tactics had to be one of the most tiresome subjects I could think of. If the witches weren't part of that equation, I might have considered leaving Dante to fend for himself, not that he minded. As general, war was his forte and his dark little heart seemed to thrive off the mere thought of violence. I loved it.

I loved sneaking into little hideaways with him even more.

I cupped Dante's cock, massaging him through his leathers, my hand instantly finding his length hardening as I worked him.

"Do you want me, Dante?" I whispered huskily. "Do you want to feel how wet I am for you?"

"Freckles, I want you to come so hard you see stars. I want you to bounce on my cock and call my name as you shatter."

I couldn't stop the small whimper that escaped me as his hand slipped down my pants, his thumb circling over the most sensitive spot. Gods, it felt so good. I was instantly wet as I rode his hand, grinding against it as he pushed one finger, two, between my folds. It wasn't enough though. I needed more.

I would always need more.

He untied the lacing of my pants and shoved them down my legs, cupping my ass in his hands. I lifted myself up, pressing against his hardened cock, teasing him as I grinded against the head of it, allowing the tip to slip inside ever so slightly.

His chest rumbled with pleasure, making me even wetter for him as I squeezed my legs together, enhancing the friction.

"Dante," I groaned.

"Shh," he crooned, pushing me gently against the wall, causing all sorts of things to clutter loudly on the floor. I couldn't help giggling and the sound just seemed to make him harder, more eager to fill me up.

Dante pumped his fingers inside me, rubbing his thumb in circles until I was panting, my chest heaving as I moaned louder and louder.

"Be quiet, or I'll have to punish you, Freckles."

I breathed in sharply, loving the way he dominated me. When he withdrew his fingers, he stuffed them in my mouth and I didn't hesitate to suck them, unreasonably turned on by something so dirty.

His eyes were hooded as he slid one calloused hand up my shirt, squeezing my nipple hard in punishment. "Say my name, Freckles. Scream it to me."

I writhed beneath his touch, hot and heavy as I came,

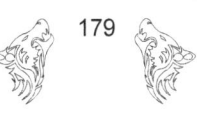

screaming out his name around his fingers as pure pleasure ripped through my being. This man was going to be the death of me. I was his good girl, and I was his to use as he wanted. Dante's cock twitched as he smiled at me darkly, removing his fingers from my mouth and claiming my lips for his own.

His kiss was bruising and I sank into it, ready to climb him and let something else sink inside me, but he wasn't done serving me just yet. He turned me around roughly, pressing my cheek against the wall. I gasped at the coolness against my skin, sticking my ass out as he rubbed a hand down my spine.

The feather-soft strokes made me shiver and he hummed in approval at the arching of my back. I knew he could see the evidence of my arousal, the slick juices glistening down my thighs. I rubbed them together slowly, tantalising him to come closer. When he licked up both upper legs, then up my centre, I shivered again, sighing softly as every nerve fired in answer. I wanted more—wanted his clever mouth on me. Shoving myself into his face, I moaned as he feasted, giving me what I wanted as he licked and sucked. I dropped a finger to my clit, circling it and biting my lip as his soft chuckle vibrated against me.

I was learning everything my body had to offer. Every twisted delight and beautiful pleasure that a few of Dante's fingers in the right places could do. I wanted him to show me more. I wanted to explore it *all*.

As if reading my thoughts, Dante shifted behind me and lapped over the most sensitive hole of my body. I jerked in

surprise, but as he stroked his thumb between my ass cheeks, my moans turned desperate. I had to bite my lip to stop the whole castle from hearing me—something that only turned me on more. There was no part of me Dante hadn't claimed. No place I would not tread with him.

"You're so wet for me, beautiful girl," he said in a low voice. "I want you to come. I want you to come all over my face."

Fuck, I was more than happy to oblige. He lapped between my ass and my clit, driving me so crazy with want I dragged my nails down the wall, my legs shaking as I felt myself getting close. "I'm close, Dante. I'm so fucking close."

"Be silent, Freckles," he whispered in my ear. "Or I won't let you finish." I bit my lip and it took all my willpower not to scream down the castle as I sucked on the finger he shoved into my mouth. I exploded, tightening as my thighs grew even more slick. He growled in approval and I knew he wouldn't have cared if I did scream. I was his. Only ever his.

But I still wanted more. To feel his cock in my mouth, to see his face as I gave him pure bliss.

My legs shook as I turned on unsteady feet, kissing him slowly. When I pulled away, I smiled softly, dropping to my knees and taking him in one hand, sliding my fingers over his cock and licking the liquid beading at the head.

When I wrapped my lips around him, he groaned, sagging as I took him as deep into my mouth as I could take him. Gods, he was so handsome. His eyes shuttered as he tipped his head back, those dark lashes whispering against his cheeks. Dante's mouth parted, that sharp jaw tilting as he opened his eyes again and looked at me. They were dark as sin, that golden ring flashing in the way that promised danger. He looked at me like nothing else in the world mattered, like he would kill anyone who would try to hurt me. And he would. Brutally and without mercy.

Just the way I liked it.

All I could do was stare as I sucked on him, captivated by this man and every ounce of pleasure I could call forth. I owned him, just like he owned me.

I was always only his to claim.

No one had ever given me pleasure like Dante and I couldn't help but smile around him as he fucked my mouth, reaching out to fist my hair and thrusting into me. He didn't look away from me once and it was so intimate, the tension between us so sparked, I knew he must be close.

I scraped my teeth against his cock ever so slightly, relaxing my throat and allowing him to slide impossibly deeper as I took him.

"Gods, Kitarni." His pace quickened and I expected him to come. Only, he lifted my chin, the slight gesture enough to have me back off and lick my lips.

I pulled him gently to the ground and climbed him, lowering myself onto his cock and riding, slow at first, a sensual sway to my hips as I grinded. I moaned at the perfect angle, the sound causing Dante to groan, his hands finding my breasts and teasing

my nipples.

My long, curly hair slid back over my shoulder as I arched my spine, stretching my body out, enjoying taking charge. I should have known Dante wouldn't allow that for long. He grabbed my hips and slammed me onto his cock, a breath gasping from my lungs as he squeezed my ass and moved me quicker.

I moaned at the faster pace and the punishing thrusts of his cock. "You're so fucking big," I said with a gasp.

He smiled darkly, meeting my eyes. "You can take it."

His chest rumbled as I cried out, reaching the edge, and a few more pumps of his dick sliding inside me had him following, diving off that cliff and spilling inside me.

When I stopped quivering and Dante's pace slowed to a stop, I rested my chest against his. He wrapped his arms around me, his cock still resting inside, fully connected.

"Is this what I can expect life as your wife to be like?" I asked playfully, twisting my neck to look at him. "Having sex in storage rooms or defiling temples?"

Dante flicked my nose, smiling. "Life with me will be whatever you wish it to be. I will give you everything you want. And I will destroy anyone in the way of you getting it."

The sincerity of his statement shuddered through my being. I looked at him intently, peering deep into those dark brown eyes. "Even if that makes you a killer? Doing things that only our enemies would?"

His hand cupped my jaw, his thumb trailing along my chin.

"There is nothing I would not do for you, Kitarni. I was born a killer, it's what I'm good at. If the price of that gift means protecting the one I love, I will gladly pay it. I'll enjoy it. For you, I would be questioner, judge, and executioner. And I won't regret any of it."

I blinked, shifting slowly as what he'd just said sank in. The enormity of that one word and how utterly fucking amazing it felt to hear him say that. I studied his face, my heart thumping beneath my ribs.

"Dante, I ..." I licked my lips, shaking my head. Some part of me found it hard to believe those words—and harder still to come to terms with what it meant after everything we'd been through.

A deep laugh rumbled through him as he watched me, those lips I loved so much curving into a crooked smile. "I've felt it for a long time now, maybe even since the first day I saw you in those woods. Your hair was wild, your eyes like pure murder as you threw a fucking dagger at my head."

"You ..." I swallowed once and the only stupid words I could manager were, "You really love me?"

"Oh, Freckles, do you really not know?" He tucked one of my stubborn curls behind my ear, shaking his head even as he smiled—the double dimple, which he seemed to save only for me. "My sword was yours the moment you asked for it. My life was yours the moment I swore to protect you. My heart? That you claimed for your own, tooth and nail and bloody beautiful murder. It was always yours. It will always be yours, from this day

to my last."

PART TWO

THE CURSE OF

FORESIGHT

EIGHTEEN

KITARNI

"You're late," Margit said sternly, a sly smile breaking her composure as she watched András, Dante and I descend into her creepy basement.

I grinned, charging like a bull as I engulfed her in my arms. She chuckled, hugging me with a lot more grace befitting her station. When I'd decided I'd squeezed her enough, I pulled back, looking at her carefully.

Her smile was true, but even beneath the classical beauty she always held, I saw the markings of sleepless nights and stress. She was thinner than I'd last seen her. Dark shadows underlined her eyes, stark against the moon-pale tone of her skin.

"Don't hold back on my account," she said drily, noting my studious gaze as she strode forward to hug both András and Dante at once. Even András—who was muscly, but not nearly as bulky and tall as Dante—dwarfed her as they greeted her warmly. "I'm the picture of good health, am I not?"

"You're beyond beautiful," I remarked. That would always remain true. "Not that you care for such things."

"You're right," she admitted, swiping a wine goblet from the table and draining it to the dregs, then patting down her gown until she found a small vial. "But my inner ego does so like to be stroked. Among other things." She huffed. "Barely back in the castle and both of you have already had more rolls in the hay than I've had in weeks."

"Always so dramatic," András said, looking around the room with disdain. "Maybe if you left this dungeon more often, you'd remember what it's like to be among the living?"

She unscrewed the vial, tipping it back like a seasoned patron who'd seen one too many taverns. Her eyes flashed a brighter blue momentarily as the liquid trickled down her throat. I'd never not find it disgusting, but if it made her visions easier to bear, I would always be fine with it. That was so long as it wasn't killing her slowly, which was something I'd been meaning to research, given I knew nothing about bloodmorphia except that the cultists thrived off it.

"András, darling, the living remind me how perfectly happy I am in my own company, with a good book and a stiff drink."

She had a good point.

"Are you okay, cousin?" Dante asked as he took a seat at her table, the rest of us following suit. "Have the visions been troubling you?"

She levelled him with a look, unimpressed as always. "Lately,

it's been just the one. Repeatedly, in waking hours or when sleeping, not that I'm getting much these days. This vision is a stubborn bastard, it won't piss off, even after trying draughts."

No wonder she looked so weary. I rubbed a hand over her back, trying to be comforting. The silence stretched in the room as we waited.

Dante cleared his throat.

András rolled his eyes. "Are you really going to make us ask?"

"Obviously." She smiled devilishly, but her shoulders sagged, and the smile crumbled like dirt slipping through one's fingers. "It's the same sequence every time, only, the person it affects varies. In one dream I will be looking through Kitarni's eyes, the next will be Dante's, myself, or you, András. There's a dance—a masquerade ball to mark Kitarni's coronation as High Witch. The covens will be there, as well as neighbouring táltosok clans. Everything is going so well, we're all so happy ..."

Her sentence trailed off as she swallowed, her hands fidgeting in her lap.

"Until?" I urged, squeezing her shoulder.

Her piercing blue eyes pinned me beneath their weight. "Until one of us is murdered."

Silence blanketed the chamber, thick and stuffy in the windowless room. Hadur's balls. Once again, it seemed like the gods were ready to fuck us over. I closed my eyes and tipped my head back, which only worsened the churning in my stomach. I knew Margit's visions were reliable, but I couldn't accept this. No

fucking way was I going to let any of them die. Not before we'd even taken our shot against Sylvie.

"Who?" I breathed. "Who does it?"

"That's just the thing." Margit sighed, drumming her nails on the table. "Kind of hard to guess the killer when everyone is wearing a mask."

"What kind were they wearing?" Dante asked slowly. "We might not guess the killer but if we know what we're looking for—"

"We can devise a plan," I finished.

"Surely we can dispense with the ball altogether?" András said, his green eyes narrowed in thought. "No ball, no stage for a murder."

I glanced at Dante, whose grimace mirrored my own. We both knew that wasn't possible. If the covens and clans were coming together, it was certainly for more than a High Witch's election. Namely, a wedding day and an excuse for all covens and clans to be present.

The ball was just a courtesy—a grand affair for the people, when really it was to tighten our alliances and secure aid for the battle that was inevitably coming. The covens had demanded a display of leadership. Marriage was the first step and the coronation, I was guessing, was the final piece to play to see us through.

"Why make it a masquerade ball then?" Dante asked. "If there are no masks, the killer cannot hide."

"Hidden by masks or shadow or in plain sight, what's the

192

difference?" Margit shook her head. "The odds remain the same, no matter how the game is changed. I have *seen* it happen, mask or not. In my dreams, the killer remains faceless. We will not discover the culprit until it's too late."

Dante growled, slamming his hand on the table. "Nothing can be done then. We're to roll over and play into Sylvie's hands?"

"There will be no avoiding it," Margit said. "Lord Sándor's mind is made up. A wedding shall be held, and the ball shall be the crown jewel of this affair. Mistvellen needs its lord, and Lord Sándor needs an heir. And the people"—her eyes flicked to me—"need a symbol of hope. A woman whose power alone may yet rival that of the Dark Queen."

I scoffed. "My magic might be strong, but I'm not stupid, Margit. Without the crown, there will be no stopping her."

She quirked a perfect brow. "A good thing then, that you came to discuss that very object."

"I came here to see you too," I protested, scowling.

"Yes, yes, everyone missed each other and we're all one big happy family," András snapped, holding out his hands as he stood. "Can we get back to the dying part? I won't deny our desperate need for allies, but are we going to ignore the fact that one of us is will soon be seeing a very excitable horseman who will delight in torturing us for all eternity?"

Dante's lips tipped up and, despite our predicament, I couldn't help but laugh at András. His frown was entirely too comical in that overly dramatic flair he always had. He sat back

down and folded his arms, muttering something about uncivilised company and death wishes.

"What mask was the murderer wearing in your vision Margit?"

"It was a sheep's face of all things." She fluffed out her hair. "Neither graceful nor regal."

I scowled. A threat. And Sylvie's not-so-subtle way of mocking my upbringing as the shepherd of my village. Baba Yaga had said to me once, right before she drove her blade into my chest and sucked the blood from my flesh, "A *wolf cares not for the sheep; we devour it.*"

Now that I thought about it, her choice of words was interesting. Wolves were a symbol of the táltosok and, before them, the loyal beasts who once guarded gods. Baba Yaga had given up her right to call herself a wolf the moment she joined the cultists. Whether she still held some love for her old home or family didn't really matter though. Her days were numbered, and I could count on one tall, dark and handsome táltos to ensure it. If he didn't, well, I'd have no problem finishing the job myself.

"If we know what mask they're wearing then we can ensure they can't get in," Dante said. "We'll double the guards, make sure the area is secure."

I smiled at him half-heartedly and Margit pursed her lips. We both knew it wouldn't be that simple, but it was something. At the very least, it seemed to calm András. I flexed my fingers, absentmindedly realising I'd been picking the skin raw around my nails while we spoke. An anxious habit I'd developed in the last

few months and one unseemly of a lady.

"There will be convoys of dignitaries, nobles, generals ... the list goes on. There's no way to ensure everyone attending has our best interests at heart. The best we can do is have the guards vet everyone attending and to keep our wits about us. Right now, I'm more interested in knowing whether this vision of yours is set in stone or if our fates might find a different path."

Everyone looked at Margit and she chewed her lip as she considered. "Honestly, I don't know. This vision is different than usual. Distorted, like looking into a rippling pond. I have never had a shared vision, which tells me our futures rely upon each other's actions. I'm sorry, I just ... I don't know."

"It's okay," I said softly, offering her a small smile. In the last five minutes, she appeared to have rapidly declined, barely clinging to consciousness as her eyes kept fluttering closed. "We have enough to go on. And once we speak to Lord Sándor and gather more information, we'll see things in a better light. We'll talk about the crown tomorrow. For now, you should get some rest. It's late and you need your strength."

She nodded, rising unsteadily, and I glanced at András with a single dip of my head. He was out of his seat and escorting her from the room in an instant. I was more grateful for his assistance now than I'd ever been. Margit was a key unit of our little family and she needed us. Goddess only knew the weight of the world was a heavy burden, not to mention holding the lives of loved ones in the palm of her hands.

I didn't envy her magic. We all had power, in our own ways, and we had all suffered much to get it. Each member of our little unit had lost loved ones. All of us carried pain and suffering, but I had to believe the bad things came with purpose. The magic I had might not be conventional, but the darkness in me could protect the ones I loved. Dante and András might not like using their necromancy, but it made them strong soldiers. Margit certainly didn't revere her gift, but she never complained about it, just shouldered it and carried on. Because we all had one thing in common. We made do with what we had and we fought for each other.

A simple thing like love could change the course of all things. Simple ... and monumental. Something Sylvie and her cronies would never understand.

Dante's hand slipped into mine and I relished every callous and bump as his skin slid against my own. It didn't matter what was coming.

We'd face it together.

NINETEEN

DANTE

"You're to marry in two days."

My father's words were weighted, his mouth set so rigidly the lines around his mouth deepened and the scar slicing through his eye puckered. I might have underestimated his impatience regarding my marriage to Kitarni.

Well ... fuck. Not a long time to prepare for either the ceremony or the nightmares to follow.

"I can't help but wonder why you two have waited so long as it is," he continued gruffly, eyeing me from his seat across the table. "It's clear you have feelings for each other—a rare gift when it comes to arrangements such as this. You are well matched, both in power and wit."

"You don't need to convince me, Father," I replied, sweeping my hair back from my face. "She is more than I deserve. I know what this marriage means for our city—for the alliances in your pocket. But does now really seem the best time to gather hundreds of people together?"

The lord looked at me sharply, his brown eyes narrowing. "What better time than that of conflict? The people need security, something to take their minds off the scourge of cultists. War isn't cheap, my son. We need the generous donations of our friends' coffers. Soldiers need food, weapons and armour, and nobles need to feel seen and heard as they fluff their feathers. This union isn't for you and Kitarni, so much as it is for everyone else."

I knew that, I did, but she deserved so much better. I wanted to give her the world and I wanted to start my life with her in truth. Whole truth, not this spectacle for the public. If I had it my way, we'd marry in a quiet corner of the grounds, surrounded only by family and friends. It's what Kitarni would want too.

I rose, striding to the balcony overlooking the gardens below. My betrothed walked the gardens arm-in-arm with her sister, the two of them thick as thieves as they bent their heads together, their laughter floating up to this level. I was glad Kitarni had her family here; the missing piece of her soul now tucked back into place in her heart.

Her sister would do well in Mistvellen. She still had dreams, still had *hope*. My father was right. It's what our people needed now—what they deserved.

"Do you love her?" my father asked as he came to my side, observing the women.

My voice was deep, but sure, as I nodded. "I do."

He turned, placing a hand on my shoulder, looking me deep

in the eyes. "When the time comes, you must do what needs to be done. I wasn't ..." He swallowed, his voice thick. "I wasn't there when Yana needed me. I think there was always a new trade route to explore, land to gain or trades to oversee. I loved your mother, I truly did, but maybe I loved this city more. I was always too busy to give her what she needed—a husband, not a king. Some small part of me will always wonder if she might have found her way back to me if I'd given her enough reason to.

"I failed her, and look what she's become. A monster. The woman we knew is gone, and I can't blame that all on the cultists. Don't make the same mistakes I did, my son. Don't let them take Kitarni like they took your mother."

I swallowed hard, ignoring the sharp pinch of splinters in my throat. "They took her, but it was her choice to stay. You could spend a lifetime thinking of the paths you could have taken or the things you might have done differently, but in the end her actions were her own. Some monsters are born and some are made. Mother chose her path and she forsook us the moment she accepted that cult."

"Maybe," he said, his eyes glassy as he looked at the lavender fields beyond the walls. A tribute neither of us could ever bear to see destroyed, despite everything. "Love is a funny thing. It burrows inside you until it's etched into your bones. You can't forsake it, nor can you deny it. The things she's done, I will never forgive; the woman she was, I will never forget." He clapped me on the back. "I hope you never truly understand how that feels."

199

My hands curled into fists where I clutched the stone wall. I knew he missed her. There would always be an ache from the hole she had left, and it had hit him hard. When Adrian passed—Kitarni's father—and Lukasz's mother, Maria, followed soon after, my father had lost his most loyal friends and loves. He would always have Lukasz and me, but some losses couldn't be filled with familial bonds.

We stood in silence for a while, sinking into memories of better times. I watched Kitarni as she walked. She gesticulated wildly as she talked and our eyes met as she spun around, her wild mess of curls fluttering in the breeze. She smirked as she bowed mockingly before raising her middle finger.

My little hellcat was so sweet.

To my surprise, my father laughed, shaking his head as we looked on. "You're going to have your hands full with that one."

"I wouldn't have it any other way."

"Hold on to that, son. You'll need it." He clasped my arm and paused, looking me in the eye. "Two days. Three nights after the wedding, we will hold a masquerade ball in your honour. I've extended invitations to our allies so that we may secure our positions in the coming days. I'd rather look a man in the eye when weighing a man's intentions. It's easier to snuff out the rats without a quill and parchment to hide behind."

How I wished it was that simple, but I nodded along. "We need the clans. All of them. I assume you've arranged with Nora to request the covens' presence too?"

His mouth twisted. "They're aware. It's a game of fate. Now to see which threads we shall tie ... and which we shall cut."

He made to move past me, but I grabbed his arm, pulling him close. "There's something you should know about the ball."

I told him everything about Margit's vision and he listened intently, not uttering a word. When I pulled away, he looked at me for a long minute and smiled. "Son, if there's one thing you should know about being a lord, it's to be one step ahead of the game. Sylvie may think she can infiltrate our castle, and maybe she's right, but she's not the only one without plans."

My brows pulled together. "What are you saying?"

"I'm saying there is more than one way to skin a snake. She wishes to assassinate my own?" He set his jaw. "Nobody comes into my house and threatens my family. I have a spy planted in her cult. Once we make the announcement about the wedding and the ball, he will send us any information he has. We will get through this Dante. All of us."

I grinned, shaking my head. "Cunning bastard. Why didn't you tell me this sooner?"

"It's a recent development." He smiled back, the grisly scar carving his cheek and brow making him look a little vicious in the moonlight cutting through the cloudy night sky above. "As for the cunning? I like to think it runs in the family."

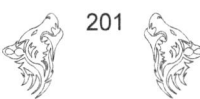

I found her in my chambers, naked, sprawled out on the bed, and wearing nothing but an extravagant necklace dripping with sapphires the size of small eggs. The gold they clung to glittered from where it plunged between her breasts.

Fucking hell. She smiled at me, a seductress if I ever saw one. "Well, aren't you a vision?" I purred, striding slowly into the room, taking my time to admire the view. "My own personal feast for me to savour. All we're missing is the trappings to pour over that delectable body."

Her grin widened. "I seem to recall you mentioning something about fucking me with jewels on. I did you one better."

She pulled a pottle out from behind her, and my dick hardened immediately as I saw what she had in mind. Honey. She took a wooden spoonful and let it drip over her chest, her kohl-lined eyes never leaving mine for a second. I watched as the sticky sweetness dripped painfully slowly over her nipples. Then she took that gods damned spoon and put it in her mouth, moaning as she tasted it.

Devious, naughty little hellcat. My cock stood to full attention and I grinned as her eyes finally darted to it. She licked her lips hungrily. "You want a taste, Freckles?"

She nodded, her eyes hooded as she scooted closer. When she bent her head to take me in her mouth, I gripped her by the throat, not hard enough to hurt, but to pull her up and move her back. She looked up at me with those innocent come-fuck-me eyes, waiting, playing.

I let my power come to the surface, the black misting around me, my eyes flashing as they always did when I was ready for a fight ... or a fuck. Her own magic met my own, tendrils of red caressing my body.

I pushed her back, claiming each breast in my mouth, lapping up the honey. She writhed in pleasure and I grinned against her soft skin, enjoying the feel of her peaked nipples against my tongue.

When I licked the last of the honey away, I kissed her hard, letting her taste the sweetness lingering on my lips. She sucked my lips greedily, twisting her tongue for every last morsel. Such a sweet tooth.

Without warning, I pulled back, grabbing her ankles tightly and lifting her up so I could meet her pussy with my tongue, sucking and nipping at that sweetness, then drowning myself in her sex. She tasted so fucking sweet. I groaned against her.

The vibration of my mouth made her moan even louder and I drove my tongue against her most sensitive nerves, circling harder and harder until she was shaking, about to break against me. "Fuck," she cried, scratching at my arms.

I loved how she liked to step over that line between pleasure and pain. She'd shown me how much she liked it hard and rough—how much she enjoyed learning what else her body could do. I wanted to push her as hard as she could go, see what limits she had. And the things I wanted to do to her weren't talked about—perhaps even known—by most gentlemen.

I wasn't a gentleman. Not when it came to the things I owned. And she was mine, body and soul. She could destroy me and I would love her still.

Her legs wrapped around me as she thrusted into my mouth, arching her back off the bed. "Greedy little witch. Are you hungry for my cock inside you?"

Her response was a garbled plea and I laughed, shoving her back and pushing her legs against her chest, thrusting inside her without mercy. She cried out, but I didn't allow her a moment to readjust, slamming deep, filling her up.

"Fuck," I groaned. "You feel so fucking tight like this." I captured her ankles again and pushed her legs back even further and she curled up, her inner walls tightening with the movement.

Sweat beaded over our skin and I palmed her breast as I rocked relentlessly, viciously, feeling my climax rising.

"Dante," she said breathlessly, "I'm going to ... I—"

Her words broke off in a moan as I slid my hand down and circled her clit. "Let go, dirty girl. I want those beautiful legs to shake."

She cried out, tightening around my cock as her body tremored, one hand going to her breast as she tilted her head back and rode the wave. I kept pumping, ready to join her as I drank in the sight of the woman arched before me.

I groaned as I spilled inside her, letting my head fall against her chest after I was spent. She cradled me against her, running her fingers through my hair, her nails massaging my scalp. My eyes

felt heavy and, for the first time in a while, I felt my body slump with a sense of ease.

Is this what life would be like with her? What peace felt like? I'd never experienced being held in a lover's arms—had never allowed anyone to hold me besides Kitarni, if I was being honest.

I'd never stayed long enough to feel a more tender touch, afraid of growing too close to those around me, afraid of learning to love and then losing that person. It had always been easier to be a lord or a commander than a lover or a friend.

Since meeting Kitarni, I wanted those deeper connections more than anything—wanted *her* more than anything. Father might have put his kingdom above all else, but after the things I'd done, I knew what was most important.

And the woman in my arms, she was it.

Sylvie threatened to take this peace—this future—away from me. Not a chance in hell. András was right. Kitarni and I had been matched for a reason. The only way to fight the Dark Queen was to combine our strengths.

With her magic and the crown's help, she was the key to ending this. We had her dark magic; it was getting the crown that would be the hard part.

I smiled. Good thing I always loved a challenge.

TWENTY

Kitarni

The dress was the most beautiful thing I'd ever seen. A combination of expert sewing and magic, courtesy of my dear sister and mother, in a fashion that was daring and wholly unique to the court. The sage bodice was tight, highlighting every curve from the dip at my breasts before it pooled out at the waist. Though sleeveless, a sheer cape covered most of my arms, the back spilling into a train behind me.

It was the detail that took my breath away. Eszter had magicked lavender and pale pink rosebuds across the gown in a starburst pattern and, I didn't know what it was, but something made the material shimmer with every swish of the dress.

My hair was pinned at the sides, spilling obediently down my waist in gentle curls—a nice change from the wild mess it usually was. They'd outdone themselves—from using my favourite colours to incorporating the sentiment of the lavender, to whatever magical spells had allowed them to create such a beautiful thing.

They'd had to have been working tirelessly to get it done in time and a pang of guilt fired through me.

It was perfection ... And it damn near made me cry.

"Oh darling," Mama said, her own cheeks wet as she perused me. "You are an image of the Goddess herself."

My cheeks reddened. "Mama," I said sheepishly. "Even you can't really mean that."

"Of course I do, I am your mother! It's my right to declare you the most beautiful woman in the world." She put an arm around Eszter's shoulder and smiled. "One of two, at least."

I grinned, embracing them both in a warm hug. We nestled into each other, just the three of us, taking a long moment to simply be together as a family. Something we might not have the luxury of doing for much longer.

When I pulled away, I looked long and hard at them, burning the image of their faces into my mind's eye. "I love you both. You give selflessly, never thinking of your own needs. The world doesn't deserve your goodness, but I must ask more of it now."

"Anything," Eszter said softly.

I took a deep breath. "There are things in motion that I cannot stop. The wheel of Fate keeps turning, and some of my actions will have consequences even I can't predict. I want you both to know that no matter what happens, I will keep you safe. Dante, Lord Sándor, they will both protect and house you. And"—I swallowed, lifting my chin—"I need to know that if I'm not ... around ... you will lead the witches. I don't trust Iren to

do so selflessly, so you will both need to step up as Acting High Witches. Erika will do whatever she can to help."

My sister's face fell. "Kit ..."

"Promise me, Eszter. Now, more than ever, I need people I can trust in my corner."

She nodded, her brown eyes—the mirror image of Mama's—emboldened and fierce. "You have my word."

Mama took my hands in her own, a sad smile on her face. "You need never ask. I will *always* look out for you."

I sighed, feeling a weight lift from my chest. It was unfair to ask this of them, knowing there would only be one reason for my absence. Both knew I'd only ever forsake them if Sylvie won the war or Death came to collect me.

The door banged open and András swept in, Margit by his side. András's eyes practically bulged out of his head and Margit looked on, scrutinising, then nodding in approval.

"By the goddess's blessed breasts, you're a vision."

Margit offered a rare, unrestrained grin. "What my dear, daft András means to say is you look beautiful, Kitarni."

Mama watched us all with a strange smile on her face, her eyes welling up again. She cleared her throat, ducking her head to hide her emotions. "I'll let you all have a moment. I'll see you at the altar, Kitarni." Quieter, so only I could hear, she said, "I love you my fire girl. And I'm so proud of you."

I sniffed, realising this was probably the first time in many years she'd seen me like this. At ease, smiling and laughing with

friends. With ... family. People who'd taken me in without a second thought, tucking me under their wings and teaching me to fly. Or perhaps it was the fact that she might not see us all like this again.

András took my hand and placed a chaste kiss to my knuckles, bowing extravagantly as he did. I snorted. He was the best dressed here, apart from me, of course. The man really did have a fondness for fine things. His blond hair was swept back neatly, his piercing green eyes standing out in a matching green tunic stitched with gold thread, his sword strapped to his waist and brown boots shining.

It was a little odd that we were all so clean for a change. If I was being honest, I kind of liked when he was dirty and covered in the blood of our enemies. A little much? Maybe, but who cared? Between him and Dante, I'd done more than a little eye fucking since I'd met them both.

Not that I'd ever tell Dante that. The possessive prick would punish me for it—a thought that sent a little wave of excitement through me. Maybe I *should* tell him. I shook my head slightly. Salivating over the man in front of my friends wasn't on my agenda for the day.

Marrying the wolf lord on the other hand ...

My stomach flipped from nerves, my skin buzzing with frantic energy. This was really happening. I was marrying the lord-in-waiting of Mistvellen. Afraid I'd crumple into a tight ball I couldn't roll out of, I focused on my friends instead, flexing my

fingers.

"A fucking masterpiece, I'd say," Margit was saying from behind me as she fussed with my dress. "This gown is truly something else. I'm rather jealous, in fact. You, Eszter, are welcome to be my seamstress anytime."

My sister blushed, bowing her head. "It would be an honour."

"Of course," Margit went on, "it's been something of a miracle for me to get her shining like she is today. The girl needed work. I'll tell you that much."

"How generous of you," I drawled, giving András the side-eye—the knowing look girls shared when gossiping or spilling secrets. I'd only ever had Eszter to do that with. It felt kind of nice to do so with another. And András was basically one of the girls. The man loved to prattle and preen over pálinka—alcohol distilled with fruits—as much as the next woman in court.

It helped that he'd bedded most of the men and women there. He was scandalous ... I loved it.

"I know that look," Margit added, moving in front of me and glaring at us both. "And I merely meant you haven't had much time to treat yourself lately, what with your little treks hunting cultists in the woods and the endless blood baths you find yourselves in. Not to mention your makeup sex after training with Dante. Yes, don't think I haven't noticed or heard."

A bubble of laughter escaped me. "My ... what?"

"Oh, don't get me started on the sex," András said, studying his own nails as if we were talking of the weather. "The pair fuck

like jack rabbits. This girl needs a gag."

"Or maybe their own dungeon," Eszter chimed in.

"Decked out with chains and handcuffs? Please, don't tempt her with a good time," András replied.

I burst out laughing. "You're all deranged. Perhaps you could find your own partners instead of investing yourselves in Dante's and my love life?"

Margit's nose scrunched up. "First of all, don't be crass. Dante is family. Secondly"—she pouted, sitting on the chair beside András—"the last time I was with a lover, I had a vision partway through and, well, let's just say he won't be warming my bed again."

I patted her knee sympathetically. Her visions were getting in the way of her sex life now. Some god had a serious vendetta against her. "Speaking of visions, have you seen anything more about the ball? If there's something different—even the smallest thing—it could help."

"Nothing has changed. All we can do is wait." She shook her head, her hands wringing in her lap. I noticed the skin around her nails was red and raw, just like my own. A hard habit to break. My heart sank as I looked at her. So beautiful and broken. Her porcelain skin was beginning to show the cracks of exhaustion and stress.

She started picking at her fingers as we sat in sombre silence, and I leaned forward, taking her hands in my own. "Margit, if you could rid yourself of your power, would you?"

When she looked up, her blue eyes burned, her sheet of long black hair shifting with the movement. "If you could rid yourself of the dark magic in you, knowing it might save someone's life or the lives of people you love, would you?" I sighed, hanging my head in defeat, because of course I wouldn't. Neither one of us would forsake our strange little family. She smiled sadly. "We don't get to choose our gifts, but we do get to decide how to use them. I show the path, the boys lead our armies, Eszter keeps everyone grounded and you, my dear, send that dark bitch back to hell."

I chuckled. "It doesn't sound so bad when you put it like that."

Her red-lined lips curved in a vicious grin. "Good. I think I'd rather like to see you do it. Drink in hand and a smile on my lips."

"Before we skip to the celebration, there's something we need to discuss."

She looked at me sceptically before eyeing off András and Eszter. "Why is she pulling that face? Why, on her wedding day, is she pulling that face?"

"Scheming expression," Eszter said, nodding. "Never a good sign."

I scowled. "I take offense to that. My plans always turn out well."

András grumbled something under his breath about demigods and cultists and folded his arms, one brow raised.

"Okay fine, some have been a little hairy, but we all still have

212

our heads, right?"

Margit just glared at me. "Out with it. Now."

"It's about those masks for the ball." I looked at Eszter. "I might have some ... changes."

I told them my plan. Margit's glare was enough to kill and András looked ready to cut my head off. My sister said nothing and her skin paled, but she nodded her acceptance. It took some convincing, but once the others settled, both seemed inclined to agree it had merit.

"I still think this is reckless and dangerous as hell," András muttered.

"Of course it is," Margit said and I was surprised to find a bit of a spark in her gaze once again. "And that's why it just might work."

"Then it's settled. Now we just wait and hope for the best," I said, pleased with my progress.

Margit pulled a vial of bloodmorphia from her dress. "I need a drink." She saluted us, tipping it back in one go before frowning. "A real fucking drink. Let's get you married ... I want to taste the good stuff."

András bounced up like an excited puppy, pressing a kiss to each of our cheeks before linking his arms in our own. "Finally, something we can all agree on."

"If I didn't know any better, I'd think you were nervous," Eszter whispered in my ear after the others had left and we had a little time between sisters. "The fierce protector, scared by a little ceremony and pomp."

I rolled my eyes, scoffing at her remark. "When it's your turn to marry Lukasz, I'll be sure to say the same thing."

She laughed, the sound melodious and soothing. Her presence alone was enough to calm the nerves dancing a jig in my stomach. Without her, I would have crumbled already or taken flight. I wasn't a runner—my days of curling in on myself were long done—but this wedding business made me want to bolt like a wayward mare.

Between Mama's fussing and the proud tears, followed by Margit's fingers pinching at me with her finishing touches this morning, it had been an ordeal.

Esther must have noticed my downward spiral, and she bumped my shoulder gently. "You don't have to do this if you don't want to. You can back out if you're not ready."

We both knew that wasn't really true. My coven depended on me, and I'd come to see the people of Mistvellen as my own, too. We needed this marriage for the stability of the city. For allies and for hope. Besides, I was never one to back down from a challenge.

I tilted my head. "It's not that I don't want to marry Dante. It's just ..."

"You wish it were under different circumstances," Eszter surmised, nodding in understanding.

"I think I love him," I blurted suddenly, pressing my fingers to my lips as if I could take it back. Because I hadn't really had the time to dissect that, not to mention him telling me he loved me. Those words from his lips meant *everything*, but I was still scared. There was still work to be done on our relationship—a lot of work that couldn't be solved by sex alone, not that I was complaining. But a girl can hardly think when she's getting fucked so hard her brains get scrambled.

Eszter's eyes widened. She looked at me so long I felt like an artwork being scrutinised for its line work. "Why do I get the feeling that scares you?"

"I ..." A lump I couldn't seem to swallow caught in my throat. My lips worked, but nothing came out. Did it scare me? Yes. I was fucking terrified of this feeling. So many secrets, so many lies—not just from Dante, but from Mama and Caitlin too. It had all been so messy, right from the very start, and gods damned was it daunting to offer all of myself to someone and risk being hurt again. It hurt too much.

Eszter held my shoulders with surprising strength. "Listen to me Kitarni. Everything you're feeling is valid. There is freedom and strength in being vulnerable. Your fears are like any other demon you might face, and I have every confidence you'll conquer them."

Tears welled in my eyes. "What if I can't? What if the very thing I'm afraid of happens?"

She shook her head. "If you think like that, you'll always live

in fear. If you know love, you'll never be alone. If you never try, you'll *always* be alone."

Kind of cryptic, but her words made an awful lot of sense. "I need to start loving myself more, I think," I said with a breathy laugh.

"A perfectly sensible first step. And maybe, just maybe, you can let the handsome lord love you too."

The golden strands in her brown hair gleamed in the sunlight streaming through the open arches in the room, and I tucked a curl back fondly. "Eszti, when you marry Lukasz, I'll have every authority to give you the best fucking wedding this city has ever seen."

She laughed. "One sister at a time, all right? Now get your big girl pants on and let's go before you ruin your makeup."

I blew out a breath as I laughed, shook my fears away, and opened the doors to my future.

 216

TWENTY-ONE

DANTE

When the doors opened, my heart skipped a beat. My warrior witch, my feisty hellcat, looking like one of those Christian angels as she walked down the aisle in a dress fit for a goddess. My goddess. She looked nervous, the pulse in her neck fluttering as she looked around at the crowded chamber, taking in the heavy stares of judgemental eyes.

I willed every inch of encouragement into my gaze and, when our eyes met, I smiled at her softly, throwing in a dimple for good measure. She took in a breath and the world melted away, nothing but the two of us in a sea of nobles, sailing to our own tempest.

Her eyes brightened and that's when I knew I had her. Her back straightened, her chin lifting high as she walked down the hall. Kitarni was always a vision, but today, with that gown, the determination in her eyes, she seemed unstoppable. She was already every inch the lady of Mistvellen and now she'd prove it to the world.

When she came to a stop next to me, I let my knuckles brush her own, the gesture feeling somehow more intimate with everyone watching, the touch eliciting a small gasp under her breath.

She looked me over approvingly, her gaze taking in the dove grey tunic beneath the black and silver doublet embroidered with wolves, my swords sheathed at my hips. She preferred me in black, I knew, but this was a wedding, after all.

Silence washed over the vast chamber and we knelt on velvet cushions before the officiant, our heads gilded in golden rays of sunlight beaming through the many slitted windows.

Out of the corner of my eye, I watched Kitarni. The tautness to her jaw and the sadness lining her eyes made my heart pang. For duty and kingdom, that's why we were here. I wanted to give her more than this. I wanted to gather every stone and star in the world and lay them at her feet, for she deserved nothing less than everything.

One day, after the war was over and the eyes of allies and enemies alike were fixed elsewhere, I would give her a reason to smile, not just on special occasions, but always.

It was only months ago that we'd first met, and yet every breath that escaped her lungs, every quirk of her lips and beat of her heart, I knew. I loved this woman more than anything and, regardless of our past, she belonged with me. *To me.* I knew it as surely as the beating organ in my own chest.

The officiant began and I bent my head, not really hearing the words until it was time to commit myself to the incredible

creature by my side.

"Do you take Kitarni Bárány as your wife and lady?" the officiant asked, and I stared at him, unblinking.

"I do."

"Do you swear to protect her, love her, and defend her under the eyes of the Mother God and all the gods above?"

Yes. A million times over, fucking yes. "I do."

The officiant nodded seriously before looking at Kitarni, and I kept my gaze straight even as my heart seemed to cease its beating as I waited.

The officiant repeated the same questions, and I felt her straighten beside me, her shoulder brushing mine ever so slightly. Her fine collarbones heaved, the delicate tendons in her neck straining as she swallowed, but her finger found my own, the barest touch.

"I do," she said. Then again, the second time, "I do."

I didn't move, but my shoulders seemed to sag at those two precious words. She was mine. Always, eternally, *mine*.

The crowd of onlookers cheered and the officiant left the dais, but it was all just background noise.

I saw only her, felt only her. Our lives were forever changed and, after that monumental shift, Kitarni remained kneeling, as if afraid of facing the gathered audience.

I lifted her chin with my finger, forcing her gaze to my own. My fingers trailed along her cheek and I pressed my thumb over those rose-tinted, full lips. I was keenly aware of the audience whispering and I ignored them easily. I only cared that she was mine.

We would celebrate with our loved ones, of course. Feast and drink and dance until our feet were sore, but really, I just wanted her to myself. Selfishly, like a dragon hoarding its treasure. And she was the most precious treasure of all.

I stretched out my hand and she slipped her palm in, letting me pull her to her feet. "Kiss me with those pretty lips, wife," I whispered in her ear. She frowned at the commanding tone, but her upper lip quirked as I pulled her against me, twisting my fingers through the hair at the nape of her neck.

"Only if you promise to make me moan from them later," she said huskily in my ear.

That's my girl. "Keep talking and you'll make me hard in front of all our friends."

She smirked, leaning in to seal our kiss, but just as our lips were about to meet the doors to the hall burst open, a soldier with wide eyes running through. "Fire! Fire in the fields. We're under attack!"

Fuck. And here I thought today couldn't be any more trying.

The hallways streamed with nobles and soldiers alike. Witches from neighbouring covens didn't hesitate to join the call to arms as the fire outside lapped hungrily at the lavender

kindling, writhing like snakes through the fields.

Water. We needed water to sate its thirst for destruction, which meant we were at the mercy of aid from the Blue Coven. Earth magic would be near useless against this threat—at least until it was staunched enough to cover with dirt—and Kitarni, for once, could do nothing with her own magic.

But it didn't mean we couldn't fight. Not bothering to change my regalia, I stormed through the winding hallways, bursting out into the courtyard where a stableboy had my horse saddled and ready. We didn't fuck around when the city was threatened.

András and Lukasz were on my tail, jumping onto their own steeds agilely and following my lead. To András I yelled, "Protect Kitarni at all costs." He nodded, not needing further direction as he barked at the stableboy to have Kitarni's horse, Arló, readied.

There was no use commanding her not to fight. She would not be told no, and I would never try again. I'd seen how well that had worked the first time.

Lukasz and I galloped down the streets, yelling at citizens to "Move" and "Make way" as the horses' hooves pounded on the cobblestone and we found ourselves charging through the gates and into the fray.

The hills surrounding us were ablaze, smoke smothering the air like a thick blanket, the heat scorching, making me sweat beneath the leather and armour. Witches waved their arms in rhythmic movements, graceful and flowing as a winding river as water poured from their palms and doused the flames.

Between them all, our enemies swarmed like rats, culling witches while they worked. Anger flared through me, hotter than the fire, swifter than the surging water. They dared attack us on today of all days, threatening my people. *My wife.*

I urged my horse onwards, killing cultists with sweep after sweep of my blade. My sword melted through bone like butter and I howled, the táltosok at my back echoing the cry. Behind the city gates and in the kennels, our great wolves joined in, their eerie, otherworldly song sending shivers down my back.

Soon I would unleash them upon this plague, but not tonight. Not until the true battle began. Body after body I cut down, swiftly ploughing through the field. "Lukasz," I yelled. "Close ranks. Herd them into—"

My horse screamed as a spear pierced its chest and we went down. I curled into a ball, trying not to stab myself with my blade as I sprawled onto the field, precariously close to the fire raging nearby.

"Dante," a shrill voice shrieked and my heart surged with panic as I realised Kitarni had joined the battle ... in her wedding gown. It was so very her I couldn't help but smile, then remembered someone could cut me down any minute. Focus, Dante.

A cultist sprinted towards me, their spear aimed at my heart as they rammed it down. I deflected just in time, plunging my sword into their throat with gritted teeth. The man's glazed eyes bulged, the stitches at his lips opening as he tried to scream, only managing garbles and chokes before he was dead moments later.

Blood spurted over my face as they fell and I shoved their body off me, swivelling on my knee to slash the stomach of another, then ducking my head and removing the legs of another man swiping at my neck.

Carnage and utter chaos. The seeds of Sylvie were indeed spreading, but I would give no mercy. I was slick with blood and I wore the cloak proudly.

My eyes snapped to our surroundings and I saw Kitarni battling with a group of cultists nearby. She was quick—what she lacked in sheer strength she more than made up for with fluid movements and flashes of fire as she scorched skin and hacked at anyone who got close to her. When the numbers kept coming, she let her beast come to the surface, snarling and snapping as that lethal red mist encircled her palms.

She closed her eyes and I sucked in a breath as, seconds later, her enemies were incinerated—there one moment and gone the next. She used that magic again and again, the cultists surging from the woods in droves eviscerated until they stopped coming altogether.

When she opened her eyes, I jolted, something altogether uncomfortable and unfamiliar surging through me. Not at the battle nor our enemies, but at the woman I loved.

Gone were the hazel eyes I could lose myself in. Instead, she looked at the world with eyes of depthless black. The hairs on my arms raised and something slithered down my spine, like an otherworldly presence was in proximity. In *her*.

Well, this was a new development.

I approached her cautiously, ignoring everything around me. "Kitarni?"

She turned, cocking her head, those black eyes gauging my worth. The beast inside her seemed to purr, then she wound her arms around my neck. "Dante," she said in a voice that was not her own. "I destroyed them. For us. For you."

"Yes, little hellcat," I said quietly. "They're gone. You can put your magic away now."

She smiled, showing all her teeth, and I had to suppress a shiver from that eerie look.

"I destroyed them," she repeated. "I'm going to destroy them all."

Then her eyes rolled back in her head and she wilted in my arms.

TWENTY-TWO

KITARNI

The bread crunched as Dante and I broke apart the huge wedding loaf decorated with branches, flowers, and fruits. We plastered smiles on our faces as the crowd cheered and clapped around us. It was hard to believe only a few hours ago we'd been under attack. The witches had stopped the fire's spread, but the lavender fields and most of the surrounding crops had been heavily damaged. We won't even speak of my gown.

After a hasty bath getting all manner of gore out of my hair and off my skin, Eszter had another gown brought in, because of course she was prepared. I now stood dressed in a navy ensemble with silver threads weaved through it that looked like starbursts and sheer, flowy sleeves. A belt with a snarling silver wolf cinched in my waist, reminding all that I would do anything to protect my pack.

If only I'd been able to save the ones we'd lost.

Another mark against Sylvie's name, and boy was she racking up the score. The forces she'd sent were too few to threaten the city walls, but the hit on our food sources was another thing entirely. Not to mention the timing. How petty of her to target us on our wedding day—a time of heralding in a new reign. I'd make damn sure she was punished for it.

Still, knowing she'd allowed caravans to enter our lands unhindered left an uncomfortable feeling in my gut, heavy and weighted like a stone I could not dislodge.

Why not attack the visiting nobles and pick off our allies? Why wait until we were all together?

I chewed on that fact, playing the gracious host as I smiled, laughed, and exchanged pleasantries with our guests. The large hall looked beautiful today, transformed into something bright and green as branches and flowers twined around arches and up walls. The greenery represented the renewal of nature and fertility, and I was glad for the distraction it had provided my coven. Many witches had been eager to help with their earth magic and I'd be lying if I didn't recognise the warm and fuzzy feeling that gave me. Oh, how things had changed now that I was High Witch. No longer the fire girl who didn't conform.

Apparently I was shifting into something much more dangerous. After the fight and the blood lust had died down, Dante had told me about my eyes shifting and the murderous little beast that seemed to take over. I remembered everything that had happened, but the eyes were certainly a new development.

It probably should have scared me, but instead I found myself delighting in the change. I felt fearsome and now my enemies would see it too. The beast was growing stronger, more eager, as if by embracing its power, it had more room to move and more teeth to show.

I gulped down my wine and looked around the chamber at my guests. Connecting with my coven was something I'd happily do, but socialising with high society? It felt like treading water. Most of the nobles present were little more than grovelling court mongers hoping for scraps to feed their status and power.

Apparently, some of the water witches felt the same, because a group left the hall all at once, giggling and talking in hushed voices. I watched them enviously, wishing I could join them for some fresh air. Unfortunately for me, I had prey to hunt, and not the kind my dark little predator could relish in.

My gaze travelled the room to land on Viktória, the High Witch of the water coven, travelled from Budapest. She was perhaps a few years older than me, with plain features and bound blonde hair. The way she held herself, the grace in which she moved and the cutting gaze of her grey eyes made me immediately mark her presence. And there was something familiar about her, but for the life of me I couldn't place what.

Beside her stood Aliz, High Witch of the fire coven in Transylvania. From what I'd heard, she was as fierce as her element. Her russet-brown skin glowed under the light of the sconces, seeming to consume the energy. Black hair hung in a long

braid down her back and I guessed her to be in her late forties, but she had aged beautifully. Many eyes followed her movements.

These two women were my marks for tonight. They would decide Mistvellen's fate, just as the lords Dante was courting would. Pretty words and promises in exchange for an army in return. If Sylvie had done one thing in our favour, though, it was unleashing her cultists on the witches. Nothing angered us more than the loss of our own. I would use that anger and exploit it.

Viktória met my gaze and crossed the floor, her sweeping gown making her appear as if she was floating. "Lady Sándor." She bowed low, her grey-blue eyes glittering, her smile sharp, but polite. "It is an honour to meet you. I've heard so much about the famed blood witch, descendant of the Dark Queen herself."

I couldn't help but notice the barbed undertone, but I smiled sweetly, forcing back my snort. As if I could help who I was born to. "The honour is mine. Our covens have been parted for too long, it was time our sisters joined in celebration once again."

"Celebration, yes," Viktória replied, "but we both know this invitation brings blood and battle. You need us for your war."

"My war?" I laughed perhaps a little unkindly, shaking my head. "Come with me, there's something I want to show you." I led her to the balcony overlooking the lavender fields and the Sötét Erdő beyond. "Corruption leaks from that forest like a festering wound left unchecked. Should Mistvellen fail, it will spread beyond our borders into Budapest, the entire Kingdom of Hungary, and then the world. Make no mistake, this is not my

war. It is all of ours."

"Oftentimes it is best to remove the limb than risk the spread," Viktória replied quietly. "Sylvie was of your coven. Her quarrel lies with you and yours, not all witchkind. What makes you think she will come for the rest of us?"

I looked Viktória up and down. Was this woman serious? "You offer Sylvie morality where she has none. Our histories recall Sylvie being judged and burned with *all* High Witches present. She will not stop until we are all dead. With the cultists at her back, Sylvie plans to reshape the world and cleanse it of humanity and witchkind alike. There will be nothing left—no walls to hide behind. Budapest will fall, just like the rest of us."

Viktória chuckled, turning to face me front on. "I've heard stories of your fire, blood witch. You make a compelling case, I'll give you that, but as it stands, Mistvellen is the only city which really profits from an alliance."

Inwardly, I seethed, wanting to shove her 'profits' right up her rigid ass. Instead, I smiled sweetly, nodding my head as if this was to be expected. Which, to be fair, it absolutely was. Dante, Farkas, and I had known we'd find some pushback from fellow covens and clans, and we'd planned for it.

"If profit is what you seek, then how about I sweeten the deal?"

Viktória's eyes glimmered, her face sharpening as she cocked her head. "I'm listening."

"Our Kingdom is mapped under the rule of a human king,

but it serves witchkind and táltosok no purpose. Our territories are drawn from a human fist, but what if we remade them to suit our needs? Why not form our own states and sovereigns? Budapest would answer to no one, having its own rules and regulations. Its own queen or king. We could increase trade with other magical beings—build new shipping routes. Perhaps even talk of reducing merchant fees and offering a more ... lucrative incentive to your people."

She was eating this up, her eyes widening, the slightest smack of her lips the only thing stopping her from drooling over the riches she was no doubt imagining up. The cat was in the bag, surely.

To her credit, she merely shrugged, pretending to contemplate my offer. "I'll tell you what, should Aliz agree to aid you, Budapest will answer the call."

"Then you'd best start making arrangements," a voice called from behind us. I turned, finding Aliz watching us from the doorway, her red skirts glimmering. I hadn't even heard her approach. "Transylvania has always been an ally to the Green Coven. We will not abandon you now."

I felt like wilting in relief, but I smiled warmly. "Mistvellen is in your debt. We will not forget this."

"I should hope not. My witches are battle trained, but it's been a long time since we've had cause to test our skills. The fire in our blood burns for a real fight." She grinned, her brown eyes twinkling. "I'm rather curious to see if the táltosok can keep up."

Oh, I liked this one. She was welcome any time. "Did you see them fight today, my lady? They are as impressive on the battlefield as they are off it."

"Perhaps I will test that for myself," she replied, eyeing the talent on display, her eyes dwelling on András.

Istenanya have mercy, she'd have her hands full with him. Though, as I watched him, I found he had eyes only for another táltos. One I recalled putting to bed alongside András when the two were too drunk to function. My gods, he wasn't subtle about the eye-fucking either.

Aliz caught my small smile and raised a brow. "A friend of yours?"

I chuckled. "We're very close. As stunning as you are tonight, I think you'll find it hard to wrench his gaze from a certain other táltos."

"Pity," Aliz said, but she was smiling. "Although I do so love a hunt. You have my promise, Kitarni. The Red Coven is at your service." She turned to Viktória. "What say you, blue sister? Will Budapest offer aid?"

Viktória's gaze was flat and hard and a smirk crossed her lips that was so uncannily familiar it made me frown, my skin prickling. She didn't see my discomfort, too busy enjoying my desperate attempt to gain allies. "My word is my honour. The blue witches will fight."

I blew out a breath. It seemed almost too easy, even if it had taken a wedding and a trial of magic to get here. Kitarni Bárány

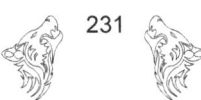

they might have refused, but the lady of Mistvellen and High Witch of the Green Coven, they could not.

I held out my hand first to Viktória, then Aliz. The former took it reluctantly, but Aliz smiled, pulling me in for a hearty embrace. Laughter rumbled out of my chest. I could see a friendship on the cards there, one that undoubtedly spelled trouble. She was a formidable woman, and my bet was she would only be more spectacular on the battlefield.

This was really happening. The covens were united, the witches were in play, and now we just needed the clans to join our army. Dante was a hard man to refuse. I had every faith he'd win the clan chieftains over.

There was still hope.

"Lady Sándor," Margit interrupted. "I need to speak with you. It's rather urgent."

I studied the excited sheen of her eyes—quite possibly a higher dose of bloodmorphia—but the anxious bobbing of her feet told me whatever it was couldn't wait, tentative friendships or not. "Please excuse me," I said to the High Witches, bowing respectively. "Enjoy the party."

Margit could barely contain her excitement as she dragged me out of the hall. When we were out of hearing distance from the chamber, I pulled her to a stop. "I hope this is worth the interruption. If you'd arrived any sooner, I might have ruined our chances, but I did it, Margit. Both covens will fight. We have our witches!"

Her smile turned devilish. "They'd have been fools not to, but you've done well. And trust me, this is worth it Kitarni. You'll be kissing my feet once I've shown you."

"Shown me what?" I frowned at her silence. "My gods, must you always be so dramatic?"

She gave me an affronted look and dragged me into her creepy dungeon where Dante and András were already waiting. My husband's gaze raked over me, ever appreciative, and I felt my cheeks pink from the hunger. The promise of *later*.

András sighed impatiently. "Finally. This better be worth it. I was in the middle of something very pleasant before."

"Or someone?" I remarked, smiling cattishly at him.

"Two someones, if this meeting hadn't so rudely interrupted."

A bark of laughter escaped me. "I saw you eyeing off your old flame in the hall not five minutes ago. You managed to find a third wheel in that time?" I clicked my tongue, doing the shape of a cross like the Christians. "Poor man whore. Your soul needs cleansing."

He batted my hand away. "Nothing wrong with spicing it up a little." András smoothed his hair back, his green eyes a little glazed from the drink. I supposed tonight could be our last chance to indulge in a little pleasure. The gods knew we wouldn't find much of it when the final battle truly began.

"I won't keep you from your dalliances for long," Margit said, shoving him out of the way as she rounded the table. She rifled through the many sheafs of ink, pulling out an open book and

233

slamming it down. "Look."

András looked down his nose at it. "A dusty tome? Really, Margit, books don't quite do it for me, so if you don't mind, I—"

"Idiot." She whacked him over the head with a frown. "Shut up and *look*, all of you."

Curiosity piqued, I squeezed in beside András, gazing down at the page before us. "Oh my gods," I gasped, shoving András along further, earning me grumbles. "You found it."

"The crown," Dante said, his voice rumbling against my back from where he towered behind me.

I leaned in closer, studying the illustration of the head piece. It was an unremarkable thing as far as crowns went. Gold, jewel-studded, like most were, but its simplicity made its secrets even curiouser.

Words jumped out at me from the page. 'Power of the ancients', 'passed down from the gods' … the more I read, the more my excitement grew.

"It belonged to the gods?" I breathed, looking up at Margit, who was bouncing on the balls of her feet.

"A priceless artefact," she said, nodding. "It renders the bearer's power essentially limitless. Whomsoever wears this crown would be unstoppable. They'd have the power of all the gods and immortality at their fingertips. Its magic is … unfathomable."

"At what cost?"

We all looked at Dante, and I was keenly reminded of Death's warning about magic. He moved around me to the other side of

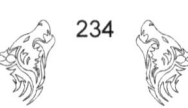

234

the table, pressing his palms flat on the surface. "Such an artefact wasn't meant for mortals to wear. Tell me Kitarni can wear this without consequence. Tell me she will still be her after using its power."

Margit swallowed as all eyes swivelled to her. "I can't."

"Margit." Dante's features darkened, and he took a deep breath, his voice low. "Explain."

She sighed. "The crown has been worn by many over the ages. All were consumed by its allure. Power of this magnitude is not meant for mortal beings. It ... takes from them. Their sanity, their morals. Even with Kitarni's power, I cannot promise she will be the same if she wears it or if she'll survive what comes out of it."

The breath caught in my lungs and I sagged against the table. Their voices melded together as they bickered, weighing every positive and negative. The truth was, I'd always known using the crown would mean sacrificing something of myself. If someone as powerful as Fate sought it, what hope did a mortal have? I was strong, but I was not immune to the gods' will, and Margit was right. This crown was never meant for lesser beings.

If we didn't use it, my power would not be enough to match Sylvie's, not to mention if she ever got her hands on it then we'd all be dead before lifting a finger. Fate too, was still hunting, which was another troubling thought. Nothing good would come of that greedy bitch overthrowing Death. He was the lesser of two evils.

At some point Dante had starting shouting, and Margit and

András were all exchanging verbal blows. My skin grew hot, my temper fraying with each passing second until I just snapped.

"Stop," I yelled. My power blasted from me in a single wave—not enough to hurt them but enough to get them to shut the hell up. I blinked, turning my hands over before shoving them down to my sides. "We all knew it wouldn't be easy, but this is my choice to make. I will find the crown, and I will use it to stop Sylvie. As far as I'm concerned, nothing has changed."

"But Kitarni," András said, seemingly fully sober now. "The cost—"

"Is mine to bear and mine alone," I replied firmly. "You cannot change my mind."

"You're wrong," Dante said quietly, taking my hand. I hadn't even noticed him move to me, but he had a habit of always knowing what I needed. "You are not alone. We'll find a way to prevent the crown from taking you. I refuse to lose you again. And I swear, I will walk to the edges of the earth, to the very bowels of hell if that's what it takes to find an answer. You are mine and I will not let it take you."

I smiled softly, stroking his skin with the pad of my thumb. "Then let us promise that if we lose each other, we'll never stop looking until we're together again. One way or the other. In this life or the next."

He cradled my head to his chest and I breathed in the leather and sandalwood scent of him. His hands clutched at me tightly, as if afraid letting go meant I would disappear entirely. Even with

everything we'd been through, I knew deep down the feeling was mutual. I buried my face in his chest, listening to the steady beating of his heart.

I shifted to see András with an arm around Margit's shoulder. Her jaw was set, her eyes burning. She knew better than anyone what toll magic could take, but understood it was necessary. Or maybe she just knew I'd let nothing stop me. I think the pair of us had always had an unspoken agreement when it came to magic, forged after I'd been so quick to judge her for her bloodmorphia addiction when we'd first met.

Her strength was something I deeply admired. The slight tremble to her chin was the only sign of her sadness and fear. The tiny crack in her façade. I took a deep breath, untangling myself from Dante's arms.

"We know what the crown is and what it can do. Do you know where it is?"

Her lips twisted, but she nodded. "As you suspected, I believe the crown is in the Under World, hidden in what's referred to as a pocket realm. The reason Fate hasn't been able to find it is because Sylvie used blood magic."

Interesting. "And Fate can't use this magic?"

Margit shook her head, her silky black hair swaying. She scrounged through her stacks of books on the table and unearthed a new one, flipping through the pages and jabbing at the one she wanted with her nail. "Like witches, who are gifted the power of an element and have a connection with the earth and its energy,

demi-gods like Fate and Death are bound by their environment. Death thrives off the pain and torment of the souls in his care, whereas Fate is granted foresight. Unlike me, she can tinker with people's fates, though obviously that doesn't always end well."

I grinned. "Not if we have anything to say about it."

"So how does this blood magic work?" Dante asked from where he'd moved to lean against the table. He looked so damn delicious in his regalia, I had to stop myself from drooling at the muscles threatening to burst out of his tunic.

"That's just it," Margit said slyly, her lips curving. "Only one with the same blood running through their veins can do the spell and enter the pocket realm. Quite clever of Sylvie, but she probably wasn't counting on her descendant fetching the crown on her behalf."

András cocked his head. "Maybe not back then, but Sylvie is no fool. She knows Kitarni will be looking for it. This could be a trap."

"Perhaps," I said, curling a strand of hair around my finger thoughtfully, "but it changes nothing. Death and Fate will have their minions hunting for the first sign of Sylvie in the Under World—maybe even set wards to keep her out. But they have no one looking for us."

András snorted. "It would be a nice change if our lovely lady can refrain from charging in palms blazing."

Everyone looked at me in varying shades of amusement. Dante's lips quirked, and András raised a brow. "What?" I said

indignantly, throwing my hands up. "I know how to be stealthy when needed."

This time they all glanced between each other and I huffed. "Fine. I promise not to burn anyone unless provoked."

"My little hellcat can't help her murderous tendencies," Dante said, pressing a kiss to my cheek. The graze of his stubble sent a soft shiver over my skin and I turned, hooking my arms around his neck.

"Only because my husband has a tendency to provoke them."

His expression darkened, his muscles tightening under my grasp. "Oh, Freckles, but you make it so hard not to."

TWENTY-THREE

DANTE

"Thank the gods for beds," Kitarni groaned, flinging herself face down on ours.

I chuckled, sitting beside her and patting her ass sympathetically. "It'll take some getting used to. Nobles are like vultures circling, waiting for the perfect moment to tear you to shreds."

She lifted her head to peer over her shoulder. "I'd rather face my enemies in battle than exchange loaded words and deal in politics. How do you do it?"

I shrugged as I slid my boots off and began peeling my shirt away. "Years of patience and knowing when to step back and regroup. Plus wine. You can never have enough wine."

Kitarni sat up and shifted, reclining as she watched me undress, her eyes roving over my body hungrily. "Patience isn't my strong suit," she said with a sly smile. "But I can help with two of those things."

"Stay," I commanded, striding over to a bench to pour us both a goblet of red and handing her one. "Drink with me." She did as I asked, tipping the wine past her red lips, her kohl-lined eyes watching me like a cat. There was something so sensual about the way she bared her throat to me. When she licked her lips, I felt myself grow hard. "Take off your dress."

She smiled, seeming to enjoy the dominance in my tone. "Is that a command, my lord?"

I flashed her my dimples, leaning against the bedpost as I looked down at her. "A suggestion, a command, call it what you will, but I would have you naked and bared before me, so that I might appreciate my latest asset."

Her eyes glittered, only the moonlight beaming through the balcony doors cresting upon her skin. "An asset, am I?" she asked dangerously. "And if I disobey?"

"You won't," I replied, leaning down to trail one finger over her calves, up her thighs, beneath her skirts. When I reached the apex of her legs, I dragged my thumb up her centre, swirling over her nerves. She was already wet for me and she smiled knowingly at my touch.

I drank my wine leisurely, still circling my finger lazily, enjoying the way her nose scrunched up as she tried to stay still and quiet. But I had her. I had all of her.

I tipped back the rest of my drink and she did the same with hers, sensing the shift as I took our goblets in one hand and leaned over her, my other hand working harder as I pressed my

lips to hers. She opened for me immediately and our tongues met. She tasted heady, earthy and rich from the red wine, and I sank into that kiss, my cock hardening even further.

She moaned against my mouth, arching her back as I slipped one finger, then two inside her, my thumb merciless in its strokes. And just as I was about to make her come, I slipped away.

A strangled noise of frustration left her and I grinned as I dragged a chair over, placing it opposite the bed. "Strip. I want to see every inch of my beautiful wife before I send you to oblivion."

Her eyes met mine, full of defiance, but my little hellcat was too flushed with the promise of pleasure to turn me down. Or so I thought. Kitarni lifted her dress ever so slowly, then peeled her undergarments away and stepped toward me.

The moonlight streaming in seemed to highlight her silhouette, bathing her in a mystical glow, shining on every dip and swell of her body. She was fucking radiant. My love. My wife. And my dirty little hellcat.

She leaned forward as if to embrace me, placing her foot on the edge of the chair and sliding it up just shy of my cock, which twitched in anticipation. Her mouth met mine and she kissed me deeply, those full lips wrapping around my own.

"Maybe," she whispered, pulling back, stroking my cock through my pants briefly. "Maybe I'll just take care of myself tonight."

Her laugh was music to my ears as she turned and climbed on the bed, arching her back and giving me full view of her

rounded ass. A rumble escaped me when she slid her fingers down, touching herself and throwing her head back in a moan. I could see the glistening wetness and fuck if the sight of her didn't make me want to explode. My pants became uncomfortably tight and I yanked them off, fisting my hand around my cock, sliding it up and down as I watched her.

She moaned, her fingers moving more frantically, her eyes closed as she indulged in her pleasure.

"Look at me," I demanded, wanting to see those pretty eyes as she worked. Her eyes snapped open, and she looked over her shoulder at me, groaning even louder at seeing the precum on my dick.

"Do you want to come with me, Dante?" she asked, her voice husky. I fucking loved it.

"Yes," I growled, "but you're not doing it alone. I hope you're prepared, Freckles, because this will be anything but gentle. Are you ready to hurt for me?"

She moaned. "Yes. Yes, I want you to use me."

In an instant I was up, shucking my pants off and pulling her back to the edge of the bed. I slicked her juices over her rear hole, sliding my thumb over it and sticking it in. The soft mewl she uttered had me grinning like a devil. She gasped as I spit on my cock and lined myself up. When I pushed my tip towards her, she blinked back at me in alarm.

"Are you ...?"

I let my darkness writhe around my wrists where I held on to her hips. "I want to claim all of you, wife. Every inch, every hole. Relax your body." She bit her lip, trembling slightly as I nudged in back and forth. Slowly, easing her body into it. She held her breath as I rocked several times. "Breathe, my love." Her body sagged, and I pushed in further, inch by inch.

"I can't fit you," she gasped, biting her lip.

I paused to kiss her back and kneaded her shoulders softly with one hand. "You can. If you want me to stop at any moment, just say the word. But push through this part and I promise you'll glide among the stars tonight."

"Yes. Take me there, Dante." Her hazel eyes turned molten at that promise, her muscles easing a little around me until I was fully seated inside her.

"Hard part's over," I whispered, twining my palm in her roots. "Now comes pleasure, my darling."

I moved, softly and slowly at first, until I heard the intake of her breath, the slight arching of her spine telling me she was enjoying it. When she was comfortable enough for me to really move, I began pumping inside of her a little faster.

"Oh, fuck," she groaned, her breath quickening. I slammed my cock harder inside her, faster, and a garbled string of curses escaped her. Then, louder, "Oh fuck!"

She slipped a finger to her front and circled while I dominated her ass, rubbing one cheek and squeezing it hard as my own pleasure rumbled out of me. I was ready to burst, but not until she rode my cock and she saw those stars I mentioned.

 244

"Come for me," I huffed against her. "I want you to scream on your wedding night."

Her breaths came in ragged pants and her body tensed up, her inner walls tightening around me as she screamed my name to the highest turret of the castle.

I continued thrusting as she climaxed, chasing her shortly after, spilling inside her and gripping onto her ass for dear life. "Fuck, Kitarni," I breathed, feeling my body let go of all the tension that had been building over the last weeks, a tiredness sweeping over me.

I was so fucking tired. What I wouldn't give to have just one day with Kitarni. No war. No castle. No duties to attend to except for my wife's pleasure and every whim. I wanted to spend every moment treating my queen, showing her I could be the man she deserved.

For now, I strode to the bathing chamber and grabbed a rag, helping her clean herself with gentle fingers. When we were done, I sprawled back on the bed, her cheek pressing to my chest. We lay there in silence for a while, comfortable in each other's arms.

"Tell me what you're feeling, Freckles. What's on your mind?" I asked, stroking her back with a featherlight touch.

"Everything," she said, a deep sigh pulling from her lips. "The war, and everyone who seeks to hurt us."

"I won't let Sylvie harm you," I promised, tilting her chin to look at me. "I will cut off her hands before she can lay a single finger on your head."

She smiled softly. "You're a bit scary when you go all possessive and protective, you know."

I hummed in my chest. "You wouldn't have it any other way."

Her answering chuckle was everything. "True. But just so you know, being married doesn't change the fact that you're an asshat."

I smiled as she traced the outline of my tattoo, her finger sliding along the sword on my chest, then along the flowers beside it. Today had been chaotic, but there was something so right about us fighting side-by-side, new allies at our back.

The tables were turning. Now to see which side would survive the summer.

TWENTY-FOUR

KITARNI

Dante's hand settled at the small of my back, his fingers brushing my ass ever so slightly as we danced. Possessive indeed, not that I could blame him. We hadn't had the luxury of basking in marital bliss, instead diving straight off the deep end into shark-infested waters.

The night of the masquerade ball was upon us and, despite the planning and security measures, I knew he was just as on edge as I was. More so, given how seriously and eagerly he took to his duty as protective and—okay, yes, pleasuring—husband.

His muscles were stiff, betraying his nerves, his brown eyes flashing gold as they scanned the room around us. With his black wolf mask covering half his face, it made him appear threatening ... dangerous.

I could feel his power rumbling through his skin, singing through his veins and lighting his body on fire. Not that it would be much help to us if we were attacked. Necromancy served little purpose with no bodies to raise. When it came to the final battle, however, my husband would be in his element. A shadow king, and a savage alpha wolf.

My own body zinged with power, the beast inside me awake and watching, sniffing for any hint of treachery. I tightened my grip on Dante's arm and thought about what had happened in the lavender fields—how my eyes had turned black and something else had seemed to take over, revelling in the death and destruction wrought by my hands.

I didn't want to think about why or how, but deep down I knew the answer. Blood magic was the stuff of darkness. It made sense that it would claim a piece of me if I didn't use it sparingly, but the truth was the beast inside me had never seemed interested in hurting *me*. The thought of losing myself to the darkness made me sick, but what could I do? To save our people, I would use every lost drop inside me. I would lose myself if it meant finding peace for Mistvellen.

Dante knew it too, his rigid shoulders carrying the burden of that knowledge. I sighed. One step at a time. Tonight we danced to a different tune. I just hoped we were all there when the song struck its last chord.

"Do you see anything?" I whispered. Dante twirled me, sending my skirts spinning as he dipped me low and pressed a kiss to my fluttering pulse. His lips were feather light, but the way he kissed me made me feel reverent. My pulse burned for him.

He lifted me back up, placing his palm in mine as we circled

each other in the dance. "Nothing yet," he remarked, his eyes ever searching. "Father increased the guards on duty, and all guests were submitted to checks upon entering. By all rights, we should be safe."

Should be. I couldn't help but focus on those two words, because we both knew that wouldn't be the case. Margit's visions never lied, which meant one of us could die tonight. That fact left a sour taste in my mouth, a lump in my throat restricting the air in my lungs.

"You know that won't change our fate," I said to him in a low voice. "Be vigilant. The killer watches in the shadows. Either cultists have somehow surpassed the guards, or we have traitors in our midst."

Dante's hand flexed against my palm. "Whoever it is, they will know my wrath before the end." He cocked his head as the song changed its tempo, the time for us to change partners approaching quickly. "Give 'em hell," he said to me and I barely had time to nod before I was spun towards another guest.

The man said nothing as he took me in his arms, his dark brown eyes glittering black in the low light of fireballs hovering mid-air. The vast hall was bedecked with greenery, flowers of all different colours and types dotting the walls, moss growing up columns and sprouting over the floor. A garden created by the earth witches' gifts. Even the blue witches had contributed, sending streams of glittering water winding around columns, lazily stretching in an endless loop.

It was utterly romantic and entirely unfitting for a murder scene. I swallowed, watching the nobles dancing, laughing, and drinking, all unaware of the treachery tonight promised. I wished to be one of them. I wished to forget, if only for a moment, so I could pretend that life was normal. That I was *safe*.

We all deserved that, didn't we? To feel safe.

My eyes roved over the man's wolf mask, which was the replica of all the other masks donned tonight. I'd had Eszter make them, enforcing guests to wear the same mask in attempt to catch any sheep in wolf's clothing. Literally, if cultists were showing up uninvited. Margit had told me it would do little to change our fate, but I'd had to do something, if only to make us all feel a little better.

The man watched me through the eyeholes, and there was something about the way he stared at me that filled me with unease. I suppressed a shiver as his cold hand shifted in my own, tightening to the point of pain.

"You're hurting my hand," I said quietly, calmly. He man remained silent, those black eyes never leaving my own. I frowned, trying to pull my hand away, but he only squeezed harder. "Let. Go."

My stomach twisted and I looked around for Dante or András, but they were further down the line, hidden behind the dancers beside me. Fuck this shit. My magic flared, and I sent a blaze of power licking out from my palm. The man hissed, raising his arm instinctively, and that's when I saw it ...

A seven-pointed star, etched into his palm. The man smiled, revealing sharp teeth, and a cold wind gusted through the room, causing the fireballs to wink out. The temperature plummeted and unnatural darkness filled the chamber as guests murmured and gasped in surprise.

Blind, I slid my hand to the dagger strapped to my thigh, pulling the blade quietly from its sheath. With my other I clicked my fingers, fire bursting from their tips to light the room.

A sheep mask appeared before me, the same glittering black eyes leering from behind it. I gasped, thrusting my blade forward on instinct. It sank between the man's ribs easily, and I slipped it up and towards his heart, twisting at the last second, making it as painful as possible.

I sighed in relief, glad to have outwitted the cultists as the man, still smiling, fell to his knees. Fucking creepy cultists. I took a step ... and stumbled. Confused, I looked to my stomach, my hand drifting up to find a dagger implanted there, blood sluicing over my fingers as I touched the wound.

How ...?

I stumbled again, bumping into other nobles as I scanned the room. The fire witches restored light to the hall as they cast more fireballs, and that's when shit really went sideways.

One scream, shrill and piercing, rang through the hall. Then another in an entirely different corner. Another scream followed, another, until shouts rang out from all around me, nobles pushing and shoving and bumping shoulders so hard that guests fell to the

floor, nearly crushed beneath the heels and boots of panicked people.

I stepped slowly through the crowd, my vision hazy as I flung my arms out uselessly, knocked back again and again. Pain flared in my side each time and I gasped, clutching my side. Where was Dante? I'd almost given up hope on finding my friends when I saw a flash of dark, reddish-brown hair, followed by the ring of steel.

"Dante," I croaked, but the din was too loud, the chaos of moving bodies silencing my cries for help. *He's okay*, I told myself. *He's fighting, which must mean he's okay.* I turned my attention towards searching for Margit. She was the one I needed now. The only one I trusted to change fate.

I burst out from the crowd, and my heart stopped in my chest. András lay with his back against the wall, his breathing ragged, his hands clutched against a wound in his chest. I crumpled at his side, wincing from the movement as I pressed my own hands next to his, trying to stop the blood seeping out. "No, no, no."

"Quite the ... plot twist ... eh?" he said with a choked laugh.

"Be still," I hushed, forbidding the hysteria from bubbling out of my throat. "I refuse to let you leave me."

He looked pointedly at my own injury, placing one bloodied hand over my own. "If you don't do something about your own wound soon, I might not want for company."

I glanced down at the blood pooling at my stomach. I didn't think any vital organs had been punctured, but then again, my

mind was becoming more muddled by the minute. I had been looking for someone ...

"Margit," I rasped. "Where?"

"I'm here." Her skirts billowed around her as she dropped to her knees, wincing as she did.

"Are you hurt?"

"A flesh wound. Dante saved me." She shook her head, tears welling in her eyes. "In my visions there was always so much blood. I'd thought it spelled our death. I'd thought only one of us would be affected. How could I have been so wrong? I never realised—"

"Stop," I whispered. "You had the same dream sequence every time. I would have thought the same. But none of that matters anymore. What's important is that we fix this." I blinked, trying to hold onto my fading energy. "Where's Eszter?"

She shook her head helplessly, and I felt a new wave of panic spread through me. "Eszter," I yelled, but I hadn't the strength to bolster the word. "Where's my sister?"

"Here," Dante called, and I swivelled too quickly, sending another spurt of blood dribbling from my stomach. My heart skipped a beat as I looked at them both. She was white as snow and her eyes were glazed, but otherwise unharmed, thank the gods. Dante had a slice to his arm but was fine.

He sank beside me, his eyes cataloguing my wounds and András's with a commander's gaze. The gold in his eyes flashed, and by Hadur, his power darkened the already dim room, lit only by sparks of fire as witches battled intruders throughout.

"Where are they?" Dante's tone was the promise of nightmares, the low rumble from his chest both haunting and dangerous. "I will cut off their heads and send them back to Sylvie."

"They're already dead," I wheezed, jerking my head behind me. The movement was too much, and I sagged, my eyes rolling back in my head.

"Both of you, stay with me. Don't you dare fucking leave me." He pulled a dagger from his belt, rolled his sleeve back, and sliced without hesitation. Blood welled, snaking down his arm in streams, forming pathways like roots of a great tree.

He nodded to Margit and she did the same without hesitation, pulling her own blade out to keep the cuts clean. My vision began to darken, and the last thing I saw before I closed my eyes was András's deathly pale face, his lips blue, his breathing so, so shallow.

It dawned on me then, what they were planning to do, and gods, it just might work. But the last time it had happened ... "No," I rasped. "I could—" I tried to speak, but the words lodged in my throat, my reflexes slow, my body beginning to fail me.

I wanted to scream, but all I could do was lie there, wait, and pray. My body was jostled, and I felt myself being lifted into Dante's arms. "Pull from me, Freckles. Pull me from me, if not for you, then for András. Save him."

My eyelashes fluttered as I tried to open my eyes. Darkness was calling me, or perhaps it was Death, taunting me, whispering sweet silken words to join him somewhere I was not ready to tread.

Well, the fucker could keep waiting. I had to save András. Had to save them all, only now I knew I didn't have to do it alone. My friends, my family, they believed in me. I would not let them down.

Dante's power bumped against my barriers, stroking a soft whisper of black against my mind. I let him in and his power surged down into the bottom-most layers of my mind, funnelling deeper than even I had imagined he could go.

I lapped it up greedily, feeling my strength return, the beast howling in delight as it unfurled inside of me and lifted its head, as if it recognised its companion—something altogether similar in mind and shape.

Our magic met in the middle, seeming to click inside me as the beast fed on that darkness, quivering with a deep-seated need. It felt so intimate this time, like a key had been unlocked and only now were the gears shifting into place. I had to suppress a moan as I writhed, feeling my body light up in every possible place.

More. I wanted more. *I wanted all of it.*

When I opened my eyes, I found myself staring into depthless black that once shone brown and gold. Dante smiled, and a cool shiver licked down my spine as I wriggled in his lap. He was covered in my blood and his own, his hands latched onto Margit and Eszter's from where they were linked together, feeding me. Their eyes remained the same blue and brown as always, shock lining those windows and their open mouths.

My stomach began knitting back together, the strength

returning tenfold. My skin glowed, reminiscent of the great goddesses above. It was not normal for mortals to feel this much power in their skin, and it felt good. Sinfully good. Only this time, I had enough sense to stop, knowing I'd kill them if they gave much more. Already, Dante was failing, his head bowed, his eyes flickering from black to brown. Margit and Eszter gasped with the effort, sweat beading on their foreheads.

I looked at András—at the chest that had nearly stopped moving altogether, and I reined myself in, remembering who I was. Remembering my purpose.

"Break the tether," I commanded, surprised by the strength of my tone. The otherworldly voice that was unrecognisable. My companions yanked away from my consciousness and I breathed in deeply, focusing only on András as the others scooted aside.

With glowing palms, I let the energy inside me morph into a different magic, one borne out of a need to restore and heal. "You're going to be okay, András," I breathed. "I am going to save you."

Golden, bright magic soared out of me into the gaping wound in his chest, a terrible mess of blood and sinew. I willed that wound to close, sending my power deeper, curious tendrils winding around muscle and tendon, closing gaps and restoring a punctured lung, then knitting skin together, piece by piece, second by second, until my friend sucked in a deep breath, his eyes snapping open to reveal that green gaze I knew and loved.

"By all the gods. That was awful!" He blinked several times,

clutching a hand to his heart as his eyes slid to mine. "And the woman I'd been dancing with was such a good dance partner."

I laughed, launching myself at him and wrapping my arms around his neck. "A great loss, I'm sure. Now please, don't fucking scare me like that again," I demanded.

He chuckled. "No need to get emotional. I'm fine, thanks to you."

His words were a little thick, betraying his feelings and I just smiled, hugging my friend harder, allowing us a small moment of reprieve despite the ruckus surrounding us.

"Dante?" Eszter's trembling voice had me whirling instantly.

My husband swayed on his feet, his eyes unfocused, but he waved her off.

"I'm okay," he said.

Right before his body tumbled to the ground.

TWENTY-FIVE

DANTE

"D ante!"

I heard my name, but I couldn't place who was calling it, nor see clearly the faces looking down at me. I'd given too much, offered too freely, but not without purpose.

There was only one way to enter the gates of hell, I was damn sure of it. Only one way to enter the realm of the Under World and find the crown. Kitarni had plotted and schemed with Margit and András, but I had plans of my own.

This time, my actions would benefit the right people. This time, I was a willing participant in this plan. A piece on a chess board, Kitarni had said of me not long ago. Only I wasn't a pawn any longer. I was a fucking lord and I would protect my lady with all I had to give.

I looked around, having enough sense to realise I was no longer in the great hall, but in Margit's lair. Her safe space and

 258

den of magics. The table I lay upon was cool against my feverish skin and I twisted my hands to set my palms against the wood, feeling every grain and dent beneath my fingers.

"Come back to me," Kitarni whispered, her voice thick with emotion. She smoothed the hair back from my brow, her palm hot against my clammy forehead. "You're so cold." She turned to Margit with wide eyes. "He's dying. I need to heal him!"

Margit's hand snaked out, catching Kitarni's wrist. "Not yet. We will heal him, I promise, but right now he is on the cusp of death, and that's exactly where he needs to be."

Kitarni shook her head. "I don't understand."

"I'm sorry, Kitarni," Margit replied, avoiding my wife's piercing gaze. My cousin kept her thoughts close to her chest, but even I knew the fear carried in those three words. She hadn't agreed to this lightly, but we both knew it wasn't me that was fated to end the Dark Queen. Only Kitarni could do that, and the risk of her not returning from the Under World was too great to take.

I might be lord, but I wasn't irreplaceable. Especially now I had a lady—a wife—as capable as any man and stronger still. The world would know her fury.

Kitarni's voice sounded far away as her pitch kicked up a notch. "What do you mean you're sorry?" A pause for a few beats, then recognition as her face twisted first into hard lines of anger, followed by despair and denial. "No. We had a deal. You promised, Margit! It was meant to be me."

"It was my choice, Freckles," I mumbled. "I do this willingly.

I need to do this, not just for all of you, but for myself." Her strangled cry only hardened my heart, fortifying my decision. "Margit will bring me back. I *will* come back to you. I promise."

My cousin looked at my wife, the sharpness to her features softening at the fear on my beloved's face. "Dante has passed too much power to you, Kitarni. His life teeters in this world and the next, which is the perfect time to conduct the spell. I do not do this lightly. I have done my research and I would stake my life on this working. His body will remain here, but his mind will travel to the Under World. Please. If we're to do this, it must be right now. I cannot make the choice for you both."

Kitarni looked at me, pain and fear swirling in those beautiful hazel eyes. "I can do this," I said softly. "I will find the crown."

She shook her head, raking her fingers through her hair and snarling in frustration. When she faced me again, she placed a kiss to my brow, then another to my lips, lingering there as if committing the moment to memory. "I know you can." She pulled away, her face set in a mask of resignation. "And just know, if you don't come back, I'm going to haunt you for all eternity."

I offered her a crooked grin, my strength waning and vision darkening until she was just a blur and a dark silhouette

Margit nodded, then grabbed a vial from the shelf, not hesitating to grab Kitarni's hand and slice it as gently as possible, stoppering the precious blood dripping from the cut. Kitarni said nothing. Didn't even wince, her eyes fixed on my own, her lips twisted with worry.

When the vial was full my cousin shoved it in my pocket, along with a scrap of parchment. She began chanting in tongues, the ancient words passing from her lips raising the hairs on my arms and neck. Dark magic. Dark and forbidden, pushing the boundaries between our world and the next.

A fey wind began to gust around the room, causing my hair to ripple, books to fly from shelves, and potions and tinctures to topple, shattering on the stone.

And then I felt it ... the pull of the unknown, a vast chasm that seemed to open beneath me. One minute I was lying on the table, the next I was falling, down, down, down.

To hell. And salvation.

The vortex spat me out on a snowy hill, a harsh wind ripping at my clothing, pulling at the hair on my scalp. I climbed to my feet, no longer feeling like death warmed up on a platter. I turned my hands before me, marvelling at the realness of the movement and the way the skin still held every callous and vein.

I was here, but also not. My body lay back in the Middle World, surrounded by family and a wife who would be sure to punish me when I returned. *If* I returned. Despite Kitarni's scheming, Margit and I had planned for the worst with the masquerade ball. That, if I was to be wounded—or worse, on my way to my deathbed—she would ensure it would be me to walk the

depths of this vast dungeon of hell. It hadn't made sense to make her go. Why bother when I was already bleeding out and perfectly primed for the trip?

Kitarni could hardly be too mad, given she'd planned on doing the same thing. And deep down, I think she knew how badly I needed to do this. How much I needed to prove, not just to her, but to myself that I could protect my people. That, in the end, I could do right by coven and clan.

The táltosok would be without their general if I didn't make it back in time, but they were in good hands with Lukasz and András. My brother and my right-hand man would ensure no one stepped out of line. I just hoped it didn't come to that. I wanted to be there beside my warrior queen, leading our people together.

I shook my head. There was little point dwelling on hope. I'd much rather be a man of action.

I looked behind me, eyes widening as I realised what I was gazing at. The door Caitlin had opened to the Under World—the gateway itself—stood proudly, stretching endlessly high into a mist that swallowed the sun and shrouded the sky.

Lightning forked with savage tongues above, thunder rumbling as the world flashed ominously. There was no light or warmth here. It was a place for the dead, and the dead received no comfort.

The door itself didn't appear like an entry one might open or shut, but a black, rippling pool that seemed to suck in the blinding light of the contrasting snow. Two stone pillars engraved

in glowing blood markings held the portal in place. I'd warrant once those glyphs went out, the portal would close and disappear.

I didn't know how to close it just yet, but that was a problem for later. Margit was clever and had a full library at her disposal. She would figure it out. For now, I had a crown to find, hopefully without alerting Death or Fate to my presence.

I jammed my hands in my armpits to stave off the biting chill. Even though my physical form remained in the Middle World, I still felt everything keenly, all my senses about me. I trudged up the snow towards a ledge to get a better bearing on my surroundings. When I reached the top, I sucked in a deep breath. It was so much worse than I could have ever imagined.

Sprawling as far as the eye could see was a maze of black rock and stalactites jutting from the ground. And between it all ... demons. Hordes of demons in varying shapes and sizes, all of them torturing, devouring, feeding on the pain and misery of the unfortunate souls trapped in this hell realm. Their screams rang out across the landscape, bouncing off the rock and echoing back to me, even above the shrill cry of the grating winds.

In the middle of the maze, perched atop a thin mountain surging towards the sky, was a castle with soaring turrets and jagged edges. On a rounded platform with no edges at the very peak, I could just make out a throne. A place to indulge in one's power and lord over underlings. Death really was a cruel bastard, even if he did have good manners.

Setting my jaw, I set out towards the maze, determined to do

my duty. I wasn't afraid to die. In fact, the only time I'd really felt true fear was seeing Kitarni bleeding, both the first time and just moments ago, before I'd been transported here. I'd told her once that I would protect her. I'd failed.

My oath to her mother still held though, and that was to give my life for Kitarni's. This was one promise I could uphold.

Even if I was afraid.

So very afraid of what came next.

TWENTY-SIX

KITARNI

Climbed the stairs out of Margit's secret passage with a heavy heart. No, with utter emptiness where my heart should be. I'd left it there with him. My husband, my lord, my partner in all things.

The frustrating thing was, I couldn't even blame him. How could I, when his actions proved how much he wanted to set things right? I knew he'd done this, not just for me, but for himself. To prove that he was more than his betrayal, that his love for the realm and for me was deeply profound.

I could choose to be angry at him, Margit and András, but the truth was, he'd done the very thing I had planned to. Dante had risked everything to find the crown, giving me a chance to rally our allies and save both Mistvellen and the Kingdom of Hungary. It made me furious, terrified, beyond sorrowful, but I understood his motives. I knew if we'd had that discussion, I would have fought him on it. I would have done something stupid and sneaky on my own terms. Dante was right; I was a stubborn creature.

And now there was every chance he wouldn't come back.

The thought of that was too much to bear; if I focused on that now, I would crumble. András walked by my side in silence, covered in blood and still a little shaken, but otherwise in good health. He would be my rock in the coming days, while Margit and Eszter watched over Dante. I knew they would both guard and protect him with their lives, which wasn't so comforting a thought, really. It seemed that no matter what we did, someone always got hurt.

My limits had been stretched. I was done with cultists. Done playing nice. Something in me had changed after connecting with Dante's power this time. The beast inside me had swelled, like it had feasted so well its presence had increased, giving me more power.

Only the gods knew if that was good or bad. If it helped me destroy those sadist pricks, I was all for it.

Lord Sándor popped into view as we stormed into the hall. Dark bags swelled under his eyes and his light brown skin was flushed, his eyes murderous. I strode directly towards him, stepping over the bodies of the fallen, cocking my head. "The cultists?"

"All dead, bar a few. The others await questioning." He shook his head. "Dante warned me this would happen. Even with Margit's foresight, I had not imagined a bloodbath like this. My spies reported no movement from Sylvie's ranks. I suspect they

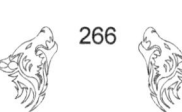

were discovered and killed. Which means—"

"There are traitors in our midst," I finished, looking around at the witches and táltosok scattered around the room.

"Any one of them could have leaked information about the ball." Farkas's eyes narrowed. "I should have cancelled it when I had the chance."

I placed a hand on his arm. "To hide behind our walls would reveal only weakness to our allies. Why should they entrust their soldiers unto us if we cannot prove our strength? We must prove how mighty Mistvellen can be. The covens and clans respect power, so show it to them. Use what happened tonight to your advantage."

The lord of the keep looked at me with intrigue. "You mean to incense our allies."

I shrugged. "You can paint a pretty picture with words like justice or honour, but there is nothing so motivating as the need for revenge. Witches and táltosok were murdered tonight. András was almost killed. Dante—"

At the mention of his son, Farkas tensed, his brows drawing together. "What happened to him?" He looked around the room and roared, "Where is my son?!"

Internally, I grimaced, wanting to flinch back from his wrath, but I held fast. "He's gone where the living cannot tread. His body holds to Margit's will, but his mind is beyond our reach. Our fate lies in your son now. All we can do is pray."

"No." Farkas's eyes narrowed, the scar puckering on his

cheek. "We can fight. We can prepare for our final stand. To enter these halls and shed blood in my castle is to suffer my wrath. I am tired of waiting for the pin to drop. It's time we show Sylvie what we can do. When next we fight, it will be upon the fields she desecrated. It's time to end this war."

We piled the dead in a heap outside the city walls. There was no distinction between witch or táltos, nothing to identify coven or clan except for the regalia or colour of dress they wore. My hands closed to fists as the fire witches set the bodies ablaze, the sickly-sweet stench of human flesh soon rising on the breeze to where I looked down from the balcony's edge.

The city gates were shut—had been shut since the last guest had entered before sundown, which meant the traitor, or group of traitors as was more likely, were still in the city. Possibly even in the castle, watching the chaos unfold and hiding secret smiles.

I looked to the skies, but even the moon and stars failed to shed light on the situation, hidden behind a veil of whisper-soft clouds. If only they whispered to me. Sighing, I turned on my heel, returning to the den of vipers and the captured cultists besides.

András, having taken it upon himself to be my bodyguard since the attack, shadowed my steps, silent and wraithlike. His anger radiated from him in waves. A smiling assassin, waiting for his mark. He was hungry for retribution—as was I, but András's

anger went deeper. A soldier who'd been bested by cheap parlour tricks like a hidden blade in a sleeve and a smile from a serpent's mouth.

We walked past the nobles gathered in the hall, some shouting angrily at guards to be allowed out, others cowering in corners. Then there were those with the promise of death in their eyes. It was the latter that drew my gaze, for I recognised the look on their face. I'd seen it in my own reflection after Sylvie had played one of her cards.

The question was, which of these guests was responsible? Whoever they were, a sheep among wolves was a dangerous place to be. I almost laughed at the mockery of those sheep masks. If the cultists who'd attacked had been wearing them upon entry, we would have known straight away. Of course, it was never that simple, though I did have a lead on who to question first. Only witch magic could have gutted the flames lighting the great hall tonight, and I distinctly recalled the moment they all went out, quickly paving the way to senseless death.

I took a breath, forcing my anger to simmer down as we descended stair after stair, until András and I were deep in the bowels of the castle. It wouldn't do to lose my head with the prisoners, but right now I wanted them to fucking burn for what they'd done.

András lay a hand on my arm. "Easy, princess. Ask questions and then deal with them as you will." His lips tightened. "Don't hold back."

We stepped into the dungeons, finding four cultists lined up against the far wall, their hands bound by iron above them, their feet shackled to the stone floor. Their eyes seemed clear, unmuddied by the bloodmorphia that had likely left their veins by now. One of them had their lips sewn shut, and I had to wonder why the guards hadn't checked beneath their masks before allowing them entry.

Sloppy. I would have Lukasz deal with them later. I stormed up to a woman, her lips twisting, causing the cracked and oozing wounds beneath the stitches to bleed. It never ceased to surprise me, how much hatred one could convey with just a look. It only made me madder.

My blood magic rose inside me, pooling at my palms and circling my arms—only this time, black writhed amongst it, fighting for space, surging forward eagerly. My eyes widened as I marvelled at the changed power. Reforged into something new. Whether that was from taking more from Dante or another unexpected development of using too much blood magic, I didn't know, but I locked that thought away to analyse later.

The room darkened as I revelled in my power. The cultist flinched back and I smiled darkly, letting it flare brighter as it snaked towards her.

I closed my eyes, soaking in the feeling of pleasure as this newfound strength coursed through me. She should be afraid. I could be terrifying if I wanted. I could be everything that hid in the shadows in the darkest part of night.

 270

"Kitarni." András's voice snapped me back to reality and I sucked in a breath, remembering where I was. His hand brushed mine hesitantly. "Kitarni," he said once more, his voice low. "Your eyes. They're black."

I blinked, realising how my magic had stretched around the woman's throat, forming a noose of sorts out of wispy black and red tendrils. With a jerk of my head, it dropped away. She seemed to choke, unable to gasp for air, her head drooping as far as the chains would allow.

The magic didn't scare me, but the momentary lapses of time and judgement did. Dante's magic was precious, but combined with the beast inside me, I was beginning to wonder what exactly was at work. Would the extra power eat away at me from the inside, stripping away who I was even faster? Perhaps the beast was enjoying the freedom to roam a little too much.

András's brows creased, but I shook my head slightly. Now wasn't the time to have *that* discussion. "Let's get this over with."

The next cultist leered at us both, then laughed manically. Deranged and clearly damaged. I stepped towards him, watching his jerky movements.

"I won't talk," he said between his laughing fit, smiling with stained yellow teeth. "So many pretty dolls with their heads cracked open and their stomachs split like sacks of grain. Whatever will the witches do now, me wonders, when dark magic comes to steal their souls?"

"Gods," I muttered to András. "She's really done a number

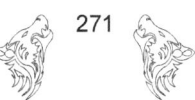

on them, hasn't she?"

"No gods," the man continued. "Only one goddess. Where she walks only dead things dwell. She is coming for you, little girl. Coming to drink your blood and take back what you took."

Now there was an interesting thought. I wanted to point out that I couldn't well take anything I was born with, but that argument was hardly worth the effort. Still, I hadn't thought of it like that—of Sylvie wanting to reclaim whatever magic remained in her bloodline.

Even though generations had passed since Sylvie was burnt at the stake, my mother had been running from the cult before I was born. I'd never stopped to question why she would suddenly flee her own people. Perhaps there was more to it than simply protecting me. If what this pitiful creature said was true, then maybe she'd been running to save her own life too, refusing to end up as a blood bag for those sadists once she realised what they were after.

There was no way to know for sure, but I had to think they knew, somehow, that the power in her hadn't been enough to resurrect Sylvie. That her child would be the key to bringing her back.

In a way, this nightmare was my fault. It was my magic that resurrected her.

I could choose to wallow in that fact, but what was the point? It was a sticky web with more players involved. Fate had Death mark me years ago, if only to serve her purposes, but that fickle

creature must have known Sylvie would always come back. Fate had probably been counting on it. And though things hadn't quite turned in her favour, I couldn't discount her entirely. Not to mention Death's hand in this.

The chained man looked at me, laughing and laughing. András's lips curled and he punched him in the face, shaking his fist afterwards as if to remove the stain of that touch.

This maniac was fast getting on my nerves and it took all my willpower not to stab him. I put a hand on my hip, glaring. "Who is the cult working with?" The man bit his lip hard enough to draw blood and started laughing again. "For fuck's sake." I punched him myself, satisfied with the crunch of bone where my fist met his nose.

"Answer her," András hissed. "We can do this all night. Nothing would make me happier than to watch you bleed."

"Snakes, snakes, flee their nest, up into the castle crest." The man giggled, pleased with his rhymes. "Spread their venom, let them loose. To kill the blood girl and tie the noose."

"What fine riddles you spin," I said calmly, crouching before him, drawing my blade slowly. It glinted in the firelight of the sconces. "Tell me, snake, how well can you hiss without a forked tongue?"

He shuffled, shaking his wrists against the chains, before leaning forward and spitting on my face. He broke into more deranged laughter. András's sword was drawn in an instant, but I put my hand out and smiled, wiping the goop from my face. "I

don't like it when pests get into my castle. Would you like to know what I do with them?" I smiled sweetly as I ran a finger down my blade, then let him see the anger flashing in my eyes. "I cut off their heads."

His eyes bore into my skull as I stood and slashed my hand, my new power effortlessly dismembering his cackling head from his neck. The woman beside him shrieked and the others had the good sense to look frightened—truly frightened at my display of power.

I'd gauge they had seen blood magic before, judging by the terror that had entered their eyes when they'd first seen my red magic. It seemed Sylvie's cultists weren't just loyal to her. They were afraid of her, of all the things she could do with the blood magic in her veins.

I turned to the woman beside him. "Who is Sylvie working with? Tell me and I'll spare you this fate."

She shivered as I stepped closer, looming over her menacingly. I let her see the conviction in my eyes, for I would not hesitate to end her in an instant. The old Kitarni would never have been so ruthless, but Sylvie had made me into a savage thing. I would not bow, I would not bend, and I certainly wouldn't allow her to break me.

"The Dark Queen has ..." The woman swallowed, looking at András for help, as if he'd fucking save her. It was almost laughable. "The Dark Queen has spies among the witches. They set this up. It was all to take out the key players."

Sure, now tell me something I didn't know. I toyed with the end of my blade, picking beneath my blood-crusted nails while I waited. The silence stretched and I knew the cultists were growing more panicked with every passing second.

"I know what they planned," I said after making the woman stew for a bit. "I know witches were involved. Give me a name or I'll see to it Death himself arranges a special welcome when you arrive in his hell."

"No," she gasped, her brown eyes wide with terror. I knew that would get a reaction, even if it was a lie. "No, wait, I ..." She banged her head back against the wall in frustration. "If I tell you, she'll kill me."

"If you don't, you'll meet your maker much sooner and, unlike your friend here, I won't make it quick."

She looked between András and me and, finally appearing to accept defeat, slumped against the wall. "It was the water coven. The High Witch Viktória planned everything. It was the perfect opportunity to cause discord from within." She licked her lips. "The water witches were supposed to give us cover to escape, only ..."

My eyes narrowed. "Only what?"

"After they doused the fire witches' light, they turned on us instead, killing any they could. In the chaos from the crowd, they were unsuccessful in completing their task."

"Gee, you think?" I scraped a hand through my hair, sighing. Betrayals within betrayals. What I didn't understand was how that

would benefit the water witch in the slightest. "So Viktória used the cult to assassinate the lord and lady in waiting of Mistvellen, as well as several of the realm's key players. And then murder the murderers?"

A smart plan, if poorly executed. Removing the cultists from the equation—and the ability for their tongues to wag—meant no blame would fall on the witches, giving them a clean getaway. My only question was ...

"Why?" András asked before I could. He cocked his blond head, his lips pursed. "Budapest is a stronghold for the water coven. They are well-equipped to deal with the threat of the cult. Assassinating you and Dante is a bold move, and highly risky. What reason do they have to turn on their kith?"

The woman shook her head in disbelief, a sly smile forming on her lips. "You are blind to what is right before your eyes."

The words struck me as odd, as though we weren't in on some little secret. A frustrated growl tore through me. "Does Viktória follow the Dark Queen? Has the coven turned to dark magic?"

"The same dark power that lives in you?"

I turned to the owner of that voice. A cultist who'd been silent, half hidden in shadow at the end of the row. "My magic is not the same as Sylvie's," I said firmly. "I am not the same."

His eyes glittered. "Not yet, but the change has already begun. You will soon heed its call if you don't die by witches' hands first."

A tremor rolled through me at those words. No, it couldn't be true. I controlled my magic. It didn't control me. But a small

voice in my head had me questioning if that was true. The black eyes, the black magic, the beast who seemed to roar louder, take up more space inside me ... Fuck.

"Silence," András barked, seeing me visibly shaken. The man just smiled, sinking back into shadow as he rested his head against the wall. He didn't seem frightened, just pleased with a job well done. They might not have succeeded in killing me and the others, but discord and the seed of doubt had indeed spread.

Why would Viktória do this? Had enough witches not died already?

Endless possibilities ran through my mind, everything falling into place, piece by piece. On my wedding night, I'd seen water witches leaving the hall not long before the bells had tolled and "Fire" had been shouted through the keep. I'd thought it odd, but hadn't investigated, assuming, like many others, they had simply wanted to walk the gardens or take fresh air.

Of course, the fires had been little more than a diversion to grant the coven good favour amongst Mistvellen. Water witches had been killed that night, which I'm sure wasn't part of the High Witch's plan, but it did make it an easy way for cultists to don witches' robes and dresses and enter our keep without question.

The first scheme. Followed by tonight's assassination attempt. I kept thinking of Viktória's face—the sharp line of her lips, those grey eyes that shone like steel. And then it clicked.

"Viktória didn't join Sylvie's ranks to protect Budapest from her wrath, did she?"

The woman looked at me, her pebble eyes gleeful as I worked through my thoughts. "She did not. The High Witch of the water coven was much more selfish in her reasoning. She didn't do it for her home, or even for her people. She did it for revenge."

I glanced at András, then turned my attention back to the cultist. "Tell me. Tell me the name of the one she avenges."

"Poor witch." The woman tutted. "You killed someone very dear to her, Kitarni of the dark blood. You know of whom I speak."

I did know. Gods save me, but I knew all too well. My heart rattled in its cage, pumping blood loudly in my ears. I almost laughed with the absurdity of it all. I hadn't even known the woman the cultist spoke of had birthed a daughter, but now the similarities between both women suddenly rang with crystal clarity. I'd recognised the familiar features. Now it was too late.

"Who?" András asked, frowning.

"Someone who burned for their crimes," I said grimly. "The High Witch tried to destroy us, my dear András, because I killed Caitlin Vargo. I killed Viktória's mother."

TWENTY-SEVEN

DANTE

S creams echoed off every crack and crevice of the black cliffs as I made my way silently through the maze. It was so dark I had to channel my inner táltos, allowing my eyes to adjust and give me a better line of sight. The maze was more complex than I'd been able to foresee from the mountain behind me.

Doorways channelled into the rock, forming prison cells and torture chambers, demons hacking at their victims with delight. I didn't look inside those cells, didn't listen to the occupants' whispered pleas or deranged babbling.

This was the Under World. A place where only the worst sinners were treated to Death's indulgent ministrations of pain. I patted my pocket for the fiftieth time, ensuring the vial of Kitarni's blood was nestled safely inside, along with the precise instructions for a spell hastily copied by Margit from the tome she'd been consulting.

If the spell didn't work ... I shook my head and set my jaw. It *would* work. Even if I didn't make it back in one piece, the crown must. My wife was awaiting my return, as was the Kingdom of Hungary. I would not let them down.

Muffled words reached my ears and I stiffened, squeezing behind a rock as best I could—which was kind of hard with my bulky frame. My palm tightened around my dagger, and I readied to fight as two demons approached.

They stopped right by my hiding place, and I held my breath as their words reached me.

"—expects her to retrieve it. It's only a matter of time."

One of the demons hissed, and I realised belatedly that it was laughing. "She won't get very far. He knows the smell of her blood. The moment she steps into this realm, he will have her."

They were talking about the crown. I released a small breath. Of course Death would know if Sylvie returned. He would have tortured her before exiling her to the endless sea of souls where she had dwelled, formless, for centuries. He would know the ripe stench of her tainted blood. I raised my eyes to the flashing skies. A small mercy, at least, that she wouldn't be stupid enough to enter his domain. One less enemy for me to watch out for.

It dawned on me that he would likely have known if Kitarni had come instead of me. If he didn't know her blood, he sure could track her through those scars on her back. Thinking of whatever horrors he might have subjected her to made my magic float around me, dark and stormy as the sky above. If I ever made

280

it out of here and Kitarni did return the crown to him, I'd make that fucker remove those scars if it was the last thing I did.

The demons' voices dropped, and I strained to hear what they were saying. All I got were three words. Crown. Queen. Bargain.

My skin prickled, a foreboding chill that had nothing to do with the freezing temperature of this realm running down my spine. A bad feeling I couldn't shake.

Fate had told Kitarni months ago that she'd wanted her to retrieve the crown—that she was the only one who could. Since then, Death had made a bargain with Kitarni, asking her to retrieve it in his stead. So why, then, were his minions prepared for Sylvie to return? Unless Death had kept some vital information to himself.

Unless he knew the crown was *here*. None of it made sense and for the life of me, I couldn't understand why he'd keep that from Kitarni. Not without having something sinister in mind for when she came hunting for it.

Anger writhed around my bones, heating my blood so much my magic rose to the surface. Black lifted in smoking tendrils from my skin. Black and ... red? I stared in alarm as blood-red smoke curled around the black tenderly, as if binding together.

Gods.

My eyes widened as the realisation hit me. We had delved too deep. Giving Kitarni too much of my magic's very essence had morphed it into something wild and untamed. Having tread so perilously close to Kitarni's source power, we'd somehow

transferred our magic, adapting into an unlikely creature.

Her power was intoxicating, alluring me like a moth drawn to flame. I wanted to unleash it, to feel the gratification of instant death. I realised what it was to hold her strength—what it felt like to have such power in my hands. She was a goddess of death, and I, the faithful servant by her side.

I stepped out from behind my stone and the demons hissed in surprise, shock widening their slitted pupils. Unlike the demon in the Middle World, I could see these ones clearly. Their forms rippled as if made from the shadows themselves, but their faces were twisted, their teeth filed into fangs, their bodies elongated and *wrong*. They reminded me of snakes that hadn't quite shed their skins, peeling and fraying at the surface.

My magic flared in my palm as I stepped towards them. They towered over me, which was a rare thing given my height. But, even so, I felt like I looked down on them, not an inch of fear flooding through me. I might have been in their realm, but I had the power here.

A commander of the dead, eager to bend them to my whims. "You're going to tell me everything I want to know," I said in a low, deep voice. "Or I'm going to drop your heads at your master's feet before I leave this place. It's your choice."

They looked between each other and I smiled nastily, letting my power flood through the valley, coating the ground in a blanket of red and black. They dipped their heads ever so slightly and my grin grew wider.

"Let's start with the crown. Then we're going to have a little chat about this so-called bargain."

I'd spent the better half of a day travelling through the maze with the demons as my guide. Unlike the one summoned by Caitlin, these ones seemed submissive—eager to be rid of my presence. I wasn't stupid enough to think it was only my newfound power that prevented them from ripping off my head and I kept my hand firmly clasped around the hilt of my dagger as we moved.

The sky remained unchanged despite the passing of time. A perpetual snowstorm, lashed with lightning and rolling dark clouds. The thundering of my heart was as loud as the booms and cracks above, and I couldn't help but feel the cold prick of fear as we drew closer to the castle on high.

We'd begun our ascent several hours ago, but it was slow going up the twisting spire as we clung to the cliff face. In many parts, the pathway had crumbled, the rockface giving way to fatal drops onto sharp black rock below.

One wrong step was all it would take.

After another few hours of biting cold and winds strong enough to send us all toppling, we made it to the castle. I stared at the looming keep, all black stone and sharp edges. If there was any light in the Under World, I knew the pitch black of the castle exterior would drink it all in.

This place was the epitome of emptiness and despair. And I was walking right into it.

The demons led me down a narrow ravine filled with a thick black substance—certainly not water, at any rate—lined with bones and skulls. A promising start.

"There isss a grate at the end which will take you into the dungeonsss. You will find what you ssseek there."

I looked at my companions and smiled. "And I suppose the minute I'm gone you'll run to your master to inform him of my presence?" They glanced at each other and my lips twitched into a grin. Right then. "I'm afraid that won't do boys. But I thank you for your trouble all the same."

Without hesitation, I kicked one square in the stomach, sending it flying off the cliff with a scream quickly drowned out by the wind. The other swiped with curved claws and I feinted, then impaled it with my dagger and charged towards the edge, pulling my blade back at the last minute before it fell.

The steel came back sticky with black blood and I wiped it on my leathers grimly, looking to the ravine filled with dead, forgotten things.

Yes, because this delightful black pool where the grate lay submerged in screamed sunshine and rainbows. I sighed. Just another day in the life. I sheathed my dagger and pulled my swords out, jumping into the ravine.

Dust flew up as my boots slapped the ground and I half-crouched, following the trail of bones. Thunder boomed

and lightning crashed moments later, not too far from where I was standing. I frowned as the storm seemed to deepen, the wind whipping at my clothes like a million clawed fingers.

Thunder split apart the sky and lightning cracked closer still. It was sign enough for me. I ran, throwing caution to the wind and sprinting as a trail of white-hot whips followed my footsteps.

Hadur give me strength. I roared, diving into the pool of black as lightning exploded right where I'd jumped, so close the hair on my head and arms rose to attention.

The not-water was cold as winter frost, immediately seizing my bones. I couldn't see, couldn't move as it sucked me down into the depths. My clothes and swords were so heavy, but I dared not drop the blades, carefully sheathing them at my back and swimming deeper.

I kicked furiously, blindly aiming for the grate as I closed my eyes and swam for dear life. My hands grazed something hard, skimming over the castle wall and I winced as the jagged surface sliced my palm, then something rounded met my hands. Bars. My fingers curled into fists around the cool metal and I pulled with all my strength, gritting my teeth as my muscles burned with the effort.

With a clank, the grate pulled free and I kicked hard, letting momentum propel me forward. I opened my eyes as the surface drew closer and a light cut through the pitch black. So close now, just a few pumps away from precious air.

I should have known better.

Something wrapped around my ankle, yanking me back towards the pool outside the castle walls. I drew a sword and slashed blindly, unable to see my attacker. Fear sank deeper than the chill in my bones and I grew sluggish from the cold. The lack of oxygen tightened my lungs, causing my vision to darken with each passing second.

I thrashed my sword wildly, meeting something solid that emitted a piercing shriek of pain, even below water. The tentacle withdrew and I took my chance, surging through the water with arm and sword, aiming for that small sliver of light. I broke the surface eagerly, gulping down air and half choking as I found purchase on solid ground and made for the safety of the keep.

Two more slimy tentacles clasped around my ankles and I stumbled once again, my sword clattering uselessly to the ground as I was swept into the air. The thing screeched below me and at last I saw it through the hole I'd just climbed from.

A thousand lidless black eyes glared at me from a bulbous face, a slimy substance dripping like acid from its body. But the teeth ... the teeth on the damn thing were like a million daggers in an endless spiral.

"Not today, you ugly fuck," I roared, grabbing a sconce from the wall and hurling it into the creature's eyes as it lifted me.

It shrieked louder this time—so loud I feared it would have every demon guard in the castle running to investigate—and dropped me into the water. Fear urged my legs to scramble out of the cess pool and onto dry land.

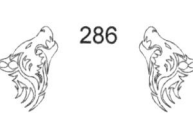

I wasn't sure what summoned the power next. Sheer determination, a kind of panicked desperation to survive, or blind rage and a desire to kill this fucking thing. I could have walked away while it burned.

I chose violence.

Magic whipped out of me, black and red and hungry for a taste of death. I felt something unfamiliar unfurl in my chest and stretch, opening its jaws wide before chomping down. I raised my palms and, where moments before I saw an ugly-ass demon, I found nothing but ash, disintegrating and sinking slowly into the blackness whence it came.

I looked at my hands in awe, turning them over slowly as the beast inside me simply yawned and curled up, having fed on its meal.

"Istenanya's tits." If this was what Kitarni felt like when using her power, I wanted more of it.

Together, we were formidable. With the crown? We'd be unstoppable.

TWENTY-EIGHT

KITARNI

My dreams were plagued with stitched faces and burning fields, the scent of smouldering lavender acrid in my nose as I gasped awake. My body was slick with sweat, my temple feverish to the touch.

I yawned, swinging my legs off the bed and putting my face in my hands. Rest wouldn't find me tonight. Perhaps a run would clear my head.

"Trouble sleeping?"

I jolted upright, snatching my blade from beneath the pillow and brandishing it before me, searching the shadows for the voice. I knew. I knew before she stepped into the dim moonlight, who it was.

"Sylvie," I hissed, looking around the room for any other threats. When satisfied, I raked my gaze over her frame, noting the odd shimmer and distortion to her body. "You're not really here, are you?"

Her full lips curved into a wicked grin as she drew closer and I held my blade higher in warning. If she'd been a vision when she was newly resurrected, she was devastating now. Her light brown skin gleamed and her cheeks flushed with colour. A gown seemingly made of smoke clung to her full figure and she watched with dark, catlike eyes lined with kohl.

"What you see is but an illusion. A little trick I learned from you." She clicked her tongue, shaking her head in amusement. "A clever spell, but all it bought you was time."

I smiled at her nastily. "Clever enough to fool you. And you're wrong, it bought much more than that."

"Ah, yes. A wedding for the ages. Covens and clans come from across the Kingdom of Hungary to support your cause, though I hear there is trouble in paradise." She cocked her head and flashed her pointed teeth. "You never really know who you can trust."

I turned my back on her—the ultimate insult, meant to show her I didn't consider her a threat. A blatant lie, obviously. I could smell her power, feel it enveloping her frame. It was terrifying, but I wouldn't tremble or shrink before her.

"Your little coup made no difference. Did you think to overthrow my cadre from within my own walls?" I shrugged. "My family are alive and well. *All of them.*"

A small hiss of annoyance came from behind me and I smiled to myself. "Just so you know, your cultists are all dead. It brought me great pleasure to incinerate them with my power. I'm short

a High Witch, but it worked out for the best. The pledge was already made, Sylvie. The Blue Coven witches answer to me now." I looked over my shoulder, lifting my chin with a satisfactory smirk. "They all do."

Sylvie bared her teeth. "It changes nothing. My cultists will swarm your fields like flies, spreading corruption from your bloated bellies. Make no mistake, blood of my blood, I will have your power and I will have your city. The witches of this kingdom shall be wiped off the face of the earth and the world will bow before their Dark Queen."

Her words dripped like poison into my ears, worming its way into my heart. I wanted to tremble at the hate rolling off her in waves, but I stood my ground, turned, and slowly stepped towards her until our faces were inches apart.

"The thing about flies is they're attracted to waste. Like you. You spin your words from pretty lips, but they fall on deaf ears, Sylvie. Because I will kill you. I will not stop until I crush your heart in your chest and melt the flesh from your body, because no one threatens the ones I love. You are a miserable, misguided creature, and it's time the world forgot your name. So keep telling me, Sylvie, how you plan to blot out everything I hold dear. It only serves as fodder to feed my rage."

Her power misted around her, the echo of my own. Blood-red and angry as an asp readying to strike. She searched my eyes and when I did not balk, she sneered. "We march on the morrow. Cherish what little time you have left, girl, because when I'm

done with you, there'll be nothing left of your soul to send the horseman." She paused, a cruel glimmer entering her dark gaze. "Perhaps I'll keep your new husband for myself. He'd be a fitting pet to entertain me."

I snapped. My power burst out of me, exploding up the walls and fanning across the ceiling like living flames of red and black, crackling and licking at her feet. Her illusion wavered, but she could not be touched.

Sylvie's eyes widened and she shrank back, half awed and half afraid as she studied the room, then studied me. I knew if I looked in the mirror, my eyes would be pitch black right now, but it didn't scare me. The knowledge that Sylvie was afraid bolstered me, giving me the confidence I had so desperately needed to face this foe. "What is this new trickery?" she asked quietly.

"It's no trick. Just a glimmer of what I can do. Now, if you don't mind, kindly get the fuck out of my room. I'll see you on the battlefield, Sylvie. And I promise you, I will not hold back."

I increased my magic, sending it searing through her form, cutting her magic at the source until she was forced to end the spell from whatever creepy cult den she resided in. When I was done, I sat back on the bed and breathed a sigh of relief, clutching my shaking hands before me.

It had taken all my false bravado to look at that bitch without my knees knocking and my body melting into a puddle of fear. My power had grown, but alone, it was not enough.

I rolled onto the bed, pawing at Dante's empty space and

grabbing a tunic I'd scrounged from his chest. It smelled like him and I inhaled the scent deeply like an obsessive stalker, clutching it to my chest.

"Wherever you are, Dante, hurry home to me," I whispered, allowing a single tear to slide down my cheek.

I'd never felt his loss more keenly than now. Even after months of not speaking, of longing stares and snide remarks, the empty space beside me seemed like a chasm. The thought of him being trapped in the Under World, of being found and tortured, was like a hand clawing at my heart, threatening to tear it from my chest.

The anger in my chest was raw and real, but it was tempered by the knowledge that he was actively trying to make things right. My dark knight. He was better than a hero in a storybook. Flawed and learning from mistakes, which only endeared him to me further. He'd gone to the Under World for me, for pity's sake, even though I knew, deep inside, that he'd done it for himself too—an act of redemption for his past actions.

But deeper than that I knew ... he did it because he loved me. He. Loved. Me.

And I'd been so caught up in the whole public affair of our wedding and the aftermath of Viktória's betrayal that I hadn't stopped to consider just how much that really meant. How much I'd been denying to myself for so long.

"Fuck." Leaping off the bed, I quickly dressed into fighting leathers, strapping on my sword, dagger, and the throwing knives

292

at my belt. A run wasn't going to cut it. I dragged a hairbrush through my unruly waves and managed a pathetic braid that would make Mama cringe.

When I threw open my door, I jumped upon finding a figure standing there. "András," I said, breathing heavily, one hand to my chest. "You scared the shit out of me. What are you doing here?"

He raised a brow. "Guarding you, obviously. After what happened on your wedding night, we haven't the luxury of feeling safe in our own home."

"Viktória has been dealt with. Even if there are witches still loyal to her, they'd be pretty stupid to try their luck at killing me now. I don't need a guard."

His next words were quiet, barely a whisper in the empty corridor. "What about a friend?"

I put my hand on my waist and popped a hip. "That I can accept. What I need right now, though, is a sparring buddy. You up for it?"

He grinned, pulling me close and pressing a kiss to my head—not in a romantic way, but a familial gesture. That's what I adored about András. He didn't give a shit about what was correct or otherwise frowned upon. He just ... was. Unapologetically so.

"Correction: you need someone to release all that pent-up Bárány rage on." I smiled sheepishly and he bumped my shoulder playfully. "You're lucky I love you enough to take the bruises."

I rolled my eyes. "So dramatic. But if it makes you feel better,

I'll make sure to refrain from whacking that pretty face of yours. We might need it to glean any gossip from the witches at court."

"Always the ulterior motive," he said, his smile suggesting he had no issue with that idea whatsoever. "I shall charm the skirts—or pants—off whomever your ladyship requires. Though I'm not sure what you hope to hear from them. After Viktória, the witches have been walking on eggshells, not a toe out of line. Do you really think there will be more attacks?"

I stopped, halting him with a hand on his arm. "Honestly? I am more concerned about how they will take orders from another High Witch. I don't know these covens, András, and I don't fully trust them. I just need us all to remain alert. Especially now that ..."

His eyes narrowed. "Don't make me make you finish that sentence Kitarni."

My stomach did an uncomfortable little lurch as I slowly looked up at him and sighed. "I had an unexpected—and unwelcome—visitor in my chambers tonight. A message from the Dark Queen. The cultists march tomorrow. We have a few days at most before war is at our gates."

András snorted. "And you call me dramatic. She should shove a trumpet up her ass to announce her if she loves an entrance so much. It would certainly be easier."

Despite my trepidation, I laughed, looping my arm around his. "Will you promise me something? Don't ever change. You're a little ball of sunshine in a fucked-up world ... and we can all use

 294

a little more light."

He reminded me of a peacock the way he preened from that comment. "I promise, Kit, I'll always be me. Who else would I be?"

My heart swelled, feeling warm and fuzzy. "That's what Eszter calls me," I said softly. "Her nickname for me."

"Then hers alone it shall be."

"No, I like it. I like being reminded that there is more to me than fire and blood."

"You are more than your magic. You can be the wrathful blood witch, the lady of Mistvellen, the High Witch of the Green Coven ... and Kit."

I chuckled. "I wonder sometimes, what it would be like to remain just Kit. The girl who, in another life, might have travelled the world and explored the ends of the earth."

András took my hand in his own, patting it fondly. "That's where you went wrong. You could never be 'just' anyone. The world is too small for even you, Kitarni. And once we get out of this mess, I'll prove it."

TWENTY-NINE

DANTE

I slunk through the halls like a mouse underfoot, darting into shadows and hiding behind crevices when voices echoed down the walkways. Thankfully, the corridors were mostly empty in the dungeons of the castle.

No one escaped Death's prison cells, so why bother guarding those destined for an eternity in hell? I could only imagine the most horrible of souls wound up in his keep, tortured by his own hands or perhaps their own waking nightmares.

Out of curiosity, I peered into several cells as I passed. The inhabitants didn't even register my passing as they looked blankly at things I couldn't see. I'd bet a full coin purse they'd been driven mad, broken beyond repair. I pitied them, but not enough to set them free.

After a time, I ducked behind a crate in what appeared to be a storage room, pulling the vial of blood from my pocket. Margit had spelled it so the blood would double as a wayfaring spell—

kind of like the crystals that had led Kitarni to me several few months ago—and my entrance to the pocket realm.

The vial glowed faintly, which was a sure sign I was getting closer to the crown. One of the cells nearby must have been Sylvie's for a time. Before she was sent to the river of souls to float, totally coherent but trapped in a form that could not touch, smell, taste ... anything that made one alive in any sense.

My lips twisted. It was a punishment I wouldn't wish on anyone. Well, okay, maybe Sylvie. She deserved everything she'd got.

I pressed the vial to my chest and straightened, listening carefully for any sounds. It was clear. The vial glimmered as I moved, spotting a stairwell descending even deeper underground. I treaded carefully, conscious of every scrape of my boots on stone.

The vial exploded with light as I made it to the bottom and I blinked a few times to adjust from the dank, dark hallway to blinding brightness.

A single cell stood at the end of the corridor and I knew in my heart that was the one. It reeked with bitterness and revenge and, perhaps it was my imagination, but I could almost smell the scent of burning flesh, as if the memory of her death followed her into the Under World.

That alone was a cruel touch. Death wasn't without finesse.

I crept along the corridor, which was silent and still as a graveyard, but I couldn't shake the sense that it had all been too easy. My hands twitched by my sides, itching to shed more blood

with my blades. Regardless of the eerie emptiness, I had no choice but to keep moving forward.

The cell door hung ajar and I stalked into the space, checking the shadows for any assailants, not that the vial—which was now lit up like a fucking sun—left room for any. This was it. I knew it as surely as I knew the back of my hands.

A shaky breath escaped me as I uncorked the stopper, smearing its liquid upon the walls of the dingy cell and the hay-lined stone floor. After pulling out the sheaf of paper crumpled in my pocket and reciting the spell, all I had to do was wait.

For a moment I thought the spell had failed me, but then a soft hum seemed to vibrate from the wall, a shimmering vortex opening where the stone surface had been. And at the end ...

A gold crown embedded with rubies and emeralds glinted from an altar at the far end of an open, unfurnished chamber. Whispers of an ancient dialect, unfamiliar to my ears, echoed through the vast space. The power that rushed out to meet me made me shiver, phantom pains skittering down my body, as well as an insatiable need to claim the crown for my own.

I took one step through the vortex, feeling the magic cling to my skin like a thin veil of snow, chilling my already dampened flesh. After shoving the vial and paper in my pocket, I stuffed my hands under my armpits and walked through the seemingly endless portal into the pocket realm.

When I emerged, my clothes and boots were fully dry, no longer sticking to me. A small mercy. My lips felt dry and cracked,

my throat raw as I looked at that crown, calling to me like a damn siren right out of one of the fantasy books in my library.

Nothing stirred in the never-ending expanse of grey that surrounded me. Not a sound followed except for that haunting melody, luring me closer, closer, like a moth to a flame. My body wanted that crown more than anything, my hand already reaching for it despite knowing how badly it could burn.

My fingers curled around the rim of that crown and I gasped as power reverberated through my body, flickers of past gods who'd once worn it flashing through my mind. Benevolent beings—kind and good—twisted into sour, bitter creatures, driven mad by power and a lust to rule.

I saw glimmers of gold and light-shrouded kingdoms, turned dark and despairing as blood rained down from the skies and spilled from the throats of other gods. The breath caught in my throat and I choked, tears streaming down my face as the horror— the fucking destruction this crown had wrought ripped at my very soul.

When the memories stopped flashing, I thudded to my knees, gasping and clutching at my heart with one hand.

Even the gods had not been saved from its lure.

What kind of man would I be to bring this crown into the world of the living? It should stay buried and forgotten, lost to anyone who would abuse its power. Especially those who already had too much of it.

I looked around me at the expanse of nothingness and yelled

my frustration, the sound seeming to echo back to me in mockery. It was the wrong question to ask.

The question I should be asking wasn't what kind of man I would be, but instead ...

"What kind of husband would I be if I gave this to my wife?!"

"I guess you'll never know."

I swivelled, turning to see Fate stepping through the portal into the pocket realm. My skin prickled as she perused me, those sapphire eyes cutting like knives before her attention shifted to the item in my hand. "The crown," she said, her voice awed, her gaze reverent. "How long I have wished to possess its power."

I stepped back, hackles raised like a cornered dog as I drew my blade. "You'll have to wait a little longer."

She smiled, the sharp cut of her blonde hair swaying as she cocked her head, a hungry gleam in her eyes. "You would stand in my way? I am immortal, boy. No mere blade can score my flesh."

"Who said anything about swords?" I let my power rise, basking in the pleasure of its eagerness to maim and murder.

Fate fell preternaturally still as she spied the black and red whisps. "That's not possible. Magic cannot be traded like common goods. How did you get this power?"

"Blood." I sneered, stepping closer, my smile widening as she stepped back. *Interesting.* "The answer has always been written in blood. And you shan't spill a drop of it. "

Her lovely face twisted into something dark and menacing. "I won't need to. The crown will destroy you and that wretched

witch. It was not made for mortals."

"Neither was it meant for your pretty head, but it didn't stop any gods before you. Kitarni and I will end this war, Sylvie will pay for her crimes, and you will remain in this realm, tied to a husband you do not want, trapped in a world you did not choose. I'll be sure to give Kitarni your best when I make it back."

The shadows pooling at Fate's feet deepened and her face flashed ever so briefly into something monstrous and dark. "Foolish táltos. You aren't going back. You aren't going anywhere."

Death stepped through the portal beside her, his robes billowing. He lifted one skeletal finger and wagged it just once. "You come into my realm uninvited, murder my guards and my pet, threaten my wife, and attempt to steal my crown. Now that's just bad manners."

I dropped to my knees as my throat closed, agonising pain rippling through my veins, crippling as my body bent against my will to bow before his feet. My teeth gritted together so hard I thought they'd snap.

He stalked closer, his hand outstretched for the crown still clutched in my fingers. Everything grew cold and impossibly dark as stars flashed behind my eyes and my vision blurred.

I sensed my end approaching and, for a moment, the paralysing fear of being stuck in this place seemed to reverberate tenfold in my mind. "You knew I was here," I managed to choke out as I clawed at my throat.

His voice sounded triumphant as he smoothed his robe

down. "From the very moment you arrived. The dead guards ... well, an unfortunate, but necessary evil. The crown is worth more than every soul in this plane."

I squeezed my eyes shut. I'd walked right into their trap even knowing something wasn't right. It was so blatantly fucking obvious now that I wanted to roar. They'd not been able to enter the pocket realm without Sylvie's blood or, in this case, that of her descendant. We may as well have handed the crown over on a silver platter.

My words were little more than garbled rasps as I struggled to speak. Death waved his hand lazily and I sucked in air, gasping and spluttering as I placed a hand to my throat. When I spoke again, my voice was hoarse and cracked.

"The demons ... you could have closed the gate Caitlin opened, you bastard. There was never any risk of them getting into the Middle Word. You manipulated us into coming here, hoping we would fall into your trap."

"Right again, wolf pup, though I was expecting the girl instead of you. Still, I'll take what I can get. My wife is ever so eager to exact her revenge. I expect it'll break Kitarni more to see you suffer."

Anger had my power flaring in an explosion of red, but Death simply waved his hand once more, erecting an invisible barrier which my magic splashed against harmlessly. He laughed cruelly. "You have no power here. You are mine until I tire of your existence and my wife requires a new plaything. Now hand

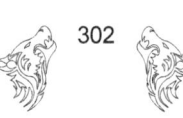

it over."

Fate grinned and I shook my head slowly. They were all the same. Sylvie, Death, Fate ... Time had done nothing to temper their greedy, petty natures. Quite the opposite in fact. But I would not rot in a fucking cell in this godsforsaken place. I would not forsake *her*.

"You want the crown?" I asked, rising to my feet. "You'll have to pry it from my head."

"No!" Death hissed, floating towards me, skeletal fingers reaching out. It all happened so fast I didn't have time to really register my movements.

What does a predator do when cornered and afraid? They bite. So I did the only reckless gods damned thing I could think of.

I put the crown on my head.

THIRTY

KITARNI

"Come back to me."

I lay my head against Dante's chest, comforted by the steady heartbeat and the gentle rise and fall of his torso. After running myself ragged with András over the last few days, then training with both sword and magic, I'd fallen asleep in a chair by Dante's side, having woken myself with a snort and an unsightly pool of dribble where my head had been resting on the table.

I sighed, scrubbing a hand over my face. The hour was late, judging by the candles that had melted down into small stubs since starting my vigil. After Sylvie's visit yesterday morning, I'd barely slept a wink and could hardly keep my eyes open during meetings with our allies. Thankfully, most of the clans had agreed to stand by Mistvellen and those too cowardly to join the fight had slunk back to their territories.

Viktória had burned for her crimes, just like her mother. An

304

ironic and fitting end for their bloodline. Several water witches involved in the coup had joined the High Witch after refusing to bend the knee, but many seemed relieved to be rid of their dictator and any agreements with the cultists.

Just in case, I had Lukasz and Erika keeping a watchful eye on them. One step—one toe—out of line, and I would incinerate them without a second thought, trials be damned.

We were in the middle of a war. I hadn't the time for rebellious witches, nor the patience, which is why I'd stayed far away from anyone likely to set a spark to my fragile temper. There was a hungry beast on permanent patrol these days and it didn't seem satisfied, no matter how many cultists I fed it. I hardly wanted it turning on allies, too, lest I really let the world see the monster I was becoming.

I sat up, stroking Dante's hand with my thumb, studying the lines of his face. A muscle in his jaw ticked, his eyes shifting beneath the lids as though dreaming. My brows pulled together, my heart constricting with worry. To any onlooker, one might mistake him for sleeping, but I knew he was living a nightmare, hunting for the crown.

He should have found it by now. He should be here, in my arms, smirking with those damn dimples or whispering dirty little nothings in my ear. Gods, I had never wanted to hear his voice so badly or look into those brown eyes ringed with gold.

My wolf lord.

Dante's body spasmed suddenly, his whole back lifting off

the table, his mouth opening in a silent scream.

"Dante!" I leapt up, my chair crashing to the floor as I leaned over him, sliding my hands under his head to prevent his skull from cracking on the table. He continued shuddering violently and I clutched him tighter, my heart threatening to crack out of my chest.

"What's going on?" Margit cried as she raced down the steps, restraining his arms as he thrashed wildly. "What's happened to him?"

"H-he just started convulsing," I stammered.

Blood began trickling out of his ears, his mouth, and all sense of calm fled from my bones. My voice sounded shrill to my own ears as I shouted, "I thought his spirit form couldn't be harmed in the Under World?"

"His body cannot, but any physical harm to the spirit can still break the mind." She shook her head, her brow creasing as she gazed down at Dante. "This is no mere demon or lesser magic. Something bigger and more powerful is causing this. Something I can't begin to understand."

I peered at her with wide eyes, tears threatening to fall down my cheeks as he shook in my arms. "I don't care what it is, he can't stay there like that. Pull him out Margit."

Margit's eyes snapped to mine as she pressed down on Dante's bulging arms. "Kitarni—"

"Pull. Him. Out."

A strangled sound of frustration clawed from her throat. "If

something is trapping his mind or he's being tethered by *someone* in the Under World, he might not come back the same. The mind is a fragile thing, it must be treated with care. You know the risk."

I bit my lip hard enough to draw blood. Dante writhed beneath me, the lines around his eyes pulling taut and his teeth gnashing. "We have no choice. If we don't get him out of there, there will be nothing left to bring back."

Her blue eyes hardened like diamonds, but she shoved her sleeves up, revealing smooth, milky skin and soft hands that she pressed to Dante's sweaty forehead. She began chanting the words to that ancient spell. Forbidden, haunting words that made the hair on my arms stand on end and a swell of magic gust around the room.

Paper tore from books and the blood dripping from Dante's ears and nose began to float above his still thrashing body. I placed my palms to his chest, ignoring the way the wind pulled at my hair and tugged at my clothes, focusing only on sending healing energy into his very soul from the golden glow at my fingertips.

Margit gasped under the onslaught of the wind, but not once did she falter or stumble. I gritted my teeth as a power stronger than any I'd ever sensed filled the room, settling over me, threatening to consume me.

At some stage, I felt András's presence beside me, his body wrapping around me like a human shield as I continued to heal Dante. My bones felt like they would snap, my skin threatening to peel away from my face.

A surge of power suddenly blasted from Dante's body, and the three of us were sent hurtling into the walls, András grabbing me to his chest and taking the brunt of the fall. When I looked up, the room was silent, but magic radiated in waves from a source in the centre of the chamber.

I crawled to Dante, one agonising elbow and knee at a time as I fought to reach my husband. Blood dripped from my nose onto the cold stone floor and the pressure in my head felt like it would explode. But I kept fighting, kept crawling and, when I had clawed my way to standing, the sight on the table made the breath whoosh from my lungs.

A golden crown bejewelled with rubies and emeralds rested on my husband's head, the sheer power and otherness of it still pumping magic out in waves. Dante's skin was paler than the moon, his flesh seeming to tighten and hollow out with every passing second.

Gritting my teeth, I reached my arm over, curled my fingers around the gilded metal, and yanked the crown from his head.

The moment he was freed, the power sucked back in on itself and the room stilled. I wilted, resting my head against Dante's chest momentarily as I panted. When I looked up, I was relieved to see colour returning to his cheeks, the skin filling in to return his smile lines and the normal set of his eyes.

He was unconscious, but breathing. After the toll the crown had taken, I suspected his body would need rest to recover from the onslaught and whatever else had happened in the Under

World.

"Goddess above. He really did it. He actually put the crown on his head." I stared at Dante, eyes wide, body trembling as belatedly, I realised what that meant. What the crown had done to him—what it would soon do to me.

This was but a taste of its power—I knew it. It was going to tear me apart, and I ... I was fucking terrified. Swallowing back my fear and triple checking Dante's chest was still moving, I glanced at the others.

"Is everyone okay?"

András groaned as he lifted himself from the floor, his hair mussed and a fresh slice in his cheek. He propped his chin on one hand, blinking profusely. "Define 'okay'."

I sighed in relief, my gaze raking over Margit. She appeared unharmed, thank the gods.

"It worked," she said, eyes wide as she shook her head. "It fucking worked." She stood, dusting off her skirts, her whole frame shuddering as a long breath escaped her. "Don't ever ask me to do that again."

"Never," I agreed.

She huffed, smoothing back her locks and immediately gathering supplies from around the room as well as a hefty tome I recognised from my village. "I'll need to close the door now that we're done with that awful place. The demons can still get through."

I watched, too tired to comment and knowing I'd just get in

her way if I tried to help. When she'd gathered all her ingredients and consulted the tome, she drew a symbol I didn't recognise on the floor, had me light a black candle, and began speaking in a language I didn't understand. Whatever it was, it sounded creepy as hell and I wanted no part in it. Judging by András's look of distrust and the way he perched as far away as possible from Margit, he agreed.

She sliced her palm, then squeezed some blood onto the circle—the blood seeming to boil where it landed. The candle's flame flared blue, then winked out, a cold breeze sighing through the room before the temperature returned to normal.

"Is it—is it done?" I asked cautiously.

Margit sighed, then looked at me tiredly. "It is done. The door is closed. No demon can enter our world unless summoned directly."

A broad grin curved my lips and I jumped on her, squeezing her tightly. She winced, and I eased off. "Sorry. I'm just so relieved. You saved his life—and he did it, Margit. We have the one thing in our possession that can defeat Sylvie."

"You can't seriously still be thinking of using the crown, are you?" András asked, squinting at me. "For whatever insane purpose, Dante used it in the Under World and barely escaped with his life. If you had waited any longer, he would probably be dead, Kitarni."

"I know that," I snapped, rubbing a hand over my face. Fuck, now I was taking my frustration and fear out on my friends. "I

 310

have no choice, András. You know that."

He shook his head. "There must be another way. If you put that crown on, if you actually use the full extent of its power ..."

"It's either that or we let Sylvie's cultists and her corruption take us. I don't know about you, but I'd rather die fighting than let those dogs tear me apart. There is no dignity in the torment she'd subject us to. If I'm to leave this world, I want it to be on my terms."

"Fuck your terms," András shouted, raking a hand through his dirty hair. "You are not replaceable. The hole you leave cannot be filled. Not for him, not for any of us. Stop with this hero complex." He pointed a shaking finger at me. "You don't need to save anyone or prove anything. You are worthy of your people, of us, of him. Of his love for you. You might have given up, but I haven't. I will not watch you die needlessly."

He stormed away, leaving me blinking like a fucking owl as his words sank in. "András," I cried after him, but Margit put her arm out.

"Leave him be. He speaks out of frustration and fear, and his heart is hurting. Seeing Dante like this was shocking for all of us."

I twisted my fingers through my skirts as I sat on the edge of the table. "Is that what he really thinks? That using the crown means I've given up?"

Margit joined me, tucking Dante's sweaty strands back from his temple. "András feels deeply. Always has. He was just a babe when Lord Sándor brought him under his wing. His father was

a drunkard and a fool, lusting for anything wet between the legs. His other love was that of the sea." She snorted. "Eventually he drowned in it."

"He told me his father abandoned him," I said, recalling the first night András had taught me to play chess. "And that his mother died during childbirth."

"Did he tell you she was a prostitute? A rare beauty, it was said." Margit scoffed. "Like all treasures, her shine was dulled by the greed of men. They had to cut the baby from her. András's father cared for him for a few months, but like all addicts, the sea was a drug he could not shake. He followed its lure to a watery grave."

I frowned. "Such a sad story. How did he come into Lord Sándor's care?"

"It was by chance your father found him. Abandoned in a box by the docks of a human village's port."

I jolted, eyes widening. "My father?"

She smiled softly, smoothing her skirts. "He was on a diplomatic mission for Lord Sándor when he came upon András. The old sap just couldn't help himself, I suppose. He brought András back to be raised in the castle. Your father, Lord Sándor and Lady Yana, all treated him like their own, not to mention the maids. It's why he's so well loved here. He's the thread that binds us all together."

What were the chances? I shook my head and laughed. "Sometimes I think my world can't get any smaller, but then a

little light shines on new shores."

Margit patted my hand gently. "In a way, it kind of feels like you were already part of this family, because of your sire. Had your mother chosen to stay in Mistvellen, we would all have grown up together."

It warmed my heart to think of the memories and mischief we would have made. How happy I might have been. But even with the traumas of growing up bullied and abused, I wouldn't change a thing about my childhood. I loved my sister and mother deeply. And the trials I'd faced? They made me who I was. Made me fiercer than I ever thought I could be.

I wrinkled my nose as another thought occurred to me. "Can you imagine if I had grown up here? Dante would have been like a brother to me. No thank you."

She laughed. "A fair point. It would have been nice to have a sister though."

"It's a good thing you've got one then," I said, looping my arm through hers. For the first time, I was shocked to see raw emotion glimmering in her eyes. A rare glimpse beneath Margit's hard exterior and iron mask. "Blood does not make family. András, more than anyone, is proof of that."

She nodded, suppressing her tears. "That he is. When you have nothing, it is easier to let go of the possibility of something. When you have everything, it's impossible to imagine having nothing. András, for all his love of finery, needs nothing but the people around him. He was abandoned once, so it's the thought of losing his loved ones that worries him again."

I looked at Dante, feeling my soul fracture into a thousand pieces. "I had little once, too. Now I have everything, yet all I want is him." I gestured at Dante, then Margit, then all around me, knowing she'd understand. "Us. This family. I would give the world to see you all safe."

She gazed at me sadly. "I trust you know then, why I do not beg of you that which you cannot give. Because I would do the same. Faced with the same odds, the same pain, I would give my life for family."

"Margit, if something happens to me, someone will need to pick up the pieces." I stared into her deep blue eyes, like endless oceans in the darkened room. "He will need you when it's done. They both will."

Our gazes turned to Dante and she took my hand in her own. "I will stand strong. I always do."

We sat there in silence for a long time, sharing vigil over Dante's sleeping form. At some point, I must have fallen asleep, because I woke with a start to find my head cradled in András's lap, Margit nestled into his side. We'd both been moved into a corner of the room, a pile of blankets cushioning the floor and draped over us.

The fact I hadn't woken when moved spoke volumes to my exhaustion, or perhaps it was simply because I felt safe when with my friends.

I blinked back my sleep-addled brain and carefully slid away

314

from András so as not to wake him. He mumbled in his sleep, his head lolling on top of Margit's at an unpleasant looking angle. I shook my head and rose to my feet, tiptoeing over to Dante.

He looked like something from a dream. All hard planes and chiselled lines, his long lashes fluttering against his cheeks as he slept, his hair mussed and that inked chest rising and falling steadily. Seeing him like this—alive and utterly perfect—all the pain and doubt I'd been holding onto melted away, my heart swelling suspiciously large. It took me a while to realise my cheeks were wet and I wiped the tears away, a happy, choked little laugh escaping me.

I pressed a gentle kiss to his lips, surprised to find them moving back, moulding to my own like a key sliding in its lock. A perfect fit.

I sank into that kiss, falling into oblivion as his tongue wrapped around mine, his lips like perfect fucking pillows against my own. Just the knowledge that he was here and safe after going to hell and back for me—quite literally—had my undergarments soaked.

"Dante," I breathed, pulling back slightly. "I love you. Do you hear me? I fucking love you. I was too afraid to say it before, and now I'm afraid I'll never be able to say it enough."

His eyes flicked open, nearly black in the darkness and ever so dangerous. His chest rumbled against my own from where I'd apparently clambered on to him, because yes, the woman downstairs was a needy bitch.

"Where you go, I go, Kitarni," he said in a husky, rasping voice. "I will follow you into darkness, or I will burn in your fire. There is no monster alive that could keep me from you."

He kissed me again, desperately and urgent, his lips bruising, his teeth scraping against my mouth so hard it drew blood. I jolted in surprise, but I'd be lying if I said it didn't make me wetter. I traced a hand down his stomach, cupping his growing cock in my hand.

Before I could stealthily show him just how much I loved him, a ruckus sounded from above, and I jumped off the table quickly, stepping into the shadows by the stairwell. Dante crept off the table, the crown in one hand and a sword in the other as he shifted in front of his family, who were still sleeping soundlessly on the floor.

"Kitarni, Margit," a voice called, and I instantly relaxed, realising it was Lukasz.

The panicked note and the shuffling of running boots made my heart skip a beat. What fucking now? I clicked my fingers, conjuring some firelight to see by, and he skidded to a halt at the top of the stairs.

"What is it?" I called, my stomach fluttering like butterfly wings as he gave me a pained expression.

"It's the Dark Queen. Her army is approaching. The final battle is upon us."

PART THREE

THE CURSE OF

A CROWN

THIRTY-ONE

DANTE

Black blotted out the horizon like a swathe of fabric stitched against the skyline. It was endless, stretching far and wide. Kitarni's palm slid into mine, warm and solid, and I rubbed my thumb over the back of her soft hand as we stood in silent solitude on the castle ramparts.

"So many," she breathed. "How long do you expect we have?"

"Half a day, maybe. They'll be here by nightfall."

"Then we haven't a moment to lose. We need to prepare our forces, come up with a plan of attack. The women and children will need shelter. And what about—"

I turned, pressing my fingers to her lips, then running my knuckles against her cheek. "It will be okay, Freckles. We will be okay."

Her eyes shone as they searched mine. "How do you know?"

I leaned down, kissing her forehead tenderly before pulling back and gazing into those hazel eyes. "Because we are together

319

and we have the crown. Because I will drive my sword into the heart of any man or monster who would try to hurt you."

She smiled, cocking her head as she roped her arms around my neck. "You're kind of sexy when you're all murderous, you know that?"

I grinned, flashing a dimple for extra measure. "Oh darling, I knew when I first heard you cuss that you were a wild and wicked thing. But this violent delight of yours? You were made for me." She licked her lips and I tracked the movement hungrily, pressing her to me, my cock swelling at the thought of what that pretty little mouth could do, how badly I wanted her lips wrapped around me.

"My lord and lady," a guard said, clearing his throat awkwardly. "You've been summoned by Lord Sándor."

A frustrated growl tore from my throat and Kitarni pouted. I pressed a kiss to her throat, licking up the column of her neck and earning a small groan. Chuckling, I turned to the guard. "Lead the way." In Kitarni's ear, I whispered, "To be continued."

She shivered against me, but made no comment as we followed the guard across the ramparts and into the castle, striding quickly down the corridors to a room dedicated for war meetings. A room I hadn't needed to visit in a long time.

My father sat at the head on the far end, Nora seated to his left and Lukasz to his right. The High Witch of the Red Coven, Aliz, paced the room, her shoulders tight, her hands balled into fists. Iren was also present, and Dominik, clan chieftain and general of

the táltosok armies of the western and eastern territories, leaned over the table.

The chieftain was well known for his swordsmanship, having seen his fair share of fights in his fifty odd years. He also had a hot head and hadn't taken much convincing to join the cause when I mentioned slaying cultists was involved. Just the mention of what Sylvie had done to our scouts back at Kitarni's village and he'd dived in the deep end of this war.

My gaze roamed over him. He was a wiry man. Plain faced and sour looking, in due part to the scar above his mouth that pulled up his top lip. His peppered black hair was cropped close to his scalp, making his features even harder. At first glance, he didn't appear threatening—didn't really warrant a lingering gaze at all—which was more the pity for anyone who underestimated him.

Everyone looked up as we entered, all but my father bowing before us. I looked at Kitarni, assessing her reaction, but gone was the cheeky woman from moments before, her chin high, her face set with determination. My hellcat come to unleash her claws.

"My son," Farkas said, his brows creased as he tracked my person, no doubt searching for any injury. "You are well?"

It was as much sentiment as he'd allow in a war meeting, but the concern was there, nonetheless. I smiled, pasting an air of nonchalance on my face. "As well as one can be on the dawn of battle."

In truth, I felt drained. The crown had ripped at my very soul, as if it had tried to suck all my power into itself. Kitarni had

321

been healing me, I knew, but I was tired. So damn tired. What I wanted was to curl up and sleep for days on end, but the people needed the face of their general and my father needed his son.

The lord nodded. "And your mission was ... successful?"

Dominik and Aliz studied me curiously, but I shrugged lazily. "On all accounts."

My father's face relaxed, some of the tension leaving his shoulders, but he would say no more on the issue. Allies the chieftain and High Witch may be, but we would not reveal our latest asset so freely. The crown would remain hidden in Margit's secret chambers under protection spells until the time was right, and the only people who knew that chamber even existed were my family.

I turned my attention to the chieftain, eager to change the subject. "What news of your forces, Dominik?"

The clan leader turned, raking a hand through his greying black hair, his scarred lips twisting even further as he scowled. Despite his thin frame, he was pure muscle, his weathered biceps lined with scars. He was renowned for his battle prowess, having defended the north against the Mongolians throughout several campaigns during the wars past. Many other commanders weren't so lucky to keep their lives.

"My men had some setbacks on the road. Human interference from nearby towns. They have seen the creatures of the Sötét Erdő and they know of Mistvellen." He growled, sounding much like the wolves we housed in the castle grounds. "Sylvie did well

enough to see to that."

"They plan to attack the city?" Kitarni asked, stepping closer.

The general looked at her sharply. "If not tonight, then on the morrow. My scouts have reported sightings from the north. The castle will be attacked on the northern and southern front."

Fuck. "Show me," I said, gesturing to the map laid out on the table.

"Sylvie's forces approach from here," he said, jabbing to the south-east of the forest before moving his finger to the north-west. "The humans are bolstering their forces and are expected to attack here."

"They mean to box us in," Lukasz said, his brown eyes hard. "Which leaves us two options: we stand our ground and defend on both fronts or send a smaller party to meet them halfway. We risk being surrounded should we stay. The alternative is a considerable dent in our defences."

"If we attack the humans, we risk the wrath of all humans in the kingdom," Nora said. "Perhaps even beyond our borders."

"I don't think we have a choice, Nora," my father said, his face grave. "Simply existing, in their eyes, is blasphemy and sin. I will be damned if I let this city crumble because of a small-minded people. We will not attack them unprovoked, but I will not hesitate to kill anyone attacking my city."

Kitarni circled to my side. "What if we can avoid bloodshed with the humans? Come to an accord? Humans can be reasoned with—more so than Sylvie, at any rate. If they can see it's in their

best interest to remain neutral, then we may be able to stay their hand."

"And who would you send to negotiate on our behalf?" Farkas folded his arms. "We have neither the time nor the resources to waste on diplomacy."

"I disagree," Nora said, standing. "Diplomacy is the best policy. I will meet with their leader. Allow me a small contingent of guards to treat with them under a white flag. They cannot harm a messenger and if they do..." She shrugged. "You will have your answer."

Kitarni stiffened beside me, but she said nothing as she watched the exchange. How could she? There were no special allowances in war for anyone not a king or queen, and we had neither in Mistvellen. All were equal in blood and war. Nora would play her part, Kitarni and I would play ours.

"Nora," Farkas said quietly, placing a hand on her arm. "You could be killed."

"And why should my life mean any more than the thousands of others in this castle? I will do this for my people. We might win the battle against the Dark Queen, but a skirmish with humans could bring about the downfall of all witchkind and táltosok. Mistvellen would perish, as would all the clans and covens beyond. We must stop this."

Iren rose, bowing before the lord. "I will go with her. You have my oath that I will defend her with my life." I blinked, noting the way Kitarni's brows shot to her hairline. Iren's face flickered

with irritation, her lips thinning. "I know we haven't always gotten along, Kitarni, but believe it or not, I care about Nora, and I care about the future of all witches. Your mother is right. If the humans involve themselves in this fight, it will only end badly for all of us."

I looked at Kitarni, who nodded her acceptance. Iren nodded back, a glimmer of mutual respect seeming to pass between the women. I had to hand it to Iren, she had done her job well in getting the covens here, even if Viktória had turned out to be a backstabbing snake.

My father glanced between Iren and Nora, considering. He could have ordered them not to go, should he really wish. I wondered if a part of him cared for Nora deeper than any friendship would allow, but what could have been would never come to pass now. Not with my marriage to Kitarni. Not when his best friend had been the love of Nora's life.

I closed my eyes, daring to dream of a day when my people were safe and the ones I loved didn't have to stick out their necks willingly on the chopping block. Nora was wise to take preventative measures. One battle with humankind today could start a war we would never win. Negotiating with them was the only way, even if it broke my heart to see my wife suffer over it.

"Go," Lord Sándor said at last. "You have my blessing."

"And the terms?" I asked, leaning my palms against the table.

My father frowned. "Humans respond to power and wealth like any other beast when presented with a free meal. Wealth,

territory ... faith. Whatever must be done, we will make them an offer they can't refuse."

The castle thrummed with activity as witches, humans, and táltosok sprinted through the corridors. Most would be headed for the armouries to be outfitted for the coming battle, but many had other parts to play to defend our keep.

Healers bustled around gathering tinctures and bandages, and witches trained in medicine and healing spells headed to the castle gates where their magic or mending would determine the fates of the wounded sure to come.

I passed them all, grunting as my shoulders were bumped time and again by panicked citizens, but I didn't care. There was only one thing—one person—on my mind right now, and it didn't matter if the war knocked down my fucking door, I would have her to myself before it ended.

I had never needed anything so much as I needed her touch right now. The sun splintered through the open arches in the corridor, sending ruby rays dancing over the floor. An omen for the blood sure to be spilled in mere hours.

The dark army was close now—so close I could hear a droning like that of a swarm of locusts, come to destroy all in their path and spread their plague upon the land. It took me a moment to realise the sound was the cultists' chanting. A low buzzing that

made the hairs on my arms stand on end and my stomach curdle in disgust.

And always, my eyes never strayed far from the forest. I hadn't forgotten about the creatures that dwelled within its depths. Sylvie was no fool. She had her cultists and she'd set the humans on us, but there more dangerous things would rear their heads tonight.

What they didn't know was how dangerous Kitarni and I could be and what tricks I had up my sleeve. I was past the point of playing nice. We may have needed it, but diplomacy was not in my nature. My blades would speak my truth. My magic would offer no mercy. Before the night was over, I would bathe in the blood of my enemies. And I knew the things that lived inside my wife and me would *like* it.

The door to my chambers slammed open and closed as I crossed the threshold. Kitarni jumped as I stormed through, her eyes widening as I grabbed her by the nape of her neck and pulled her to me, kissing her like the world was ending.

Maybe it was. There were no promises in war. No guarantees. So I'd give my everything to this woman, to the only white light in this sea of darkness.

She groaned, wrapping her legs around my waist as I hoisted her up, her fingertips sliding beneath my shirt and up my chest. "Dante," she said in a husky voice and it only made me more desperate to plunge inside her.

I pressed kisses beneath her ear, licking and sucking as I trailed down her neck. She wriggled beneath my touch, panting,

 327

and I grinned against her, whispering in her ear, "Such a needy, wet little cunt. What would you like me to do to it?"

"Fill me up. Show me that you own me, Dante."

My hands roved down her dress, cupping her breasts, growling at the fabric blocking my access. "This," I said, turning her quickly, "will simply not do." I shifted her hair to the side, untying the stays of her gown slowly.

"Dante," Kitarni said slowly. "If you don't hurry up and fuck me now, I'll be forced to satisfy myself."

I breathed against her neck, making my little hellcat shiver. "So bossy. Touch yourself, Freckles. Tell me how wet your needy little cunt is." I allowed her enough room to bend and slip a hand under her dress, her soft whimpers making me even harder. "Show me."

She lifted a hand up and I leaned forward, sucking her finger into my mouth, then licking my lips. Fuck this gown. I quickened my pace, unravelling the ribbons at her back until the dress slipped from her shoulders and she stepped out of it in all her glory.

Her long curly hair rippled down her spine, whispering against the small of her back. For a moment I stepped back and enjoyed the masterpiece that was my wife. Every curve an artful stroke, every freckle or scar a mark in time of a painter's beautiful creation. Even the three black scars shimmering across her spine were beautiful, though the thought of who'd caused them made me want to tear heads off.

Kitarni shifted under my touch as I trailed a thumb down

her bare shoulders, the roundness of her ass, then around and lower still as I slid my fingers through her wetness. She squeezed her legs together, making a frustrated noise as I pulled my hands higher up. I slapped her cheek hard enough to leave a print and she moaned in surprise.

Kicking her legs apart, I bent her over and kneeled before my queen, feasting on her, lapping before sucking at her clit. She was so gods damned wet. "I'm close," she whispered breathily, and I smiled against her.

"Scream for me darling."

She shuddered against my lips, crying out, her palms slapping against the stone as she bent over, giving me better access to her as I drowned in her juices. But I wasn't done yet. Not nearly.

I picked my hellcat up and lay her gently on the bed, placing my palms either side of her head as I kissed her deeply, then moved to her shapely breasts. I pinched one peaked nipple, then the other, sucking on each one to lessen the hurt. She groaned at the pain-turned-pleasure, bucking into my touch as I put one finger inside her, pumping before adding a second, then a third, filling her up.

Her hands roved over her breasts before she grabbed my scalp, raking her fingernails over my hair. I hummed at the massage, rewarding her as I removed my fingers and circled her most sensitive nerves, switching between flicking with my tongue and my finger. She only shoved my head against her harder, and I chuckled as her back arched and she climaxed again, her hands

329

fisting the furs on the bed.

Kitarni smiled at me when she was finished, licking her lips with a hungry gleam in her eye. "Stand up," she commanded. I did as she said, a crooked grin on my face at her bossiness.

She untied my pants and I shucked them off lazily, groaning as she slid her hand over my cock, licking the precum beading at the tip. Her eyes danced with mischief as she rose, circling around me before pressing a hand to my chest and pushing me to sitting at the edge of the bed.

Her knees hit the stone and I gasped as her hand curled around my base. She slipped me into her mouth, sucking slowly, rubbing her thumb over the head intermittently. I groaned, drinking in the sight of her, the way the sunset streaming in made her brown eyes appear golden, the green speckles dotted like constellations in her eyes.

I could drown in that gaze. Instead, I mapped every freckle across the bridge of her nose, the slope of her cheeks, the way her lips puckered as she moved. She took me deeper and I had to force myself to keep from spilling inside her mouth.

"Kitarni. If you keep that up, I'll be spent before I can really give you what you need."

She pulled back and licked her lips, a cheeky smile on her face. "And what do I really need?"

I grinned in answer, moving back onto the bed and pulling her with me, turning so she was beneath me. She made to line me up, but I slammed home, giving her no time to adjust as I moved

hard and fast, setting a punishing pace as I lifted and dipped my hips and gave her what she really wanted.

Not one to be entirely dominated, she grappled my arms and moved me beneath her, pressing her nails into my chest so hard I hissed. Then she started rocking, sliding along my cock until she was filled to the brim. I could feel every inch of her inner walls, groaning at the friction. I tweaked her nipple as she moved, the other hand moving round to grab her ass as I slammed her down on me again and again.

She cried out, screaming my name as her release came. I continued pumping, riding out her orgasm until I followed not long after, grunting as I spilled inside her. We both crumpled into a heap, gasping as our limbs tangled and she rested her head upon my chest.

Her fingertips traced the sword inked from my chest to the vee above my pants, and I stilled her hand, clenching it to my heart as we lay together.

"Are you afraid, Dante? Of what's to come?"

She turned to look at me, concern clouding her eyes, and I tucked a strand of hair behind her ears. "I am not afraid to die."

"Then what are you afraid of?"

I paused, considering her question. "I'm afraid of the unknown. I'm afraid of what comes in the after—whether the gods would permit me a place in brighter lands, or if my destiny lies in the Under World."

Her lips pursed together. "What's it like? I didn't get a chance

to ask what happened when we pulled you back. Why you were wearing the crown."

I sighed. "It was a trap. Death and Fate knew the crown had been hidden there—I'm guessing Sylvie had told Fate as part of their bargain, but when Sylvie was resurrected, Fate never had a chance to interfere before Death whisked her back to the Under World."

Kitarni grinned. "Tied up like a hog, no less. I'm sure it took some convincing from Death for her to forgive him."

"Evil little witch," I said, kissing her wrist. "But you're correct in one sense. Death would never have allowed Fate to wear the crown, so I think you were the next best thing he could offer. She might be forbidden to lay a hand on you in the Middle World, but the rules don't apply in their domain. Only the dead are meant to walk in hell. The demons roaming free, the supposed spell you needed to close the gate? It was all a ploy to get your blood so they could open the pocket realm where the crown was stored."

"And when we sent you down instead, they had to resort to other measures," Kitarni said, her eyes widening. "There was never any risk of the demons walking the Middle Realm, was there? No price to be paid or balance to restore after Caitlin was burned. It was all to get my blood."

I nodded. "I made it to the crown, but once a portal had been opened to allow me into the realm, Fate and Death had access too. If I hadn't put it on, Death would have destroyed me or kept me as Fate's pet. It's safe to say there are now two demi-gods

332

wanting my head."

She snorted. "Death can be a real prick sometimes. He won't come for you until your time here is done. He'd consider it ... impolite."

"He will come for the crown, though." I shook my head. "It's little more than a trinket to assert his right as ruler of the Under World, but he would not risk losing his throne. Fate, on the other hand, wants the crown out of pure greed."

"That bitch will hold a grudge as long as we live," Kitarni replied, sighing. "Power is all she's ever wanted."

"She will never have it. Death would never allow his consort to wear the crown. You were meant to be her consolation prize." I chuckled, remembering Fate's face when I'd put the crown on my head. If looks could kill, those blue eyes of hers would have sliced more than my head off. "Their marriage is certainly odd."

Kitarni was silent for a time, then she wrinkled her nose. "How does their relationship work, anyway? Do you think he has any equipment to ... you know?"

My chest rumbled with a gruff laugh as I shuffled on the bed. "I'd prefer you didn't think about Death's skeletal knob, thank you very much. As far as I'm concerned, he's missing that particular bone."

Kitarni laughed, her eyes lighting up with mischief. "He is a demi-god though. A powerful one at that. Demi-gods must have some seriously epic sex."

"My twisted little creature." I let a dark smile carve my lips. "I

would cut his hands off before he could touch you."

She nestled into me, a smirk on her face. "I love it when you talk dirty."

"And I love you."

Her curls rippled like ocean waves as she rested her elbow on the bed, propping her chin on her hand. I traced my fingers over her curves, touching every dip and swell, admiring her nakedness. Her eyes pinned me with burning intensity. "Say it again. It sounded good."

"I. Love. You."

Her eyes glimmered with amusement as she moved closer and pressed a kiss to my lips. Long, sensual and sinful as the hell I'd been to. Wetness touched my cheeks and I pulled away in alarm, reaching a hand to her chin. "Does that truth scare you so?"

Her composure cracked and she shook her head. "I thought I'd lost you Dante. When you were bleeding on that table, the crown upon your head, I thought I'd never see you again. It made me realise some things." I waited as she looked away, lost to her thoughts. When her eyes met mine again, they were filled with sorrow. "I spent months being miserable and angry—the pain not yet buried between us. After András forced us to reconcile, I drowned my doubts in your arms and was so consumed with everything around us that it was easy to shove my fears aside. But when we said our vows, I married you with doubt in my heart. Doubt that our broken pieces would fit, that this marriage would

334

survive behind closed doors. I was wrong."

My hand moved up her jawline, across her cheek, down the side of her face and around her curls. But still I stayed silent, knowing she needed to voice this, that it could well be our last chance for honesty together. For redemption.

She released a shaky breath and nuzzled into my hand, cocking her head as she looked at me. "I forgive you for everything. I don't care about what was. Only what will be ... or what could be if we make it out of this war alive. I—" Her throat bobbed as she swallowed, and she shook her head, chuckling nervously. "Oh fuck a duck. I love you, Dante. My heart is yours. It beats for you, and it will die with only you. I just needed to let you know in case—"

I kissed her before she could finish, my own heart thumping a war drum in my chest. There was still so much I wanted to do with my wife. I wanted her to spread those wings like she'd always wished. To explore the seas and the sands, to conquer our enemies and start a new reign that was fair and just. We'd danced around each other for too long, only for the last grains of sand in the hourglass to count down what time we had left.

So I'd just have to smash the damn thing. Fuck demi-gods and dark queens. My future was lying right beside me. András had said he'd believed our fates to be wound together and that the gods had bigger plans, and I believed it now more than ever. Our souls—our very beings—were as one, merged after our magic had collided and bonded together. From our suffering *and* from our

love, we'd become something new. A fierce spell no dark magic could imitate.

"No fire could ever burn so bright as what I feel for you," I said fiercely. "We will get through this. You will always be with me, like the magic coursing through my veins. That beast you're so afraid of, it lives in me too. And if it means saving you, I'd let it cut down every last man standing in my way."

I pulled her to me, pressing my forehead to hers as we breathed each other in. "You're wrong, Dante," she said quietly. "I'm not afraid of it anymore. It's a part of me. The good, the evil, every ugly facet—it's all me. I'm tired of holding back every part of myself. I want to unleash it. I want to see the carnage it can wreak—both of our magics."

A horn sounded in the distance and we bolted upright, our eyes burning.

"Get your gear on, Freckles. You're about to get your chance."

THIRTY-TWO

Kitarni

The breath left my chest in a sudden rush. Cultists spread as far as the eye could see, their black robes billowing in the night breeze. Crows circled above, a bad omen for the bloodshed soon to be spilled. The damned chanting never ceased as the cultists formed line after line on the opposite side of the field, their torches dotting the sea of black.

The scent of burnt lavender and grass clung to my nostrils, cloying and sickly sweet—a smell that would only deepen as the hours passed, joined by death and rot and carrion fodder. I swallowed the lump in my throat, taking courage in my comrades around me. Witches and táltosok joined together at last, brothers and sisters and lovers-in-arms.

In first joining coven and clan, our ancestors started something special long ago and I would die knowing we'd truly brought them together again ... but not before we raised a little hell along the way.

My hip tingled where the crown rested in a leather bag and I shuddered as the magic pulsed through me, calling me. The hairs on my arms stood on end, a chill settling over my neck that defied the balmy breeze in the summer night's sky.

Arló shifted uneasily and I patted his neck comfortingly, leaning forward in my saddle. "Easy, boy. No running off on me tonight, okay?"

He nickered softly in answer and I smiled grimly. Dante and I sat abreast on our horses, an army of táltosok knights at our back. Witches formed ranks behind us, organised in units of fire, water, and earth witches. Their magic combined with the necromantic skills of the táltosok would be the turning point for this battle.

Until I slipped the crown on at least. Our little family had agreed I wouldn't use it until it was clear any chances at victory were lost. Maybe that made us selfish to wait so long—to risk the lives of others—but the devastation it could wreak unchecked would take more than my life. Until I had a clear shot at Sylvie, I wouldn't risk its power. There was no telling what it would do once I put it on or if I'd have total control. The risk of wiping out not just the cultists but our own was too great.

A desperate measure—that's what the crown was. A last-ditch effort to destroy that monstrosity and her many minions. I didn't allow myself time to think about what came next ... or what didn't. More than my life was at stake. That's all that mattered.

I scanned the army of shadows for a glimpse of the Dark Queen, and ... there. She stood near the treeline, bedecked in

black armour with a seven-pointed-star etched in red that looked suspiciously like blood.

Our eyes met and she sneered, her gaze turning hungry as we stared each other down. Slowly, she ran a single finger along her throat and flashed those sharpened teeth.

Noted. If I lost, she'd have a merry old time draining me of my blood. I suspected she'd be using those fucking fangs to do so.

My knuckles whitened where I gripped the reins, my magic rising in me with every angry beat of my heart.

A low horn echoed over the plains and our forces began moving, the militia breaking free from the front lines in a slow jog towards the beginning of the end. A hand found my thigh and I looked to Dante, finding comfort in his determined gaze. So steadfast and sure, like he was lounging on a throne. He was a pillar of strength. The calm before the storm. One that offered no quarter this night.

Archers lined up on the ramparts of the outer city walls, loosing arrows from longbows in a flutter of black-and-grey fletching. The arrows hit their marks, embedding deep into chests and eye sockets as cultists crumpled to the ground.

I forced myself to breathe like those archers might. In and out. Slow and steady. The seconds ticked on by as both sides of the field came to meet in the middle.

Three.

Two.

One.

Bang.

Swords clapped like thunder as steel clashed against steel, cultists and táltosok surging like the molten fires of a forge. I forced myself to remain still, my shoulders tense and my posture stiff as I awaited Dante's signal.

András caught my eye and winked. I smiled back, something wild and wicked in my heart galloping with the change of atmosphere. Was it wrong that adrenaline surged through me? That I sought to wet my blade and feed the beast inside me?

Maybe. But I didn't care anymore. Dead things didn't lie or scheme or threaten everything I loved. I squeezed my hilt, eager to join the fray, and looked to Dante. He was already watching me, the glimmer in his eyes telling me he was just as bloodthirsty and vicious as me.

He was magnificent, dressed in full black leathers, greaves, gauntlets, and boots. The silver wolf spaulder snarled on his shoulder, a red cloak at his back clasped by the skeletal hand-and-flame symbol at his throat. His black breastplate embroidered with silver wolves sparkled like starlight, and his magic—red and black—smoked around him. My husband. My lord. A fucking death god if I ever saw.

We made a wicked pair. I wore the same black outfit and red cloak, the only difference being the wolf-and-floral breastplate I wore, gifted to me months ago by Margit as a sign of acceptance into the Wolfblood Clan. Into the *family*.

I would do that little deviant proud.

340

Dante's lips quirked as he saw me drink him in, his brown hair swept back by a simple leather cord atop his temple. His eyes softened, the love and devotion in his gaze passing so quickly I almost missed it. Then he set his jaw and hardened his features, the gold ring in his eyes flashing.

Farkas thundered past the cavalry on his black stallion, his sword raised and his black regalia glimmering as it drank in the light of the torches. "For Mistvellen! For home and glory! For witches and táltosok and all the spirits of the land. Fight!"

Dante, András and I howled, feral grins on our faces as we charged, the clans at our backs answering the call. Arló's hooves ate up the ground, pounding like the frantic beating of my heart as we closed in. Reality hit me before my brain had a chance to catch up.

Spears raced towards us and I slung low over my saddle, nearly falling out of my seat as I righted myself. Others weren't so lucky, the sharp points embedded in chests of táltosok and horse alike, the steeds tumbling to the ground with whinnies and panicked shrieks.

I raced onwards, trampling all cultists in my path, Dante swinging his sword and lopping off heads from his horse beside me. When we reached the middle of the fray, I had little time to think.

My sword moved of its own accord as I slashed, arcing downwards at torsos and necks. Blood splattered, and weapons sang, accompanied by moans and screams of the dying.

Hands grabbed at me, trying to pull me off my saddle and I cried out, kicking and wriggling. Fear climbed my throat as I struggled to find purchase and I readied to tumble to the ground when an earth-shattering bellow sounded somewhere nearby.

I looked into the eyes of one of the cultists and gasped as a sword plunged through his throat, the man's eyes widening as blood bubbled from his mouth. The man toppled forward as Dante kicked him and slashed at the others, his face dark with fury.

It shouldn't have warmed my heart to see him all protective and murderous, but there was something undeniably alluring about him in full-death mode. His magic simmered around his hands, but he didn't unleash it.

We'd agreed to save it towards the end when we'd need our full power to wipe Sylvie from existence. Besides, for him to use his necromancy, we needed to rack up more bodies to make it effective. Something I was more than happy to assist with.

Tearing my eyes from him, I focused back on the battle, my stomach sinking with dismay as I noted the overwhelming mass of cultists against our own. We were vastly outnumbered. If Mama couldn't get the humans to stand down, the fight would be over in a blink.

A flash of blond caught my eye and I gritted my teeth as a cultist lunged towards András, who was busy fighting in the other direction, his back vulnerable to attack. With a scream of fury, I turned Arló and galloped towards my friend. I had good aim, but

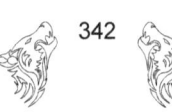

342

there were no assurances in battle.

Arló reared up, whinnying as he struck the cultist in the head with his two front hooves, sending the man to the dirt. I grinned like a crazed person as his hooves came slamming down onto the man's skull. My horse had found his courage after all. With a satisfied smirk, I saluted András and scanned our forces. The táltosok were toppling too quickly. It was time for some real action.

I lit a fireball and tossed it straight into the air, giving the signal for my brethren. "Witches," I yelled at the top of my lungs. "Show no mercy. Make them suffer." Whether they heard me or not, fireballs and water jets lit up the sky like shooting stars. I turned my attention back to the cultists. "Time to see what real magic is made of."

The ground began to rumble, grass, dirt, and lavender trembling beneath us. I watched in awe as a sound like splitting trees cracked all around me, then roots began stretching up and out of the dirt, latching onto cultists and dragging them underground.

Vines snaked around our enemies' throats, choking them to death or tripping up their feet. I didn't hesitate to gallop towards them and slice through the subdued cultists, downing every man and woman who dared stand against us.

Arló screamed, and I shrieked as I was tossed off, rolling into a ball to protect my neck. "Arló, no!" I rammed my blade through a cultist's chest, vaulting over another one's back and sinking my sword into his gut. My horse's body heaved with shaking breaths, his nostrils flaring as his wide brown eyes blinked with utter fear. Blood coated his flank, an arrow sticking out of his side. "Easy boy," I whispered, running my hands over him.

Damn it all, I would not let him die. Snapping the shaft, I pulled the arrow in one quick movement, gritting my teeth as blood spurted out from the wound. I conjured my light—the goodness of my father's gift—and cleansed the source, spearing healing energy into my horse.

Sweat beaded on my forehead and lip, dribbling down my back and between my breasts. I was exposed and unable to protect myself, but green vines kept sprouting up beside me, forming a protective barrier from any approaching cultists.

I looked through the cracks and grinned upon seeing Erika's face, one hand splayed towards me, her attention divided between protecting her High Witch and slaying all in her path. A warrior woman ... and my bad bitch teacher.

My attention shifted back to Arló, who snuffled at my fingers and jumped up, his side healed. I sighed in relief, then slapped his flank. "Get out of here. Back to the castle."

Not that he needed any encouragement. He galloped away with flaring nostrils.

I spotted Erika and nodded my thanks; she dipped her head in answer before engaging another cultist, her braids lashing like whips as she swivelled.

Erika's shield crumpled to dust and I leapt to my feet, pissed

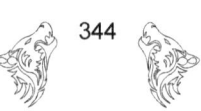

and utterly done with swordplay. That was Dante's domain. My heart was all fire.

Conjuring flames to my fingertips, I let rage bolster my strength, using the rivets in the ground to channel my scorching fire through. Everything it touched instantly lit up and cultists screamed as their robes burst into beacons, their skin purged in my unholy fire.

I lost myself to the dance, letting my beast poke its head out just enough to feel its extra power flood my system. My blood magic shrouded my shoulders like a veil, threatening anyone who came too close. A warning unheeded, apparently, as a group of cultists charged me, their eyes glazed from bloodmorphia, their skin pale and sweaty and pocked with blistering pustules and infection from self-inflicted wounds in the name of their cult.

Fuckers. I clicked my fingers and they disintegrated without a second thought, but not before something sliced my calf. I stumbled as hot blood dripped down my leg, hissing in pain as I turned to find a glaring cultist with sewed lips.

He snatched at my raised hand, curling my fingers into a fist to prevent the blast of my magic, his dark eyes menacing as he stared me down. Our swords clashed and I grunted as we struggled against each other. He was stronger than me, but high on bloodmorphia, the fool. A muffled grunt sounded from behind his lips and I clenched my teeth as I jerked my wrist and slid my sword along his, slicing his hand off.

He fell to his knees and I didn't hesitate to squeeze with my

freed fist, something unexpected happening. The beast inside me growled, the power latching on to, not only the man's blood, but the organ pumping in his chest. I could feel it beating, feel the hurried strain of panic. So I wrapped my power around that heart and pulled it from his fucking chest.

I tossed it aside and turned.

A cultist in a bull's head stood over me, his spear angled towards my heart.

I jumped to the side ...

And screamed as the tip sank into my flesh.

THIRTY-THREE
Dante

Her scream ripped me apart from the inside. It didn't matter that the battlefield was awash with the roaring of men and the crackling of magic. I'd know her voice anywhere.

I kicked my attacker, sending them soaring into a group of cultists, and swivelled, hacking off the arm of the opponent nearest me, then slashing the throat of another.

My attention honed-in on my wife, somehow knowing where she was in the undulating pit of people. I caught a flash of her red cloak, then glimpsed the bull-headed man towering over her. What was it with these sadists and bulls?

Something careened into my cheek and my head whipped back from the impact. I didn't even flinch, just turned slowly, eyeing my prey with the biggest death stare I could conjure. The cultist flinched and I smiled darkly.

With my twin blades, I lunged forward and slashed both

 347

down, removing his head from his body. The skull rolled along the ground, Lukasz's boot halting it. My brother's dark skin was slick with blood, his black armour somehow even darker with the congealing gore.

"We're losing ground," he said, panting. "Our warriors are overrun."

"Fall back. Pull the táltosok into ranks. It's time."

He nodded, then crossed the distance between us, clasping my arm. "Don't die on me, brother."

I grinned. "And let you have all the fun? Never."

His answering smile was devious and he shook his head with a raspy laugh. "It's always a competition with you."

I winked, not bothering to answer as the horn he blew into drowned out any words I might have shared. Táltosok came running back, and they moved around me like water in a river bend as I stalked towards the bull threatening Kitarni.

She rolled, over and over, barely missing the blows from that beastly man as he hefted his weapon, thudding it into the earth. When I caught up, I gripped his arm tightly, wrenching the man's arm back so fast it almost ripped out of its socket.

When I faced the bull—dried blood and clumps of skin still clinging to the mask—I leaned in close and whispered in his ear. "Not my fucking wife."

Both my blades plunged deep into his eye sockets and out the back of his head. A quick death, but a gruesome one. The man deserved no less.

 348

I removed my swords, flicking the blood from my blades with a quick shake of my wrist, then ran to Kitarni. She groaned, pressing a hand to her side to staunch the bleeding.

"Let me see."

The wound was bleeding freely, but it wasn't deep. A surface cut to one side of her waist that wasn't life threatening. It did, however, need dressing. Of course, there would be no telling her what to do. She batted my hand away and managed a smile in between panting. "Paws off, you over-bearing chicken. I'll be fine."

I sighed, ripping a strip of my shirt off and binding it around her waist. Not ideal, but it would do the job. I extended a hand and hauled her to her feet, brushing away the hair plastered to her face. "Pull from me."

She huffed, but didn't argue, clasping my forearm. The breath rushed out of me as she drew, not even needing to draw my blood as that foreign creature inside me opened its eyes and surged to meet hers. The exchange took mere seconds—just enough to stop the bleeding and allow her to fight without hindered movement. The wound would likely scar, not that either of us cared about that.

"Thank you, darling," she said, reaching on her toes to plant a kiss on my cheek. When she pulled back, her eyes were wide. "Dante." Her low voice sent a shard of ice spearing through my stomach. "We've got company."

She squared her jaw, staring at something over my shoulder. I turned, expecting to see more cultists coming our way. Instead, I

349

found a stampede of forest creatures sprinting our way. Lidércek, tündérek, and all manner of supernatural creatures stormed towards us, their eyes black and their skin slick with oozing corruption.

Fuck.

"Run," I barked, pulling her along by the wrist. "Get back to the frontlines."

She kept pace beside me, racing back to our brethren as the horde at our back advanced. Shrieks and hisses rent the air and even my bones went cold at the unearthly howls. Sorrow filled me too, that it had come to this. That we'd be forced to turn on once gentle spirits and beings that hunted only within their own borders.

But nothing was worth Kitarni's life. I'd kill them all if it meant protecting my own.

We had almost formed ranks with the others when a flash of movement to the right caught my eye. My father was stuck mid-fight with a group of men, his longsword glinting in the night. I cried out his name and his gaze turned to me.

It all happened so fast.

One moment he was blocking a cultist's blow, the next a sword was sticking out his chest. My heart skipped a beat and I found myself changing direction, running towards him with all the strength I had to give.

"Protect your lord," I cried. "Protect the lord of the keep."

Táltosok instantly answered the call, sprinting towards the

ring of cultists surrounding my father, but they were too far away. I saw glimpses of him through the throng and my rage amplified, so hot that the beast inside me finally roused from its slumber and sought to answer my pain.

I caught Lukasz's eye from across the field, his brown eyes stricken with fear, his brows pulled taut. The muscled chest beneath the bloodied breastplate he wore heaved as he sprinted, his dark skin slick with sweat as his black boots pounded across the dirt.

My brother's throat bobbed as a million emotions seemed to pass over his face, and when he looked at me once more, his shoulders sagged, the realisation seeming to hit us both like a blow to the face.

We were too far. Too far to do anything but watch as the enemy closed in around the man who'd been the best damn parent we ever could've asked for. My chest constricted as Lukasz's eyes shuttered. Seeing him resigned to Father's fate … it was enough to crack something in my chest.

My eyes flickered and that deep well of power inside me—Kitarni's power—yawned open, the magic bursting outwards, curving like the moon as it disintegrated all cultists in its path. I didn't have time to be awed by its might, because once the bodies blocking my vision turned to ash, I was left with the image of my dead father, ravaged by what seemed like a hundred scores to his flesh.

His hand still clung to his blade, his eyes wide and unseeing as they stared into the night.

Tears threatened to fall, but I blinked them back, resting a firm hand on my brother's shoulder as we both sank to our knees in the blood and dirt, ignoring the battle around us.

"We will avenge him," I swore. "He will not have died in vain."

Lukasz's brown eyes glimmered, a stray tear sliding down his cheek. "Father only ever thought of his family and of this kingdom. Nothing he ever did was in vain," he said softly. "His legacy lives on. We will make him proud, Brother. *You* will make him proud."

My emotions caught in my throat—a lump I couldn't swallow down or cough up. Everything felt unbearably stretched. My skin was too tight over my bones, my heart pumping too hard for my body to keep up with. Pain, I realised. Utter pain I had never quite known, even when the woman I'd called Mama had forsaken me.

Choking, I slid to my father's side, gazing at the sky above for some small scrap of reason.

The lord of Mistvellen was dead. Resting a hand on his chest, I prayed Hadur would welcome him in the beyond.

"Avenge him, Brother," Lukasz said. He squeezed my arm just once and that small act was enough to return my wits and spur my rage.

I howled at the sky, setting my eyes on my next targets as hundreds of bone chilling calls echoed my own, none more emotional than the man by my side.

To the east and west, the lupus—our great black wolves and protectors of the old gods—stretched along the hillsides, looking down with golden eyes from their giant black bodies.

"I will show them why we call ourselves the Wolfblood," I whispered to my father. "I will show them what we're really made of."

THIRTY-FOUR

KITARNI

I watched in awe as the huge wolves descended the hillsides, sprinting out and around the approaching creatures, surrounding them entirely. Hope sparked in my chest at the sight of these graceful beasts, but my heart ached for Dante and the loss of my father-in-law. After never really knowing my own father—thanks to Caitlin's antiquated laws—I'd hoped to find that bond in Farkas, but it would never be.

The wolves were a mighty sight to behold as they fought with gnashing teeth and paws the size of giant clubs. I didn't even know where they'd been hiding in Mistvellen's walls, but I was never more grateful for their presence.

They worked efficiently as a pack, tearing out throats and covering each other's tails as they fought. With our own lines reformed, we would soon re-join them.

Dante stood before us, his cloak rippling in the wind, one of his swords planted in the ground as he held his hands out, palms down, and began to summon. My lips parted as the shadowy smoke of his own power blotted out my red while he called forth the dead. My skin tingled, like it was covered in a thousand scurrying spiders, as an otherworldly wind gusted over the army.

When he looked over his shoulder at me, his eyes were pitch-black and my stomach flipped at the cruel smile curving his lips. I'd expected to see bodies rising from the battlefield, but what I saw was so much better.

A portal opened in front of him and I gasped as demons poured out in droves. Creatures both scaled and furred released from that gate, spilling out in wave upon wave. Evil wrapped steel claws around my heart, but I gritted my teeth and rode out the spine-tingling magic that ensnared me.

When Death stepped out of that portal, I just about died of shock. His robes billowed as the shrieking wind ripped at our clothes and nearly tore the hair from our scalps. I stood my ground and stared as the horseman turned towards me, somehow narrowing down on my power, the scars on my back rippling painfully. The prick could probably sense the crown still pulsing annoyingly at my hip.

I gasped as Death's magic flared and András stepped to my side silently, angling his body in front of mine. I rolled my eyes. Typical protective male syndrome. "If he wants me dead," I said between sharp inhalations, "I'd be gone already."

András grunted but didn't move. Thankfully, Death's burning gaze—yeah, I could feel it, even if the fucker didn't have

 355

eyes—passed from me as he moved to observe the battle on the hillside. Apparently, he still couldn't intervene.

His demons, however? I didn't know how Dante had managed to get them on our side, but I hoped whatever bargain he'd made was worth it.

András lifted his hands, mimicking Dante's movement, only this time the bodies of the fallen reanimated. I looked around at the other táltosok mirroring these actions, their magic beckoning their lost brothers to return.

Transfixed by so much power radiating through the air, I stood rooted to the spot as my soldiers called upon their gifts. The crown's vibrations seemed to increase in urgency, as if responding to so much dark magic around us. It took all my willpower to ignore that taunting call and put the damned thing on my head.

To end them all.

I shook my head and sheathed my sword, ignoring the stab of pain that panged up my side as I twisted my hands, summoning my blood magic. The red circled my wrists and I stepped forward slowly, joining Dante while he worked.

We linked hands, the connection somehow strengthening my power, as I knew it did his. He looked at me, his black eyes giving him a sinister edge, and I smiled, knowing my eyes would be the same.

I turned towards the succubi advancing on stained, black hooves and unleashed my power.

Red misted out from my free hand, curling around our allies

and only striking down the approaching beasts. Flesh one moment and ash the next, stirred up on the wind still gusting from Dante.

The demons kept pouring from that void, flooding out in a wave of darkness as creatures on both sides gnashed their teeth and swiped claws and tails. Blood spurted everywhere, and beasts began to feed on flesh, ripping and tearing. My insides baulked at the sight, but I didn't turn away, blasting again and again until that moral voice inside me was but a memory of a witch.

I relished in my fury, sinking into a deep bliss of magic so addictive and pleasurable, I lost all sense of time and meaning as I killed. And killed. And killed.

It wasn't until a horn blasted that I snapped out of my revelry and looked behind me, startled by the unfamiliar call and hoping to hell that whoever it was, they were on our side.

Blue banners rippled in the wind, the turul—the Kingdom of Hungary's bird and national symbol—mid-flight on the sigil. Row upon row of humans equipped with swords, spears, and shields overlooked the fields, their torches raised high.

Several pikes raised above the others and I squinted to see the objects placed on top, not quite close enough to make them out until …

"Oh my gods. No. No, no, no, no."

My hands trembled, my chest constricting as I struggled to breathe, my forehead cold with sweat.

Because those were heads stuck on the pikes and, in the middle of them all, beside one blonde head with a sharp bob, was

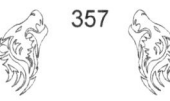

my mother's.

I fell to my knees and rocked, my hands ripping at the hair on my scalp as I stared at what remained of my mother.

And I screamed.

And screamed.

And screamed.

THIRTY-FIVE

DANTE

K itarni fell to the ground beside me, inconsolable as she screamed until her voice went hoarse, her fingers wet with her own blood as I pulled them from her skull and lifted her into my arms.

"Shh. I've got you." I held her close, stroking her hair, ignoring the chaos surrounding us. For those few moments, there was nothing but my wife and her pain—raw and utterly consuming.

Anger coursed through me, poisonous and crippling, but rather than give in I let it stoke my flames. They'd mutilated the whole diplomatic party and I looked at each face on those pikes— faces that belonged to soldiers, friends, and loyal allies.

Humans had done this. Humans so blinded by faith they'd revealed themselves to be true monsters born from fear. Nora had treated with them under a white flag and they'd *murdered* her. Ignored the rules and mutilated her body. I would not stand for it.

We had lost our only parents.

The humans had lost their rights to mercy.

I cradled Kitarni in my arms, pressing a kiss to her bloodied brow. When her sobs quieted, she pulled back, a glazed, blank look in her eyes. "She's gone," she whispered, so quiet I almost didn't catch it. "Her body is ... she's gone," she repeated, almost like she couldn't believe what she was seeing.

Her whole body shook as she tried to gasp down air and I rubbed her shoulders. "You're in shock. Deep breaths, my love." She did as I bade, her shoulders heaving until that golden breath filled her lungs. I sighed in relief, stroking her cheek with the pad of my thumb. "Make them pay, Kitarni. Make them suffer."

Those hazel eyes hardened as she looked once more at the humans descending the hill. I knew she'd destroy them all to avenge her mother's death. I *wanted* her to. She set her jaw, rising to her feet and rolling her shoulders. I watched as she strode through the ranks to the rear end of the army.

When she reached the other side, she planted her feet in the ground and looked at Erika, the two of them speaking quickly before the latter conjured a platform of interwoven roots and vines from the earth. Kitarni stepped onto it and the damn thing lifted her into the air, suspending her over the oncoming army.

I didn't go to her, try to hold her back or help. This was something she needed to do on her own. My hellcat was more powerful than any of us and that wasn't even considering the crown. Sylvie was the only one who posed a real threat.

They were only a few hundred strong—no match for us normally, but with the losses we'd sustained, their presence could be troublesome. Being surrounded was the worst-case scenario, but if the castle gates held strong, Mistvellen would be safe.

Kitarni raised her hands and the very air seemed to hold its breath as all but the demons and the reanimated dead stopped fighting and looked to her—my blood witch, my queen.

Thunder rumbled in the skies and lightning lashed with forked tongues, the first drops of rain suddenly pattering down, tinkling on armour as the armies paused to see her might. Red exploded out of her hands and my gaze flicked to the humans quivering in their damn boots and painting the sign of the cross across their small-minded heads.

The humans? Nothing but fodder for Kitarni's beast to feed on.

Something inside me shivered, demanding I head towards her and I obeyed without hesitation, breaking through the lines hurriedly to reach my girl.

Her power washed over them in a cloud of red so mighty it blocked out all else. When it passed, dust scattered and their weapons and armour tumbled to the earth, forgotten, never to be held by human hands again.

Hadur's. Fucking. Blade. Hundreds of humans gone, just like that. Whispers broke out among the soldiers, then our army cheered, chanting her name and pumping their fists into the air.

'Wolfblood Witch', they called her. My chest puffed with

pride to hear their acceptance, their loyalty to this woman.

Kitarni stumbled and I sprinted as she dropped, holding out my arms and catching her before she could dash her skull on the dirt. She was out cold and I crouched, laying her head against my lap.

"Come back to me, Freckles. Don't you dare give in yet." Her eyelashes fluttered and I stroked her hair, whispering sweet nothings in her ear. She groaned, muttering something unintelligible, and I held her tighter, putting my ear to her lips. "What did you say?"

"I said you're choking me. And not in a good way." She half-smiled as her eyes snapped open and I laughed, kissing her deeply on the lips. By the gods, I'd take her right then and there if the world wasn't watching. Maybe even then, but we had cultists to kill.

"You are—" I shook my head, in total awe of this creature before me. "You're a goddess."

She rose, dusting herself off and taking a minute to lean against me as she collected herself. The spell had drained her, but I knew better than to think she was spent. "Dante. Look." Her voice dripped with venom as she locked eyes on something in the distance. I turned to find her squinting at the one person who could end all this.

Sylvie stood at the forefront of her army, disintegrating demons and the undead with lazy waves of her hands. Blood dripped down her chin, as if she'd just fed and I gritted my teeth.

She probably had, restoring her power on the blood of a witch.

Her eyes met mine, then slid with cold indifference to Kitarni. My táltos vision was better than a witch's, so the taunting smile that dark bitch offered made my insides boil. My muscles flexed with the urge to rip off her head.

My gaze shifted to the woman who stepped beside her, every killer instinct inside me awakening upon one look at that smirking face—once beautiful and kind, now just an ugly reminder of everything I hated. My mother.

"This ends now," Kitarni said. She turned, looking at me with adoration, her hand reaching up to cup my cheek. The sounds of battle quieted to nothing as I focused on her gorgeous face. "I fucking love you, Dante Sándor. I would go to hell and back for you, but I guess you already did that." She smirked, her freckled nose puckering. "So I'll do you one better. I'll send that wretch there instead."

I narrowed my eyes. "Kitarni—"

"Don't." She pressed her fingers to my lips. "Don't try and stop me. Don't say goodbye. Just ... kiss me. Kiss me like you own me."

"I do own you, Freckles. From the tip of your toe to the very top of that precious, stubborn head of yours."

Our lips crashed together and I devoured the taste of her, the feel of her tongue curling against mine, the arch of her back, the lingering scent of lavender in her hair. The kiss lasted a lifetime and a split second all at once.

 363

When we pulled apart, she looked at me for a long moment, then turned and disappeared amongst the fray.

Unbidden tears lined my eyes. My chest ached with a hurt so deep and profound I could feel my inner resolve crumbling. Fireballs and water jets lobbed in the air around me and all I could do was stand there. Utterly useless. I closed my eyes and tried to block out reality, but a chasm opened in my heart, swallowing me whole.

For once in my life, I had no idea what to do. I should have held on. I should have ... Fuck. I shook my head, refusing to believe this was farewell—that once she put that crown on, it would all be over. It couldn't end like this.

My hands curled into fists as I watched the bloodshed around me, refocusing on Baba Yaga as she made her way across the battlefield, her sights set on me. There was my answer. *My justice.*

I let her come to me until she stood mere feet away, staring me down, almost imploring as she gazed at her only son. "Dante, my sweet, sweet boy. You must understand—"

"I understand," I spat. "I understand you abandoned your family when you had every opportunity to come home. I understand you manipulated a child's love into doing your bidding. I understand you used me, coerced me and forced me to obey your every command by holding my brother as bait. And most of all, I understand you hurt the woman I love. You disgust me."

Yaga shook her head, her brown eyes wide. "Please. I did this

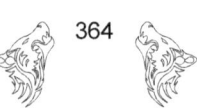

all for you. So that one day, when the Dark Queen reigns, she would spare you. You will see, in time, that the cult is the true path. Dante, I love—"

I stiffened, my head heating with the pure rage coursing through me. "Don't you dare. Don't you fucking dare say those words to me. You lost that right long ago when you decided dark magic was more endearing than your own child. There is a debt owed that you can never repay."

"Then tell me," she cried, raising her arms, her gaze imploring. All I could focus on was the blood stained down her chin, the teeth filed into sharp points. Teeth that had sank into witch flesh and drained them of their blood. All I could see was *red*. "What can I do to make this right?"

I sneered, letting my power flash. "You can die."

Before she could blink, I rushed her, my two blades sinking through her chest and out the other side. Her mouth parted, her eyes bulging as she stared at me in shock, fresh blood trickling down her chin in the same path as before. With one hand, I clasped her back and pulled her closer, deeper down the swords until we were nearly chest to chest.

A sickening, choking noise bubbled out of her mouth as she tried to speak, but the words didn't come. Just before she took her last breath, I pulled her closer, whispering in her ear, "Burn in hell."

She died in my arms. The last embrace I'd ever offer and one she didn't deserve. When I pulled my blades free, I felt nothing

365

but satisfaction at what I'd done. No remorse or regret, just a weight lifted from my shoulders that this monster would never hurt me and mine again.

The moment was freeing, but entirely short lived as I looked at the carnage around me.

My brothers and sisters fell by the dozen as Sylvie unleashed her blood magic. The faeries and creatures of the woods pounced, never tiring, always hungry for more flesh.

The portal I'd conjured began shaking violently, cracking in two like an earthquake, and I sucked in a breath as it shattered entirely. The demons fighting winked out of existence, likely having returned to their own realm. We were fighting a losing battle and Kitarni had known it.

Soldiers I'd grown up with littered the fields, their limbs or heads severed, their eyes open and mouths wide in a silent scream. The lupus fought on, but even they were outnumbered as creatures leapt upon their hides, stabbing and slicing.

Their howls of pain cleaved my heart in two and, as I watched the river of red running through the dirt beneath my feet, my resolve hardened. The power of the táltosok was mostly spent and the witches were tiring, their magic dwindling or fizzling out. Our forces would not last the night.

But we could fight with sword and axe and fire in our hearts.

We could die with honour.

I sprinted through the throng of moving bodies, grabbing the reins of a riderless horse and swinging up onto its back with all my

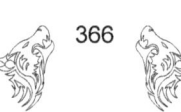

strength. I spotted Lukasz and András fighting back-to-back, their teeth gritted as they parried and countered, their path to safety blocked by a circle of cultists.

Snatching the reins of another panicked horse, I urged my steed through the masses, trampling all enemies in my path. Sword raised, my blade cleaved a woman's arm off, then I stabbed another through the heart, urging my horse to turn abruptly to bump another man off his feet.

I swore as a knife plunged into my leg, then ducked a projectile soaring past where my neck had just been. *Fuck.* My magic flared and I sent a burst of blood magic out, wiping away the closest cultists. The well of power inside me was precariously low, but I had little choice. My family needed me.

"Get on," I barked, tossing the reins to Lukasz, who swiftly mounted and held an arm out to András to hoist him up behind him. My horse's flanks were slick beneath me and I patted his sides. "We're not giving up."

"Only death can stop us now," Lukasz agreed, dipping his head at me.

András nodded sullenly at his back, his green eyes bright. "For Mistvellen."

I thumped my fist over my heart and raced to the arrowhead of our army. "This is it," I cried, my horse thundering down the lines. "We are wolves! We are Wolfblood! And we never hunt alone. Push the attack. Fight. Fight. *Fight!*"

My men roared, the entire army racing behind Lukasz, András

and me, the wolves turning and sprinting in line with my horse.

This was it. This was the end.

A detached calm settled over me and I descended into the madness, my sword raised and ready.

It wasn't until our warriors had swarmed the enemies' next line of defence that I saw them.

Kitarni and Sylvie faced off against each other, their blood magic surging, both witches' arms outstretched as they stood fast beneath the weight of immense power clashing in a mighty blast.

Kitarni bent beneath Sylvie's, her waves of magic faltering against the Dark Queen's tide. She cried out and I redirected my horse, trying and failing to make my way through the endless mass of bodies. She was so close ... so close, and yet so far.

Desperation filled me and my heart raced against the clock as I watched my wife stumble, Sylvie's power mere inches from consuming her entirely.

No!

Frenzied panic hit me as I slashed and hacked at anything that moved.

Kitarni turned, her eyes shuttering between black and hazel and the look on her face cracked the heart beneath my ribs. She smiled gently, a kind of resignation settling over her eyes, and then she mouthed four words that stole the breath from my lungs.

"I love you, Dante."

She turned back to Sylvie, the Dark Queen's eyes widening with horror as Kitarni pulled the crown from its pouch. I could

see her screaming, but the words didn't reach me as everything around me seemed to slow.

Then Kitarni put the crown on her head and the world exploded.

THIRTY-SIX

KITARNI

I stormed towards Sylvie, not tearing my eyes from her for a second as I waved my hands, destroying everything in my path. My magic was fading, but the beast inside me seemed to dig deeper, both in anticipation and recognition of the predator facing me.

It bared its teeth and gnashed and I fed from that rage, using it to gather every last drop of my power until I stopped several feet away from her.

Sylvie smiled, that stunning face morphing into cold malice as she cocked her head at me. "Blood witch," she purred. "We meet in the flesh at last."

I pressed a finger to my lips. "Hmm. Well, you weren't at your best, but I recall that time when I was bleeding out on a stone slab to resurrect you. The first meeting was more than enough."

Her grin deepened, emphasising the filed points of her vampiric teeth, still covered in blood from her most recent meal.

Fire sprang to my palms, crackling in warning as we began circling each other.

"I have waited an age for this day," Sylvie said, her footsteps graceful as a large cat as she prowled. "You have something of mine and I want it back."

"Oh, this old thing?" I asked, letting my blood magic coil around my wrists. "You want it bad enough? Come and claim it."

Sylvie laughed and I had to repress the shiver wanting to skitter down my spine. "You're a fierce little creature. Powerful, even without my gifts running through your veins. I shall enjoy breaking that spirit. Perhaps after I tear your lover limb from limb, I'll let you watch as I feed on his heart."

I trembled with rage. "Lay a hand on a single strand of his hair and I'll make Death's torture seem like child's play."

Her eyes glittered in response, the only sign of her fear being a quick glance at said entity from where he watched the battlefield from the hillside. *Good*. Maybe he'd be more forgiving if I gave him his old toy to play with.

"You could join me, little girl. We could be a force this world has never known. With our power, we could rule the Under World. Take back the crown and reach for the land of the gods. We'd be unstoppable."

I wrinkled my nose and yawned. "A lifetime in your company? No thanks. I'd rather stab my eye out than spend a single minute by your side."

"Then you will die with the rest of your witch filth."

"Why do you hate them so?" I frowned, looking her up and down. "What damaged that shrivelled soul of yours so much that you sought to destroy your own kith?"

Sylvie laughed, a cold and ugly sound that slithered down my spine like slick oil. "I was never a sheep to be herded and controlled by dictators. The old coven leaders clung to their seat of power, unwilling to step aside when their time to rule was up. Like stubborn weeds, they did not relent." She sneered, her brown eyes burning. "When my power kept growing and my knowledge of the arts surpassed their own, they grew afraid. They tried to kill me. Sent paid assassins to my bed to murder me in the night. Miserable wretches didn't even have the stomach to do it themselves."

I blinked, unable to believe what I was hearing. "The High Witches tried to murder you?"

"Oh yes. They smelled the change in me. They *feared* what I'd become. I killed the assassins easily, of course, and when that didn't quench my hunger, I turned to dark magic. It's a gift, Kitarni. Witches are so limited, but this cult ... it transcends the coven. Opens doors to new realms and opportunities. Why settle for one kingdom when I could conquer the world?"

Any pity I felt for her died instantly. "Your cult is a plague. A sickness spreading to the weak-minded. The old faith was wrong in so many ways, but those witches got something right. They should've finished the job when they had the chance."

"Perhaps. But it matters not. Your fate remains the same."

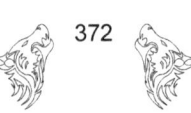

For a moment we stared at each other, the sounds of swords ringing, accompanied by the howl and screech of various monsters as they fought. Sylvie's fists shook by her sides, but when she collected herself, a small smile graced her lips. Coy and cunning, as if she knew something I did not.

"I see you already received my other gift," she continued, nodding to the hill where the humans had been. "I only wish I could have heard your mother scream as the humans severed that pretty head from her shoulders. No matter. It was quite the show watching you wipe them out. I should thank you for removing that future problem for me. And for using so much magic."

A sharp pain cleaved my chest, but I forced my face to remain blank as I stared at her. Her eyes flashed with anger when I didn't take the bait and I straightened, looking her dead in the eyes. "You're pathetic and I grow tired of your company." I tilted my head and pasted a cocky grin on my face. "So, are we going to stand here and talk all night, or shall we get this over with?"

She pursed her lips like a spoiled brat, but shrugged her shoulders nonchalantly. "You're right. One shouldn't play with their food. Give me your best, girl."

I scoffed, flexing my fingers, sensing the change in the static air as magic gathered from us both. "Like I needed any encouragement."

As one, our power burst from our hands, a brilliant flare of blood-red coursing out from our fingertips and thrashing wildly in the middle. I grunted against Sylvie's magic. She was strong. So

 373

fucking strong and, apparently, as stubborn as I was.

We battled it out, our magic ebbing and flowing, pushing and pulling in what seemed like a war of wills. Sweat dripped down my back, my palms slick with the effort, brows pulled in and teeth gritted so hard I feared they would break.

My bones felt like they would snap, my stomach twisting with nausea as my power funnelled out of me. I was weakening, wilting like a flower before frost.

Sylvie's smile widened, sensing my losing battle and I flagged, bending further and further until it truly hit me. I was never going to win this fight. I hadn't allowed myself to dwell on what it really meant, or what my next move would really mean.

For me? Nothing. I would die a saviour. A martyr. But who the fuck wanted that? I wanted to live, to wake up every morning by my husband's side, to laugh with my sister, to joke with András and to be scolded by Margit. I wanted a life in Mistvellen, to explore every corner of the earth.

I wanted.

But it wouldn't happen for me. Fate was probably laughing as she threaded this future in the Under World. Well, that bitch had something coming. I'd haunt her ass for all eternity if that's where I was headed.

I steeled my shoulders and pushed all my remaining power into one hand as I turned, looking behind me on the battlefield for my reason for living ... and for dying.

Dante battled like a knight possessed, swinging his sword,

mounted on a horse like a vengeful demon prince. His eyes caught mine and a breath escaped me as that connection between us almost seemed to pulse, as if afraid of that tether breaking.

His eyes widened as understanding dawned on his face, then his gaze turned panicked. I knew it would break him, but all I could wish for was that he'd move on and find happiness. Because my sacrifice would ensure his life. The asshat just had to *live* it.

My heart shattered into a thousand shards of glass as I looked at his handsome face and I mouthed four words, willing every ounce of my love into my eyes.

"I love you, Dante."

Pain flitted over his features, his spirit breaking before my eyes. I turned before I could let myself wallow in that sorrow and I did the one thing that would save the coven and clan.

I pulled the crown from its pouch ...

"No," Sylvie screamed. "How do you have that? It's not possible. No!"

... and lifted the cursed thing to my head.

"Bring it on, bitch."

I barely heard her answering scream as the crown unleashed its power. Wave upon wave of magic burst out of my very being, consuming, devouring, stretching out as far as the eye could see and even blasting into the heavens.

Pain lanced through my veins like fire, burning me from the inside out. I forced myself to stay standing, raising my arms up, gritting my teeth. My eyes felt like they might pop from my sockets as the pressure built within my body, but still I let it take me.

I turned my gaze on Sylvie and smiled as the magic tore through her, devouring her power and stretching her so thin her body exploded, bits of blood and body parts splattering everywhere.

Holy fuck.

My body spasmed as hot blood trickled down my nose and out my ears. My eyes would leak soon and I knew, before long, my body would break down until there was nothing left. With great effort, I managed to move my legs so I could see the armies, willing with all my might for that unfathomable power to bend around my allies.

Somehow, some-fucking-how, it did as commanded, coiling round the cultists and wiping them from existence. I could feel it peeling back the corruption in the forest and as far as the outer cities it had begun consuming—what remained of my old village among them.

Vaguely, I registered the moment the power had vanquished all our enemies, a small sliver of relief filling my subconscious at that thought. I tried to pull back, to staunch the power and lift my hand to my head, but the magic was unstoppable, my body nothing but a vessel for its might.

Hands grasped at my arms, swivelling my body around and I stared at Dante's face, his features etched with desperation and sheer panic.

"Let go, Kitarni," he roared. "Don't let it consume you. Fight

back."

I tried to move my lips, but they were frozen in a silent scream as my back bowed and I threw my head back to the sky, holding on with everything I had to stop that magic from harming him.

His hands found my cheeks, forcing me to look him in the eye even as I stood there helplessly. "You are my person, Kitarni. Mine. I will not let you go. Please. Please don't go."

I could sense his pain, his magic reaching out with tender fingers against my own. András stood by his side, his mouth wide with horror and Lukasz stood beside him, his gentle brown eyes downcast.

My person. It was all I could focus on while my lifeforce drained away, as I burned and burned and burned.

Dante grabbed my hand. I gasped as the crown's power flooded into him and he instantly cried out in pain. The sound echoed in my bones and I shook my head, finally able to speak with the pressure lessened. "Let go. You cannot do this Dante. We will *both* die!"

His eyes flashed, that stubborn golden ring flaring. "Then I will have you in death as I did in life."

Damn that man. Poetic bastard. My throat choked up with tears and I lifted my face, that same stubbornness flaring inside me. I hadn't come all this way for both of us to die.

"Or ..." Dante said through gritted teeth, somehow managing a crooked smile. "Or you can ... buckle up ... Freckles. Fight. It."

I panted in frustration, my muscles straining as I fought

 377

against the power. The dark magic of that crown hissed and lashed out, doubling down on its efforts to take me. Dante only bit back harder, taking the brunt of my pain, his nose and ears bleeding.

My fingers twitched, my hand moving ever so slowly towards the crown as memories flashed before my eyes. Cooking in Mama's kitchen, watching Eszter sew, lying by the fire with Laszlo, Jazmin and Lili's smiling faces as they taught me how to weave nets and catch fish.

Tears streamed down my face as the pain wore me down, my vitality slipping like grains of sand through my fingers.

"Look at me," Dante said fiercely. "You can do this. You always could."

More memories surged through my mind's eye—of him consoling me in the abandoned cabin, of us lying in the lavender fields and eating bejgli, of our wedding day when he'd looked at me like a god's gift, even when he'd betrayed me in the cultist camp.

Every moment of happiness, sadness, and joy flashed before my eyes, because each moment was precious. Each moment made me stronger, not the magic inside me.

That was just a bonus.

I dug deep and threw the gate wide open for that beast inside me. No leash, no restraint, just pure permission to control me. It uncoiled, growing as it filled me up, taking every available space offered. My vision fluttered and I let go, fully giving in to that dark part of myself.

Vaguely, I sensed the beast take charge and almost cried with sorrow at what I felt. It was simply a misunderstood creature who'd only ever wanted to find a place to call home. Well, we'd found it, and we weren't letting go. Blood magic hidden within the deepest recesses of my body filled my palms and the beast gnashed its teeth, snarling as its jaws yawned wide and it latched on to the crown's darkness.

The pain was unimaginable and I screamed in agony as the two powers fought, ripping and tearing at my insides.

The muscles in my arms suddenly released and, without hesitation, I ripped the crown from my skull, hurling the damned thing away from me. All at once, the power sucked back in on itself and the battlefield fell silent.

My legs gave out and I fell into Dante's arms. He grabbed me, cradling my head against his chest as we both gasped for air.

"By all the gods," András whispered from somewhere close by, but I only had eyes for Dante.

He stroked my face, kissing and squeezing me as if afraid to let me go.

"You saved me," I croaked, letting myself slump further in his embrace and looking up at him.

He smiled, two dimples winking at me, melting my damn heart. Gods, I was the luckiest woman alive to have this man.

"No, Freckles," he said, leaning forward and kissing me tenderly, his mouth lingering for a while before he pulled back. "You saved me. You saved us all."

 379

THIRTY-SEVEN
DANTE

For a while we just sat and held each other, both too shocked to move. The agony caused by the crown had faded, but a dull ache still throbbed in my veins, like poison pumping through my body.

Seeing her screaming, her body bending and breaking, had snapped something inside of me. I would never forget the look on her face—defeated resignation. I never wanted to see it again and, hopefully, I would never have to.

András joined our group huddle and Kitarni chuckled as he nuzzled into us, pulling Lukasz in too, his arms wrapping around us hesitantly. I knew our soldiers awaited us, not to mention a certain horseman, but for now the contact was grounding, reminding me of what we had achieved.

All that was missing was a certain black-haired seer and a kind and gentle sister. My heart ached with grief for those we'd lost but, right now, I could only focus on the living. As we pulled

apart, rising to our feet, we stared at the ravaged field lined with bodies, then at the rows of men and women waiting beyond.

I untied the pouch at Kitarni's waist, walked to the crown and cautiously slipped it into the bag. No way was I touching that hateful thing after the damage it had wrought. If I could destroy it here and now, I would do so without hesitation. Of course, that would only cause further problems with the man downstairs.

Sighing, I turned, stretching my arm out to my wife as she approached, her eyes narrowed on the bag at my waist. Kitarni took my hand gently and, slowly, we walked towards our people and the future beyond. When we reached the front lines, they started cheering, hugging each other and celebrating our victory.

And then they did something I hadn't expected. Lukasz and András joined the masses, turning to face us, a smile on each of their faces. András lifted his arms, beckoning for quiet, and the soldiers fell silent, leaving nothing but the sound of our banners rippling in the wind.

He bent the knee, bowing his head in reverence. "All hail the Wolfblood Witch. Our lady and saviour."

The army followed suit and I held my breath as line after line of táltosok and witch alike bowed before Kitarni. "Hail! Hail! Hail!"

Lukasz looked up, his brown eyes swimming with pride, a lopsided grin on his face. "Long live the lord and lady of Mistvellen."

My people echoed the call riotously. The sound made my

heart soar, my bones singing with joy. I glanced at Kitarni, finding her smiling with tears in her eyes, and I squeezed her hand, letting her know I was here. *Always.*

Her hand squeezed back and I wrapped my arm around her waist, tugging her to me. She rolled her eyes as if to say 'possessive táltos' and I grinned, going one step further and kissing her passionately in front of our people. She might be lady of Mistvellen, but she would always be *my lady.*

Red light filtered over the horizon and I looked to the sunrise, breathing in the new day. The gates beyond the army creaked open and streams of women, children and the elderly came running out, curiosity on their faces.

When all were gathered, I smiled at my people, taking the time to look at as many faces as I could.

"The Dark Queen is dead. Our enemies are vanquished. We stand victorious in the absence of tyranny, but we lost many in the fight. My father, the lord of Mistvellen, is dead. And so begins a new age for Mistvellen. An age where covens and clans can prosper on these lands together." I looked to Kitarni, who nodded, realising where my speech was heading.

She lifted her chin, giving an air of queenly authority as she spoke. "No longer will witches in my coven remain separated from their loved ones. Where you go is your choice. Mistvellen welcomes all witches and clansmen, all races and stations. This I swear to you."

The cheers were deafening as families embraced, lovers kissed

and friends clapped each other on the back. How had anyone ever thought to enforce such archaic constructs? We were stronger together. Witch and táltos. Allies for eternity.

"Today, we offer respect to the fallen. At dusk, we shall light the bonfires for their passing and tonight, we give thanks to our friends and allies. Let us celebrate our victory with a feast and honour the warriors who made it so."

I turned to Kitarni, finding her haunted eyes glued to the hillside. I cursed internally, jerking my chin at my brothers, who nodded and took off without needing explanation. What remained of Nora and the others were still staked there and I'd be damned if I let the crows feed on their flesh.

"Freckles," I said gently, lifting her chin with my finger. "Look at me."

She blinked rapidly, wiping her dirty cheeks, her eyes slowly rising to meet my own. "Is it really over?"

Gods, how I wished I could say yes, but I sighed, shaking my head and turning to the entity waiting in the distance. "There's one more thing we have to do."

She followed my line of sight, setting her jaw upon seeing Death still watching us. "Let's go."

We walked across the field in silence, our hands clasped tightly together. When we reached him, I shielded her subtly, my hand reaching for my sword. Though drained, my magic felt different, and I suspected Kitarni's gifts would never surface again. Just as well. Her blood magic was her gift, not mine. We didn't need

magic to bind us, our souls were intwined already.

Death's raspy voice grated over my ears as he smoothed his robe down. "I suppose I should thank you for returning my favourite plaything."

"See that she remains leashed this time," Kitarni snapped. "No more resurrections for your little pet. In fact, I will have the covens spell her remains before burning them to ensure she never rises again."

He chuckled, his breath reeking of rot and decay. I had to swallow a gag. "Do not fear, little witch," Death replied with a wave of his bone fingers. "Her suffering shall be endless."

"Good. And our bargain?" I asked in a low voice.

Death sighed, picking a piece of lint from his attire. The bastard had the nerve to seem bored, treating this deal like a conversation over a lazy lunch. "I shall hold to my word."

"That would be a first," Kitarni mumbled, placing her hands on her hips.

Death's curling tendrils of black smoke rippled out from him, the balmy morning air dropping in temperature. "Do not forget whose crown helped you win this fight."

She rolled her eyes. "Right. Because you weren't betting on it killing me in the process."

If I could see his face, I had the distinct feeling Death was smiling right now. "Semantics. You know how I love them so." He tapped beneath his hood and cocked his head. "Had you asked, I might have told you Fate had already woven your thread before this

battle. You were never destined to die, Kitarni of the Wolfblood. At least not today. When you unwittingly bound yourself to Dante through your blood magic, you forged a connection transcending your body's limitations. When Dante freely offered his life to you once the crown was on your head, your power combined broke the spell's thrall."

"Because my magic living inside him saved us?"

Death hummed as he considered. "Not exactly, but it certainly helped. Magic always has a price. The crown's is power for life and life for power. Do you know why so many before you died when wearing it? Because, in their arrogance, they thought themselves indestructible. You, on the other hand, expected to die. You knew the cost, and it was that sacrifice—a shared sacrifice—that saved you. Sometimes, I'm surprised to find mortals are wiser than their years and more giving than any god.

"Regardless, this simple truth did save the lives of few bearers before you, but such acts were rare. Istenanya, Goddess of Wisdom, once wore the crown herself. It was her family who pulled her back from oblivion. By her wisdom, the crown was cast beyond the Upper Realm, passing from many hands until it fell into my own for safekeeping. Now, it remains a symbol of my status." He held out his arm, his skeletal fingers curling out. "I kept my side of the bargain, Lord Sándor. Give me the crown."

"King Sándor," I said with a sly smile.

The freckles on Kitarni's nose rippled as she scrunched her nose at me, frowning. "What bargain? And wait … *king*?"

I laughed, pressing a kiss to her temple and grinning as I untied the bag from my hip. "When I put the crown on my head, the monarchy in the Under World changed. Death and Fate no longer held dominion over the realm, nor their minions. The demons who fought on the battlefield? They were answering to me. The king of the Under World."

"Istenanyás tits." Her wide eyes glimmered, a smirk curving her lips. "So I guess that makes me a—"

"Queen," I finished smugly.

"Damn," she replied, directing her gaze at the horseman. "Royalty feels good. I think I'll keep it."

Death hissed in warning, and she laughed. "Don't worry, bonebag, you can have your pretty little trinket back." She looked at me with pure love and adoration in her gaze, a sparkle in her eyes I'd not yet seen. "We have no interest in the dead. We've got a whole lot of living to do."

I tossed it to him casually and he clasped it, hugging it to his chest like a child on Szent-este. "And our other terms?"

Death sighed and waved his free hand. A ripple of magic pulsed in the air, and Kitarni gasped beside me, her body trembling. "They have been removed, as promised. As for my darling Fate, you have my word she will not interfere with mortal affairs. You are safe."

"Good. Then if you don't mind, I'd like to celebrate this victory with my wife. We're done here."

Death watched us silently, then shook his head. "For what

it's worth, blood witch, I always placed my bets on you."

Kitarni grinned. "As heart-warming as that sentiment is, and as pleasurable the company, I hope to never see your not-face again. Farewell Death."

"My lady," he said with a rasping laugh. Death bowed—actually bowed to a mortal being—and snapped his fingers, disappearing from sight.

Those two had the weirdest relationship I could never pretend to understand. I shook my head and turned to my hellcat, a smile on my face. "Lift up your shirt, gorgeous."

"Dante," she said, batting my hands away. "A girl's got needs, but it can probably wait until we get back to the castle."

I chuckled, trying not to think of those very needs right now as I boxed her in. "Just trust me."

She huffed, but allowed me to remove her breastplate and finally, to lift the back of her shirt. I ran my palm up her spine, smiling at the textured skin. The scars remained, but the rippling black was gone, leaving white skin in its wake.

"The magic in them is gone, isn't it?" she whispered, shivering under my touch as I stroked her spine. When she turned, her eyes were lined with silver. "You made him remove them."

I nodded, at a loss for words as I stared at the stunning creature before me. She was more beautiful than ever now. Dirty and bloodied and exhausted, her eyes alight with happiness and hope. The fact she was standing before me, alive and utterly real ... I struggled to speak. "It was past time he removed his claws

from your life."

"Dante, I—" Kitarni swallowed, shaking her head. "I can't believe you're mine."

I smiled. "Well you'd best start believing, Freckles, because we've got our whole lives ahead of us. And not a day will go by when—"

"Dante." She pressed her fingers to my lips and smiled coyly. "Shut up and kiss me."

I smiled crookedly. "As my lady commands."

Our mouths clashed together and she opened for me, letting my tongue sweep inside, our kiss passionate and desperate at first, then unhurried and sensual as we both seemed to come to the conclusion that we had the rest of our lives to do this.

My cock hardened as I pushed against her and she giggled, holding me tight as I lifted her into my arms, her legs wrapping around my waist.

She moaned as I pressed kisses to her neck, my fingers squeezing her ass. "First order of business, Freckles? I'm going to wash that irresistible body of yours and stake my claim over you."

"I thought you'd already done that when we married," she said, tilting her head.

I grinned. "Not as the lord of Mistvellen, I haven't. And I mean to service my lady."

Her answering smile was all danger and she bopped me on the nose. "I thought it was king. But, husband of mine, I give you full permission to do just that. Only if I can claim you right back."

I bit her neck hard enough to leave a mark and pulled back, flashing the dimples I knew she loved. "Freckles? I thought you'd never ask."

THIRTY-EIGHT

KITARNI

ante's hands massaged my scalp and I groaned, utterly at his mercy as he washed my hair with the lavender soap, working the suds through the matted, bloodied ends.

We should be helping to gather the dead and prepare the bonfires, but the thought of stepping back onto that field seemed so morbid and horrifying, I couldn't bring myself to suggest it. After decimating the human forces and blasting Sylvie into oblivion, I kind of figured I'd get a free pass on this one.

Besides, I wasn't ready to face reality yet. I'd only drown in my grief—allowing that pain in would mean I'd be a boneless mess of tears come dusk. Not exactly the stuff of leaders. So, I squashed those thoughts with the next best distraction. Mine just happened to come in the form of a stack of muscles. Naked. With something hard pressed against my back.

"Have I ever told you how good you are with your hands?" I asked flirtatiously.

His deep chuckle sent a wave of excitement flooding through me and I adjusted my position in the tub, pretending to get comfortable as I grinded my ass against his cock. His chest rumbled as he hummed and his fingers stopped their ministrations. "Not lately, Freckles. We'll have to do something about that."

He lifted me into his lap, reaching around to slip a finger straight into my cunt. I groaned, sticking my breasts out and arching my back. He latched onto my back, biting me gently.

His finger pumped lazily—far too slowly for my liking—and I uttered a sound of frustration, wriggling to give him more room to play. He smiled against my neck and cupped my breast, slipping another finger in and pulsing faster.

I moaned, already so wound up I knew my release would shatter me soon. Instead, he lifted me from his lap and perched me at the other end of the tub, moving me gently so I draped backwards over the edge, my legs spread wide, putting me on full display.

He groaned in appreciation, his warm tongue sliding up my centre, lapping and sucking until I writhed beneath him. I panted while he worked me with both fingers and tongue. Blood rushed to my head, the dizzying effect making me even wilder as I bucked against him. My thighs squeezed around his head and an earth-shattering orgasm sped through me.

"Fuck, Dante," I screamed, my legs quivering, my body soaring with the pleasure. When I came back down to Earth I smiled coyly. "Take me to the bed chambers."

He lifted me easily, disregarding our dripping wet bodies and all but throwing me on the bed with a dangerous grin. When he was on the bed, I took him in my hand, swiping at the pre-cum and sucking my finger. His eyes flared, watching me like a hawk while I took his shaft and pumped slowly.

I leaned back, running a hand over my breast and down, circling my most sensitive flesh. "I want you to fuck my mouth. Remind me who I belong to."

He shifted, climbing over me and thrusting his cock into my mouth so hard I gagged on his thick length. Exactly the kind of distraction I wanted. He pumped into the back of my throat, the dirty sounds filling the chamber as I took him, letting him grip the back of my head and shove in deeper.

My hand found its way downwards and I played with myself, nearly panting around Dante's cock as another orgasm built. Dante groaned and the sound only excited me more, drenching my already wet upper thighs.

His pace quickened and he thrust without mercy until his release hit the back of my throat and I swallowed it greedily, licking my lips once he pulled out. "You're so beautiful," he said, eying me from head to toe, watching me hungrily as I continued pleasuring myself. "My sweet girl."

I smiled, drinking in his praise, putting on a show as I worked my fingers and squeezed my full breast with one hand. "I want ..." I gasped as a wave of pleasure rippled through me.

Dante's gaze turned dangerous, his cock already hard again as

he stroked it. "What do you want, sweet thing?"

"I want you inside me."

He growled in approval and shifted back onto the bed, resting on his elbows. I wet my lips and crawled towards him, turning and lowering myself onto his length. He slapped my ass and a sharp sting marked my flesh, making me shiver. I moaned and he whispered behind me, "Do you like that, Freckles?"

I moaned again as he slapped harder this time and I sank deeper onto him, his cock hitting me at an incredible angle that immediately had me panting, the pleasure inside me building. "Fuck, I'm gonna—"

Another orgasm ripped through me, but Dante lifted my cheeks, bouncing me up and down as he slammed into me again and again. My legs grew weak. I let him move my body as my vision grew spotty and I felt deliriously drunk on pleasure.

Silly me thought that was it.

He grabbed me and, quicker than I could blink, was smearing my juices up my backside, sliding his finger against my rear hole before sticking it inside, stretching me. When he was satisfied, he slid his cock home and a whole new world of pleasure opened before me.

"Hadur's blade," I groaned, bouncing back against his dick, panting with the friction. Dante grunted, thrusting deep inside me, harder and faster until my mouth opened in a silent scream.

He moved my body, pressing my chest into the bed, my face buried in the softness as he took charge, thrusting into me again and again.

Dante followed me into oblivion, spilling inside me before he stilled and pressed kisses down my spine. He winked at me, a smug grin that said 'I own you now' plastered on his face.

Sure, sure. We both knew I was the one who really wore the pants. He came back and helped me clean up. Someone knocked on the door and I looked at him in alarm, but he only grinned knowingly.

He exchanged words with a woman—not even bothering to hide his nakedness, the poor old dear—then re-entered our chambers with a basket under his arm. "Gifts," he explained. "From our old friend Imre."

My stomach grumbled at the mere thought of the baker. We hadn't eaten in over a day and food had been the last thing on my mind after the lingering nausea following the battle. But now that it was here ...

I sniffed, the mouth-watering scent of freshly baked bread and sugary sweetness filling my nostrils. "Oh my gods," I said, feeling hopeful. "Do I smell bejgli?"

Dante chuckled. "You're in luck, my little pastry thief. He spoils you."

It's true. Imre knew my bad habits and fed them all too eagerly. A fact which only made me love that gentle soul even more.

I rifled through the basket, lifting a bejgli to my mouth and biting into the sweet pastry, groaning as the taste of walnut and

poppyseeds exploded in my mouth.

For a while we just sat there, eating our fill quietly, Dante toying with my hair with his free hand.

"Stupid question I know but ... Are you okay?" he asked after I'd lapsed into silence, my thoughts returning to darker things.

"Not really, but I will be. It's not the death that scares me, but what comes next." I sighed and shifted so I was lying on my side, thinking of the humans I'd so easily wiped out. "I don't regret what I did, but there will be consequences."

"The humans had their chance," he replied, scanning my face. "We offered peace and they answered with brutality."

"Perhaps, but more will come to settle the score. This isn't over."

"Then we'll restore the wards," Dante said, his voice tight. "The barriers kept us hidden for many years. When the humans come looking, they'll find no evidence of Mistvellen."

"I hope you're right." I reached for his hand, soaking in his warmth. He smiled at me and it was the most beautiful sight I'd ever seen—the most beautiful feeling, knowing I'd get to wake up and see it every day. That simple gesture alone made it all worth it, but it also made my stomach twist with stark reminder at the smiles I'd lost in the process.

His hand found my cheek and he pressed a kiss to my lips, gentle and lingering. When he pulled back, he smiled softly once more, encouraging and patient.

I chewed my lip, knowing we both needed to talk about

 395

what happened. It was real and ignoring it, pretending it wasn't so wouldn't change the fates of those who'd passed on. "Things are going to change now, Dante. It scares me, knowing so many people are going to look to us as their leaders, now that—that—" *Now that our parents are dead.* Tears burned my eyes, only this time, I let them fall gladly, my shoulders shaking as that last gruesome image of my mother sped through my mind.

His own eyes glistened as he wiped my cheek with his knuckles, his lips pulled down. "I know it hurts, and it probably always will, but they died knowing their legacy lives on. You were your mother's pride and joy, Kitarni. You and Eszter. Not every son or daughter can say the same."

His kindness only made me cry harder. How did I end up with someone so caring, so selfless? "I already miss her so much."

"I know." He pulled me closer, and I tucked myself into his chest, nestling into his warmth and the steady beating of his heart. "I'm not sure I'll ever forget seeing him like that on the battlefield," he said, his voice low and haunted. "That look on my brother's face ... I never want to see Lukasz like that again."

I nodded against his chest, eternally grateful Eszter would never know the horror of today. "You will need each other in the days to come. I'm glad—so damned glad—you have each other to get through this."

"And the rest of our unlikely little family. You know how much András would sook if you didn't count him in that equation."

A smile pulled at my lips, thinking of my dearest friend. Of

all the blessed days I'd have with them ahead. It was enough to make my broken heart stitch itself back together, just a little. Just enough. "As if there was ever a chance."

We lapsed into silence for a few minutes as Dante stroked my hair and I drew little patterns down his shoulder.

"I promise, Kitarni. Everything is going to be all right. We'll deal with the humans and we'll excel in our new reign."

And Gods help me, but I believed him. Despite the darker topic, I shook my head, unable to stop myself from chuckling. "You're always so sure of yourself. Cocky bastard."

Dante laughed. "*Your* cocky bastard. From this day, until my last."

I smiled, realising that would hopefully be many, many years from now. A future I'd never really allowed myself to imagine and, although there was certain darkness to come from today's actions, I could see it being a bright one.

Feeling a little better now, I helped myself to another bejgli, munching away in silent contentment and grinning at Dante when he looked at me with a knowing smirk.

His shoulders started shaking and it took me a second to figure out that he was laughing, the sound booming from his chest. It was so addictive—and so uncontained— I couldn't stop staring as the sound filled the room. A sound I'd never tire of.

"What?" I asked in confusion and he pointed a trembling finger at me. His joy only made me giggle along, and he started laughing even harder.

"Kitarni," he wheezed between breaths. "Poppyseed ... in your ... teeth."

I frowned, then grinned even wider, leaning forward to spot several stuck in his own teeth. We both laughed until tears streamed down my eyes and a heaviness lifted from my chest. This was why we'd fought so hard. This was but a taste of what was to come.

Dante pulled me closer and kissed me on my brow, then on my lips, holding me close, keeping me safe. This was what dreams were made of. Only now, it had come true.

I looked at my husband, smiling, my heart full.

"Mine," I agreed with his earlier sentiment. "Until the end of time."

EPILOGUE

KITARNI

A week after the battle, I found myself dressing for a coronation. My gown was midnight black in a simple velvet. A mourning gown for the ones we'd lost, and the one I'd miss most on this special day.

We'd burned the dead and held a ceremony in their honour. But for Mama, Eszter and I had held our own private vigil in the gardens nearest my chambers. We'd buried her ashes beneath the loving embrace of a wisteria tree and Eszter had magicked her own small meadow to bloom forever at its feet.

Farkas's body slept within the stone mausoleum beneath the castle, kept in good company with other rulers past. Never far, should we need their guidance.

My sister had taken Mama's death surprisingly well upon first glance, but I knew her steps were haunted and she felt our mother's absence keenly. A big sister could only fill so much space and mothers could never be replaced.

Lukasz, for his part, had hardly left her side. He was a good match for her, one I approved wholeheartedly. I knew my sister would thrive in Mistvellen and I still had high hopes that she'd open her own business. The world needed her gift and she needed to follow her passions.

Eszter tied the silver stays at the back of my dress and I studied her in the mirror, trying hard not to scrutinise every detail. With her brows pinched together and her lips set in concentration, she looked so like our mother. A dull ache throbbed inside my chest as I watched her.

She caught my gaze and smiled. "She'd be so proud of you, you know."

My stomach dipped. "I know she would. I just wish she were here to see it. I wish I could see her smile, just one last time."

Eszter nodded in understanding, lifting a hand to squeeze my shoulder. "I bet she's watching. Somewhere in the beyond, she looks down on you with that smile. Mama was many things, but she was stubborn as hell. She'd not miss this coronation for the world."

She wrinkled her nose, and I laughed. "You're right about that."

A door opened behind us and Laszlo bounded in, his tail knocking Eszter's sewing supplies onto the floor. "Hey boy," I said, smiling at his golden-brown eyes. "What do you think? Is it time to be crowned?"

He uttered a soft 'wuff' and I scratched him behind the ears,

giving him all the love. Margit entered, looking a little frazzled as she frowned at my furry companion. "Please tell me you're not bringing the dog to the ceremony."

I grinned, happy to see my friend. Since the battle, she'd had no visions and there was a healthy glow about her skin. I'd warrant she'd never slept better—and it was showing.

"Of course he's coming! I've got to have my best boy in attendance."

She rolled her eyes, a small smile quirking her lips. "Look, if it means getting you out of this room, then by all means bring the excitable mutt. You can't hide in here forever."

"I'm not hiding," I said indignantly. "Just ... going out there makes it all real, you know? Why do I even need a coronation? It seems so pompous and unnecessary."

"If I recall," Margit said slowly, "you're the one who suggested crowning sovereigns for each clan and coven territory as a bargaining chip for getting the covens on our side in the first place."

Oh right. I'd forgotten about that little bribery. But since the humans had turned on us, it felt right crowning territories by our own magical rule, rather than answering to a human king to whom we owed no allegiance.

"Okay, fine, you might be right, but—"

"But nothing," Margit said with a click of her tongue. "Mistvellen is the largest city populated by táltosok and witches in the Kingdom of Hungary. You made this peace possible. You're

going out there."

She tugged my sleeve and I let her pull me up, huffing out a breath. "Fiiine. But if everyone starts bowing again, we're going to have problems."

"Out. Now."

Eszter laughed, her brown curls bouncing. "Are you ready?"

"As I'll ever be," I groaned. "Let's get this over with."

To Margit and Eszter's credit, the vast hall where the coronation was being held was utterly breathtaking as we stepped through the doors. Vines wrapped around pillars and flowers in whites and purples hung in garlands draping from the high ceiling. Candles littered corners and lined a carpet running the length of the hall to the dais at the end.

The dais, where my husband stood proudly, his dark hair gleaming with streaks of red in the light of the sun's rays streaming through arched windows. The light made it appear as if he was already crowned, his olive skin glowing. He popped a dimple—bastard—and gave me a knowing smile.

I straightened my shoulders, feeling bolstered by that simple act of encouragement, and began the long walk to the dais, refraining from rolling my eyes as everyone bowed when I passed them. Gods dammit. My hands trembled, but I held them clasped before me until someone joined my side, looping an arm through mine.

András nodded, his blond hair shining and his green eyes glittering with amusement as he guided me down the hall. An

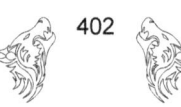

honour. It was an honour to be escorted by this man who'd given nothing short of everything since I'd first walked through the doors of this castle.

The smiling faces of friends and allies were blurry as we passed, but I nodded and smiled to all of them. They deserved nothing less than my utmost respect for all they had sacrificed.

Every step seemed to boom in time with the frantic beating of my heart and, when I reached the dais, I all but sagged as I turned and András placed my hand in Dante's. We kneeled together and his thumb rubbed soothing circles on my palm, my body relaxing slightly at his touch.

I'd recited the words many times in anticipation for the ceremony, but when Erika stepped forward, I nearly jolted in surprise and relief. We didn't have archbishops or priests, so I nearly wept with joy to find a friendly face conducting the ceremony—someone I trusted with my whole heart.

She smiled, her dark brown eyes glimmering. When she began, I found myself speaking without really needing to think at all. It was only when a page boy handed her a red cushion with a crown on it that I sucked in a breath.

A silver crown inlaid with rubies. Simple, yet elegant. It suited Dante perfectly.

"Speak your truth to the gods and their denizens, so they may bless you with this gift."

"I, Dante Sándor, swear upon my father and his father before him, to protect these lands, honour thy people and rule with a

 403

just hand."

He leaned forward and Erika smiled as she placed the crown upon his head. "By the gods' grace, so shall it be."

Another page boy stepped forward, this time with a dainty silver crown with swirling lines shaped like little flowers, sapphires inlaid into the metal—sapphires exactly like the pendant lying between my breasts, gifted to me by Dante.

My heart could have burst with the love I held for him. He'd been thoughtful from the start, even if my stubborn, pig-headed brain had taken a while to see that. So, when Erika bid me to recite the same lines, her arms stretching out to place that crown upon my head, he squeezed my hand hard enough to hurt, distracting me from the utter fear filling my being.

Because the thought of another crown being placed on my head was nearly enough for me to break down sobbing in front of the gathered crowd. My cheeks heated—not from embarrassment, but from fear. Sweat beaded on my upper lip, the walls seeming to close in as my limbs failed to move. I licked my lips, willing myself to breathe and forcing myself to *move*.

My hand trembled in Dante's and he squeezed harder still, grounding me, instilling all his love into that simple touch. With a shaky breath, I nodded, bent my neck and bit my lip as the cool metal settled on my head.

When it was obvious magic wasn't about to start eviscerating everyone I loved, my breathing calmed and I gave Dante a grateful look.

"Rise," Erika said, "Dante Sándor, Lord of Mistvellen. Rise, Kitarni Sándor, Lady of Mistvellen and High Witch of the Green Coven. Long may you reign."

"Hail, Dante, Lord of Mistvellen! Hail, Kitarni, Lady of Mistvellen!"

Dante and I stood and my heart swelled to see the genuine excitement of the gathered crowd—to see my family speak those words, my friends, and my coven. My life as that lonely girl in a village where no one wanted her seemed far away as Dante led me out of the hall and towards the large balcony overlooking the city.

We looked over the streets lined with citizens below—táltosok and witch and other creatures besides—and a sense of pride filled me as I looked at what we'd already achieved.

Unity. Together, and for all our people.

There would be repercussions for what I'd done to the humans, but that was a problem for another day. Dante and I had a long reign ahead of us, no doubt wrought with many complications to come. But, for now, I would enjoy this moment of peace.

Once, I'd longed to explore the world and experience all life had to offer. I'd longed for a home—somewhere I belonged.

I looked at Dante beside me, my heart singing with the smile he gave me, the endearment shining brighter than the sun in those brown eyes. And I realised I didn't need anything more than the little circle I'd made, surrounded by family.

I didn't need to sail the seas or climb the highest mountain, because my home was in Dante, András and Margit, Eszter and

Lukasz, Erika and all the other souls who made life worth living.

And the world?

Mine was already by my side, dressed in black, wearing a coy smile and flashing me two damn dimples that could make butter melt.

He was only the beginning, but for the first time I had faith that we could write our own endings.

Hand in hand, soul by soul, and one bejgli after another.

Want to find more of Chloe's books and to stay in touch? Eager to hear more of Chloe's upcoming Urban Fantasy Why Choose series?

Join the facebook group at Chloe Hodge's Reading Coven! https://www.facebook.com/groups/chloesreadingcoven

Language Guide

A dictionary of Hungarian terms, and explanations of Hungarian folklore/mythical creatures. Note: There are items using Hungarian language that, for the purposes of this book, are entirely fictional.*

Aliz (AH-leez) – *High Witch of the fire coven.*

András (AHRN-drash) – *Dante's second in command.*

Arló (AH-low) – *Kitarni's horse.*

Árnyalat (ARN-yah-laht) – *Shade/Shadow. An ancient order of protectors, tasked with protecting the old gods.* *

Elátkozottak Napja (Narp-yah) – *The Day of the Cursed.* As punishment for the Dark Queen's treachery, Death comes once a year to claim the souls of wayward witches. If a witch has not warded her home with the required spells, he may lay claim to their souls.*

Banya/Baba Yana (BA-nyuh/BA-buh YA-nuh) – *Protector of the witch coven.*

Baba Yaga (BA-buh Yah-guh) – *Leader of the cultists.*

Boszorkány/Boszorkányok (BAH-sarh-kahn-yah / BAH-sarh-kahn-yah-) – *Witch/Witches.*

Bejgli (BAY-glee) – *Walnut or poppyseed sweet roll.*

Caitlin Vargo (KATE-linn Vah-go) – *Chief elder in Kitarni's village.*

Dante Sándor (DUN-tay SHAN-dorh) – *Eldest son of Farkas Sándor and Kitarni's betrothed.*

Dominik (DOM-in-ick) – *Clan chieftain*

Eszter Bárány (ES-ter BARH-ray-nee) – *Kitarni's sister.*

Erika (Eh-ree-kuh) – Elder and magic tutor in Kitarni's village.

Farkas Sándor (FOR-kosh SHAN-dorh) – The lord of Mistvellen.

Garabonc (GURRA-bonz) – A mythical being with likeness to the táltos but born with all its teeth. The garabonc will visit homes asking for milk and eggs. If the owner lies about not having any, they will earn its wrath.

Guta (Guhr-TAH) – Hungarian demon

Hanna (HA-nah) – a witch from Kitarni's village.

Hadúr (HAH-duhr) – The god of war, also known as the blacksmith god.

Imre (IM-ray) – A baker in Mistvellen.

Iren (EYE-ren) – Elder and spymaster of Kitarni's village.

Isten (ISH-ten) – The Golden Father, ruler of the Middle World.

Istenanya (ISH-ten-ahn-yah) – Goddess of the moon, fertility and childbirth.

Jazmin (JAZZ-min) – A water faerie residing in the Sötét Erdő. Twin to Lili.

Kakaós csiga (KAH-kow-tsee-gah) – Sweet rolls in spirals of melted chocolate.

Kitarni Bárány (KEE-tah-nee BAHR-ray-nee)

Kürtős kalács (Keur-twos KOHL-ahsh) – A spit cake made from sweet dough and rolled with sugar.

Laszlo (LAHZ-low) – Kitarni's dog.

Lidérc/Lidércek (LEE-dertsk/LEE-der-tsek) – A supernatural being in Hungarian folklore. There are several traditional versions of this creature, but in this tale the lidérc acts as an incubus, attaching itself to a lover and sometimes inducing nightmares or sucking blood.

Lili (LI-lee) – A water faerie residing in the Sötét Erdő. Twin to Jazmin.

Napkirály (NAHP-kihr-ah-lee) – King of the Sun and rider of his beloved silver-haired horse.

Margit (MARH-git) – Seer and lady of Mistvellen. She is also Dante's cousin.

Mistvellen (MIST-vell-en) – Stronghold of the Táltosok and home to the Sándor family.

Palacsinta (PAHL-ah-shin-tah) – A thin pancake rolled or folded into triangles, and often filled with chocolate, fruit, nuts, cream, or custard.

Pálinka (PAH-link-ah) – A traditional spirit made with fruits.

Sötét Erdő (SHO-tay-et AIR-do) – dark wood. *

Sylvie Morici (SILL-vee MORE-ee-chee) – the Dark Queen.

Szaloncukor (Tsalon-zoo-korh) – A traditional Hungarian Christmas candy made from fondant and covered in chocolate.

Szélkirály (SEE-al-key-rai) – King of the Wind, charged with the winds, rain, and storms.

Szenteste (CEN-tesh-teh) – Holy Eve/Christmas Eve.

Táltos/ Táltosok (TAHL-tosh/TAHL-tosh-ock) – A mythical being with likeness to a shaman. Their power is spiritual in nature. In this book, the traditional táltos has been adapted to have necromantic power.

Tündér/ Tündérek (TUHN-dehr/TUHN-derh-eck) – Faery/ Faeries.

Turul (TUH-rool) – Mythological bird of prey often depicted as an eagle. It is a national symbol of Hungary.

Viktória (Vik-tor-ee-yuh) – High Witch of the water coven

A SMALL FAVOUR...

Readers make the world go round—authors' worlds, that is. Without you, we wouldn't be able to do what we love! Your opinions, posts, stories, videos, shares and reviews help us find our place in the book world, and our book into new hands. If you enjoyed this book, please leave a review on your preferred websites. Sites like Goodreads and Amazon drive new eyes to our books, and ultimately, traffic to our sales pages. As always, thank you for your incredible support. That's true magic, that.

MORE BOOKS BY CHLOE HODGE

The Guardians of the Grove trilogy
-Epic YA Fantasy -
Vengeance Blooms
Retribution Dies
Fury Burns

The Cursed Blood duology
-NA Fantasy Romance-
The Cursed and the Broken
The Fated and the Damned

The Terrulian Trials
-Why Choose Urban Fantasy-
A Sky of Storms
A Forest of Fire (Coming October 2023)

ACKNOWLEDGEMENTS

I can't believe we're finally here, at the end of the road for this duology. It's certainly been a year of ups and downs and strange circumstances, but it's been a hell of a ride for some big wins too.

As I type this, I'm currently on the couch in my pyjamas, Netflix on and tea on standby. Oh, and spiralling into the abyss that is covid. Can we talk about the temperatures? Yeesh.

Hanging out with Kitarni and Dante makes the crappy times a bit better, so a big thank you to you all for championing those two stubborn asses and letting this story shine.

A huge thanks to my editor and salty graham cracker, Aidan. I made this book super spicy just for you. You're welcome.

To my cover designer, Franziska, thank you, thank you, thank you! I didn't think the cover for The Cursed and the Broken could be topped but my gods, this one is pretty damn sexy. You're the best!

A shout-out to my best writing buddy and friend, Rebecca Camm, for doing my formatting and putting up with my rants and rambles. You are stellar.

There are so many other people I could thank, but we'd be here all day. My beta team, ARC readers, street team, Bookstagram family, Booktokers, my reading coven, all you wonderful readers, you are seriously amazing. Thank you.

And as always, much love to my darling Jason. I'll keep climbing that mountain.

Much love and see you all soon for my next adventure! It's going to be a doozy.

ABOUT THE AUTHOR

Chloe Hodge has always had a fondness for the fantastical. Before her love of books led her to publish the Guardians of the Grove trilogy, she completed a Bachelor of Journalism and Professional Writing and worked as a journalist. She currently lives in Adelaide, Australia, crafting new worlds, running editing business, Chloe's Chapters, drinking copious amounts of tea, and playing video games.

Stay in touch!
Instagram @chloeschapters
TikTok @chloehodgeauthor
www.chloehodge.com

Join my reading group!
https://www.facebook.com/groups/chloesreadingcoven